Christop[her Priest is th]e author of ten previous novels
and two collections of short stories. His novel *The
Prestige* won the 1995 James Tait Black Memorial Prize
for Best Novel and the World Fantasy Award, and was
shortlisted for the Arthur C. Clarke Award. His novel
The Glamour won the 1988 Kurd Lasswitz Best Novel
Award.

Christopher Priest lives in Hastings with his wife and
twin children.

BOOKS BY CHRISTOPHER PRIEST

The Extremes
The Prestige
The Quiet Woman
The Glamour
The Affirmation
A Dream of Wessex
The Space Machine
Inverted World
Fugue For a Darkening Island
The Dream Archipelago
The Christopher Priest Omnibus 1

INVERTED WORLD
&
FUGUE FOR A
DARKENING ISLAND
Omnibus 2

Christopher
PRIEST

EARTHLIGHT

LONDON · SYDNEY · NEW YORK · TOKYO · SINGAPORE · TORONTO

www.earthlight.co.uk

First published in this omnibus edition in Great Britain by Earthlight,
1999
An imprint of Simon & Schuster UK Ltd
A Viacom Company

Simon & Schuster UK Ltd
Africa House
64 - 78 Kingsway
London
WC2B 6AH

Simon & Schuster Australia
Sydney

A CIP catalogue record for this book is available from the British
Library.

ISBN 0-671-03390-5

1 3 5 7 9 10 8 6 4 2

Printed and bound in Great Britain by Caledonian International Book
Manufacturing, Glasgow

CONTENTS

INVERTED WORLD

Illustrations by Andrew Stephenson

to my Mother and Father

Part One

1

I had reached the age of six hundred and fifty miles. Beyond the door the guildsmen were assembling for the ceremony in which I would be admitted as a guild apprentice. It was a moment of excitement and apprehension, a concentration into a few minutes of all that my life had been until then.

My father was a guildsman, and I had always seen his life from a certain remove. I regarded it as an enthralling existence, charged with purpose, ceremony, and responsibility; he told me nothing of his life or work, but his uniform, his vague manner, and his frequent absences from the city hinted at a preoccupation with matters of utmost importance.

Within a few minutes the way would be open for me to join that life. It was an honour and a donning of responsibility, and no boy who had grown up inside the confining walls of the crèche could fail to respond to the thrill of this major step.

The crèche itself was a small building at the very south of the city. It was almost totally enclosed: a warren of corridors, rooms, and halls. There was no access to the rest of the city, except by way of a door which was normally locked, and the only opportunities for exercise existed in the small gymnasium and a tiny open space, bounded on all four sides by the high walls of the crèche buildings.

Like the other children I had been placed in the charge of the crèche administrators soon after my birth, and knew no other world. I had no memories of my mother: she had left the city soon after my birth.

It had been a dull but not unhappy experience. I had made some good friends, and one of them – a boy a few miles older than me called Gelman Jase – had become an apprentice guildsman a short time before me. I was looking forward to seeing Jase again. I had seen him once since his coming of age, when he returned briefly to the crèche, and already he had adopted the slightly preoccupied manner of the guildsmen, and I had learned nothing from him. Now that I too was about to become an apprentice I felt that he would have much to tell me.

The administrator returned to the ante-room in which I was standing.

'They're ready,' he said. 'Can you remember what you have to do?'

'Yes.'

'Good luck.'

I discovered that I was trembling, and the palms of my hands were moist. The administrator, who had brought me from the crèche that morning, grinned at me in sympathy. He thought he understood the ordeal I was suffering, but he knew, literally, only half of it.

After the guild ceremony there was more in store for me. My father had told me that he had arranged a marriage for me. I had taken the news calmly because I knew that guildsmen were expected to marry early, and I already knew the chosen girl. She was Victoria Lerouex, and she and I had grown up together in the crèche. I had not had much to do with her – there were not many girls in the crèche, and they tended to keep together in a tight-knit group – but we were less than strangers. Even so, the notion of being married was a new one and I had not had much time to prepare myself mentally for it.

The administrator glanced up at the clock.

'O.K., Helward. It's time.'

We shook hands briefly, and he opened the door. He walked into the hall, leaving the door open. Through it I could see several of the guildsmen standing on the main floor. The ceiling lights were on.

The administrator stopped just beyond the door and turned to address the platform.

'My Lord Navigator. I seek audience.'

'Identify yourself.' A distant voice, and from where I was standing in the ante-room I could not see the speaker.

'I am Domestic Administrator Bruch. At the command of my chief administrator I have summoned one Helward Mann, who seeks apprenticeship in a guild of the first order.'

'I recognise you, Bruch. You may admit the apprentice.'

Bruch turned and faced me, and as he had earlier rehearsed me I stepped forward into the hall. In the centre of the floor a small podium had been placed, and I walked over and took up position behind it.

I faced the platform.

Here in the concentrated brilliance of the spotlights sat an elderly man in a high-backed chair. He was wearing a black cloak

12

decorated with a circle of white stitched on the breast. On each side of him stood three men, all wearing cloaks, but each one of these was decorated with a sash of a different colour. Gathered on the main floor of the hall, in front of the platform, were several other men and a few women. My father was among them.

Everyone was looking at me, and I felt my nervousness increase. My mind went blank, and all Bruch's careful rehearsals were forgotten.

In the silence that followed my entrance, I stared straight ahead at the man sitting at the centre of the platform. This was the first time I had ever seen – let alone been in the company of – a Navigator. In my immediate background of the crèche such men had sometimes been spoken of in a deferential way, sometimes – by the more disrespectful – in a derisory way, but always with undertones of awe for the almost legendary figures. That one was here at all only underlined the importance of this ceremony. My immediate thought was what a story this would be to tell the others . . . and then I remembered that from this day nothing would be the same again.

Bruch had stepped forward to face me.

'Are you Helward Mann, sir?'

'Yes, I am.'

'What age have you attained, sir?'

'Six hundred and fifty miles.'

'Are you aware of the significance of this age?'

'I assume the responsibilities of an adult.'

'How best can you assume those responsibilities, sir?'

'I wish to enter apprenticeship with a first-order guild of my choice.'

'Have you made that choice, sir?'

'Yes, I have.'

Bruch turned and addressed the platform. He repeated the content of my answers to the men assembled there, though it seemed to me that they must have been able to hear my answers as I gave them.

'Does anyone wish to question the apprentice?' said the Navigator to the other men on the platform.

No one replied.

'Very well.' The Navigator stood up. 'Come forward, Helward Mann, and stand where I can see you.'

Bruch stepped to one side. I left the podium, and walked forward to where a small white plastic circle had been inlaid into the carpet. I stopped with my feet in the centre of it. For several seconds I was regarded in silence.

The Navigator turned to one of the men at his side.

'Do we have the proposers here?'

'Yes, My Lord.'

'Very well. As this is a guild matter we must exclude all others.'

The Navigator sat down, and the man immediately to his right stepped forward.

'Is there any man here who does not rank with the first order? If so, he will grace us with his absence.'

Slightly behind me, and to one side of me, I noticed Bruch make a slight bow towards the platform, and then he left the hall. He was not alone. Of the group of people on the main floor of the hall, about half left the room by one or other of the exits. Those left turned to face me.

'Do we recognise strangers?' said the man on the platform. There was silence. 'Apprentice Helward Mann, you are now in the exclusive company of first-order guildsmen. A gathering such as this is not common in the city, and you should treat it with appropriate solemnity. It is in your honour. When you have passed through your apprenticeship these people will be your peers, and you will be bound, just as they are, by guild rules. Is that understood?'

'Yes, sir.'

'You have selected the guild you wish to enter. Please name it for all to hear.'

'I wish to become a Future Surveyor,' I said.

'Very well, that is acceptable. I am Future Surveyor Clausewitz, and I am your chief guildsman. Standing around you are other Future Surveyors, as well as representatives from other first-order guilds. Here on the platform are the other chief guildsmen of the first order. In the centre, we are honoured by the presence of Lord Navigator Olsson.'

As Bruch had earlier rehearsed me I made a deep bow towards the Navigator. The bow was all I now remembered of his instructions: he had told me that he knew nothing of the details of this part of the ceremony, only that I should display appropriate respect towards the Navigator when formally introduced to him.

'Do we have a proposer for the apprentice?'

'Sir, I wish to propose him.' It was my father who spoke.

'Future Surveyor Mann has proposed. Do we have a seconder?'

'Sir, I will second the proposal.'

'Bridge-Builder Lerouex has seconded. Do we hear any dissent?'

14

There was a long silence. Twice more, Clausewitz called for dissent, but no one raised any objection to me.

'That is as it should be,' said Clausewitz. 'Helward Mann, I now offer you the oath of a first-order guild. You may – even at this late stage – decline to take it. If, however, you do swear to the oath you will be bound to it for the whole of the rest of your life in the city. The penalty for breaching the oath is summary execution. Is that absolutely clear in your mind?'

I was stunned by this. Nothing anyone had said, my father, Jase, or even Bruch, had said anything to warn me of this. Perhaps Bruch had not known ... but surely my father would have told me?

'Well?'

'Do I have to decide now, sir?'

'Yes.'

It was quite clear that I would not be allowed a sight of the oath before deciding. Its content was probably instrumental in the secrecy. I felt that I had very little alternative. I had come this far, and already I could feel the pressures of the system about me. To proceed as far as this – proposal and acceptance – and then to decline the oath was impossible, or so it seemed to me at that moment.

'I will take the oath, sir.'

Clausewitz stepped down from the platform, walked over to me, and handed me a piece of white card.

'Read this through, clearly and loudly,' he told me. 'You may read it through to yourself before, if you wish, but if you do so you will be immediately bound by it.'

I nodded to show my understanding of this, and he returned to the stage. The Navigator stood up. I read the oath silently, familiarising myself with its phrases.

I faced the platform, aware of the attention of the others on me, not least that of my father.

'I, Helward Mann, being a responsible adult and a citizen of Earth do solemnly swear:

'That as an apprentice to the guild of Future Surveyors I shall discharge whatever tasks I am given with the utmost effort;

'That I shall place the security of the city of Earth above all other concerns;

'That I shall discuss the affairs of my guild and other first-order guilds with no one who is not himself an accredited and sworn apprentice or a first-order guildsman;

'That whatsoever I shall experience or see of the world beyond

15

the city of Earth will be considered a matter of guild security;

'That on acceptance as a full guildsman I shall apprise myself of the contents of the document known as Destaine's Directive, and that I shall make it my duty to obey its instructions, and that further I shall pass on the knowledge obtained from it to future generations of guildsmen.

'That the swearing of this oath shall be considered a matter of guild security.

'All this is sworn in the full knowledge that a betrayal of any one of these conditions shall lead to my summary death at the hands of my fellow guildsmen.'

I looked up at Clausewitz as I finished speaking. The very act of reading those words had filled me with an excitement I could hardly contain.

'Beyond the city . . .' That meant I would leave the city, venture as an apprentice into the very regions which had been forbidden me, and were even yet forbidden to most of those in the city. The crèche was full of rumours about what lay outside the city, and already I had any number of wild imaginings about it. I was sensible enough to realise that the reality could never equal those rumours for inventiveness, but even so the prospect was one that dazzled and appalled me. The cloak of secrecy that the guildsmen placed around it seemed to imply that something dreadful was beyond the walls of the city; so dreadful that a penalty of death was the price paid for revealing its nature.

Clausewitz said: 'Step up to the platform, Apprentice Mann.'

I walked forward, climbing the four steps that led up to the stage. Clausewitz greeted me, shaking me by the hand, and taking away from me the card with the oath. I was introduced first to the Navigator, who spoke a few amiable words to me, and then to the other chief guildsmen. Clausewitz told me not only their names but also their titles, some of which were new to me. I was beginning to feel overwhelmed with new information, that I was learning in a few moments as much as I had learned inside the crèche in all my life to that date.

There were six first-order guilds. In addition to Clausewitz's Future Surveyors guild, there was a guild responsible for Traction, another for Track-Laying and another for Bridge-Building. I was told that these were the guilds primarily responsible for the administration of the city's continued existence. In support of these were two further guilds: Militia and Barter. All this was new to me, but now I recalled that my father had sometimes referred in passing to men who bore as titles the names of their guilds. I had heard of the Bridge-Builders, for instance, but until this ceremony I had had no conception that the building of a bridge was an event surrounded by an aura of ritual and secrecy. How was a bridge fundamental to the city's survival? Why was a militia necessary?

Indeed, what was the future?

I was taken by Clausewitz to meet the Future guildsmen, among them of course my father. There were only three present; the rest, I was told, were away from the city. With these introductions finished I spoke to the other guildsmen, there being at least one representative from each of the first-order guilds. I was gaining the impression that the work of a guildsman outside the city was a major occupier of time and resources, for on several occasions one or other of the guildsmen would apologise for there being no more of their number at the ceremony, but that they were away from the city.

During these conversations one unusual fact struck me. It was something that I had noticed earlier, but had not registered consciously. This was that my father and the other Future guildsmen appeared to be considerably older than the others. Clausewitz himself was strongly built, and he stood magnificently in his cloak, but the thinness of his hair and his lined face betrayed a considerable age; I estimated him to be at least two thousand five hundred miles old. My father too, now I could see him in the company of his contemporaries, seemed remarkably old. He was of an age similar to Clausewitz, and yet logic denied this. It would mean that my father would have been about one thousand eight hundred miles at the time I was born and I already knew that it was the custom in the city to produce children as soon after reaching maturity as possible.

The other guildsmen were considerably younger. Some were evidently only a few miles older than myself; a fact which gave me some encouragement as now I had entered the adult world I wished to be finished with the apprenticeship at the earliest opportunity. The implication was that the apprenticeship had no fixed term, and if, as Bruch had said, status in the city was as a result of ability, then with application I could become a full guildsman within a relatively short period of time.

There was one person missing, whom I would have liked to be there. That was Jase.

Speaking to one of the Traction guildsmen, I asked after him.

'Gelman Jase?' he said. 'I think he's away from the city.'

17

'Couldn't he have come back for this?' I said. 'We shared a cabin in the crèche.'

'Jase will be away for many miles to come.'

'Where is he?'

The guildsman only smiled at this, infuriating me . . . for surely, now I had taken the oath I could be told?

Later, I noticed that no other apprentices were present. Were they all away from the city? If so, that probably meant that very soon I too could leave.

After a few minutes talking to the guildsmen, Clausewitz called for attention.

'I propose to recall the administrators,' he said. 'Are there any objections?'

There was a sound of general approval from the guildsmen.

'In which case,' Clausewitz continued, 'I would remind the apprentice that this is the first occasion of many on which he is bound by his oath.'

Clausewitz moved down from the platform, and two or three of the guildsmen opened the doors of the hall. Slowly, the other people returned to the ceremony. Now the atmosphere lightened considerably. As the hall filled up I heard laughter, and in the background I noticed that a long table was being set up. There seemed to be no rancour from the administrators about their exclusion from the ceremony that had just taken place. I assumed that it was a common enough event for it to be taken as a matter of course, but it crossed my mind to wonder how much they were able to surmise. When secrecy takes place in the open, as it were, it lays itself open to speculation. Surely no security could be so tight that merely dismissing them from a room while an oath-taking ceremony took place would keep them in the dark as to what was happening? As far as I could tell, there had been no guards at the door; what was there to prevent someone eaves-dropping while I spoke the oath?

I had little time to consider this for the room was filled with activity. People spoke together in an animated way, and there was much noise as the long table was laid with large plates of food and many different kinds of drink. I was led from one group of people to another by my father, and I was introduced to so many people that I was soon unable to remember names or titles.

'Shouldn't you introduce me to Victoria's parents?' I said, see-ing Bridge-Builder Lerouex standing to one side with a woman administrator who I assumed was his wife.

'No . . . that comes later.' He led me on, and soon I was shaking hands with yet another group of people.

I was wondering where Victoria was, for surely now that the guild ceremony was out of the way our engagement should be announced. By now I was looking forward to seeing her. This was partly due to curiosity, but also because she was someone I already knew. I felt outnumbered by people both older and more experienced than me, and Victoria was a contemporary. She too was of the crèche, she had known the same people as me, was of a similar age. In this room full of guildsmen she would have been a welcome reminder of what was now behind me. I had taken the major step into adulthood, and that was enough for one day.

Time passed. I had not eaten since Bruch had woken me, and the sight of the food reminded me of how hungry I was. My attention was drifting away from this more social aspect of the ceremony. It was all too much at once. For another half an hour I followed my father around, talking without much interest to the people to whom I was introduced, but what I should really have welcomed at that moment was some time left to myself, so that I could think over all that I had learned.

Eventually, my father left me talking to a group of people from the synthetics administration (the group which, I learned, was responsible for the production of all the various synthetic foods and organic materials used in the city) and moved over to where Lerouex was standing. I saw them speak together briefly, and Lerouex nodded.

In a moment my father returned, and took me to one side.

'Wait here, Helward,' he said. 'I'm going to announce your engagement. When Victoria comes into the room, come over to me.'

He hurried away and spoke to Clausewitz. The Navigator returned to his seat on the platform.

'Guildsmen and administrators!' Clausewitz called over the noise of the conversations. 'We have a further celebration to announce. The new apprentice is to be engaged to the daughter of Bridge-Builder Lerouex. Future Surveyor Mann, would you care to speak?'

My father walked to the front of the hall and stood before the platform. Speaking too quickly, he made a short speech about me. On top of everything else that had happened that morning this came as a new embarrassment. Uneasy together, my father and I had never been so close as he made out by his words. I wanted to stop him, wanted to leave the room until he had finished, but it was clear I was still the centre of interest. I wondered if the guildsmen had any idea how they were alienating me from their sense of ceremony and occasion.

To my relief, my father finished but stayed in front of the platform. From another part of the hall Lerouex said that he wished to present his daughter. A door opened and Victoria came in, led by her mother.

As my father had instructed I walked over and joined him. He shook me by the hand. Lerouex kissed Victoria. My father kissed her, and presented her with a finger-ring. Another speech was made. Eventually, I was introduced to her. We had no chance to speak together.

The festivities continued.

2

I was given a key to the crèche, told that I might continue to use my cabin until accommodation could be found in guild quarters, and reminded once more of my oath. I went straight to sleep.

I was awakened early by one of the guildsmen I had met the previous day. His name was Future Denton. He waited while I dressed myself in my new apprentice's uniform, and then led me out of the crèche. We did not take the same route as that along which Bruch had led me the day before, but climbed a series of stairs. The city was quiet. Passing a clock I saw that the time was still very early indeed, just after three-thirty in the morning. The corridors were empty of people, and most of the ceiling lights were dimmed.

We came eventually to a spiral staircase, at the top of which was a heavy steel door. Future Denton took a flashlight from his pocket, and switched it on. There were two locks to the door, and as he opened it he indicated that I should step through before him.

I emerged into coldness and darkness, such extremes of both that they came as a physical shock. Denton closed the door behind him, and locked it again. As he shone his flashlight around I saw that we were standing on a small platform, enclosed by a handrail about three feet high. We walked over and stood at the rail. Denton switched off his light, and the darkness was complete.

'Where are we?' I said.

'Don't talk. Wait . . . and keep watching.'

I could see absolutely nothing. My eyes, still adjusted to the comparative brightness of the corridors, tricked my senses into detecting coloured shapes moving about me, but in a moment these stilled. The darkness was not the major preoccupation; already the movement of the cold air across my body had chilled me and I was trembling. I could feel the steel of the rail in my hands like a spear of ice, and I moved my hands trying to minimise the discomfort. It was not possible to let go though. In that absolute dark the rail was my only hold on the familiar. I had never before been so isolated from what I knew, never before been confronted with such an impact of things unknown. My whole body was

21

tense, as if bracing itself against some sudden detonation or physical shock, but none came. All about me was cold and dark and overwhelmingly silent bar the sound of the wind in my ears.

As the minutes passed, and my eyes became better able to adjust, I discovered I could make out vague shapes about me. I could see Future Denton beside me, a tall black figure in his cloak, outlined against the lesser darkness of what was above him. Beneath the platform on which we stood I could detect a huge, irregularly shaped structure, black and black on black.

Around all this was impenetrable darkness. I had no point of reference, nothing against which I could make distinctions of form or outline. It was frightening, but in a way which struck emotionally, not in such a way that I felt at all threatened physically. Sometimes I had dreamed of such a place, and then I had awakened still experiencing the after-images of an impression such as this. This was no dream; the bitter cold could not be imagined, nor could the startling clarity of the new sensations of space and dimension. I knew only that this was my first venture outside the city – for this was all it could be – and that it was nothing like I had ever anticipated.

Fully appreciating this, the effect of the cold and dark on my orientation became of subsidiary importance. I was outside . . . *this* was what I had been waiting for!

There was no further need for Denton's admonition to silence; I could say nothing, and had I tried the words would have died in my throat or been lost on the wind. It was all I could do to look, and in looking I saw nothing but the deep, mysterious cape of a land under the clouded night.

A new sensation affected me: I could smell the soil! It was unlike anything I had ever smelled in the city, and my mind conjured a spurious image of many square miles of rich brown soil, moist in the night. I had no way of telling what it was I could actually smell – it was probably not soil at all – but this image of rich, fertile ground had been one that endured for me from one of the books I had read in the crèche. It was enough to imagine it and once more my excitement lifted, sensing the cleansing effect of the wild, unexplored land behind the city. There was so much to see and do . . . and even yet, standing on the platform, it was still for those few precious moments the exclusive domain of the imagination. I needed to see nothing; the simple impact of this fundamental step beyond the city's confines was enough to spark my underdeveloped imagination into realms which until that moment had been fed only by the writings of the authors I had read.

Slowly, the blackness became less dense, until the sky above me was a dark grey. In the far distance I could see where the clouds met the horizon, and even as I watched I saw a line of the faintest red begin to etch the shape of one small cloud. As if the impact of the light was propelling it, this cloud and all the others were moving slowly above us, borne on the wind away from the direction of the glow. The redness spread, touching the clouds for a few moments as they moved away, leaving behind a large area of clear sky which was itself coloured a deep orange. My whole attention was rivetted on this sight, for it was quite simply the most beautiful thing I had experienced in my whole life. Almost imperceptibly, the orange colour was spreading and lightening; still the clouds which moved away were singed with red, but at the very point at which the horizon met the sky there was an intensity of light which grew brighter by the minute.

The orange was dying. Far more quickly than I would ever have guessed, it thinned away as the source of light brightened. The sky now was a blue so pale and brilliant that it was almost white. In the centre of it, as if growing up from the horizon, was a spear of white light, leaning slightly to one side like a toppling church steeple. As it grew it thickened and brightened, becoming as the seconds passed so brilliant and incandescent that it was not possible to stare directly at it.

Future Denton suddenly gripped my arm.

'Look!' he said, pointing to the left of the centre of brilliance.

A formation of birds, spread out in a delicate V, was flapping slowly from left to right across our vision. After a few moments, the birds crossed directly in front of the growing column of light, and for a few seconds they could not be seen.

'What are they?' I said, my voice sounding coarse and harsh.

'Just geese.'

They were visible again now, flying slowly on with the blue sky behind them. After a minute or so they became lost to sight beyond high ground some distance away.

I looked again at the rising sun. In the short time I had been looking at the birds it had been transformed. Now the bulk of its body had appeared above the horizon, and it hung in sight, a long, saucer-shape of light, spiked above and below with two perpendicular spires of incandescence. I could feel the touch of its warmth on my face. The wind was dropping.

I stood with Denton on that small platform, looking out across

23

the land. I saw the city, or what part of it was visible from the platform, and I saw the last of the clouds disappearing across the horizon farthest from the sun. It shone down on us from a cloudless sky, and Denton removed his cloak.

He nodded to me, and showed me how we could climb down from the platform, by way of a series of metal ladders, to the land below. He went first. As I stepped down, and stood for the first time on natural ground, I heard the birds which had nested in the upper crannies of the city begin their morning song.

3

Future Denton walked with me once around the periphery of the city, then took me out across the ground towards a small cluster of temporary buildings which had been erected about five hundred yards from the city. Here he introduced me to Track Malchuskin, then returned to the city.

The Track was a short, hairy man, still half-asleep. He didn't seem to resent the intrusion, and treated me with some politeness.

'Apprentice Future, are you?'

I nodded. 'I've just come from the city.'

'First time out?'

'Yes.'

'Had any breakfast?'

'No . . . the Future got me out of bed, and we've come more or less straight here.'

'Come inside . . . I'll make some coffee.'

The interior of the hut was rough and untidy, in contrast to what I had seen within the city. There cleanliness and tidiness seemed to be of great importance, but Malchuskin's hut was littered with dirty pieces of clothing, unwashed pots and pans, and half-eaten meals. In one corner was a large pile of metal tools and instruments, and against one wall was a bunk, the covers thrown back in a heap. There was a background smell of old food.

Malchuskin filled a pan with water, and placed it on a cooking-ring. He found two mugs somewhere, rinsed them in the butt, and shook them to remove the surplus water. He put a measure of synthetic coffee into a jug, and when the water boiled filled it up.

There was only one chair in the hut. Malchuskin removed some heavy steel tools from the table, and moved it over to the bunk. He sat down, and indicated that I should pull up the chair. We sat in silence for a while, sipping the coffee. It was made in exactly the same way as it was in the city, and yet it seemed to taste different.

'Haven't had too many apprentices lately.'

'Why's that?' I said.

'Can't say. Not many of them coming up. Who are you?'

'Helward Mann. My father's – '

25

'Yeah, I know. Good man. We were in the crèche together.'

I frowned to myself at that. Surely, he and my father were not of the same age? Malchuskin saw my expression.

'Don't let it bother you,' he said. 'You'll understand one day. You'll find out the hard way, just like everything else this god-damn guild system makes you learn. It's a strange life in the Future guild. It wasn't for me, but I guess you'll make out.'

'Why didn't you want to be a Future?'

'I didn't say I didn't want it . . . I meant it wasn't my lot. My own father was a Tracksman. The guild system again. But you want it hard, they've put you in the right hands. Done much manual work?'

'No . . .'

He laughed out loud. 'The apprentices never have. You'll get used to it.' He stood up. 'It's time we started. It's early, but now you've got me out of bed there's no point being idle. They're a lazy lot of bastards.'

He left the hut. I finished the rest of my coffee in a hurry, scalding my tongue, and went after him. He was walking towards the other two buildings. I caught him up.

With a metal wrench he had taken from the hut he banged loudly on the door of each of the other two buildings, bawling at whoever was inside to get up. I saw from the marks on the doors that he probably always hit them with a piece of metal.

We heard movement inside.

Malchuskin went back to his hut and began sorting through some of the tools.

'Don't have too much to do with these men,' he warned me. 'They're not from the city. There's one of them, I've put him in charge. Rafael. He speaks a little English, and acts as interpreter. If you want anything, speak to him. Better still, come to me. There's not likely to be trouble, but if there is . . . call me. O.K.?'

'What kind of trouble?'

'They don't do what you or I tell them. They're being paid, and they get paid to do what we want. It's trouble if they don't. But the only thing wrong with this lot is that they're too lazy for their own good. That's why we start early. It gets hot later on, and then we might as well not bother.'

It was already warm. The sun had risen high while I had been with Malchuskin, and my eyes were beginning to water. They weren't accustomed to such bright light. I had tried to glance at the sun again, but it was impossible to look directly at it.

'Take these!' Malchuskin passed me a large armful of steel

26

wrenches, and I staggered under the weight, dropping two or three. He watched in silence as I picked them up, ashamed at my ineptitude.

'Where to?' I said.

'The city, of course. Don't they teach you anything in there?'

I headed away from the hut towards the city. Malchuskin watched from the door of his hut.

'South side!' he shouted after me. I stopped, and looked round helplessly. Malchuskin came over to me.

'There.' He pointed. 'The tracks at the south of the city. O.K.?'

'O.K.' I walked in that direction, dropping only one more wrench on the way.

After an hour or two I began to see what Malchuskin had meant about the men who worked with us. They stopped at the slightest excuse, and only Malchuskin's bawling or Rafael's sullen instructions kept them at it.

'Who are they?' I asked Malchuskin when we stopped for a fifteen-minute break.

'Local men.'

'Couldn't we hire some more?'

'They're all the same round here.'

I sympathised with them to a certain degree. Out in the open, with no shade at all, the work was vigorous and hard. Although I was determined not to slacken, the physical strain was more than I could bear. Certainly, it was more strenuous than anything I had ever experienced.

The tracks at the south of the city ran for about half a mile, ending in no particular place. There were four tracks, each consisting of two metal rails supported on timber sleepers which were in turn resting on sunken concrete foundations. Two of the tracks had already been considerably shortened by Malchuskin and his crew, and we were working on the longest one still extant, the one laid as right outer.

Malchuskin explained that if I assumed the city was to the front of us, the four tracks were identified by left and right, outer and inner in each case.

There was little thought involved. What had to be done was routine, but heavy.

In the first place the tie-bars connecting the rail to the sleepers had to be released for the whole length of the section of rail. This was then laid to one side, and the other rail similarly released. Next we tackled the sleepers. These were attached to the concrete

27

foundations by two clamps, each of which had to be slackened and removed manually. When the sleeper came free it was stacked on a bogie which was waiting on the next section of track. The concrete foundation, which I discovered was prefabricated and re-usable, then had to be dug out of its soil emplacement and similarly placed on the bogie. When all this was done, the two steel rails were placed on special racks along the side of the bogie.

Malchuskin or I would then drive the battery-powered bogie up to the next section of track, and the process would be repeated. When the bogie was fully loaded, the entire track-crew would ride on it up to the rear of the city. Here it would be parked, and the battery recharged from an electrical point fitted to the wall of the city for this purpose.

It took us most of the morning to load the bogie and take it up to the city. My arms felt as if they had been stretched from their sockets, my back was aching, I was filthy dirty and I was covered with sweat. Malchuskin, who had done no less work than any of the others – probably more than any of the hired labour – grinned at me.

'Now we unload and start again,' he said.

I looked over at the labourers. They looked like I felt, although I suspected I too had done more work than they, considering I was new to it and hadn't yet learnt the art of using my muscles economically. Most of them were lying back in what little shadow was afforded by the bulk of the city.

'O.K.,' I said.

'No . . . I was joking. You think that lot'd do any more without a bellyful of food?'

'No.'

'Right, then . . . we eat.'

He spoke to Rafael, then walked back across towards his hut. I went with him, and we shared some of the heated-up synthetic food that was all he could offer.

The afternoon started with the unloading. The sleepers, foundations, and rails were loaded on to another battery-powered vehicle which travelled on four large balloon tyres. When the transfer was completed, we took the bogie down to the end of the track and began again. The afternoon was hot, and the men worked slowly. Even Malchuskin had eased up, and after the bogie had been refilled with its next load he called a halt.

'Like to have got another load in today,' he said, and took a long draught from a bottle of water.

'I'm ready,' I said.

'Maybe. You want to do it on your own?'

'But I'm willing,' I said, not wanting to reveal the exhaustion I was feeling.

'As it is you'll be useless tomorrow. No, we get this bogie un-loaded, run it down to the track-end, and that's it.'

That wasn't quite it, as things turned out. When we returned the bogie to the track-end, Malchuskin started the men filling in the last section of the track with as much loose soil and dirt as we could find. This rubble was laid for twenty yards.

I asked Malchuskin its purpose.

He nodded over towards the nearest long track, the left inner. At its end was a massive concrete buttress, stayed firmly into the ground.

'You'd rather put up one of those instead?' he said.

'What is it?'

'A buffer. Suppose the cables all broke at once . . . the city'd run backwards off the rails. As it is the buffers wouldn't put up much resistance, but it's all we can do.'

'Has the city ever run back?'

'Once.'

Malchuskin offered me the choice of returning to my cabin in the city, or remaining with him in his hut. The way he put it didn't leave me much choice. He obviously had low regard for the people inside the city and told me he rarely went inside.

'It's a cosy existence,' he said. 'Half the people in the city don't know what's going on out here, and I don't suppose they'd care if they did know.'

'Why should they have to know? After all, if we can keep working smoothly, it's not their problem.'

'I know, I know. But I wouldn't have to use these damned local men if more city people came out here.'

In the near-by dormitory huts the hired men were talking noisily; some were singing.

'Don't you have anything at all to do with them?'

'I just use them. They're the Barter people's pigeon. If they get too lousy I lay them off and get the Barters to find me some more. Never difficult. Work's in short supply round here.'

'Where is this?'

'Don't ask me . . . that's up to your father and his guild. I just dig up old tracks.'

I sensed that Malchuskin was less alienated from the city than

29

he made out. I supposed his relatively isolated existence gave him some contempt for those within the city, but as far as I could see he didn't have to stay out here in the hut. Lazy the workers might be, and just now noisy, but they seemed to act in an orderly manner. Malchuskin made no attempt to supervise them when there was no work to be done, so he could have stayed in the city if he chose.

'Your first day out, isn't it?' he said suddenly.

'That's right.'

'You want to watch the sunset?'

'No . . . why?'

'The apprentices usually do.'

'O.K.'

Almost as if it were to please him I went out of the hut and looked past the bulk of the city towards the north-east. Malchuskin came up behind me.

The sun was near the horizon and already I could feel the wind cold on my back. The clouds of the previous night had not returned, and the sky was clear and blue. I watched the sun, able to look at it without hurting my eyes now that its rays were diffused by the thickness of the atmosphere. It had the shape of a broad orange disk, slightly tilted down towards us. Above and below, tall spires of light rose from the centre of the disk. As we watched it sank slowly beneath the horizon, the upper point of light being the last to vanish.

'You sleep in the city, you don't get to see that,' Malchuskin said.

'It's very beautiful,' I said.

'You see the sunrise this morning?'

'Yes.'

Malchuskin nodded. 'That's what they do. Once a kid's made it to a guild, they throw him in at the deep end. No explanation, right? Out in the dark, until up comes the sun.'

'Why do they do that?'

'Guild system. They believe it's the quickest way to get an apprentice to understand that the sun isn't the same as he's been taught.'

'Isn't it?' I said.

'What were you taught?'

'That the sun is spherical.'

'So they still teach that. Well, now you've seen that the sun isn't. Make anything of it?'

'No.'

'Think about it. Let's go and eat.'

30

We returned to the hut and Malchuskin directed me to start heating up some food while he bolted another bunk-frame on top of the vertical supports around his own. He found some bedding in a cupboard, and dumped it on the bunk.

'You sleep here,' he said, indicating the upper bunk. 'You restless at night?'

'I don't think so.'

'We'll try it for one night. If you keep moving around, we'll change over. I don't like being disturbed.'

I thought there was little chance I would disturb him. I could have slept on the side of a cliff that night, I was so tired. We ate the tasteless food together, and afterwards Malchuskin talked about his work on the tracks. I paid him scant attention, and a few minutes later I lay on my bunk, pretending to listen to him. I fell asleep almost at once.

4

I was woken the next morning by Malchuskin moving about the hut, clattering the dishes from the previous evening's meal. I made to get out of the bunk as soon as I was fully conscious, but at once I was paralysed by a stab of pain in my back. I gasped.

Malchuskin looked up at me, grinning.

'Stiff?' he said.

I rolled over on to my side, and tried to draw my legs up. These too were stiff and painful, but with a considerable effort I managed to get myself into a sitting position. I sat still for a moment, hoping that the pain was cramp and that it would pass.

'Always the same with you kids from the city,' Malchuskin said, but without malice. 'You come out here, keen I'll grant you. A day's work and you're so stiff you become useless. Don't you get any exercise in the city?'

'Only in the gymnasium.'

'O.K. . . . get down here and have some breakfast. After that, you'd better go back to the city. Have a hot bath, and see if you can find someone to give you a massage. Then report back here.'

I nodded gratefully and clambered down from the bunk. This was no easier and no less painful than anything else I'd attempted so far. I discovered that my arms, neck, and shoulders were as stiff as the rest of me.

I left the hut thirty minutes later, just as Malchuskin was bawling at the men to get started. I headed back towards the city, limping slowly.

It was the first time I had been left to my own devices away from the city. When in the company of others, one never sees as much as when alone. The city was five hundred yards from Malchuskin's hut, and that was an adequate distance to be able to get some impression of its overall size and appearance. Yet during the whole of the previous day I had been able to afford it only the barest of glances. It was simply a large, grey bulk, dominating the landscape.

Now, hobbling alone across the ground towards it I could inspect it in more detail.

From the limited experience I had had of the interior of the city, I had never given much thought to what it might look like from outside. I had always conceived of it as being large, but the reality was that the city was rather smaller than I had imagined. At its highest point, on the northern side, it was approximately two hundred feet high, but the rest of it was a jumble of rectangles and cubes, fitted into what seemed to be a patternless arrangement of varying elevations. It was a dull brown and grey colour, made as far as I could tell from many different kinds of timber. There seemed to be very little use of concrete or metals, and nothing was painted. This external appearance contrasted sharply with the interior – or at least, those few areas I had seen – which were clean and brightly decorated. As Malchuskin's hut was directly to the west of the city, it was impossible for me to estimate the width as I walked towards it, though I estimated its length to be about one thousand five hundred feet. I was surprised how ugly it was, and how old it appeared to be. There was much activity about, particularly to the north.

As I came near to the city it occurred to me that I had no idea how I could enter it. Yesterday, Future Denton had taken me around the exterior of the city, but my mind had been so swamped with new impressions that I had absorbed very few of the details pointed out to me. It had looked so different then.

My only clear memory was that there was a door behind the platform from which we had observed the sunrise, and I determined to head for that. This was not as easy as I imagined.

I went to the south of the city, stepping over the tracks which I had been working on the previous day, and moved round to the east side, where I felt sure Denton and I had descended by way of a series of metal ladders. After a long search I found such an access, and began to climb. I went wrong several times, and only after a long period of clambering painfully along catwalks and climbing gingerly up ladders did I locate the platform. I found that the door was still locked.

I had no alternative but to ask. I climbed down to the ground, and went once more to the south of the city where Malchuskin and the gang of men had started work again on dismantling the track.

With an air of aggrieved patience, Malchuskin left Rafael in charge, and showed me what to do. He led me up the narrow space between the two inner tracks, directly beneath the lip of the city's edge. Underneath the city it was dark and cool.

We stopped by a metal staircase.

33

'At the top of that there's an elevator,' he said. 'You know what that is?'

'Yes.'

'You've got a guild key?'

I fumbled in a pocket and produced an irregularly shaped piece of metal that Clausewitz had given me. It opened the lock on the crèche door. 'Is this it?'

'Yes. There's a lock on the elevator. Go to the fourth level, find an administrator, and ask if you can use the bathroom.'

Feeling very stupid I did as he directed. I heard Malchuskin laughing as he walked back towards the daylight. I found the elevator without difficulty, but the doors would not open when I turned the key. I waited. A few moments later the doors opened abruptly, and two guildsmen came out. They took no notice of me, and went down the steps to the ground.

Suddenly, the doors began to close of their own accord, and I hurried inside. Before I could find any way of controlling the elevator, it began to move upwards. I saw a row of keyed buttons placed on the wall near the door, numbered from one to seven. I jabbed my key into number four, hoping that this was the right one. The elevator-car seemed to be moving for a long time, but then it halted abruptly. The doors opened and I stepped forward. As I came out into the passageway, three more guildsmen stepped into the car.

I caught a glimpse of a painted sign on the wall opposite the car: SEVENTH LEVEL. I had come too far. Just as the doors were closing, I hurried inside again.

'Where are you going, apprentice?' one of the guildsmen said.

'Fourth level.'

'O.K., relax.'

He used his own key on number four, and this time when the car stopped it was on the right level. I mumbled my thanks to the guildsman who had spoken to me, and stepped out of the elevator.

In my various preoccupations I had been able to overlook the discomforts in my body for the last few minutes, but now I felt tired and ill once more. In this part of the city there seemed to be so much activity: many people moving about the corridors, conversations going on, doors opening and closing. It was different from outside the city, for there was a timeless quality to the still countryside, and although people moved and worked out there the atmosphere was more leisurely. The labours of men like Malchuskin and his gang had an elemental purpose, but

34

here, in the heart of the upper levels which had for so long been forbidden to me, all was mysterious and complicated.

I remembered Malchuskin's instructions and, choosing a door at random, I opened it and went inside. There were two women inside; they were amused but helpful when I told them what I wanted.

A few minutes later I lowered my aching body into a bathful of hot water, and closed my eyes.

It had taken me so much time and effort to get my bath, that I had wondered whether I would benefit by it at all; the fact was that when I had towelled myself dry and dressed again the stiffness was not nearly as bad. There were still traces of it when I stretched my muscles, but the tiredness had gone from my body.

My early return to the city had inevitably brought Victoria to mind. The glimpse I had had of her at the ceremony had heightened my curiosity. The thought of returning immediately to dig old sleepers out of the ground paled somewhat – although I felt I shouldn't stay away from Malchuskin for too long – and I decided to see if I could find her.

I left the bathroom, and hurried back to the elevator. It was not in use, but I had to summon it to the floor I was on. When it arrived I was able to study its controls in rather more detail. I decided to experiment.

I travelled first to the seventh level, but from a brief excursion into its corridors I could see no immediately obvious difference from the level I had just left. The same was true for most of the other levels, though there was more apparent activity on the third, fourth, and fifth. The first level was the dark tunnel actually beneath the city itself.

I travelled up and down a couple of times, discovering that there was a surprisingly long distance between the first and second levels. All other distances were very short. I left the elevator at the second level, feeling intuitively that this would be where I would find the crèche, and that if I was wrong I would go in search of it on foot.

Opposite the elevator entrance on the second level was a flight of steps descending to a transverse corridor. I had a vague recollection of this from when Bruch had taken me up to the ceremony, and soon I came across the door leading into the crèche.

Once inside, I locked the door with the guild key. It was all so familiar. I realised that until the moment I shut the door my movements had been guarded and cautious, but now I felt at home. I hurried down the steps, and walked along the short corridor of the area I knew so well. It looked different from the rest of the city, and it smelt different. I saw the familiar scratches on the walls, where generations of children before me had inscribed their names, saw the old brown paint, the worn coverings on the floors, the unlockable doors to the cabins. Out of long habit I headed straight for my cabin, and went inside. Everything here was untouched. The bed had been made up, and the cabin was tidier than it had ever been when I was using it regularly, but my few possessions were still in place. So too were Jase's, though there was no sign of him.

I looked round once more, then returned to the corridor. The purpose of the visit to my cabin had been fulfilled: I had no purpose. I headed on down the corridor, towards the various rooms where we had been given lessons. Muted noises came through the closed doors. I peered through the circular glass peepholes, and saw the classes in progress. A few days earlier, I had been in there. In one room I saw my erstwhile contemporaries; some of them, like me, no doubt headed for an apprenticeship with one of the first-order guilds, most of them destined for administrative jobs in the city. I was tempted to go in and take their questions in my stride, maintaining a mysterious silence.

There was no segregation of the sexes in the crèche, and in each room I peered into I searched for a sight of Victoria; she did not appear to be there. When I had checked all the classrooms I went down to the general area: the dining-hall (here there was background noise of the midday meal being prepared), the gymnasium (empty), and the tiny open space, which gave access only to the blue sky above. I went to the common-room, that one place in the whole extent of the crèche which could be used for general recreation. Here there were several boys, some of whom I had been working with only a few days before. They were talking idly – as was usual when left alone for the purposes of private study – but as soon as they noticed me I became the centre of attention. It was the situation I had just now resisted.

They wanted to know which guild I had joined, what I was doing, what I had seen. What happened when I came of age? What was outside the crèche?

Curiously, I wouldn't have been able to answer many of their questions, even if I had been able to break the oath. Although

36

I had done many things in the space of a couple of days. I was still a stranger to all that I was seeing.

I found myself resorting – as indeed Jase had done – to concealing what little I knew behind a barrier of crypticism and humour. It clearly disappointed the boys, and although their interest did not diminish the questions soon stopped.

I left the crèche as soon as I could, since Victoria was evidently no longer there.

Descending by way of the elevator, I returned to the dark area beneath the bulk of the city, and walked out between the tracks to the sunlight. Malchuskin was exhorting his unwilling labourers to unload the bogie of its rails and sleepers, and he hardly noticed that I had returned.

5

The days passed slowly, and I made no more return visits to the city.

I had learned the error of my ways by throwing myself too enthusiastically into the physical side of the track-work. I decided to follow Malchuskin's lead, and confined myself in the main to supervising the hired labourers. Only occasionally would he and I pitch in and help. Even so, the work was arduous and long, and I felt my body responding to the new labours. I soon felt fitter than I had ever done in my life before, my skin was reddening under the rays of the sun, and soon the physical work became less of a strain.

My only real complaint was with the unvarying diet of synthesised food and Malchuskin's inability to talk interestingly about the contribution we were making to the city's security. We would work late into the evenings, and after a rough meal we would sleep.

Our work on the tracks to the south of the city was nearly complete. Our task was to remove all the track and erect four buffers at a uniform distance from the city. The track we removed was carried round to the north of the city where it was being re-laid.

One evening, Malchuskin said to me: 'How long have you been out here?'

'I'm not sure.'

'In days.'

'Oh . . . seven.'

I had been trying to estimate it in terms of miles.

'In three days' time you get some leave. You have two days inside the city, then you come back here for another mile.'

I asked him how he reckoned the passage of time in terms of both days and distance.

'It takes the city about ten days to cover a mile,' he said. 'And in a year it will cover about thirty-six and a half.'

'But the city isn't moving.'

'Not at the moment. It will be soon. Anyway, we don't take account of how much the city has actually moved, so much as

38

how much it *should* have moved. It's based on the position of the optimum.'

I shook my head. 'What does that mean?'

'The optimum is the ideal position for the city to be. To maintain that it would have to move approximately a tenth of a mile every day. That's obviously out of the question, so we move the city towards optimum whenever we can.'

'Has the city ever reached optimum?'

'Not as long as I can remember.'

'Where's the optimum now?'

'About three miles ahead of us. That's about average. My father was out here on the tracks before me, and he told me once that they were then about ten miles from optimum. That's the most I've ever heard.'

'But what would happen if we ever reached optimum?'

Malchuskin grinned. 'We'd go on digging up old tracks.'

'Why?'

'Because the optimum's always moving. But we're not likely to reach optimum, and it doesn't matter that much. Anywhere within a few miles of it is O.K. Put it this way . . . if we could get ahead of optimum for a bit, we could all have a good long rest.'

'Is that possible?'

'I guess so. Look at it this way. Where we are at the moment the ground is fairly high. To get up here we had to go through a long stretch of rising country. That was when my father was out here. It's harder work to climb, so it took longer, and we got behind optimum. If we ever come to some lower country, then we can coast down the slope.'

'What are the prospects of that?'

'You'd better ask your guild that. Not my concern.'

'But what's the countryside like here?'

'I'll show you tomorrow.'

Though I hadn't followed much of what Malchuskin said, at least one thing had become clear, and that was how time was measured. I was six hundred and fifty miles old; that did not mean that the city had moved that distance during my lifetime, but that the optimum had.

Whatever the optimum was.

The next day Malchuskin kept his promise. While the hired labourers took one of their customary rests in the deep shadow of the city, Malchuskin walked with me to a low rise of land some distance to the east of the city. Standing there we could see almost the whole of the immediate environment of the city.

It was at present standing in the centre of a broad valley, bounded north and south by two relatively high ridges of ground. To the south I could see clearly the traces of the track which had been taken up, marked by four parallel rows of scars where the sleepers and their foundations had been laid.

To the north of the city, the tracks ran smoothly up the slope of the ridge. There was not much activity here, though I could see one of the battery-driven bogies rolling slowly up the slope with its load of rail and sleepers and its attendant crew. On the crest of the ridge itself there was a considerable degree of activity, although from this distance it was not possible to determine exactly what was going on.

'Good country this,' Malchuskin said, but then immediately qualified it. 'For a trackman, that is.'

'Why?'

'It's smooth. We can take ridges and valleys in our stride. What gets me bothered is broken ground: rocks, rivers, or even forests. That's one of the advantages of being high at the moment. This is all very old rock around here, and it's been smoothed out by the elements. But don't talk to me about rivers. Then I get agitated.'

'What's wrong with rivers?'

'I said don't talk about them!' He slapped me good-humouredly on the shoulders, and we started our walk back towards the city. 'Rivers have to be crossed. That means a bridge has to be built unless there's one already there, which there never is. We have to wait around while the bridge is made ready, and that causes a delay. Usually, it's the Track guild that gets the blame for delays. But that's life. The trouble with rivers is that everyone's got mixed feelings about them. The one thing the city's permanently short of is water, and if we come across a river that solves one problem for the time being. But we still have to build a bridge, and that gets everyone nervous.'

The hired labourers did not look exactly pleased to see us when we returned, but Rafael moved them and work soon recommenced. The last of the tracks had now been taken up, and all we had left to do was build the last buffer. This was a steel erection, mounted above and across the last section of track, and utilising three of the concrete sleeper foundations. Each of the four tracks had a buffer, and these were placed in such a way that if the city were to roll backwards it would be supported. The buffers were not in a line, owing to the irregular shape of the southern side of the city, but Malchuskin assured me that they were an adequate safeguard.

'I shouldn't like them to have to be used,' he said, 'but if the city did roll these should stop it. I think.'

With the completion of the buffer our work was finished.

'What now?' I said.

Malchuskin glanced up at the sun. 'We ought to move house. I'd like to get my hut up across the ridge, and there are the dormitories for the workers. It's getting late, though. I'm not sure that we could get it done before nightfall.'

'We could do it tomorrow.'

'That's what I'm thinking. It'll give the lazy bastards a few hours off. They'd like that.'

He spoke to Rafael, who consulted the other men. There was little doubt about the decision. Almost before Rafael had finished speaking to them, some of the men had started back towards their huts.

'Where are they going?'

'Back to their village, I expect,' said Malchuskin. 'It's just over there.' He pointed towards the south-east, over beyond the southern ridge of high ground. 'They'll be back, though. They don't like the work but there'll be pressure in the village, because we give them what they want.'

'What's that?'

'The benefits of civilisation,' he said, grinning cynically. 'To wit, the synthetic food you're always griping about.'

'They *like* that stuff?'

'No more than you do. But it's better than an empty belly, which is what most of them had before we happened along here.'

'I don't think I'd do all that work for that gruel. It's tasteless, it's got no substance, and – '

'How many meals a day did you eat in the city?'

'Three.'

'And how many were synthetic?'

'Only two', I said.

'Well, it's people like those poor sods who work their skins off just so you can eat one genuine meal a day. And from what I hear, what they do for me is the least of it.'

'What do you mean?'

'You'll find out.'

Later that evening, as we sat in his hut, Malchuskin spoke more on this subject. I discovered that he wasn't as ill-informed as he tried to make out. He blamed it all on the guild system, as ever. It had been a long established practice that the ways of

41

the city were passed down from one generation to the next not by tuition, but on heuristic principles. An apprentice would value the traditions of the guilds far more by understanding at first hand the facts of existence on which they were based than by being trained in a theoretical manner. In practice, it meant that I would have to discover for myself how the men came to work on the tracks, what other tasks they performed, and in fact all other matters concerning the continued existence of the city.

'When I was an apprentice,' Malchuskin said, 'I built bridges and I dug up tracks. I worked with the Traction guild, and rode with men like your father. I know myself how the city continues to exist, and through that I know the value of my own job. I dig up tracks and re-lay them, not because I enjoy the work but because I know why it has to be done. I've been out with the Barter guild and seen how they get the local people to work for us, and so I understand the pressures that are on the men who work under me now. It's all cryptic and obscure . . . that's the way you see it now. But you'll find out that it's all to do with survival, and just how precarious that survival is.'

'I don't mind working with you,' I said.

'I didn't mean that. You've worked O.K. with me. All I'm saying is that all the things you've probably wondered about – the oath, for instance – have a purpose, and by God it's a sensible purpose!'

'So the men will be back in the morning.'

'Probably. And they'll complain, and they'll slacken off as soon as you or I turn our backs . . . but even that's in the nature of things. Sometimes, though, I wonder . . . '

I waited for him to finish his sentence, but he said nothing more. It was an uncharacteristic sentiment, for Malchuskin did not seem to me to be in any way a pensive man. As we sat together he fell into a long silence, broken only when I got up to go outside to use the latrine. Then he yawned and stretched, and kidded me about my weak bladder.

Rafael returned in the morning with most of the men who had been with us before. A few were missing, though the numbers had been brought up to strength by replacements. Malchuskin greeted them without apparent surprise, and at once began supervising the demolition of the three temporary buildings.

First, all the contents were moved out, and placed in a large pile to one side. Then the buildings themselves were dismantled; not as difficult a task as I'd imagined, as they had evidently been

42

designed to be taken down and put up again easily. Each of the walls was joined to the next by a series of bolts. The floors broke down into a series of flat wooden slats, and the roofs were similarly bolted into place. Fittings such as doors and windows were part of the frames in which they sat. It took only an hour to demolish each cabin, and by midday everything was done. Well before then Malchuskin had gone off by himself, returning half an hour later in a battery-powered truck. We took a short break and ate a meal, then loaded the truck with as much of the material as it would hold and set off towards the ridge, Malchuskin driving. Rafael and a few of the workers clung to the sides of the truck.

It was some way to the ridge. Malchuskin steered a course that brought us diagonally towards the nearest part of the track, and we drove the rest of the way towards the ridge alongside it. There was a shallow dip in the breast of the ridge, and it was through this that the four pairs of rails had been laid. There were many men working on this part of the track: some hacking manually at the ground to each side of the track – presumably to widen it sufficiently to take the bulk of the city as it passed through – and others toiled with mechanical drills, trying to erect five metal frames, each bearing a large wheel. Only one had been so far securely laid, and it stood between the two inner tracks, a gaunt, geometrical design with no apparent function.

As we passed through the dip Malchuskin slowed the truck, looking with interest at how the work was proceeding. He waved to one of the guildsmen supervising the work, then accelerated again as we passed over the summit of the ridge. From here there was a shallow downhill slope towards a broad plain. To east and west, and on the far side of the plain, I could see hills which were much higher.

To my surprise the tracks ended only a short distance beyond the ridge. The left outer track had been built for about a mile, but the other three were barely a hundred yards long. There were two teams already at work on these tracks, but it was immediately clear that progress was slow.

Malchuskin stared round. On our side of the tracks – that is, on the western side – there was a small cluster of huts, presumably the living quarters for the track-teams already here. He headed the truck in that direction, but drove some way past before stopping.

'This'll do,' he said. 'We want the buildings up by nightfall.'

I said: 'Why don't we put them up by the others?'

'It's my policy not to. I have trouble enough with these men as it is. If they have too much contact with the others they drink more and work less. We can't stop them mixing together when they're not working. but there's no point in clustering them together.'

'But surely they have a right to do what they want?'

'They're being bought for their labour. That's all.'

He clambered down from the cabin of the truck, and began to shout at Rafael to start the work on the huts.

The truck was soon unloaded, and leaving me in charge of the re-building, Malchuskin drove the truck back over the ridge to collect the rest of the men and the materials.

As nightfall approached, the re-building was nearly completed. My last task of the day was to return the truck to the city and connect it to one of the battery-recharging points. I drove off, content to be alone again for a while.

As I drove over the ridge, the work on the raised wheels had finished for the day and the site was abandoned but for two militiamen standing guard, their crossbows slung over their shoulders. They paid no attention to me. Leaving them behind, I drove down the other side towards the city. I was surprised to see how few lights were showing and how, with the approach of night, the daytime activities ceased.

Where Malchuskin had told me I would find recharging points I discovered that other vehicles were already connected up, and no other places were available. I guessed that this was the last truck to be returned that evening, and that I would have to look around for more points. In the end, I found a spare point on the south side of the city.

It was now dark, and after I had attended to the truck I was faced with the long walk back alone. I was tempted not to return, but to stay the night inside the city. After all, it would take only a few minutes to get back to my cabin in the crèche . . . but then I thought of Malchuskin and the reaction I would get from him in the morning.

Reluctantly, I walked around the perimeter of the city, found the tracks leading northwards and followed them up to the ridge. Being alone on the plain at night was a rather disconcerting experience. It was already cold and a strong breeze was blowing from the east, chilling me through my thin uniform. Ahead of me I could see the dark bulk of the ridge, set against the dull radiance of the clouded sky. In the dip, the angular shapes of the wheel structures stood on the skyline, and pacing to and fro in their lonely vigil were the two militiamen. As I walked up to them I was challenged.

'Stop right there!' Both men had come to a halt, and although I could not see for certain I had an instinct that the crossbows were pointing in my direction. 'Identify yourself.'

'Apprentice Helward Mann.'

'What are you doing outside the city?'

'I'm working with Track Malchuskin. I passed you just now in the truck.'

'Oh yes. Come forward.'

I walked up to them.

'I don't know you,' one of them said. 'Have you just started?'

'Yes . . . about a mile ago.'

'Which guild are you in?'

'The Futures.'

The one who had spoken laughed. 'Rather you than me.'

'Why?'

'I like a long life.'

'He's young though,' the other said.

'What are you talking about?' I said.

'Been up future yet?'

'No.'

'Been down past yet?'

'No. I only started a few days ago.'

A thought occurred to me. Although I could not see their faces in the dark I could tell by the sound of their voices that they were not much older than me. Perhaps seven hundred miles, not much more. But if that was so, then surely I should know them for they would have been in the crèche with me?

'What's your name?' I said to one of them.

'Conwell Sturner. Crossbowman Sturner to you.'

'Were you in the crèche?'

'Yes. Don't remember you, though. But then you're just a kid.'

'I've just left the crèche. You weren't there.'

They both laughed again, and I felt my temper weakening. 'We've been down past, son.'

'What does that mean?'

'It means we're men.'

'You ought to be in bed, son. It's dangerous out here at night.'

'There's no one around,' I said.

'Not now. But while the softies in the city get their sleep, we save 'em from the tooks.'

'What are they?'

45

'The tooks? The dagos. The local thugs who jump out of shadows on young apprentices.'

I moved past them. I wished I'd gone into the city and hadn't come this way. Nevertheless my curiosity was aroused.

'Really . . . what do you mean?' I said.

'There's tooks out there who don't like the city. If we didn't watch them, they'd damage the track. See these pulleys? They'd have them down if we weren't here.'

'But it was the . . . tooks who helped put them up.'

'Those as work for us. But there's a lot as doesn't.'

'Get to bed, son. Leave the tooks to us.'

'Just the two of you?'

'Aye . . . just us, and a dozen more all over the ridge. You hurry on down to bed, son, and watch you don't get a quarrel between the eyes.'

I turned my back on them and walked away. I was seething with anger, and had I stayed a moment longer I felt sure I would have gone for one or the other of them. I hated their manly patronisation of me, and yet I knew I had needled them. Two young men armed with crossbows would be no defence against a determined attack, and they knew it too, but it was important for their self-esteem not to let me work it out for myself.

When I judged I was out of their earshot I broke into a run, and almost at once stumbled over a sleeper. I moved away from the track and ran on. Malchuskin was waiting in the hut, and together we ate another meal of the synthetic food.

6

After two more days' work with Malchuskin the time came for
my period of leave. In those two days Malchuskin spurred the
labourers on to more work than I had ever seen them do, and
we made good progress. Although track-laying was harder work
than digging up old track, there was the subtle benefit of seeing
the results, in the shape of an ever-extending section of track.
The extra work took the form of having to dig the foundation-
pits for the concrete blocks before actually laying the sleepers
and rail. As there were now three track-crews working to the
north of the city, and each of the tracks was approximately the
same length, there was the additional stimulus of competition
amongst the crews. I was surprised to see how the men responded
to this competition, and as the work proceeded there was a certain
amount of good-natured banter among them as they toiled.

'Two days,' Malchuskin said, just before I left for the city.
'Don't take any longer. They'll be winching soon, and we need
every man available.'

'Am I to come back to you?'

'It's up to your guild . . . but yes. The next two miles will be
with me. After that you transfer to another guild, and do three
miles with them.'

'Who will it be?' I said.

'I don't know. Your guild will decide that.'

'O.K.'

As we finished work late on the last night I slept in the hut.
There was another reason too: I had no wish to walk back to the
city after dark and pass through the gap guarded by the militiamen. During the day there was little or no sign of the Militia,
but after my first experience of them Malchuskin had told me
that a guard was mounted every night, and during the period
immediately prior to a winching operation the track was the
most heavily guarded area.

The next morning I walked back along the track to the city.

It was not difficult to locate Victoria now that I was authorised

47

to be in the city. Before, I had been hesitant in looking for her, for at the back of my mind there had been the thought that I should have been getting back to Malchuskin as soon as I could. Now I had two whole days of leave, and was relieved of the sense of evading what my duties should have been.

Even so, I still had no way of knowing how to find her . . . and so had to resort to the expedient of asking. After a few misroutings I was directed to a room on the fourth level. Here, Victoria and several other young people were working under the supervision of one of the women administrators. As soon as Victoria saw me standing at the door she spoke to the administrator, then came over to me. We went out into the corridor.

'Hello, Helward,' she said, shutting the door behind her.

'Hello. Look . . . if you're working I can see you later.'

'It's all right. You're on leave, aren't you?'

'Yes.'

'Then I'm on leave too. Come on.'

She led the way down the corridor, turned off into a side passage, and then went down a short flight of steps. At the bottom was another corridor, lined on both sides by doors. She opened one of them and we went inside.

The room beyond was much larger than any private room I had so far seen inside the city. The largest single piece of furniture was a bed placed against one of the walls, but the room was also well and comfortably furnished with a quite surprising amount of floor space. Against one wall was a wash-basin and a small cooker. There was a table and two chairs, a cupboard to keep clothes in, and two easy chairs. Most unexpected of all, there was a window.

I went over to it immediately and looked out. There was an area of open space beyond, bounded on the opposite side by another wall with many windows. The space extended to left and right, but the window was small and I could not see what lay at the sides of the space.

'Like it?' Victoria said.

'It's so large! Is it all yours?'

'In a sense. Ours, once we're married.'

'Oh yes. Someone said I'd have quarters to myself.'

'This is probably what they meant,' said Victoria. 'Where are you living at the moment?'

'I'm still in the crèche. But I haven't stayed there since the ceremony.'

'Are you outside already?'

48

'I . . .'

I wasn't sure what to say. *Outside?* What could I tell Victoria, bound as I was to the oath?

'I know you go outside the city,' said Victoria. 'It's not such a secret.'

'What else do you know?'

'Several things. But look, I've hardly spoken to you! Can I make you some tea?'

'Synthetic?' I immediately regretted the question; I did not wish to seem ungracious.

'I'm afraid so. But I'm going to be working with the synthetics team soon, so I might be able to find some way of improving it.'

The atmosphere relaxed slowly. For the first hour or two we addressed each other coolly and almost formally, politely curious about one another, but soon we were able to take more things for granted; Victoria and I were not such strangers, I realised.

The subject of conversation turned to our life in the crèche, and this immediately brought a new doubt to the surface. Until I had actually left the city, I had had no clear idea of what I would find. The teaching in the crèche had seemed to me – and to most of the others – dry, abstract, and irrelevant. There were few printed books, and most of those were fictional works dealing with life on Earth planet, so the teachers had relied mainly on texts written by themselves. We knew, or thought we knew, much about everyday life on Earth planet, but we were told that this was not what we would find on this world. A child's natural curiosity immediately demanded to know the alternative, but on this the teachers had kept their silence. So there was always this frustrating gap in our knowledge: what by reading we learned of life on a world which was not this one, and what by surmise we were left to imagine of the ways of the city.

This situation led to much discontent, evidenced by a surplus of unspent physical energy. But where, in the crèche, was the outlet? Only the corridors and the gymnasium gave space enough to move, and then with severe limitations. The release was manifest in unrest: in the younger children emotional outbursts and disobedience, in older children fighting and passionate devotion to what few sports could be played in the tiny gymnasium . . . and in those in their last few miles before coming of age a premature carnal awareness.

There were token efforts at control by the crèche administrators, but perhaps they understood these activities for what they were. In any event, I had grown up in the crèche, and I no less than anyone else had taken part in these occasional outbursts. In the last twenty miles or so before coming of age I had indulged myself in sexual relationships with some of the girls – Victoria not among them – and it had not seemed to matter. Now she and I were to marry, and suddenly what had gone before did matter.

Perversely, the more we talked the more I found that I was wishing we could lay this ghost from the past. I wondered if I should detail my various experiences, explain myself. Victoria, however, seemed to be in control of the conversation, directing it along channels of mutual acceptability. Perhaps she too had her ghosts. She told me something of life in the city, and I was of course interested to hear this.

She said that as a woman she was not automatically granted a responsible position, and only her engagement to me had made her present work possible. Had she become engaged to a non-guildsman, she would have been expected to produce children as often as possible, and spend her time on routine domestic chores in the kitchens, or making clothes or whatever other menial tasks came along. Instead, she was now able to have some control over her future, and could probably rise to the position of a senior administrator. She was currently involved in a training procedure similar in structure to mine. The only difference was that there appeared to be less emphasis on experience, and more on theoretical education. Consequently, she had already learnt far more about the city and how it was run internally than I had.

I didn't feel free to speak of my work outside, so I listened to what she said with a great deal of interest.

She said that she had been told that there were two great shortages in the city: one was water – which I knew from what Malchuskin had said – and the other was population.

'But there are plenty of people in the city,' I said.

'Yes . . . but the rate of live births has always been low, and it's getting worse. What makes this even more serious is that there is a predominance in the live births of male babies. No one is really sure why.'

'It's the synthetic food,' I said sardonically.

'It might be.' She had missed the point. 'Until I left the crèche, I had only vague notions of what the rest of the city might be like . . . but I had always assumed that everyone in it had been born here.'

'Isn't that so?'

'No. There are a lot of women brought into the city in an effort to boost the population. Or, more specifically, in the hope they'll produce female babies.'

50

I said: 'My mother came from outside the city.'

'Did she?' For the first time since we had met Victoria looked ill at ease. 'I didn't know that.'

'I thought it would be obvious.'

'I suppose it was, but somehow I never thought . . . '

'It doesn't matter,' I said.

Abruptly, Victoria fell silent. It really wasn't of much concern to me, and I regretted having mentioned it.

'Tell me more about this,' I said.

'No . . . there's not much more. What about you? What's your guild like?'

'It's O.K.,' I said.

Quite apart from the fact that the oath forbade me to speak about it, I felt no inclination to talk. In that abrupt silence from Victoria I had gained a distinct impression that there had been more to say, but that some discretion prevented her from doing so. For the whole of my life – or at least as much of it as I could remember – the absence of my mother had been treated as a matter of fact. My father, whenever we spoke of it, talked factually about it, and there seemed to be no stigma attached. Indeed, many of the boys in the crèche had been in the same situation as I and, what is more, most of the girls. Until the subject had provoked this reaction in Victoria, I'd never thought about it.

'You're something of an oddity,' I said, hoping to get her to return to the subject by approaching it from a different direction. 'Your mother is still in the city.'

'Yes,' she said.

So that was to be the end of it. I decided to let it drop. In any event, I hadn't especially wanted to discuss matters outside ourselves. I had come to the city to spend my time getting to know Victoria, not to talk about genealogy.

But the feeling persisted; the conversation had died.

'What's out there?' I said, indicating the window. 'Can we go there?'

'If you like. I'll show you.'

I followed her out of the room, and along the corridor to where a door led to the outside. There was not much to see: the open space was no more than an alley running between the two parts of the residential block. At one end of it there was a raised section, reached by a wooden staircase. We walked first to the opposite end, where another door led back into the city; returning, we climbed the steps and came out on a small platform, where several wooden seats were placed, and where there was room to

51

move with some freedom. On two sides the platform was bounded by higher walls, presumably containing other parts of the city's interior, and the side by which access was gained looked down over the roofs of the residential blocks and along the alleyway. But on the fourth side the view was uninterrupted, and it was possible to see out into the surrounding countryside. This was a revelation to me: the terms of the oath had implied that no one but guildsmen should ever see outside the city.

'What do you think?' Victoria said, sitting down on one of the seats which looked out across the view.

I sat next to her. 'I like it.'

'Have you been out there?'

'Yes.' It was difficult; already I was finding myself in conflict with the terms of the oath. How could I talk to Victoria about my work without breaking what I had sworn?

'We're not allowed up here very often. It's locked at night, and only open at some hours of the day. Sometimes it's locked for several days on end.'

'Do you know why?'

'Do you?' she said.

'It's probably . . . something to do with the work out there.'

'Which you're not going to talk about.'

'No,' I said.

'Why not?'

'I can't.'

She glanced at me. 'You're very tanned. Do you work in the sun?'

'Some of the time.'

'This place is locked when the sun's overhead. All I've ever seen of it is when the rays touch the higher parts of the buildings.'

'There's nothing to see,' I said. 'It's very bright, and you can't stare at it.'

'I'd like to find that out for myself.'

I said: 'What are you doing at the moment? In your work, I mean?'

'Nutrition.'

'What's that?'

'It's determining how to work out a balanced diet. We have to make sure that the synthetic food contains enough protein, and that people eat the right amount of vitamins.' She paused, her voice having reflected a general lack of interest in the subject. 'Sunlight contains vitamins, you know.'

'Does it?'

52

'Vitamin D. It's produced in the body by the action of sunlight on the skin. That's worth knowing if you never see the sun.'

'But it can be synthesised,' I said.

'Yes . . . and it is. Shall we go back to the room and have some more tea?'

I said nothing to this. I don't know what I had expected by seeing Victoria, but I had not anticipated this. Illusions of some romantic ideal had tempted me during my days working with Malchuskin, and from time to time these had been tempered by a feeling that perhaps she and I might have to adapt to each other; in any event it had never occurred to me that there would be such an undercurrent of resentment. I had seen us working together towards realising the intimate relationship formed for us by our parents, and somehow shaping it in such a way that it would become a realistic and perhaps even loving relationship. What I had not foreseen was that Victoria had seen us both in larger terms: that I would be forever enjoying the advantages of a way of life forbidden to her.

We stayed on the platform. Victoria's remark about returning to the room had been ironic, and I was sensitive enough to identify it. Anyhow, I felt that for different reasons we would both prefer to stay on the platform; I did, because my work outside had given me a taste for fresh air, and by contrast I now found the interior of the city buildings claustrophobic, and I supposed Victoria did, for this platform was as near as she could come to leaving the city. Even so, the undulating countryside to the east of the city served as a reminder of the newly discovered difference that separated us.

'You could apply to transfer to a guild,' I said in a moment, 'I'm sure – '

'I'm the wrong sex,' she said abruptly. 'It's men only, or didn't you realise that?'

'No . . . '

'It hasn't taken me long to work a few things out,' she went on, speaking quickly and barely suppressing her bitterness. 'I'd seen it all my life and never recognised it: my father always away from the city, my mother working in her job, organising all those things we took for granted, like food and heating and disposal of sewage. Now I *have* recognised it. Women are too valuable to risk outside. They're needed here in the city because they breed, and they can be made to breed again and again. If they're not lucky enough to be born in the city, they can be brought from outside and sent away when they've served their

53

purpose.' The sensitive subject again, but this time she didn't falter. 'I know that the work outside the city has to be done, and whatever it is it's done at risk . . . but I've been given no option. Just because I'm a woman I have no choice but to be kept inside this damned place and learn fascinating things about food production, and whenever I can I have to give birth.'

I said: 'Do you not want to marry me?'

'There's no alternative.'

'Thanks.'

She stood up, walked angrily towards the steps. I followed her down, and walked behind her as she returned to her room. I waited in the doorway, watching her as she stood with her back to me, looking out of the window at the narrow alleyway between the buildings.

'Do you want me to go?' I said.

'No . . . come in and close the door.'

She didn't move as I did this.

'I'll make some more tea,' she said.

'O.K.'

The water in the pan was still warm, and it took only a minute or so to bring it back to boiling.

'We don't have to marry,' I said.

'If it's not you it'd be someone else.' She turned and sat beside me, taking her cup of the synthetic brew. 'I've nothing against you, Helward. You should know that. Whether we like it or not, my life and yours is dominated by the guild system. We can't do anything about that.'

'Why not? Systems can be changed.'

'Not this one! It's too firmly entrenched. The guilds have the city sewn up, for reasons I don't suppose I'll ever know. Only the guilds can change the system, and they never will.'

'You sound very sure.'

'I am,' she said. 'And for the good reason that the system which runs my life is itself dominated by what goes on outside the city. As I can never take part in that I can never do anything to determine my own life.'

'But you could . . . through me.'

'Even you won't talk about it.'

'I can't,' I said.

'Why not?'

'I can't even tell you that.'

'Guild secrecy.'

'If you like,' I said.

54

'And even as you're sitting here now, you're subscribing to it.'

'I have to,' I said simply. 'I was made to swear –'

Then I remembered: the oath itself was one of the terms of the oath. I had breached it, and so easily and naturally that it had been done before I'd thought.

To my surprise, Victoria reacted not at all.

'So the guild system is ratified,' she said. 'It makes sense.'

I finished my tea. 'I think I'd better go.'

'Are you angry with me?' she said.

'No. It's just –'

'Don't go. I'm sorry I lost my temper with you . . . it's not your fault. Something you said just now: through you I could determine my own life. What did you mean?'

'I'm not sure. I think I meant that as the wife of a guildsman, which I'll be one day, you'd have more of a chance of . . .'

'Of what?'

'Well . . . seeing through me whatever sense there is in the system.'

'And you're sworn not to tell me.'

'I . . . yes.'

'So first-order guildsmen have it all worked out. The system demands secrecy.'

She leaned back and closed her eyes.

I was very confused, and angry with myself. I had been an apprentice for ten days, and already I was technically under sentence of death. It was too bizarre to take seriously, but my memory of the oath was that the threat had been a convincing one at the time. The confusion arose because unwittingly Victoria had involved the tentative emotional commitment we had made to each other. I could see the conflict, but could do nothing about it. I knew from my own life inside the crèche the subtle frustrations that arose through being allowed no access to the other parts of the city; if that were extended to a larger scale – allowed a small part in the running of the city, but given a point beyond which no actions were possible – that frustration would continue. But surely this was no new problem in the city? Victoria and I were not the first to be married in this way. Before us there must have been others who had encountered the same rift. Had they simply taken the system as it appeared to them?

Victoria didn't move as I left the room and went towards the crèche.

Away from her, away from the inescapable syndrome of reaction and counter-reaction by talking to her, the concerns she expressed faded and I became more worried about my own situation. If the oath were to be taken at all seriously I could be killed if word were to reach one of the guildsmen. Could breaching the oath be that dreadful a thing to do?

Would Victoria tell anyone else what I had said? On thinking this my first impulse was to go back to see her, and plead for her silence . . . but that would have made both the breach and her own resentment more serious.

I wasted the rest of the day, lying on my bunk and fretting about the entire situation. Later I ate in one of the dining-rooms of the city, and was thankful not to see Victoria.

In the middle of the night, Victoria came to my cabin. My first awareness was of the sound of the door closing, and as I opened my eyes I saw her as a tall shape standing beside the bed.

'Wha – ?'

'Ssh. It's me.'

'What do you want?' I reached out to find the light-switch, but her hand came across and took my wrist.

'Don't turn on the light.'

She sat down on the edge of the bed, and I sat up.

'I'm sorry, Helward. That's all I've come to say.'

'O.K.'

She laughed. 'You're still asleep, aren't you?'

'Not sure. Might be.'

She leaned forward, and I felt her hands press lightly against my chest and then move up until they were behind my neck. She kissed me.

'Don't say anything,' she said. 'I'm just very sorry.'

We kissed again, and her hands moved until her arms were tight around me.

'You wear a night-shirt in bed.'

'What else?'

'Take it off.'

She stood up suddenly, and I heard her undoing the coat she was wearing. When she sat down again, much closer, she was naked. I fumbled with my night-shirt, getting it caught as it came over my head. Victoria pulled back the covers, and squeezed in beside me.

'You came down here like that?' I said.

'There's no one about.' Her face was very close to mine. We kissed again, and as I pulled away my head banged against the

56

cabin wall. Victoria cuddled up close to me, pressing her body against mine. Suddenly she laughed loudly.

'Christ! Shut up!'

'What's up?' she said.

'Someone will hear.'

'They're all asleep.'

'They won't be if you keep laughing.'

'I said don't talk.' She kissed me again.

In spite of the fact that my body was already responding eagerly to her, I was stricken with alarm. We were making too much noise. The walls in the crèche were thin, and I knew from long experience that sounds transmitted readily. With her laughter and our voices, the fact that of necessity we were squeezed in the bunk against the wall, I was certain we'd awaken the whole crèche. I pushed her away and told her this.

'It doesn't matter,' she said.

'It does.'

I flung back the bed-covers, and scrambled over her. I turned on the light. Victoria shielded her eyes against the glare, and I tossed her coat to her.

'Come on . . . we'll go to your room.'

'No.'

'Yes.' I was pulling on my uniform.

'Don't put that on,' she said. 'It smells.'

'Does it?'

'Abominably.'

She sat up and as she did so I stared at her, admiring the neatness of her naked body. She pulled the coat around her shoulders, then got out of the bed.

'O.K.,' she said. 'But let's be quick.'

We left my cabin and let ourselves out of the crèche. We hurried along the corridors. As Victoria had said, this late at night there was no one about, and the corridor lights were dimmed. In a few minutes we had reached her room. I closed the door, and bolted it. Victoria sat down on the bed, holding her coat around her.

I took off my uniform and climbed into the bed.

'Come on, Victoria.'

'I don't feel like it now.'

'Oh, Christ . . . why not?'

'We should have stayed where we were,' she said.

'Do you want to go back?'

'Of course not.'

'Get in with me,' I said. 'Don't sit there.'

'O.K.'

She undid her coat and dropped it on the floor, then climbed in beside me. We put our arms around each other, and kissed for a moment, but I knew what she meant. The desire had left me as rapidly as it had come. After a while we just lay there in silence. The sensation of being in bed with her was pleasant, but although I was aware of the sensuality of it nothing happened.

Eventually, I said: 'Why did you come to see me?'

'I told you.'

'Was that all . . . that you were sorry?'

'I think so.'

'I nearly came to see you,' I said. 'I've done something I shouldn't. I'm frightened.'

'What was it?'

'I told you . . . I told you I had been made to swear something. You were right, the guilds impose secrecy on their members. When I became an apprentice I had to take an oath, and part of it was that I had to swear I would not reveal the existence of the oath. I broke it by telling you.'

'Does it matter?'

'The penalty is death.'

'But why should they ever find out?'

'If . . .'

Victoria said: 'If I say anything, you mean. Why should I?'

'I'm not sure. But the way you were talking today, the resentment at not being allowed to lead your own life . . . I felt sure you would use it against me.'

'Until just now it meant nothing to me. I wouldn't use it. Anyway, why should a wife betray her husband?'

'You still want to marry me?'

'Yes.'

'Even though it was arranged for us?'

'It's a good arrangement,' she said, and held me tighter for a few moments. 'Don't you feel the same?'

'Yes.'

A few minutes later, Victoria said: 'Will you tell me what goes on outside the city?'

'I can't.'

'Because of the oath?'

'Yes.'

'But you're already in breach of it. What could matter now?'

'There's nothing to tell anyway,' I said. 'I've spent ten days doing a lot of physical work, and I'm not sure why.'

'What kind of physical work?'

'Victoria . . . don't question me about it.'

'Well tell me about the sun. Why is no one in the city allowed to see it?'

'I don't know.'

'Is there something wrong with it?'

'I don't think so. . . . '

Victoria was asking me questions I should have asked myself, but hadn't. In the welter of new experiences, there had been hardly time to register the meaning of anything I'd seen, let alone query it. Confronted with these questions – quite aside from whether or not I should answer them – I found myself demanding the answers. Was there indeed something wrong with the sun that could endanger the city? Should this be kept secret if so? But I had seen the sun, and . . .

'There's nothing wrong with it,' I said. 'But it doesn't look the same shape as I'd thought.'

'It's a sphere.'

'No it's not. Or at least it doesn't look like one.'

'Well?'

'I shouldn't tell you, I'm sure.'

'You can't leave it like that,' she said.

'I don't think it's important.'

'I do.'

'O.K.' I had already said too much, but what could I do? 'You can't see it properly during the day, because it's so bright. But at sunrise or sunset you can see it for a few minutes. I think it's disk-shaped. But it's more than that, and I don't know the words to describe it. In the centre of the disk, top and bottom, there's a kind of shaft.'

'Part of the sun?'

'Yes. A bit like a spinning-top. But it's difficult to see clearly because it's so bright even at those times. The other night, I was outside and the sky was clear. There's a moon, and that's the same shape. But I couldn't see that clearly either, because it was in phase.'

'Are you sure of this?'

'It's what I've seen.'

'But it's not what we were taught.'

'I know,' I said. 'But that's how it is.'

I said no more. Victoria asked more questions but I pushed

them aside, pleading that I did not know the answers. She tried to draw me further on the work I was doing, but somehow I managed to keep my silence. Instead, I asked her questions about herself and soon we had moved away from what was for me a dangerous subject. It could not be buried forever, but I needed time to think. Some time later we made love, and shortly afterwards we fell asleep.

In the morning Victoria made some breakfast, then left me sitting naked in her room while she took my uniform to be laundered. While she was away I washed and shaved, then lay on the bed until she returned.

I put my uniform on again: it felt crisp and fresh, not at all like the rather stiff and odorous second skin it had become as a result of my labours outside.

We spent the rest of the day together, and Victoria took me to show me around the interior of the city. It was far more complex than I had ever realised. Most of what I had seen until then was the residential and administrative section, but there was more to it than this. At first I wondered how I should ever find my way around until Victoria pointed out that in several places plans of the lay-out had been attached to the walls.

I noted that the plans had been altered many times, and one in particular caught my attention. We were in one of the lower levels, and beside a recently drawn revised plan was a much older one, preserved behind a sheet of transparent plastic. I looked at this with great interest, noting that its directions were printed in several languages. Of these I could recognise only the French language in addition to English.

'What are these others?' I asked her.

'That's German, and the others are Russian and Italian. And this – ' she pointed to an ornate, ideographic script ' – is Chinese.'

I looked more closely at the plan, comparing it with the recent one next to it. The similarity could be seen, but it was clear that much alteration work had been carried out inside the city between the compiling of the two plans.

'Why were there so many languages?'

'We're descended from a group of mixed nationals. I believe English has been the standard language for many thousands of miles, but that's not always been the case. My own family is descended from the French.'

'Oh yes,' I said.

On this same level, Victoria showed me the synthetics plant.

60

It was here that the protein-substitutes and other organic surrogates were synthesised from timber and vegetable products. The smell in here was very strong, and I noticed that all the people who worked here had to wear masks over their faces. Victoria and I passed through quickly into the next area where research was carried out to improve texture and flavour. It was here, Victoria told me, she would soon be working.

Later, Victoria expressed more of her frustrations at her life, both present and future. More prepared for this than previously I was able to reassure her. I told her to look to her own mother for example, as she led a fulfilled and useful life. I promised her – under persuasion – that I would tell her more of my own life, and I said that I would do what I could, when I became a full guildsman, to make the system more open, more liberal. It seemed to quiet her a little, and together we passed a relaxed evening and night.

7

Victoria and I agreed that we should marry as soon as possible. She told me that during the next mile she would find out what formalities we had to undergo, and that if it were possible we would marry during my next period of leave, or during the one after. In the meantime, I had to return to my duties outside.

As soon as I came out from underneath the city it was obvious that much progress had been made. The immediate environment of the city had been cleared of most of the impedimenta of the work. There was none of the temporary buildings in sight, and no battery-operated vehicles stood against the recharging points, all, presumably, in use beyond the ridge. A more fundamental difference was that leading out from the northern edge of the city were five cables, which lay on the ground beside the tracks and disappeared from view over the hump of the ridge. On guard beside the track, pacing up and down, were several militiamen.

Suspecting that Malchuskin would be busy I walked quickly towards the ridge. When I reached the summit my suspicions were confirmed, for in the distance, where the tracks ended, there was a flurry of activity concentrated around the right inner track. Beyond this, more crews were working on some metal structures, but from this distance it was impossible to determine their function. I hurried on down.

The walk took me longer than I had anticipated as the longest section of track was now more than a mile and a half in length. Already the sun was high, and by the time I found Malchuskin and his crew I was hot from the walk.

Malchuskin barely acknowledged me, and I took off the jacket of my uniform and joined in with the work.

The crews were labouring to get this section of track extended to a length equal to the others, but the complication was that a patch of ground with a rock-hard subsoil had been encountered. Although this meant that the concrete foundations were not necessary, the pits for the sleepers could only be dug with the greatest difficulty.

I found a pickaxe on a near-by truck, and started work. Soon, the more sophisticated problems I had encountered inside the city seemed very remote indeed.

In the periods of rest I gathered from Malchuskin that apart from this section of track all was nearly ready for the winching operation. The cables had been extended, and the stays were dug. He took me out to the stay-emplacements and showed me how the steel girders were buried deep into the ground to provide a sufficiently strong anchor for the cables. Three of the stays were completed and the cables were connected. One more stay was in the process of completion, and the fifth was being erected now.

There was a general air of anxiety amongst the guildsmen working on the site, and I asked Malchuskin the cause of this.

'It's time,' he said. 'It's taken us twenty-three days since the last winching to lay the tracks this far. On present estimates we'll be able to winch the city tomorrow if nothing else goes wrong. That's twenty-four days. Right? The most we can winch the city this time is just under two miles . . . but in the time we've taken to do that the optimum has moved forward two and a half miles. So even when we've done this we'll still be half a mile farther behind optimum than we were at the last winching.'

'Can we make that up?'

'On the next winching, perhaps. I was talking to some of the Traction men last night . . . they reckon we can do a short winch next time, and then two long ones. They're worried about those hills.' He waved vaguely in a northern direction.

'Can't we go round them?' I said, seeing that a long way to the north-east the hills appeared to be slightly lower.

'We could . . . but the shortest route towards optimum is due north. Any angular deflection away from that just adds a greater distance to be covered.'

I didn't fully understand everything he told me, but the sense of urgency came across clearly.

'There's one good thing,' Malchuskin went on. 'We're dropping this crowd of tooks after this. The Future guild has found a bigger settlement somewhere up north, and they're desperate for work. That's how I like them. The hungrier they are, the harder they'll work . . . for a time, at least.'

The work continued. That evening we didn't finish until after sunset, Malchuskin and the other Track guildsmen driving on the labourers with bigger and better curses. I had no time to react one way or another, for the guildsmen themselves, and I, worked no less hard. By the time we returned to the hut for the night I was exhausted.

In the morning, Malchuskin left the hut early, instructing me to bring Rafael and the labourers across to the site as soon as possible. When I arrived he and three other Track guildsmen were in argument with the guildsmen preparing the cables. I set Rafael and the men to work on the track, but I was curious about the dispute. When Malchuskin eventually came over to us he said nothing about it but threw himself into the work, shouting angrily at Rafael.

Some time later, when we took a short break, I asked him about the argument.

'It's the Traction men,' he said. 'They want to start winching now, before the track's finished.'

'Can they do that?'

Yes . . . they say that it'll take some time to get the city up to the ridge, and we could finish off here while that's going on. We won't allow it.'

'Why not? It's sounds reasonable.'

'Because it'd mean working under the cables. There's a lot of strain on the cables, particularly when the city's being winched up a slope, like the one before the ridge. You've never seen a cable break, have you?' It was a rhetorical question; I didn't know before this that cables were even used. 'You'd be cut in half before you heard the bang,' Malchuskin finished sourly.

'So what was agreed?'

'We've got an hour to finish, then they start winching anyway.'

There were still three sections of rail to lay. We gave the men a few more minutes' rest and then the work started again. As there were now four guildsmen and their teams concentrated in one area, we moved quickly, but even so it took most of the hour to complete the track.

With some satisfaction, Malchuskin signalled to the Traction men that we were ready. We collected our tools, and carried them to one side.

'What now?' I said to Malchuskin.

'We wait. I'm going back to the city for a rest. Tomorrow we start again.'

'What shall I do?'

'I'd watch if I were you. You'll find it interesting. Anyway, we ought to pay off these men. I'll send a Barter guildsman out to you later today. Keep them here until he arrives. I'll be back in the morning.'

'O.K.,' I said. 'Anything else?'

'Not really. While the winching is taking place the Traction

64

men are in charge out here, so if they tell you to jump, jump. They might need something done to the tracks, so you'd better be alert. But I think the tracks are O.K. They've been checked already.'

He walked away from me towards his hut. He looked very tired. The hired men went back to their own huts, and soon I was left to my own devices. Malchuskin's remark about the danger of a breaking cable had alarmed me, so I sat down on the ground at what I considered was a safe distance from the site.

There was not much activity in the region of the stay-emplacements. All five of the cables had been connected up, and now ran slackly from the stays across the ground parallel to the tracks. Two Traction guildsmen were by the emplacements, carrying out what I presumed was a final check on the connections.

From the region of the ridge a group of men appeared, and walked in two orderly files towards us. From this distance it was not possible to see who they were, but I noticed that one of their number left the file at approximately one hundred yard intervals, and took up a position at the side of the track. As the men approached I saw that they were militiamen, each equipped with a crossbow. By the time the group reached the stay-emplacements only eight of them were left, and these took up a defensive formation around them. After a few minutes one of the militiamen walked over to me.

'Who are you?' he said.

'Apprentice Helward Mann.'

'What are you doing?'

'I've been told to watch the winching.'

'All right. Keep your distance. How many tooks are there here?'

'I'm not sure,' I said. 'About sixty, I think.'

'They been working on the track?'

'Yes.'

He grinned. 'Too bloody tired to do any harm. That's O.K. Let me know if they cause any trouble.'

He wandered away and joined the other militiamen. What kind of trouble the labourers would cause wasn't clear to me, but the attitude of the Militia towards them seemed to be curious. I could only presume that at some time in the past the tooks had caused some kind of damage to the tracks or the cables, but I couldn't see any of the men with whom we'd been working presenting a threat to us.

The militiamen on guard beside the tracks seemed to me to be dangerously near the cables, but they showed no sign of any awareness of this. Patiently, they marched to and fro, pacing their allotted sections of the track.

I noticed that the two Traction men at the emplacements had taken up a position behind metal shields, just beyond the stays. One of them had a large red flag, and was looking through binoculars towards the ridge. There, beside the five wheel-pulleys, I could just make out another man. As all attention seemed to be on this man I watched him curiously. He had his back towards us as far as I could make out at this distance.

Suddenly, he turned and swung his flag to attract the attention of the two men at the stays. He waved it in a wide semi-circle below his waist, to and fro. Immediately, the man at the stays with the flag came out from behind his shield and confirmed the signal by repeating the movement with his own flag.

A few moments later I noticed that the cables were sliding slowly across the ground towards the city. On the ridge I could see the wheel-pulleys turning as the slack was taken up. One by one, the cables stopped moving although the major part of their length still ran across the ground. I presumed this was the weight of the cables themselves, for in the region of the stays and the pulleys the cables were well clear of the ground.

'Give them the clear!' shouted one of the men at the stays, and at once his colleague waved his flag over his head. The man on the ridge repeated the signal, then moved quickly to one side and was lost to view.

I waited, curious to see what was next . . . although from all I could see nothing was happening. The militiamen paced to and fro, the cables stayed taut. I decided to walk over to the Traction men to find out what was going on.

No sooner was I on my feet and walking in their direction than the man who had been signalling waved his arms at me frantically.

'Keep clear!' he shouted.

'What's wrong?'

'The cables are under maximum strain!'

I moved back.

The minutes passed, and there was no evident progress. Then I realised that the cables had been slowly tightening, until they were clear of the ground for most of their length.

I stared southwards at the dip in the ridge: the city had come into sight. From where I was sitting, I could just see the top corner of one of the forward towers, bulking up over the soil and

66

rocks of the ridge. Even as I watched, more of the city came into view.

I moved in a broad arc, still maintaining a healthy distance from the cables, and stood behind the stays looking along the tracks towards the city. With painful slowness it winched itself up the farther slope until it was only a few feet away from the five wheel-pulleys which carried the cables over the crest of the ridge. Here it stopped and the Traction men began their signalling once more.

There followed a long and complicated operation in which each of the cables was slackened off in turn while the wheel-pulley was dismantled. I watched the first pulley removed in this way, then grew bored. I realised I was hungry, and suspecting that I was unlikely to miss anything of interest I went back to the hut and heated up a meal for myself.

There was no sign of Malchuskin, although nearly all his possessions were still in the hut.

I took my time over the meal, knowing that there were at least another two hours before the winching could be resumed. I enjoyed the solitude and the change from the strenuous work of the past day.

When I left the hut I remembered the militiaman's warning about potential trouble from the men, and walked over to their dormitory. Most of them were outside sitting on the ground, watching the work on the pulleys. A few were talking, arguing loudly and gesticulating, but I decided the Militia saw threats where none existed. I walked back towards the track.

I glanced at the sun: it was not long to nightfall. I reasoned that the rest of the winching should not take long once the pulleys were out of the way, for it was clear that the rest of the tracks led along a downhill gradient.

In due course the final pulley was removed, and all five cables were once again taut. There was a short wait until, at a signal from the Traction man at the stays, the slow progress of the city continued . . . down the slope towards us. Contrary to what I had imagined, the city did not run smoothly of its own accord on the advantageous gradient. By the evidence of what I saw the cables were still taut; the city was still having to pull itself. As it came closer I detected a slackening of tension in the manner of the two Traction men, but their vigilance didn't alter. Throughout the operation they concentrated their whole attention on the on-coming city.

Finally, when the huge construction was no more than about

67

ten yards from the end of the tracks, the signaller raised his red flag and held it over his head. There was a large window running across the breadth of the forward tower, and here one of the many men who stood in view raised a similar flag. Seconds later, the city halted.

There was a pause of about two minutes, and then a man came through a doorway in the tower and stood on a small platform overlooking us.

'O.K. . . . brakes secured,' he called down. 'We're slackening off now.'

The two Traction men came out from behind their metal shelters, and stretched their limbs exaggeratedly. Undoubtedly, they had been under considerable mental strain for several hours. One of them walked straight over to the edge of the city and urinated against its side. He grinned back at the other, then hauled himself up on to a ledge and clambered up the super-structure of the city itself until he reached the platform. The other man walked down past the cables – which were now visibly slacker – and disappeared under the lip of the city itself. The militiamen were still deployed in their defensive formation, but even they seemed to be more relaxed now.

The show was over. Seeing the city so near I was tempted to go inside myself, but I wasn't sure whether I should. There was only Victoria to see, and she would be occupied with her work. Besides, Malchuskin had told me to stay with the men, and I thought I ought not disobey him.

As I was walking back towards the hut, a man came over to me from the direction of the city.

'Are you Apprentice Mann?' he said.

'Yes.'

'Jaime Collings, from the Barter guild. Track Malchuskin said there were some hired men here who were to be paid off.'

'That's right.'

'How many?' said Collings.

'In our crew, fifteen. But there are several more.'

'Any complaints?'

'What do you mean?' I said.

'Complaints . . . any trouble, refusal to work.'

'They were a bit slow, and Malchuskin was always shouting at them.'

'Did they ever refuse to work?'

'No.'

'O.K. Do you know who their squad leader was?'

'There was one called Rafael, who spoke English.'

'He'll do.'

Together we walked over to the huts, and we found the men. At the sight of Collings, silence fell abruptly.

I pointed out Rafael. Collings and he spoke together in Rafael's language, and almost at once one of the others shouted back angrily. Rafael ignored him, and spoke to Collings, but it was clear that there was a lot of animosity. Once again someone shouted, and soon many of the others had joined in. A crowd gathered around Collings and Rafael, some of the men reaching through the packed bodies and jabbing at Collings.

'Do you need any help?' I shouted over the row at him, but he didn't hear. I moved closer and shouted the question again.

'Get four of the Militia,' he called out in English. 'Tell them to keep it low.'

I stared at the arguing men for a moment, then hurried away. There was still a small group of the Militia in the area of the cable-stays, and I went in that direction. They had evidently heard the noise of the argument, and were already looking towards the crowd of men. When they saw me running over to them, six of the men started out.

'He wants four militiamen!' I said, gasping from my running.

'Not enough. Leave that to me, sonny.'

The man who had spoken, who was evidently in charge, whistled loudly and beckoned towards some more of his men. Four more militiamen left their position near the city and ran over. The group of ten soldiers now ran towards the scene of the argument, with me trailing in the rear.

Without waiting to consult Collings, who was still in the centre of the mêlée, the militiamen charged into the group of men, swinging their drawn crossbows as clubs. Collings turned round suddenly, shouted at the militiamen, but was seized from behind by one of the men. He was dragged to the ground and the men moved in, kicking at him.

The militiamen were obviously trained for this kind of fighting, for they moved expertly and quickly, swinging their improvised clubs with great precision and accuracy. I watched for a moment, then struggled into the mass of men, trying to reach Collings. One of the hired men grabbed at my face, his fingers closing over my eyes. I tried to snatch my head away, but another man helped him. Suddenly I was free . . . and saw the two men who had attacked me fall to the floor. The militiamen who had rescued me made no sign of recognition, but carried on with their brutal clubbing.

The crowd was swelling now, as the other local men came to give assistance. I paid no heed to this and turned back into the thick of it, still trying to reach Collings. A narrow back was directly in front of me, clad in a thin white shirt sticking wetly to the skin. Unthinkingly, I slammed my arm around the man's throat, pulled his head back, and punched him roughly in the ear. He fell to the ground. Another man was beyond him, and I tried the same tactic, but this time before I could land a blow I was kicked roughly by another man and I fell to the floor.

Through the mass of legs I saw Collings's body on the ground, still being kicked. He was lying face-down, his arms defensively over his head. I tried to push my way across to him, but then I too was being kicked. Another foot slammed against the side of my head, and for a moment I blacked out. A second later I was conscious again, and fully aware of the vicious kicks being hurled at my body. Like Collings, I covered my head with my arms but pushed myself forward in the direction I had last seen him.

Everything around me seemed to be a surging forest of legs and bodies, and everywhere there was the roar of raised voices. Lifting my head for a moment I saw that I was only a few inches from Collings, and I pushed my way through until I was crouched on the ground beside him. I tried to stand, but was immediately felled by another kick.

Much to my surprise I realised Collings was still conscious. As I fell against him I felt his arm go over my shoulders.

'When I say,' he bawled in my ear, 'stand up!'

A moment passed, and I felt his arm grip my shoulder more tightly.

'*Now!*'

With a massive effort we pushed ourselves upwards and at once he released me, swinging his fist round and catching one of the men full in the face. I did not have his same height, and the best I could manage was an elbow jab into someone's stomach. For my trouble I was punched in the neck, and once more I fell to the ground. Someone grabbed me, and hauled me to my feet. It was Collings.

'Hold it!' He put both his arms around me, and pulled me against his chest. I held him myself, more weakly. 'It's O.K.,' he said. 'Hold it.'

Gradually the jostling around us eased, then stopped. The men moved back and I slumped in Collings's arms.

I was very dazed, and as I saw a red mist building up in my sight I caught a glimpse of a circle of militiamen, their armed

crossbows raised and aimed. The hired men were moving away.
I passed out.

I came round about a minute later. I was lying on the ground,
and one of the militiamen was standing over me.

'He's O.K.,' he shouted, and moved away.

I rolled painfully on to my side and saw that a short distance
away Collings and the leader of the Militia were arguing angrily.
About fifty yards away, the hired men were standing in a group,
surrounded by the militiamen.

I tried to stand up, and managed it on my second attempt.
Dazedly, I stood and watched while Collings continued to argue.
In a moment the Militia officer walked away towards the group
of prisoners, and Collings came over to me.

'How do you feel?' he said.

I tried to grin, but my face was swollen and painful. All I could
do was stare at him. He had a huge red bruise up one side of his
face, and his eye was beginning to close. I noticed that he held one
arm around his waist.

'I'm O.K.,' I said.

'You're bleeding.'

'Where?' I raised my hand to my neck – which was hurting
abominably – and felt warm liquid. Collings moved over and
looked at it.

'It's just a bad graze,' he said. 'Do you want to go back to the
city and have treatment?'

'No,' I said. 'What the hell happened?'

'The Militia over-reacted. I thought I told you to bring four.'

'They wouldn't listen.'

'No, they're like that.'

'But what was it all about?' I said. 'I've worked with those
men for a long time and they've never attacked us before.'

'There's a lot of built-up resentment,' said Collings. 'Specifically,
it was that three of the men have wives in the city. They weren't
going to leave without them.'

'Those men are from the *city*?' I said, not sure I had heard
properly.

'No . . . I said that their wives are there. These men are all
locals, hired from a nearby village.'

'That's what I thought. But what are their wives doing in the
city?'

'We bought them.'

8

I slept uncomfortably that night. Alone in the hut I undressed carefully and looked at the damage. One side of my chest was a mass of bruises, and there were several deep and painful scratches. The wound on my neck had stopped bleeding, but I washed it in warm water and put on it some ointment I found in Malchuskin's first-aid box. I discovered that in the fight one of my fingernails had been badly torn, and my jaw ached when I tried to move it.

I thought again about returning to the city as Collings had suggested – it was, after all, only a matter of a few hundred yards away – but in the end thought better of it. I had no wish to draw attention to myself by appearing in the sterile-clean surroundings of the city looking as if I had just come out of a drunken brawl. The truth wasn't too far from that, but even so I thought I would lick my own wounds.

I tried to sleep, only managing to doze off for a few minutes at a time.

In the morning I was awake early, and got up. I didn't wish to see Malchuskin before I had had a chance to clean myself up further. My whole body ached, and I could move only slowly.

When he arrived, Malchuskin was in a bad mood.

'I heard,' he said straight away. 'Don't try to explain.'

'I can't understand what happened.'

'You were instrumental in starting a brawl.'

'It was the Militia . . .' I said weakly.

'Yes, and you ought to know by now that you keep the Militia away from the tooks. They lost a few men some miles back, and there are a few scores to settle. Any excuse, and those stupid bastards go in and start clubbing.'

'Collings was in trouble,' I said. 'Something had to be done.'

'All right, it wasn't entirely your fault. Collings says now that he could have handled it if you hadn't brought the Militia in . . . but he also admits that he told you to fetch them.'

'That's right.'

'O.K. then, but think next time.'

'What do we do now?' I said. 'We've no labourers.'

'There are more coming today. The work will be slow at first, because we'll have to train them for it. But the advantage is that the resentments won't start at once, and they'll work harder. It's later, when they get time to think, that the trouble begins.'

'But why do they resent us so? Surely, we pay for their services.'

'Yes, but at our price. This is a poor region. The soil's bad, and there's not much food. We pass by in our city, offer them what they need . . . and they take it. But they get no long-term benefit, and I suppose we take more than we give.'

'We should give more.'

'Maybe.' Malchuskin looked indifferent. 'That's none of our concern. We work the track.'

We had to wait several hours for the new men to arrive. During that time Malchuskin and I went to the dormitory huts vacated by the previous men and cleaned them out. The previous occupants had been hustled away by the militiamen during the night, but they'd been given time to collect their belongings. There was a lot that was left though: mainly old and worn garments and scraps of food. Malchuskin warned me to keep an eye open for any kind of message that might have been left for the new men; neither he nor I discovered anything of this sort.

Later, we went outside and burned anything that had been left.

Around midday a man from the Barter guild came over to us and said that the new labourers would be with us shortly. We were made a formal apology about what had happened the previous evening, and told that in spite of much discussion it had been decided that the Militia guard would be strengthened for the time being. Malchuskin protested, but the Barter guildsman could only agree: the decision had been taken against his own opinion.

I was in two minds about this. On the one hand I had no great admiration for the militiamen, but if their presence could avert a repetition of the trouble then I supposed it was inevitable.

Malchuskin was beginning to fret about the delay. I presumed that this was because of the ever-present necessity to make up lost time, but when I mentioned this he was not as concerned about this as I'd thought.

'We'll make time on the optimum on the next winching,' he said. 'The delay last time was because of the ridge. That's behind us now and the land's fairly level ahead of us for the next few miles. I'm more concerned about the state of the track behind the city.'

'The Militia will be protecting it,' I said.

'Yes . . . but they can't stop it buckling. That's the main risk, the longer it's left.'

'Why?'

Malchuskin looked at me sharply. 'We're a long way south of optimum. You know what that means?'

'No.'

'You haven't been down past yet?'

'What does that mean?'

'A long way south of the city.'

'No . . . I haven't.'

'Well when you go down there you'll find out what happens. In the meantime, take my word for it. The longer we leave the track laid south of the city, the more risk there is of it becoming unusable.'

There was still no sign of the hired men, and Malchuskin left me and went over and spoke to two more Track guildsmen who had just come out of the city. In a while he returned.

'We'll wait another hour, and if no one's come by then we'll second some men from one of the other guilds and start work. We can't wait any longer.'

'Can you do that, use other guilds?'

'Hired men are a luxury, Helward,' he said. 'In the past the track-laying was done by guildsmen alone. Moving the city's the main priority and nothing stands in the way. If we had to, we'd have everyone in the city out here laying the tracks.'

Suddenly he seemed to relax, and lay back on the ground and closed his eyes. The sun was almost directly overhead and it seemed hotter than usual. I noticed that over to the north-west there was a line of dark clouds, and that the air felt stiller and more humid than normal. Even so, the sun was still untouched by clouds and with my body still sore from its beating I would rather lie here lazily than be working on the track.

A few minutes later Malchuskin sat up and looked northwards. Coming towards us was a large band of men, led by five of the Barter guildsmen wearing their regalia of cloaks and colours.

'Good . . . now we start work,' said Malchuskin.

In spite of his barely concealed relief there was much that had to be done before work could begin. The men had to be organised into four groups, and an English-speaking one appointed leader. Then bunks had to be allotted in the huts, and their possessions stowed away. Malchuskin looked optimistic throughout all this, in spite of the additional delays.

'They're looking hungry,' he said. 'Nothing like an empty belly to keep them working.'

They were indeed a dishevelled lot. They all had clothes of sorts but very few had any shoes, and most of them wore their hair and beards long. Their eyes were deep-sunken in their faces, and several sported stomachs swollen by lack of proper food. I noticed that one or two walked with discomfort, and one had a mutilated arm.

'Are they fit to work?' I asked Malchuskin quietly.

'Not properly. But a few days of work and a proper diet, and they'll be O.K, A lot of tooks look like this when we first hire them.'

I was shocked by the condition they were in, and reflected that the local standard of living must be as bad as Malchuskin had made out. If this were so I could better understand the way resentment grew against the people of the city. I supposed that what the city gave in return for the labourers was a long way beyond what they were generally accustomed to, and this gave them a glimpse of a better fed, more comfortable life. As the city passed on, they would have to revert to their former primitive existence, the city meanwhile having taken of the people's best.

More delays, as the men were given food, but Malchuskin was looking more optimistic than ever.

Finally, we were ready to begin. The men formed themselves into four groups, each headed by a guildsman. We set off for the city, collected the four track bogies, and headed south down the tracks in grand style. To each side of the rails the militiamen continued their guard, and as we crossed the ridge we saw that down in the valley we had recently vacated there was a strong guard around the track buffers.

With four track-teams now at work there was the additional incentive of competition I had noticed before. Perhaps it was too early for the men to respond to this, but that would come later.

Malchuskin stopped the bogie a short distance before the buffer, and explained to the group leader – a middle-aged man named Juan – what had to be done. Juan related this to the men, and they nodded their understanding.

'They haven't the vaguest idea what they've got to do,' Malchuskin said to me, chuckling. 'But they'll pretend to understand.'

The first task was to dismantle the buffer, and move it up the tracks to a position just behind the city. Malchuskin and I had only just started to demonstrate how the buffer was dismantled when the sun went in abruptly and the temperature dropped.

Malchuskin glanced up at the sky. 'We're in for a storm.'

After this remark he paid no more attention to the weather, and we continued with the work. A few minutes later we heard the first distant grumble of thunder, and a short while after that the rain began to fall. The hired men looked up in alarm, but Malchuskin kept them going. Soon the storm was on top of us, the lightning flashing and the thunder cracking in a way that terrified me. We were all soon drenched, but the work continued. I heard the first complaints, but Malchuskin – through Juan – stilled them.

As we were taking the component parts of the buffer back up the track, the storm cleared and the sun came out again. One of the men began to sing, and soon the others joined in. Malchuskin looked happy. The day's work finished with erecting the buffer a few yards behind the city; the other crews also stopped work when they had built theirs.

The next day we started early. Malchuskin still looked happy but expressed his desire to get on with the work as fast as we could.

As we tried to take up the southernmost part of the track, I saw at first hand the cause of his worry. The tie-bars holding the rails to the sleepers had bent, and had to be wrenched away manually, bending them beyond re-use. Similarly, the action of the pressure of the tie-bars against the sleepers had split the wood in many places – though Malchuskin declared they could be used again – and many of the concrete foundations had cracked. Fortunately, the rails themselves were still in a usable condition; although Malchuskin said they had buckled slightly, he reckoned they could be straightened again without too much difficulty. He held a brief conference with the other Track guildsmen, and it was decided to dispense with the use of the bogies for the moment, and concentrate on digging up the track before any more of it became distorted. As it was still some two miles between where we were working and the city, each journey in the bogie took a long time and this decision made sense.

By the end of that day we had worked our way up the track to a point where the buckling effect was only just beginning to be felt. Malchuskin and the others declared themselves satisfied. we loaded the bogies with as many of the rails and the sleepers as they would hold, and called a halt again.

And so the track-labours continued. By the time my ten-day period came to an end, the track-removal was well advanced, the hired men were working well as teams, and already the new track to the north of the city was being laid. When I left Malchuskin he was as contented as I had ever seen him, and I felt not in the least guilty about taking my two days' leave.

9

Victoria was waiting for me in her room. By this time the bruises and scratches from the fracas had mostly healed, and I had decided to say nothing of it. Word of the scuffle had evidently not reached her, for she did not ask me about it.

After leaving Malchuskin's hut in the morning I had walked across to the city, enjoying that early part of the morning before it became too hot, and with this in mind I suggested to Victoria that we could go up to the platform.

'I think it'll be locked at this time of day,' she said. 'I'll go and see.'

She was gone for a few seconds, then returned to confirm that this was so.

'I suppose it'll be open some time after midday,' I said, thinking that by this time the sun would have passed from the view of the platform.

'Take your clothes off,' she said. 'They need laundering again.'

I started to undress but suddenly Victoria came over to me and put her arms around me. We kissed, spontaneously realising that we were pleased to see each other.

'You're putting on weight,' she said, as she slipped the shirt from my shoulders and ran her hand lightly across my chest.

'It's all the work I'm doing,' I said, and began to unbutton her clothes.

As a consequence of this change in our plans it wasn't until some time later that Victoria took my clothes away to be laundered, leaving me to enjoy the comforts of a proper bed.

After we had eaten some lunch we discovered that the way to the platform was now open, and so we moved up there. This time we were not alone; two men from the education administration were there before us. They recognised us both from our days in the crèche, and soon we were involved in a bland conversation about what we had been doing since coming of age. From Victoria's expression I gathered that she was as bored as I was with this, but neither of us liked to make a move to finish it.

In due course the men bade us farewell and returned to the interior of the city.

Victoria winked at me, then giggled.

'God, I'm glad we're not still in the crèche,' she said.

'So am I. And I thought they were interesting when they were teaching us.'

We sat down together on one of the seats and looked out across the landscape. From this part of the city it was not possible to see what was happening immediately at the side of the city, and even as I knew the track-crews would be carting the rails from the southern side to the north, it was not possible to see them.

'Helward . . . why does the city move?'

'I don't know. Not exactly, anyway.'

She said: 'I don't know what the guilds imagine we think about this. No one ever says anything about it, though one has only to come up here to see the city has moved. And yet if you ask anyone about it you're told it's not the concern of an administrator. Are we not supposed to ask questions?'

'They tell you nothing?'

'Nothing at all. A couple of days ago I came up here and discovered that the city had moved. A few days before that the platform had been locked for two days on end, and word was passed round to secure loose property. But that was all.'

'O.K.,' I said, 'you tell me something. At the time the city was moving, were you aware of it?'

'No . . . or I think not. Remember, I didn't realise until afterwards. Thinking back, I don't recall anything unusual the day it must have been moved, but I've never left the city and so I suppose all the time I was growing up I must have got used to occasional moves. Does the city travel along a road?'

'A system of tracks.'

'But why?'

'I shouldn't tell you.'

'You promised you would. Anyway, I don't see what harm it would do to tell me how it moves . . . it's pretty clear it does.'

The old dilemma again, but what she said made sense even though it was in conflict with the oath. Gradually, I was coming to wonder about the continued validity of the oath, even as I felt it eroding about me.

I said: 'The city is moving towards something known as the optimum, which lies due north of the city. At the moment the city is about three and a half miles south of optimum.'

'So it will stop soon?'

'No . . . and that's what isn't clear to me. Apparently, even if the city ever did reach optimum it couldn't stop as the optimum itself is always moving.'

'Then what's the point of trying to reach it?'

There was no answer to that, because I didn't know.

Victoria continued to ask questions, and in the end I told her about the work on the tracks. I tried to keep my descriptions to the minimum, but it was difficult to know how far I was breaching the oath, in spirit if not in practice. I found that everything I said to her I qualified immediately afterwards with a reference to the oath.

Finally, she said: 'Look, don't say any more about this. You obviously don't want to.'

'I'm just confused,' I said. 'I'm forbidden to talk, but you've made me see that I don't have any right to withhold from you what I know.'

Victoria was silent for a minute or two.

'I don't know about you,' she said eventually, 'but in the last few days I've begun to develop a rather strong dislike for the guild system.'

'You're not alone. I haven't heard many advocate it.'

'Do you think it could be that those in charge of the guilds keep the system in operation after it has outlived its original purpose? It seems to me that the system works by suppression of knowledge. I don't see what that achieves. It has made me very discontented, and I'm sure I'm not alone.'

'Perhaps I'll be the same when I become a full guildsman.'

'I hope not,' she said, and laughed.

'There is one thing,' I said. 'Whenever I've asked Malchuskin – he's the man I'm working with – the sort of questions you've asked me, he says that I'll find out in due course. It's as if there is a good reason for the guilds, and it relates in some way to the reason the city has to move. So far, all I've learnt is the city does have to move . . . but that's all. When I'm out there it's all work, and no time to ask questions. But what is clear is that moving the city is the first priority.'

'If you ever find out, will you tell me?'

I thought for a moment. 'I don't see how I can promise that.'

Victoria stood up abruptly and walked to the far side of the platform. She stood at the rail, looking out across the roof of the city building below at the countryside. I made no move to join her; it was an impossible situation. Already I had said too much, and in her demands that I say more Victoria was placing too great a burden on me. And yet I couldn't deny her.

After a few minutes she returned to the seat and sat down beside me.

'I've found out how we get married,' she said.

'Another ceremony?'

'No, it's much simpler. We just have to sign a form and give a copy to each of our chiefs. I've got the forms downstairs ... they're really very straightforward.'

'So we could sign them right away.'

'Yes.' She looked at me seriously. 'Do you want to?'

'Of course. Do you?'

'Yes.'

'In spite of everything?'

'What do you mean?' she said.

'In spite of the fact that you and I can't seem to talk without coming across something I either can't or shouldn't tell you, and the fact that you seem to blame me for it.'

'Does it worry you?' she said.

'A lot, yes.'

'We could postpone getting married if you prefer.'

'Would that solve anything?' I said.

I was uncertain of what it would mean if Victoria and I broke off our engagement. Because the guilds had been instrumental in formally introducing us, what new breach of the system would it imply to say now that we did not intend to marry? On the other hand, once the formal introduction was out of the way there appeared to be no pressure on us to marry immediately. As far as she and I were concerned the vexations of the limitations placed by the oath were the only differences between us. Without those, we seemed to be perfectly suited to each other.

'Let's leave it for a while,' said Victoria.

Later in the day we returned to her room and the mood lightened considerably. We talked a lot, carefully skirting those topics of conversation we both knew caused problems ... and by the time we went to bed our attitude had changed. When we woke up in the morning we signed the forms and took them along to the guild leaders. Future Clausewitz was not in the city but I found another Future guildsman, and he accepted it on Clausewitz's behalf. Everyone seemed pleased, and later that day Victoria's mother spent a lot of time with us, telling us of what new freedoms and advantages we would enjoy as a married couple.

Before I left the city to rejoin Malchuskin on the tracks I cleared what remained of my possessions from the crèche, and moved in officially with Victoria.

I was a married man, and I was six hundred and fifty-two miles old.

10

For the next few miles my life settled into a routine that was for the most part agreeable. During my visits to the city my life with Victoria was comfortable, happy, and loving. She would tell me much of her work, and through her I came to learn how the day-to-day life of the city was administered. Sometimes she would ask me about my work outside, but her early curiosity had either faded or she now thought better of asking me, for the resentments never again became as obvious as at first.

Outside, my apprenticeship progressed. The more work outside the city I participated in, the more I realised how much of a mutual effort the city's moving was.

At the end of my last mile with Malchuskin I was transferred on order of Clausewitz to the Militia. This came as an unpleasant surprise, as I had assumed that on completion of my training on the tracks I would start work with my own guild of Futures. However, I discovered that I was to be transferred to another first-order guild every three miles.

I was sorry to leave Malchuskin, for his simple application to the strenuous work on the tracks had an undeniable appeal. After we were past the ridge the terrain had been easier for track-laying, and as the new group of hired men continued to labour without untoward complaint his discontent had seemed to fade.

Before reporting to the Militia I sought out Clausewitz. I did not wish to make too much of an issue, but I asked him for the reason behind the decision.

'It's standard practice, Mann,' he said.

'But, sir, I thought by now I should be ready to enter my own guild.'

He sat in a relaxed manner behind his desk, not in the least disturbed by my mild protest. I guessed that such a query was not unusual.

'We have to maintain a full Militia. Sometimes it becomes necessary to draft other guildsmen to defend the city. If so, we do not have the time then to train them. Every first-order guildsman has served time in the Militia, and so must you.'

There was no argument with that, and so I became Crossbowman Second Class Mann for the next three miles.

I detested this period, fuming at the waste of time and the apparent insensitivity of the men I was forced to work with. I knew that I was only making life difficult for myself, and so it was, for within a few hours I was probably the most unpopular recruit in the entire Militia. My only relief was the presence of two other apprentices – one with the Barter guild and another with the Track guild – who seemed to share my outlook. They, however, had the fortunate ability to adapt to the new company and suffered less than I.

The quarters for the Militia were in the area next to the stables at the very base of the city. These consisted of two large dormitories, and we were obliged to live, eat, and sleep in conditions of intolerable overcrowding and filth. During the days we went through apparently endless periods of training involving long marches across the countryside; and were taught to fight unarmed, taught to swim rivers, taught to climb trees, taught to eat grass, and any number of other futile activities. At the end of the three miles I had learned to shoot with a crossbow, and I had learned how to defend myself when unarmed. I had made myself some bitter personal enemies, and I knew I should have to keep out of their way for some considerable time to come. I wrote it off to experience.

After this I was transferred to the Traction guild, and at once I was much happier. Indeed, from this point to the end of my apprenticeship my life was pleasant and fruitful.

The men responsible for the traction of the city were quiet, hard-working, and intelligent. They moved without haste, but they saw that the work for which they were responsible was done, and done well.

My one previous experience of their work – when watching the city being winched – had not revealed to me the extent of their operations. Traction was not simply a question of moving the city but also involved its internal affairs.

I discovered that a large nuclear reactor was situated in the centre of the city, on the lowest level. It was from this that the city derived all its power, and the men who operated it were also responsible for the city's communication and sanitary systems. Many of the Traction guildsmen were water-engineers, and I learned that throughout the city there was a complicated system of pumping which ensured that almost every last drop of water was continually recycled. The food-synthesiser, I discovered to my horror, was based on a sewage filtration device, and although it was operated and programmed by administrators inside the city, it was in the Traction pumping-room that the quantity (and in some respects the quality) of synthesised food was ultimately determined.

It was almost as a secondary function that the reactor was used to power the winches.

There were six of these, and they were built in a massive steel housing running east-west across the city's base. Of the six, only five were used at any one time, the other being overhauled by rotation. The primary cause for concern with the winches was the bearings, which, after many thousands of miles' use, were very worn. During the time I was with the Traction men there was a certain amount of debate on the subject of whether the winching should be carried out on four winches – thus allowing more time for bearing servicing – or should be increased to all six winches, thus reducing wear. The consensus seemed to be to continue with the present system, for no major decisions were taken.

One of the jobs I worked on with the Traction men was checking the cables. This too was a recurring task for the cables were as old as the winches, and breakages happened more frequently than was ideal, which was never. Each of the six cables used by the city had been repaired several times, and in addition to the weaknesses this caused there were several parts of each cable which were beginning to fray. Before each winching, therefore, each of the five cables to be used had to be checked over foot by foot, cleaned and greased, and bound where frays occurred.

Always in the reactor-room, or working outside on the cables, the talk was of catching up the lost ground towards the optimum. How the winches might be improved, how new cables might be obtained. The entire guild seemed to be alive with ideas, but they were not men fond of theories. Much of their work was concerned with mundane matters; for instance, while I was with the guild a new project was begun to construct an additional water-reservoir in the city.

One pleasurable benefit of this aspect of my apprenticeship was that I was able to spend the nights with Victoria. Although I came back to the room at night hot and dirty from my work, I was for this short period enjoying the comforts of a domestic existence and the satisfactions of a worthwhile job.

One day, working outside the city as one of the cables was being hauled mechanically out towards the distant stay-emplacement, I

85

asked the guildsman I was with about Gelman Jase.

'An old friend of mine, apprenticed to your guild. Do you know him?'

'About your age is he?'

'A bit older.'

'We had a couple of apprentices through a few miles back. Can't remember their names. I can check, if you like.'

I was curious to see Jase. It had been a long time since I'd seen him, and it would be good to compare notes with someone who was going through the same process as myself.

Later that day I was told that Jase had been one of the two apprentices the man had mentioned. I asked how I could contact him.

'He won't be around for a while.'

'Where is he?' I said.

'He's left the city. Down past.'

Too soon, my time with the Traction guild ended and I was transferred to the Barter guild for the next three miles. I greeted this news with mixed feelings, having witnessed one of their operations at first hand. To my surprise I learnt I was to work with Barter Collings, and to my further surprise I discovered it was he who had requested I work with him.

'I heard you were joining the guild for three miles,' he said. 'Thought I'd like to show you our work isn't all dealing with rioting tooks.'

Like the other guildsmen, Collings had a room in one of the forward towers of the city, and here he showed me a long roll of paper with a detailed plan drawn on it.

'You needn't take too much notice of most of this. It's a map of the terrain ahead of us, and it's compiled by the Futures.' He showed me the symbols for mountains, rivers, valleys, steep gradients – all vital information for those who planned the route the city would take on its long slow journey towards optimum. 'These black squares represent settlements. That's what we're concerned with. How many languages do you speak?'

I told him that I had never found languages easy when in the crèche, and only spoke French, and that haltingly.

'As well you're not planning to join our guild permanently,' he said. 'Ability with languages is our stock in trade.'

He told me that the local inhabitants spoke Spanish, and that he and the other Barter guildsmen had to learn this from one of the books in the city library as there were no people of Spanish descent in the city. They got by, but there were recurring difficulties with dialects.

Collings told me that of all the first-order guilds only the Track guild used hired labour regularly. Sometimes the Bridge-Builders had to hire men for short periods, but by and large the major part of the Barters' work was in hiring manual labourers for the track-work . . . and what Collings referred to as 'transference.'

'What is that?' I said immediately.

Collings said: 'It's what makes us so unpopular. The city looks for settlements where food is short, where poverty is widespread. Fortunately for the city this is a poor region, so we have a strong bargaining position. We can offer them food, technology to help their farming, medicines, electrical power; in return, the men labour for us, and we borrow their young women. They come to the city for a short while, and perhaps they will give birth to new citizens.'

'I've heard of this,' I said. 'I can't believe it happens.'

'Why not?'

'Isn't it . . . immoral?' I said hesitantly.

'Is it immoral to want to keep the city peopled? Without fresh blood we would die out within a couple of generations. Most children born to people in the city are male.'

I remembered the fight that had started. 'But the women who transfer to the city are sometimes married, aren't they?'

'Yes . . . but they stay only to give birth to one child. After that, they are free to leave.'

'What happens to the child?'

'If it is a girl, she stays in the city and is brought up in the crèche. If it is a boy, the mother may take it with her or may leave it in the city.'

And then I understood the diffidence with which Victoria had spoken on this subject. My mother had come to the city from outside, and afterwards had left. She had not taken me with her; I had been rejected. But there was no pain in this realisation.

The Barter guildsmen, like those of the Futures guild, rode out across the countryside on horses. I had never learnt to ride, and so when we left the city and headed north I walked beside Collings. Later, he showed me how to ride the horse, telling me that I would need to ride when I joined my father's guild. The technique came slowly; at first I was frightened of the horse and found it difficult to control. Gradually, as I realised the animal was docile and good-natured, my confidence grew and the horse – as if under-standing this – responded better.

We did not travel far from the city. There were two settlements to the north-east, and we visited them both. We were greeted with some curiosity, but Collings's assessment was that neither settlement displayed any great need for the commodities the city could offer, and so he made no attempts to negotiate. He told me that the city's needs for labour were met for the moment, and that there were enough transferred women to be going on with.

After the first journey away from the city – which took nine days, and during which we lived and slept rough – I returned to the city with Collings, to hear the news that the Council of Navigators had given the go-ahead for a bridge to be built. According to the interpretation Collings gave me, there were two possible routes ahead of the city. One angled the city towards the north-west, and although avoiding a narrow chasm led through hilly country with much broken rock; the other led across more level country but required a bridge to be built across the chasm. It was this latter course which had been selected, and so all available labour was to be diverted temporarily to the Bridge-Builders guild.

As the bridge was now the major priority, Malchuskin and another Track guildsman and each of their gangs were drafted, about one half of the entire Militia force was relieved of other duties to assist, and several men from the Traction guild were to supervise the laying of the rail-way across the bridge. Ultimate responsibility for the design and structure of the bridge lay with the Bridge-Builders guild itself, and they requested fifty additional hired labourers from the Barter guild.

Collings and another Barter guildsman left the city at once, and headed for the local settlements; meanwhile, I was taken north to the site of the bridge, and was placed in the charge of the supervising guildsman, Bridges Lerouex, Victoria's father.

When I saw the chasm I realised that the bridge presented a major engineering problem. It was wide – about sixty yards across at the point selected for the bridge – and the chasm walls were crumbly and broken. A fast-running stream lay at the bottom. In addition, the northern side of the chasm was some ten feet lower than the southern side, which meant that the track would have to be laid across a ramp for some distance after the chasm.

The Bridge-Builders guild had decided that the bridge must be suspended. There was insufficient time to build an arch or cantilever bridge, and the other favoured method – that of a timber scaffolding support in the chasm itself – was impracticable owing to the nature of the chasm.

Work started immediately on the building of four towers: two each to north and south of the chasm. These were apparently insubstantial affairs, built of tubular steel. During the construction one man fell from a tower and was killed. The work continued without delay. Shortly after this I was allowed to return to the city for one of my periods of leave and while I was there the city was winched forward. It was the first time I had been inside the city knowing that a winching operation was taking place, and I was interested to note that there was no discernable sensation of movement, although there was a slight increase in background noise, presumably from the winch motors.

It was during this leave too that Victoria told me she was pregnant; an announcement that caused her mother much joy. I was delighted, and for one of the few times in my life I drank too much wine and made a fool of myself. No one seemed to mind.

Back outside the city, I saw that the usual work on tracks and cables continued – if with a general shortage of labour – and that we were now only two miles from the site of the bridge. Speaking to one of the Traction guildsmen as I passed, I learnt that the city was only one and a half miles from optimum.

This information did not register until later, when I realised that the bridge itself must actually be to the *north* of optimum by about half a mile.

There followed a long period of delay. The bridge-building proceeded slowly. After the accident more stringent safety precautions were introduced, and there were recurring checks by Lerouex's men on the strength of the structure. As we worked, we learnt that the track-laying operations at the city were going slowly; in one sense this suited us, as the bridge was a long way from being ready, but in another it was a cause for anxiety. Any time lost in the endless pursuit of the optimum was not good.

One day, word passed around the site that the bridge itself was at the point of optimum. This news caused me to look anew at our surroundings, but there seemed to be nothing unusual about optimum. Once again, I wondered what its special significance was, but as the days passed and the optimum moved on in its arcane way northwards it moved also from my thoughts.

With the resources of the city now being concentrated on the bridge, there was no chance of furthering my apprenticeship. Every ten days I was allowed my leave – as were all guildsmen on the site – but there was no thought now of my acquiring a general knowledge of the functions of the various guilds. The bridge was the priority.

Other work continued, though. A few yards to the south of the bridge a cable-stay emplacement was built, and the tracks were run up to it. In due course the city was winched along the tracks, and it stood silently near the chasm waiting for the completion of the bridge.

The most difficult and demanding aspect of the bridge-building came with running the chains across the chasm from the south towers to the north, then suspending the rail-way from them. Time was passing and Lerouex and the other guildsmen grew worried. I understood this was because as the optimum moved slowly northwards away from the bridge, the construction of the bridge itself would soon be laying itself open to the same problem that Malchuskin had shown me with the tracks to the south of the city: it was liable to buckle. Although the design of the bridge was intended to compensate for this to a certain extent, there was a definite limit to how long we could delay the crossing. Now work continued through the nights, lit by powerful arc-lamps powered from within the city. Leave was suspended, and a system of shifts devised.

As the slabs of the rail-way were laid, Malchuskin and the others put down tracks. Meanwhile, cable-stays were being erected on the northern side, just beyond the elaborate ramps that had been built.

The city was so close by, we were able to sleep in our quarters inside it, and I found a confusing difference between the extreme activity of the bridge site and the comparatively calm and normal atmosphere of everyday work inside the city. My behaviour evidently reflected this confusion, because for a while Victoria's questions about the work outside were renewed.

Soon, though, the bridge was ready. There was a further delay of a day while Lerouex and the other Bridges guildsmen carried out a series of elaborate tests. Their expressions stayed concerned, even as they pronounced the bridge safe. During the hours of the night the city prepared for the winching.

As dawn was breaking, the Traction men signalled the clear . . . and with infinite stealth the city inched forward. I had taken a vantage point on one of the two suspension towers on the south side of the chasm, and as the city's forward wheels moved slowly on to the tracks on the rail-way itself I felt a tremble of vibration through the tower as the chains took the strain. In the weak light of the rising sun I saw the suspension chains being tugged into a deeper curve by the weight, the rail-way itself clearly sagging with the immense burden being placed on it. I looked at the Bridges guildsman nearest to me, who was squatting on the tower a few yards away from me. His whole attention was on a load-meter, which was connected to the overhead chains. No one watching the delicate operation moved or spoke, as if the slightest interruption could disturb the balance. The city moved on, and soon the entire length of the bridge rail-way was bearing the weight of the city.

The silence was broken abruptly. With a loud cracking noise that echoed round the rocky walls of the chasm one of the winching cables snapped, and whiplashed back, slicing through a line of militiamen. A physical tremor ran through the structure of the bridge, and from deep inside the city I heard the rising whine of the suddenly free winch, sharply cut off as the Traction man controlling the differential drive phased it out. Now on only four cables, and moving visibly slower, the city continued on its way. On the northern side of the chasm, the broken cable lay snaked across the ground, curling over the bodies of five of the militiamen.

The most critical part of the crossing was done: the city moved between the two northern towers, and began to slide slowly down the ramps towards the cable-stays. Soon it stopped, but no one spoke. There was no sense of relief, no cry of celebration. On the far side of the chasm the bodies of the militiamen were being placed on stretchers, ready to be taken into the city. The city itself was safe for the moment, but there was much to be done. The bridge had caused an unavoidable delay, and now the city was four and a half miles behind optimum. The tracks had to be taken up, the broken cable repaired. The suspension towers and chains had to be dismantled, and saved for possible future use.

Soon the city would be winching again . . . ever onward, ever northwards, heading for the optimum that managed somehow to be always a few miles ahead.

Part Two

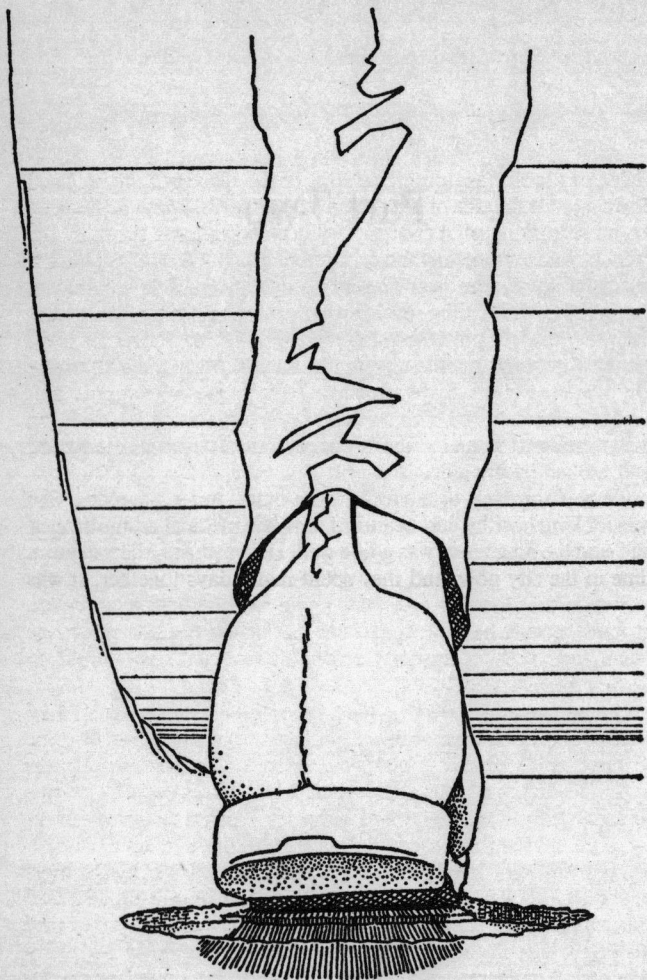

1

Helward Mann was riding. Standing in the stirrups, with his head down against the side of the neck of the large tan mare, he rejoiced in the sensations of speed: the wind blowing back his hair, the crunch of hooves against the pebbly soil, the rippling of the beast's muscular loins, the ever-present anticipation of a stumble, a throw. They were riding south, away from the primitive settlement they had just left, down through the foothills and across the plain towards the city. As the city of Earth came into view behind a low rise of ground, Helward slowed the horse to a canter and guided her in a broad turn so that they headed back north. Soon they were walking, and as the day grew hotter Helward dismounted and walked by her side.

He was thinking of Victoria, now many miles pregnant. She was looking healthy and beautiful, and the medical administrator had said the pregnancy was going well. Helward was allowed more time in the city now, and they spent many days together. It was fortunate that the city was once again moving across unbroken ground, because he knew that if another bridge became necessary, or an emergency of any sort arose, his time with her would be curtailed drastically.

He was waiting now for his apprenticeship to end. He had worked hard and long with all the guilds save one: his own, the Futures guild. Barter Collings had told him the end of the apprenticeship was approaching, and later the same day he was to see Future Clausewitz and formally discuss his progress so far. The apprenticeship couldn't end soon enough for Helward. Though still an adolescent in his emotional outlook, by the ways of the city he was deemed an adult; he had indeed worked and learned for that status. Fully aware of the city's external priorities, if still not sure of their rationale, he was ready to be accorded his title of full guildsman. In the last few miles his body had grown muscular and lean, and his skin had tanned to a deep healthy golden. He was no longer stiff after a day of labour, and he welcomed the sensation of well-being that followed a difficult task well done. With most of the guildsmen he had worked under he had become respected and liked for his willingness to work hard and without question, and as his domestic life in the city settled down to a steady and loving relationship with Victoria he became well known and accepted as a man with whom the city's security could soon be entrusted.

With Barter Collings in particular. Helward had established a good and amicable working partnership. When he had served his obligatory three mile periods with each of the other guilds he had been allowed to choose a further period of five miles with any one of the guilds but his own, and he had immediately asked to work with Collings. The Barter work attracted him, for it enabled him to see something of the way of life of the local people.

The area through which the city was currently passing was high and barren, and the soil was poor. Settlements were few, and those that they approached were almost invariably clustered around one or another collection of ramshackle buildings. The squalor was terrible, and disease was widespread. There appeared to be no kind of central administration, for each of the settlements had its own rituals of organisation. Sometimes they were greeted with hostility, and at other times the people hardly seemed to care.

The Barter work was one largely of judgement: assessing the particular outlook and needs of a chosen community, and negotiating along those lines. In most cases, negotiations were fruitless; the one thing all settlements seemed to share was an abiding lethargy. When Collings could initiate any kind of interest, the needs became immediately apparent. By and large, the city could fulfil them. With its high degree of organisation, and the technology available to it, the city had over the miles accumulated a large stockpile of foodstuffs, medicines, and chemicals, and it had also learnt by experience which of these were most required. So with offers of antibiotics, seeds, fertilisers, water-purifiers – even, in some cases, offers of assistance to repair existing implements – the Barter guildsmen could lay the groundwork for their own demands.

Collings had tried to teach Helward to speak Spanish, but he had little ability with languages. He picked up a handful of phrases, but contributed very little to the often lengthy periods of negotiation.

Terms had been agreed with the settlement they had just left. Twenty men could be raised to work on the city tracks, and another ten were promised from a smaller settlement some distance away. In addition, five women had either volunteered or been coerced – Helward was uncertain which, and he did not question Collings – to move into the city. He and Collings were now returning to the city to obtain the promised supplies, and prepare the various guilds for the new influx of temporary population. Collings had decided that all of the people should be medically examined, and this would place an additional burden on the medical administrators.

Helward liked working to the north of the city. This would soon be his territory, for it was up here, beyond the optimum, that the Future guild did its work. He often saw Future guildsmen riding north, away into the distant territory where one day the city would have to travel. Once or twice he had seen his father, and they had spoken briefly. Helward had hoped that with his experience as an apprentice, the unease which dogged their relationship would vanish, but his father was apparently as uncomfortable as ever in his company. Helward suspected that there was no deep and subtle reason for this, because Collings had once been talking about the Future guild, and had mentioned his father. 'A difficult man to talk to,' Collings had said. 'Pleasant when you get to know him, but he keeps to himself.'

After half an hour Helward remounted the horse, and walked her back along their previous path. Some time later he came across Collings, who was resting in the shade of a large boulder. Helward joined him, and they shared some of the food. As a gesture of goodwill, the leader of the settlement had given them a large slab of fresh cheese, and they ate some of it, relishing the break from their more normal diet of processed, synthesised food.

'If they eat this,' Helward said, 'I can't see that they would have much use for our slop.'

'Don't think they eat this all the time. This was the only one they had. It was probably stolen from somewhere else. I saw no cattle.'

'So why did they give it to us?'

'They need us.'

Some time later they continued on their way towards the city. Both men walked, leading the horse. Helward was both looking forward to returning to the city, and regretting that this period of his apprenticeship had ended. Realising that this was probably the last time he would have with Collings, he felt the stirrings of an old and long buried intention to talk to him about something that still caused him to fret from time to time, and of all the men he had met outside the city Collings was the only one with whom he could discuss it. Even so, he turned over the problem in his mind for some time before finally deciding to raise it.

'You're unnaturally quiet,' said Collings suddenly.

'I know . . . sorry. I'm thinking about becoming a guildsman. I'm not sure I'm ready.'

'Why?'

'It's not easy to say. It's a vague doubt.'

'Do you want to talk about it?'

'Yes. That is . . . can I?'

'I don't see why not.'

'Well . . . some of the guildsmen won't,' said Helward. 'I was very confused when I first came outside the city, and I learnt then not to ask too many questions.'

'It depends what the questions are,' said Collings.

Helward decided to abandon trying to justify himself.

'It's two things,' he said. 'The optimum and the oath. I'm not sure about either of them.'

'That's not surprising. I've worked with dozens of apprentices over the miles, and they all worry about those.'

'Can you tell me what I want to know?'

Collings shook his head. 'Not about the optimum. That's for you to discover for yourself.'

'But all I know about it is that it moves northwards. Is it an arbitrary thing?'

'It's not arbitrary . . . but I can't talk about it. I promise you that you'll find out what you want to know very soon. But what's the problem with the oath?'

Helward was silent for a moment.

Then he said: 'If you knew I'd broken it – if you knew at this moment – you'd kill me. Is that right?'

'In theory, yes.'

'And in practice?'

'I'd worry about it for days, then probably talk to one of the other guildsmen and see what he advised. But you haven't broken it, have you?'

'I'm not sure.'

'You'd better tell me about it.'

'All right.'

Helward started to talk about the questions Victoria had asked him at the very beginning, and tried to confine his account to vague generalities. As Collings stayed silent. Helward began to go into more and more detail. Soon he found himself recounting, almost word for word, everything he had told her.

When he had finished, Collings said: 'I don't think you've anything to worry about.'

Helward experienced a feeling of relief, but the nagging problem could not be dispelled as quickly as that.

'Why not?'

'No harm has come of your saying anything to your wife.'

The city had come into view as they walked, and they could see the customary signs of activity around the tracks.

'But it can't be as simple as that,' said Helward. 'The oath is very firm in the way it is worded, and the penalty is hardly a light one.'

'True . . . but the guildsmen who are alive today inherited it. The oath was passed to us, and we pass it on. So will you in your turn. This isn't to say the guilds agree with it, but no one has yet come up with an alternative.'

'So the guilds would like to dispense with it if possible?' said Helward.

Collings grinned at him. 'That's not what I said. The history of the city goes back a long way. The founder was a man named Francis Destaine, and it is generally believed that he introduced the oath. From what we can understand of the records of the time such a regimen of secrecy was probably desirable. But today . . . well, things are a little more lax.'

'But the oath continues.'

'Yes, and I think it still has a function. There are a large number of people in the city who may never know what goes on out here, and will never need to know. These are the people who are mainly concerned with the running of the city's services. They come into contact with the people from outside the city – the transferred women, for example – and if they were to speak too freely, perhaps the true nature of the city would become common knowledge with the people outside. We already have trouble with the locals, the tooks as the militia calls them. You see, the city's existence is a precarious one, and has to be guarded at all costs.'

'Are we in danger?'

'Not at the moment. But if there were any sabotage, the danger would be immediate and great. We're unpopular as things stand . . . there's no profit in allowing that unpopularity to be compounded with a local awareness of our vulnerability.'

'So I can be more open with Victoria?'

'Use your judgement. She's Lerouex's daughter, isn't she? Sensible girl. So long as she keeps to herself whatever you tell her, I can't see any harm. But don't go talking to too many people.'

'I won't,' said Helward.

'And don't go talking about the optimum moving. It doesn't.'

Helward looked at him in surprise. 'I was told it moved.'

'You were misinformed. The optimum is stationary.'

'Then why does the city never reach it?'

'It does, from time to time,' said Collings. 'But it can never stay there for long. The ground moves away southwards from it.'

2

The tracks extended about one mile to the north of the city. As Helward and Collings approached they saw one of the winch-cables being hauled out towards the stay-emplacements. Within a day or two the city would move forward again.

They led the horse over the tracks, and walked down towards the city. Here on the north side was the entrance to the dark tunnel that ran beneath the city, and which gave the only official access to the interior.

Helward walked with Collings as far as the stables.

'Goodbye, Helward.'

Helward took the proffered hand, and they shook warmly.

'You make that sound very final,' said Helward.

Collings shrugged in an off-hand way. 'I shan't be seeing you for some time. Good luck, son.'

'Where are you going?'

'I'm not going anywhere. But you are. Just take care, and make of it what you can.'

Before Helward could reply the man had turned away and hurried into the stables. For a moment Helward was tempted to go after him, but an instinct told him that it would serve no purpose. Perhaps Collings had already told him more than he should.

With mixed feelings, Helward continued down the tunnel to the elevator and waited for the car. When it arrived he went straight to the fourth level to look for Victoria. She was not in their room, so he went down to the synthetics plant to find her. She was now more than eighteen miles pregnant, but was planning to continue working for as long as possible.

When she saw him she left her bench, and they returned to the room together. There were still two hours to spare before Helward was to see Future Clausewitz, and they passed the time with inconsequential conversation. Later, when the door was unlocked, they spent a few minutes together on the outside platform.

At the appointed time Helward went up to the seventh level,

and gained access to the guild block. He was now no stranger to this part of the city, but he visited it infrequently enough to feel still slightly in awe of the senior guildsmen and Navigators.

Clausewitz was waiting in the Future guild room, and was alone. When Helward arrived he greeted him cordially, and offered him some wine.

From the Futures' room it was possible to see through a small window towards the north of the city. Ahead, Helward could see the rising ground he had been working in during the last few days.

'You've settled in well, Apprentice Mann.'

'Thank you, sir.'

'Do you feel ready to become a Future?'

'Yes, sir.'

'Good . . . from the guild's point of view there's no reason why you shouldn't. You've earned yourself some good reports.'

'Except from the Militia,' Helward said.

'You needn't concern yourself with that. Military life doesn't suit everyone.'

Helward felt a small relief; his bad showing in the Militia had made him wonder if word of it had got back to his guild.

'The purpose of this interview,' Clausewitz went on, 'is to tell you what is to happen next. You still have a nominal three miles' apprenticeship to serve with our guild, but as far as I am concerned that will be a mere technicality. Before that, though, you are to leave the city. It's a part of your training. You will probably be away for some time.'

'May I enquire for how long?' said Helward.

'It's difficult to say. Several miles, certainly. It might be as few as ten or fifteen, or it might be as long as a hundred miles of time.'

'But Victoria – '

'Yes, I understand she's expecting a child. When is it due?'

'In about nine miles,' said Helward.

Clausewitz frowned. 'I'm afraid you will have to be away at that time. There's really no alternative.'

'But couldn't it be left until afterwards?'

'I'm sorry, no. There's something you have to do. You know by now that from time to time the city is obliged to barter for the use of women from the outside. We keep these women for as short a time as possible, but even so they are rarely here for less than thirty miles. It is part of the bargain we strike that they are given safe conduct back to their settlements . . . and there are now three women who wish to leave. It is the custom of the city to use the apprentices to conduct them back, particularly as we now see this as an important part of the training process.'

Helward had been forced, by the very nature of his work, to become more sure of himself. 'Sir, my wife is expecting her first baby. I must be with her.'

'It's out of the question.'

'What if I refuse to go?'

'You will be shown a copy of the oath you swore, and you will accept the punishment it prescribes.'

Helward opened his mouth to reply, but hesitated. This was evidently not the time to debate the validity of the oath. Future Clausewitz was clearly restraining himself, for on Helward's resistance to the instruction his face had turned a deep pink, and he had sat down, resting his hands palm down on the table-top. Instead of saying what was on his mind, Helward said: 'Sir, can I appeal to your reason?'

'You can appeal, but I cannot be reasonable. You swore in your oath to place the security of the city above all other matters. Your guild training is a matter of city security, and that's the end if it.'

'But surely it could be delayed? As soon as the child is born, I could leave.'

'No.' Clausewitz turned round, and pulled forward a large sheet of paper, covered in part with a map, and in part with several lists of figures. 'These women must be returned to their settlements. In the nine miles or so of time it will take for your wife to deliver her baby, the settlements will be dangerously distant. They are already more than forty miles to the south of us. The plain fact is that you are the next apprentice on this schedule, and it is you who must go.'

'Is that your last word, sir?'

'Yes.'

Helward put down his untouched glass of wine, and walked towards the door.

'Helward, wait.'

He paused at the door. 'If I am to leave, I would like to see my wife.'

'You have a few more days yet. You leave in half a mile's time.'

Five days. It was almost no time.

'Well?' said Helward, no longer feeling the need to display customary courtesies.

'Sit down, please.' Reluctantly, Helward complied. 'Don't think I'm inhuman, but ironically this expedition will reveal to you why some of the city's customs might seem to be inhuman.

It is our way, and it is forced on us. I understand your concern for . . . Victoria, but you must go down past. There is no better way for you to understand the situation of the city. What lies there to the south of us is the reason for the oath, for the apparent barbarisms of our ways. You are an educated man, Helward . . . do you know of any civilised culture in history which has bartered for women for the simple, uncomplicated reason of wanting one gestation from them? And then, when that gestation is completed, to return them?'

'No, sir.' Helward paused. 'Except –'

'Except primitive tribes of savages who raped and pillaged. Well, maybe we're a little better than that, but the principle's no less savage. Our barter is one-sided, for all that the contrary may seem to be. We propose the bargain, call our own terms, pay the price, and move on our way. What I am telling you must be done; that you abandon your wife at a time when she needs you most is one small inhumanity that stems from a way of life that is itself inhuman.'

Helward said: 'Neither one excuses the other.'

'No . . . I'll grant you that. But you are bound by your oath. That oath stems from the causes of the major inhumanities, and when you make your personal sacrifice you will understand better.'

'Sir, the city should change its ways.'

'But you will see that's impossible.'

'By travelling down past?'

'Much will become clear. Not all.' Clausewitz stood up. 'Helward, you've been a good apprentice so far. I can see that in the miles to come you will continue to work hard and well for the city. You have a good and beautiful wife, a lot to live for. You aren't under threat of death, I promise you that. The penalty of the oath has never been invoked as far as I know, but I ask that this task that the city calls upon you to do is done, and done now. I have done it in my time, so has your father . . . and so have all other guildsmen. Even now there are seven of your colleagues – all apprentices – down past. They have had to face similar personal hardships, and not all have faced them willingly.'

Helward shook hands with Clausewitz, and went in search of Victoria.

3

Five days later, Helward was ready to leave. That he would go
had never been in serious doubt, but it had not been easy to
explain to Victoria. Although at first she had been horrified by
the news, her attitude had changed abruptly.

'You have to go, of course. Don't use me as an excuse.'

'But what about the child?'

'I'll be all right,' she said. 'What could you do if you were
here? Stand around and make everyone nervous? The doctors
will look after me. This isn't the first pregnancy they've had to
deal with.'

'But . . . don't you want me to be there with you?' he said.

She had reached out and taken his hand in hers.

'Of course,' she said. 'But remember what you said. The oath
isn't as rigid as you thought. I know you're going, and when
you get back there'll be no mystery any more. I've got plenty to
do here, and if what Barter Collings told you about the oath was
true, you'll be able to talk to me about what you see.'

Helward had not been sure what she meant by this. For some
time he had been in the habit of confiding in her much of what
he saw and did outside the city, and Victoria listened with great
interest. He no longer saw the harm in talking to her, though it
worried him that she should continue to be so interested, particularly when so much of what he said was confined to what he
considered to be routine details.

The result was that on his own personal score he no longer
had a motive to try to avoid the journey down past, and indeed
the idea excited him. He had heard so much of it, mostly by
implication and half-reference, and now the time had come for
him to venture that way himself. Jase was down past; perhaps
they would meet. He wanted to see Jase again. So much had
happened since they last saw each other. Would they even recognise each other?

Victoria did not come to see him leave. She was in the room
when he left her, still in bed. During the night they had made
love tenderly and gently, making half-hearted jokes about making

105

it 'last.' She had clung to him when he kissed her goodbye, and as he closed the door and went into the corridor he thought he heard her sobbing. He paused, debating whether to go back to her, but after a moment's hesitation he went on his way. He saw no benefit in prolonging the situation.

Clausewitz was waiting for him in the Futures' room. In one corner a modest pile of equipment had been laid, and spread out on the table-top was a large plan. Clausewitz's manner was different from that of the previous interview. As soon as Helward let himself into the room, Clausewitz led him to the desk and without preamble explained what he was to do.

'This is a composite plan of the land to the south of the city. It's based on a linear scale. You know what that means?'

Helward nodded.

'Good. One inch on this is roughly equivalent to one mile . . . but linearly. For reasons you'll discover, that won't help you later. Now, the city is here at the moment, and the settlement you have to find is here.' Clausewitz pointed to a cluster of black spots at the other end of the plan. 'As of today that's exactly forty-two miles from here. Once you leave the city you will find that distances are confusing, and so are directions. In which case the best advice I can give you, as we give all our apprentices, is to follow the tracks of the city. When you go south they are the only contact you will have with the city, and the only way you will find your way back. The pits dug for the sleepers and the foundations should still show. Have you got that?'

'Yes, sir.'

'You are making this journey for one main reason. You must see that the women we entrust to you arrive safely at their village. When that has been done, you return to the city without delay.'

Helward was occupied with mental calculations. He knew how long it took him to walk a mile . . . just a few minutes. On a full day's march in hot weather he could hope to cover at least twelve miles; with the women to slow him up, half that. Six miles a day, and that took seven days for the outward trip, three or four days for the return. At best, he could be back at the city within ten days . . . or one mile, as the city measured elapsed time. Suddenly he wondered why he had been told that he could not be back in time for the birth of his child. What had Clausewitz said the other day? That he would be gone ten or fifteen miles . . . perhaps even as long as a hundred? It didn't make sense.

'You'll need some way of measuring distance, so that you'll know when you're in the region of the settlement. Between the city

106

and the settlement there are thirty-four old sites of our stay-emplacements. They're marked on this plan as straight lines across the tracks. You shouldn't have much difficulty in locating them; although the tracks are built over the sites after they've been used, they leave quite distinct marks in the ground. Keep to the left outer track. That is, as you walk southwards, the one farthest to the right. It is on this side of the track that the settlement is situated.'

'Surely the women will recognise the area where they used to live?' said Helward.

'That's correct. Now . . . the equipment you will need. It's all here, and I suggest you take it all. Don't think you can dispense with any of it, because we know what we're doing. Is that clear?'

Once again Helward confirmed that he understood. With Clausewitz he went through the equipment. One pack contained nothing but dehydrated synthetic food and two large canteens of water. The other pack contained a tent and four sleeping-bags. In addition, there was a length of stout rope, grappling irons, a pair of metal-studded boots . . . and a folded crossbow.

'Are there any questions, Helward?'

'I don't think so, sir.'

'You're quite sure?'

Helward looked again at the pile of equipment. It was going to be a devil of a weight to carry, unless he could share some of it with the women, and the sight of all that dried food had set his stomach lurching. . . .

'Could I not live off the land, sir?' he said. 'I find the synthetic food rather tasteless.'

'I would advise you to eat *nothing* that is not in these packs. You can supplement your water-ration if you have to, but make sure the source is running water. If you eat anything that grows locally once you're out of sight of the city, it will probably make you ill. If you don't believe me you can try. I did, when I was down past, and I was sick for two days. This isn't vague theory I'm giving you, it's advice based on hard experience.'

'But we eat local foods in the city.'

'And the city is near optimum. You're going a long way south of optimum.'

'That changes the food, sir?'

'Yes. Is there anything else?'

'No, sir.'

'Good. Then there's someone who would like to see you before you go.'

He gestured towards an inner door, and Helward walked over to it. Beyond it was a smaller room, and here his father was waiting for him.

Helward's first reaction was surprise, immediately followed by one of incredulity. He had seen his father last not more than ten days ago as the man was riding north; now, in that short period, it seemed to Helward that his father had aged suddenly and horribly. As he walked in his father stood up, balancing himself with an unsteady hand on the seat of his chair. He turned painfully, and faced Helward. His whole manner was marked with advanced age: he stood hunched, his clothes hung on him badly and the hand that came forward was trembling.

'Helward! How are you, son?'

The manner had changed too. There was no trace of the diffidence to which Helward had grown so accustomed.

'Father . . . how are you?'

'I'm fine, son. I've got to be taking it easy now, the doctor says. I've been north once too often.' He sat down again, and instinctively Helward stepped forward and helped him into his seat. 'They tell me you're going down past. Is that right?'

'Yes, father.'

'You be careful, son. There's a lot down there will give you thought. Not like up future . . . that's my place.'

Clausewitz had followed Helward, and was now standing in the doorway.

'Helward, you ought to know that your father has been given an injection.'

Helward turned away from his father.

'What do you mean?' he said.

'He came back to the city last night, complaining of chest pains. It's been diagnosed as angina, and he's been given a pain-killer. He ought to be in bed.'

'O.K. I shan't be long.'

Helward knelt on the floor beside the chair.

'Do you feel all right now, father?' he said.

'I told you . . . I'm fine. Don't worry about me. How's Victoria?'

'She's getting on fine.'

'Good girl, Victoria.'

'I'll tell her to visit you,' said Helward. It was a terrible thing to see his father in this condition. He had no idea that his father was growing so old . . . but he had not looked like this a few days ago. What had happened to him in the meantime? They talked for a few more minutes, but soon his father's attention began to wander. Eventually, he closed his eyes and Helward stood up.

'I'll get one of the medics,' said Clausewitz, and hurried out of the room. When he returned a few minutes later there were two of the medical administrators with him. Gently, they picked the old man up and carried him out to the corridor, where a wheeled trolley draped in white was waiting.

'Will he be all right?' said Helward.

'He's being looked after, that's all I can say.'

'He looks so old,' said Helward, unthinkingly. Clausewitz himself was in advanced years, though in demonstrably better health than his father.

'An occupational hazard,' said Clausewitz.

Helward glanced at him sharply, but there was no further information forthcoming. Clausewitz picked up the metal-studded boots, and pushed them towards Helward.

'Here . . . try these on,' he said.

'My father . . . will you ask Victoria to visit him?'

'Don't worry about that. I'll deal with it.'

4

Helward rode in the elevator to the second level, the packs and equipment loaded in beside him. When the car stopped he keyed the door-hold button, and went along to the room to which Clausewitz had directed him. Here, four women and a man were waiting for him. As soon as he entered the room, Helward realised that only the man and one of the women were city administrators.

He was introduced to the other three, but they glanced at him briefly and looked away. Their expressions revealed a suppressed hostility, deadened by an indifference that until that moment Helward himself had felt. Until entering the room he had given no thought as to who the women might be, nor even had he speculated about their appearance. In fact, he recognised none of them, but hearing Clausewitz speak of them Helward had associated them in his mind with the women he had seen in the settlements while riding north with Barter Collings. Those women had been in general thin and pallid, their eyes deep-sunk over prominent cheekbones, their arms scrawny, and their chests flat. Dressed more often than not in ragged, filthy clothes, flies crawling over their faces, the women of the villages outside were pitiful wretches.

These three had none of these characteristics. They wore neat, well-fitting city clothes, their hair was clean and well cut, their flesh was round and full, and their eyes were clear. To his barely concealed surprise Helward saw that they were very young indeed: scarcely older than himself. The people of the city spoke of the women who were bartered from outside as if they were mature . . . but these were nothing more than girls.

He knew he was staring at them, but they paid him no attention. What struck him hardest was the growing suspicion that these three had once been similar to the wretches he had seen in the villages, and that by being brought to the city they had been restored temporarily to an approximation of the health and beauty that might have been theirs had they not been born into poverty.

The woman administrator gave him a brief description of

110

their background. Their names were Rosario, Caterina, and Lucia. They spoke a little English. Each had been in the city for more than forty miles, and each had given birth to a baby. There were two boys and a girl. Lucia – who had given birth to one of the boys – did not wish to keep the child, and it was to stay in the city and be brought up in the crèche. Rosario had chosen to keep her baby boy, and it would be going with her back to the settlement. In Caterina's case there had been no choice . . . but in any event she had expressed indifference about losing her baby daughter.

The administrator explained that Rosario was to be given as much of the powdered milk as she asked for, because she was still suckling the baby. The other two would have the same food as himself.

Helward tried a friendly smile on the three girls, but they took no notice of him. When he tried to look at Rosario's baby, she turned her back on him and clutched it to her possessively.

There was nothing more to be told. They walked along the corridor towards the elevator, the three girls carrying their few belongings. They crowded into the car and Helward keyed the button to take them to the lowest level.

The girls continued to ignore him, and spoke to each other in their own language. When the car opened on to the dark passageway beneath the city, Helward struggled to remove the equipment. None of the girls helped him, but watched with amused expressions. With difficulty Helward picked up the various packs and staggered towards the southern exit.

Outside, the sun was dazzlingly bright. He put down the packs and glanced round.

The city had been winched since he was last outside, and now track-crews were taking up the rails. The girls shaded their eyes, and looked about them. It was probably their first sight of the outside since coming to the city.

The baby in Rosario's arms began to cry.

'Will you help me with this?' Helward said, meaning the stack of food and equipment. The girls stared at him uncomprehendingly. 'We ought to share the load.'

They made no reply so he squatted down on the ground, and opened the pack containing the food. He decided it would not be right to expect Rosario to carry any extra weight, so he divided the food into three packets, giving one each to the other two and returning the rest to his pack. Lucia and Caterina reluctantly found room for the food packets in their holdalls. The length of rope was the most unwieldy part of the load and so Helward

111

contrived to wind it into a tighter roll, and stuffed it into the pack. The grapple and pitons he managed to get into the pack containing the tent and the sleeping-bags. Now his load was more manageable but not much lighter, and in spite of what Clausewitz had said Helward felt tempted to abandon most of it.

The baby was still crying, and Rosario appeared unconcerned.

'Come on,' he said, feeling irritated with them. He set off, walking southwards parallel to the tracks, and in a moment they followed him. They stayed together, keeping a distance of a few yards between them and him.

Helward tried to set a good pace, but after an hour he realised that his calculations about how long the expedition would take had been over-optimistic. The three girls moved slowly, complaining loudly about the heat and the surface of the ground. It was true that the shoes they had been given were unsuited for walking over this rough terrain, but he was afflicted no less by the heat. In fact, in his uniform and weighed down by the bulk of the equipment, he was most unpleasantly warm.

They were still in sight of the city, the sun was still only approaching its midday heat, and the baby had not stopped crying. His only relief so far had been a few moments speaking to Malchuskin. The trackman had been delighted to see him – still full of complaints about his hired labourers – and had wished Helward well in his expedition.

True to form, the girls had not waited for Helward, and he had spoken to Malchuskin for only a minute or two before he hurried after them.

Now he decided to call a rest.

'Can't you stop him crying?' he said to Rosario.

The girl glared at him, and sat down on the ground.

'O.K.,' she said. 'I feed.'

She stared at him defiantly, and the other two girls waited at her side. Taking the point, Helward moved some distance away, keeping his back turned discreetly while she fed the baby.

Later, he opened one of the water-canteens and passed it round. The day was impossibly hot, and his temper was no better than that of the girls. He took off the jacket of his uniform, and laid it over the top of the packs, and although this meant he felt the bite of the straps more deeply, it helped him keep a little cooler.

He was impatient to move on. The baby had fallen asleep, and two of the girls made a makeshift cot out of one of the sleeping-bags, carrying it slung between them. Helward had to relieve them of their holdalls, and although he was now over-burdened with things to carry he gladly exchanged the extra discomfort for the welcome silence.

They walked for another half an hour, and then he called another halt. By now he was drenched with sweat, and it gave him little comfort to realise that the girls were no cooler.

He glanced up at the sun. It seemed to be almost directly overhead. Near where they were standing was an outcrop of rock, and he went over and sat down in the shade. The girls joined him, still complaining to each other in their own language. Helward regretted he had not taken more trouble to learn the language; he could pick out one or two phrases, but only enough to discover that he was the butt of most of their complaints.

He opened a packet of the dehydrated food, and moistened it with water from the canteen. The resultant grey soup looked and tasted like sour porridge. Perversely, he derived pleasure from the girls' renewed complaints . . . here was one occasion they were justified, and he wasn't going to give them the satisfaction of letting them see he agreed.

The baby was still asleep, but fretting in the heat. Helward guessed that if they moved again it would wake up, so when the girls stretched out on the ground for a nap he made no effort to dissuade them.

While they were relaxing Helward stared back at the city, still clearly visible a couple of miles away. He realised that he had not been taking note of the marks left by the stay-emplacements. They would have passed only one so far, and now he thought about it he saw what Clausewitz had meant by saying they left clearly distinguishable scars in the earth. He recalled that they had passed one a few minutes before they had halted. The marks left by the sleepers were shallow depressions some five feet in length by twelve inches across, but where the cable-stays had been buried were deep pits, surrounded by upturned soil.

Mentally, he marked off the first one. Thirty-seven to go.

In spite of their slow progress he still saw no reason why he should not be back in the city in time for the birth of his own child. After he had seen the women back to their village he could make good progress on his own, however unpleasant the conditions.

He decided to allow the girls an hour for their rest, and when he

113

estimated that it had passed he went and stood over them.

Caterina opened her eyes, and looked up at him.

'Come on,' he said. 'I want to move on.'

'Is too hot.'

'Is too bad,' he said. 'We're moving.'

She stood up, stretching her body elaborately, then spoke to the other two. With similar reluctance they stood up, and Rosario went and looked at the baby. To Helward's dismay she woke it, and lifted it up . . . but fortunately the crying did not start again. Without delay, Helward gave back the two holdalls to Caterina and Lucia, and picked up his own two packs.

Away from the shade, the full heat of the sun came down on them, and within a few seconds the benefit of the rest in the shade seemed to vanish. They had gone only a few yards when Rosario passed the baby to Lucia.

She went back to the rocks and disappeared behind them. Helward opened his mouth to ask where she had gone . . . but then realised. When she returned, Lucia went, and then Caterina. Helward felt his anger returning. They were deliberately delaying him. He felt a pressure in his own bladder, aggravated by realising what the girls had been doing, but his anger and pride would not allow him to relieve himself. He decided to wait until later.

They walked on. The girls had now discarded the jackets that were common apparel inside the city, and wore only the trousers and shirts. The thin material, damp with perspiration, adhered to their bodies and Helward noticed this with a despondent interest, reflecting that under different circumstances he might have found the phenomenon of considerable potential. As things were he registered this new development only so far as to appreciate that each of the girls was of fuller figure than Victoria; Rosario in particular had large, pendulous breasts with protuberant nipples. Later, one of the girls must have noticed his occasional glance, for soon all three of them were walking with their jackets held over their chests. It made no difference to Helward . . . he just wanted to be rid of them.

'We have water?' said Lucia, crossing over to him.

He rummaged in the pack and gave her the canteen. She drank some, and then moistened the palms of her hands and splashed water over her face and neck. Rosario and Caterina did likewise. The sight and sound of the water was too much for Helward, and his bladder protested anew. He looked around. There was no cover, so he walked some yards away from the girls and relieved

114

himself on to the soil. Behind, he heard them giggling.

When he returned, Caterina held out the canteen to him. He took it and raised it to his lips. Suddenly, Caterina tipped it from below, and the water splashed over his nose and eyes. The girls roared with laughter as he sputtered and choked. The baby started crying again.

5

They passed two more stay-emplacement marks before evening, and then Helward decided to pitch camp for the night. He selected a site near a clump of trees two or three hundred yards from the scars made by the tracks. A small brook passed nearby, and after testing it for purity – he had no guide other than his own palate – he declared it safe for drinking to conserve the supply in the canteens.

The tent was relatively simple to erect, and although he started the work on his own the girls helped him finish off. As soon as it was up he laid the sleeping-bags inside, and Rosario went in to feed the baby.

When the baby had gone to sleep again, Lucia helped Helward reconstitute the synthetic food. The result this time was an orange-coloured soup and it tasted no better than before. As they were eating, the sun set. Helward had lit a small fire, but soon a wind blew up from the east, chilling them. Finally, they were forced to go inside the tent and lie down inside their sleeping-bags for warmth.

Helward tried to strike up a conversation with the girls but either they did not answer, or they giggled, or made joking references to each other in Spanish, so he soon abandoned the idea. There were a few small candles in the pack of equipment, and Helward lay in the light of these for an hour or two, wondering what possible benefit the city could derive from this pointless expedition of his.

He fell asleep at last, but was wakened twice in the night by the baby crying. On one occasion he could just make out the shape of Rosario against the dim glow from outside, sitting up in her sleeping-bag and suckling the baby.

They were awake early, and set off as soon as they could. Helward wasn't sure what had happened, but the mood of the girls today was obviously different. As they walked Caterina and Lucia sang a little, and at their first stop for a drink they tried again to spill the water on him. He moved back to avoid them, but in doing so stumbled on the uneven ground ... and spluttered and choked once more for their amusement. Only Rosario maintained a distance, pointedly ignoring him as Lucia and Caterina played up to him. He didn't enjoy being teased – for he could think of no way of replying – but he preferred it to the bad feeling of the day before.

As the morning progressed and the temperature rose, their mood became more careless. None of the three girls wore her jacket, and at the next stop Lucia undid the top two buttons of her shirt and Caterina opened hers all the way down the front, holding it in place with a large knot and so baring her midriff.

By now Helward could not mistake the effect they were having on him. As familiarity grew, so the atmosphere eased further. Even Rosario did not turn her back on him the next time she suckled her baby.

Relief from the heat came with another patch of woodland, one which Helward could remember helping to clear for the track-layers some miles before. They sat down in the shadows, waiting for the worst of the heat to pass.

They had now passed a total of five cable-stay marks: thirty-three to go. Helward's mood of frustration at the slowness of their journey was easing; he saw that to travel faster was hardly possible, even if he had been alone. The ground was too hard, the sun too hot.

He decided to wait for two hours in the shadow of the trees. Rosario had moved some way away from him, and was playing with her baby. Caterina and Lucia sat together under a tree. They had taken off their shoes and were talking quietly together. Helward closed his eyes for a few minutes, but soon became restless. He walked out of the trees on his own, and went down to the scars left by the four lines of track. He looked left and right, north and south: the line ran straight and true, undulating slightly with the rise and fall of the ground, but always maintaining its direction.

Enjoying the comparative solitude he stood there for some time, wishing the weather would change and the sky would cloud over, if only temporarily. He debated with himself for a while, trying to decide whether it might be better to rest during the days and travel at night . . . but considered on balance it would be too risky.

He was about to turn back to the trees when he suddenly saw a movement about a mile to the south of him. At once he was on his guard, and dropped to the ground, lying behind a tree-stump. He waited.

117

In a moment he saw it again: someone was walking up the track towards him.

Helward remembered his crossbow, folded inside the pack ... but already it was too late to go back for it. There was a bush just a yard or two to the side of the stump, and he wriggled over until he was behind it. Now better covered he hoped he might not be seen.

The figure was still coming towards him, and in a few minutes Helward saw to his surprise that the man was wearing the uniform of a guild apprentice. His first impulse was to come out of hiding, but he fought this back and stayed put.

When the man was less than fifty yards away, Helward recognised him. It was Torrold Pelham, a boy several miles older than him who had left the crèche a considerable time before.

Helward broke cover and stood up.

'Torrold!'

At once, Pelham was on his guard. He raised his crossbow and aimed it at Helward ... then slowly lowered it.

'Torrold ... it's me. Helward Mann.'

'God, what are you doing here?'

They laughed together, realising that they were both here for the same reason.

'You've grown up,' said Pelham. 'You were just a kid the last time I saw you.'

'Have you been down past?' said Helward.

'Yes.' Pelham stared past him, northwards up the track.

'Well?'

'It's not what I thought.'

'What's there?' said Helward.

'You're down past now. Can't you feel it?'

'Feel what?'

Pelham looked at him for a moment. 'It's not so bad here. But you can feel it. Perhaps you can't recognise it yet. It builds up quickly further south.'

'What does? You're talking in riddles.'

'No ... it's just impossible to explain.' Pelham glanced towards the north again. 'Is the city near here?'

'A few miles. Not far.'

'What happened to it?' Have they found some way to make it move faster? I've only been gone a short time, and the city's moved much farther than I thought it would.'

'It's gone no faster than normal.'

'There's a creek back there where a bridge had been built. When was that done?'

'About nine miles ago.'

Pelham shook his head. 'It doesn't make sense.'

'You've lost your sense of time, that's all.'

Pelham suddenly grinned. 'I expect that's it. Listen, are you on your own?'

'No,' said Helward. 'I've got three girls with me.'

'What are they like?'

'They're O.K. It was a bit difficult at first, but we're getting to know each other now.'

'Good lookers are they?'

'Not bad. Come and see.'

Helward led the way back through the trees until the girls came into view.

Pelham whistled. 'Hey . . . they're all right. Have you . . . you know?'

'No.'

They walked back towards the track.

Pelham said: 'Are you going to?'

'I'm not sure.'

'Take a tip, Helward . . . if you're going to, do it soon. Otherwise it'll be too late.'

'What do you mean?'

'You'll see.'

Pelham gave him a cheery grin, then continued on his way northwards.

Thoughts and intentions in the direction to which Pelham had been alluding were put out of Helward's mind almost at once. Rosario fed her baby before they set off, and they had been walking only a few minutes when the child was violently sick.

Rosario hugged it to her, crooning quietly, but there was little anyone could do. Lucia stood by her, speaking sympathetically to her. Helward was worried, because if the child were seriously ill there was not much else they could do but return to the city. Soon, though, the baby stopped retching, and after a lusty crying session it quietened down.

'Do you want to go on?' Helward said to Rosario.

She shrugged helplessly. '*Si.*'

They walked on more slowly. The heat had not abated much, and several times Helward asked the girls if they wanted to stop. Each time they said no, but Helward detected that a subtle change

119

had come over all four of them. It was if the minor tragedy had drawn them together.

'We'll camp tonight,' said Helward. 'And rest all day tomorrow.'

There was agreement to this and when Rosario fed the baby again a little later, this time it kept the milk down.

Just before nightfall they passed through countryside which was more hilly and rocky than that they had seen so far, and suddenly they came to the chasm that had caused so much trouble to the Bridge-Builders. There was not much sign now of where the bridge had been, although the foundations of the suspension towers had left two large scars in the ground on this side.

Helward remembered a patch of level ground on the northern bank of the stream at the bottom of the chasm, and he led the way down.

Rosario and Lucia fussed over the baby, while Caterina helped Helward erect the tent. Suddenly, while they were laying out the four sleeping-bags inside, Caterina put a hand on his neck and kissed him lightly on the cheek.

He grinned at her. 'What's that for?'

'You O.K. with Rosario.'

Helward stayed put, thinking that the kiss might be repeated, but Caterina crawled backwards from the tent and called the others.

The baby looked better, and fell asleep when it was put into its makeshift cot inside the tent. Rosario said nothing about the child, but Helward could tell she felt less worried. Perhaps it had been wind.

The evening was much warmer than the night before, and after they had eaten they stayed outside the tent for some time. Lucia was concerned with her feet, rubbing them continually, and the other girls seemed to be making much of this. She showed her feet to Helward, and he saw that large calluses had appeared on the outer sides of her toes. Feet were compared at great length, the other girls saying that theirs were sore too.

'Tomorrow,' said Lucia, 'no shoes.'

That seemed to be the end to it.

Helward waited outside the tent as the girls crawled inside. The previous night it had been so cold that all of them had slept with their clothes on inside the sleeping-bags, but as it was now warm and humid that was clearly out of the question. A certain coyness in Helward made him resolve that he would keep his own clothes on, and sleep on top of the bag, but a fast-developing interest in the girls led his thoughts to wilder fantasies about what they might do. After a few minutes, he crawled into the tent. The candles were alight.

Each of the three girls was inside her own bag, although Helward saw from the pile of clothes that they had undressed. He said nothing to them, but blew out the candles and undressed in the dark, stumbling and falling clumsily in the process. He lay down, only too aware of Caterina's body lying close beside him in the next sleeping-bag. He stayed awake for a long time, trying to rid himself of a fierce manifestation of his arousal. Victoria seemed to be a long way away.

6

It was daylight when he awoke and, after a futile attempt to get dressed while still in his sleeping-bag, Helward scrambled out of the tent naked and dressed hurriedly outside. He lit the camp-fire, and began to heat some water to make synthetic tea.

Here at the bottom of the chasm it was already warm, and Helward wondered again whether they should move on, or rest for a day as he had promised.

The water boiled, and he sipped his tea. Inside the tent he heard movement. In a moment Caterina came out, and walked past him towards the stream.

Helward stared after her: she was wearing only her shirt, which was unbuttoned all down the front and swinging open, and a pair of pants. When she reached the water, she turned and waved back at him.

'Come!' she called.

Helward needed no further bidding. He went down to her, feeling clumsy in his uniform and metal-studded boots.

'We swim?' she said, and without waiting for an answer slipped her shirt off, stepped out of her pants and waded down into the water. Helward glanced back at the tent: nothing moved.

In a few seconds he had taken his clothes off, and was splashing through the shallows towards her. She turned and faced him, grinning when she saw the response in him she had caused. She splashed water at him, and turned away. Helward leaped at her, getting his arms around her . . . and together they fell sideways full-length into the water.

Caterina wriggled away from him, and stood up. She skipped away from him through the shallows, throwing up a huge spray. Helward followed, and caught her at the bank. Her face was serious. She raised her arms around his neck, and pulled his face down to hers. They kissed for a few moments, then clambered up out of the water and into the long grass growing on the bank. They lay down together and started to kiss again, more deeply.

By the time they had disentangled, got dressed, and returned to the tent, Rosario and Lucia were eating a pile of yellow gruel.

Neither of them said anything, but Helward saw Lucia smile at Caterina.

Half an hour later the baby was sick again . . . and as Rosario was holding it concernedly, she suddenly thrust the baby into Lucia's arms and rushed away. A few seconds later, she could be heard retching beside the stream.

Helward said to Caterina: 'Do you feel O.K.?'

'Yes.'

Helward sniffed the food they had been eating. It smelt normal . . . unappetising, but not tainted. A few minutes later, Lucia complained of intense stomach pains, and she went very pale.

Caterina wandered away.

Helward was desperate. The only course open to them now seemed to be to return to the city. If their food had become foul, how could they survive the rest of the journey?

After a while, Rosario returned to the camp-site. She looked weak and pale, and she sat down on the ground in the shade. Lucia gave her some water from the canteen. Lucia herself looked white and was holding her stomach, and the baby continued to scream. Helward was not prepared to cope with a situation like this, and hadn't the least idea of what to suggest.

He went in search of Caterina, who had seemed to be unaffected.

About a hundred yards down the chasm he came across her. She was walking back towards the camp-site with an armful of apples which, she said, she had found growing wild. They looked red and ripe, and Helward tasted one. It was sweet and juicy . . . but then he remembered Clausewitz's warning. His reason told him Clausewitz was wrong, but reluctantly he gave it to Caterina and she ate the rest.

They baked one of the apples in the embers of the fire, and then pulped it. In tiny mouthfuls, they fed it to the baby. This time it kept the food down and made happy noises. Rosario was still too weak to attend to it, so Caterina laid it down in its cot and within minutes it was asleep.

Lucia was not sick, although her stomach continued to give her pain for most of the morning. Rosario recovered more quickly, and ate one of the apples.

Helward ate the rest of the yellow synthetic food . . . and it did not make him ill.

Later in the day, Helward climbed up to the top of the creek and walked along its northern side. Here, a few miles back in time,

123

lives had been lost in the cause of getting the city to cross this chasm. The scene was still familiar to him, and although most of the equipment used by the city had been collected, those long days and nights spent racing to complete the bridge were still very vivid in his memory. He looked across to the southern side, at the very place where the bridge had been built.

The gap did not look as wide as it had done then, nor did the chasm look so deep. Perhaps his excitement at the time had exaggerated his impression of the obstacle the chasm presented.

But no . . . surely the chasm *had* been wider?

He remembered that when the city had been crossing the bridge the rail-way itself had been at least sixty yards long. Now it seemed that at the point the bridge had been built the chasm was only about ten yards wide.

Helward stood and stared at the opposite edge for a long time, not understanding how this apparent contradiction could occur. Then an idea came to him.

The bridge had been built to quite exact engineering specifications; he had worked for many days on the building of the suspension towers, and he knew that the two towers on each side of the chasm had been built an exact distance apart to allow the city to pass between them.

That distance was about one hundred and thirty feet, or forty paces.

He went to the place where one of the northern towers had been built, and walked over towards its twin. He counted fifty-eight paces.

He went back, trying again: this time it was sixty paces.

He tried again, taking larger steps: fifty-five paces.

Standing on the edge of the chasm he stared down at the stream below. He could remember with great clarity the depth of the creek when the bridge was being built. Standing here, the bottom of the chasm had seemed to be a terrifying depth below; now it was an easy climb down to where they had camped.

Another thought struck him and he walked northwards to where the ramp had been brought the city down into contact with the soil again. The traces of the four tracks still showed clearly, from this point running parallel northwards.

If the two towers were now apparently farther apart, what of the tracks themselves?

From long hours working with Malchuskin, Helward knew intimately every detail of the tracks and their sleepers. The gauge of the tracks was three and a half feet, resting on sleepers five feet long. Looking now at the scars left in the ground by the sleepers, he saw that they were much bigger than this. He made a rough measurement, and estimated that they were now at least seven feet long, and shallower than they ought to be. But he knew that could not be so: the city used standard length sleepers, and the pits dug for them were always roughly the same size.

To make sure he checked several more, and found they were all apparently two feet longer than they should be.

And too close together. The sleepers were laid by the track-crews at four feet intervals . . . not about eighteen inches apart, as these were.

Helward spent a few more minutes making similar measurements, then scrambled down the chasm, waded through the stream (which now seemed to him to be narrower and shallower than it had been before), and climbed up to the southern edge.

Here too the measurements he made of the remains of the city's passage were in stark conflict with what he knew should be so.

Puzzled, and more than a little worried, he returned to the camp.

The girls were all looking healthier, but the baby had been sick yet again. The girls told him that they had been eating the apples Caterina had found. He cut one in half, and inspected it closely. He could see no difference between it and any other apple he had ever eaten. Once again, he was tempted to eat it, but instead he passed it to Lucia.

An idea had suddenly occurred to him.

Clausewitz had warned him of eating local foods; presumably this was because he was of the city. Clausewitz had said it was all right to eat local foods when the city was near optimum, but here, some miles to the south, it was not so. If he ate the city food, he would not be ill.

But the girls . . . they were not of the city. Perhaps it was his food which was making them ill. They could eat city food when they were near the optimum, but not now.

It made a kind of sense, but for one thing: the baby. With the exception of the few tiny mouthfuls of apple, it had had nothing but its mother's milk. Surely that could not harm it?

He went with Rosario to see the baby. It lay in its cot, its face red and tear-stained. It was not crying now, but it fretted weakly. Helward felt sorry for the tiny creature, and wondered what he could do to help.

Outside the tent, Lucia and Caterina were in good spirits.

125

They spoke to Helward as he emerged, but he walked on past them and went to sit beside the stream. He was still thinking about his new idea.

The only food had been its mother's milk . . . Suppose the mother was different now, because they were away from the optimum? She was not of the city, but the baby was. Could that make a difference? It did not make much sense – for surely the baby was of the mother's body? – but it was a possibility.

He went back to the camp and made up some synthetic food and dried milk, being careful to use only water he had brought from the city. He gave it to Rosario, and told her to try feeding the baby with it.

She resisted the idea at first, but then relented. The baby took the food, and two hours later it was sleeping peacefully once more.

The day passed slowly. Down in the creek the air was still and warm, and Helward's feeling of frustration returned. He saw now that if his supposition was correct he could no longer offer the girls any of the food. But with thirty or more miles to walk, they couldn't survive on apples alone.

Later, he told them what was on his mind, and suggested that for the moment they should eat very small amounts of his food, and supplement this with whatever they could find locally. They seemed puzzled, but agreed to this.

The sweltering afternoon continued . . . and Helward's restlessness was transmitted to the girls. They became light-hearted and frisky, and teased him about his bulky uniform. Caterina said she was going for another swim, and Lucia said she would go too. They stripped off their clothes in front of him, and then turned on him playfully and made him undress. They splashed about naked in the water for a long time, joined later by Rosario whose attitude towards him no longer seemed to be one of suspicion.

For the rest of the day they lay on the ground beside the tent, sunbathing.

That night, Lucia took Helward's hand just as he was about to go inside the tent, and led him away from the camp-site. She made love to him passionately, holding him tight against her as if he were the only force of reality in her world.

In the morning, Helward sensed a growing jealousy between Lucia and Caterina, and so he broke camp as early as possible.

He led them across the stream and up to the higher land to the south. Following the left outer track they continued their

126

journey. The surrounding countryside was now familiar to Helward, as this was the region through which the city had been passing when he first worked outside. Up ahead, some two miles to the south, he could see the ridge of high ground that the city had had to climb during the first winching he had witnessed.

They stopped for a rest half-way through the morning, and then Helward remembered that only two miles to the west of where they were was a small local settlement. It occurred to him that if food could be obtained there, the problem of what the girls could eat would be solved. He suggested this to them.

The problem arose of who was to go. He felt he should go himself because of his responsibility, but would need one of the girls because she could speak the language. He did not wish to leave just one of the girls alone with the baby, and he felt that if he went with either Caterina or Lucia, the one left behind would show more obviously what he had guessed was their shared jealousy over him. In the end, he suggested that Rosario should go with him, and by the reception with which this was greeted Helward felt it was the right choice.

They set off in the approximate direction Helward remembered the village to be, and found it without difficulty. After a long conversation between Rosario and three of the men in the village, they were given some dried meat and some green, raw vegetables. Everything went remarkably smoothly – Helward wondered what kind of persuasions she had used – and soon they were returning to the others.

Walking along a few yards behind Rosario, Helward noticed something about the girl he had not seen before.

She was built rather more heavily than the other two girls, and her arms and face were round and well-fleshed. The girl did have a slight tendency to plumpness, but it suddenly seemed to Helward that this was much more noticeable than before. With casual interest at first, and greater attention later, he saw that the fabric of her shirt was stretched tightly across her back. But her clothes had not been as tight as that before . . . they had been given to her in the city, and had fitted her well. Then Helward noticed the trousers she was wearing: they were tight across the seat, but the legs scuffed against the ground as she walked. True, she was without shoes, but even so he did not remember them being as long as this before.

He caught up with her, and walked at her side.

The shirt was tight across her chest, compressing her breasts . . . and the sleeves were too long. Also, the girl seemed to be far

127

shorter than he remembered her from even the day before . . .

When they joined the others, Helward noticed that their clothes too were now fitting them badly. Caterina had her shirt knotted across her stomach as before, but Lucia's was buttoned and the tightness of the fit caused the fabric to part between the buttons.

He tried to put the phenomenon out of his mind, but as they continued southwards it seemed to become more and more obvious . . . and with comic results. Bending down to attend to the baby, Rosario split the seat of her trousers. One of Lucia's buttons popped off as she raised the canteen of water to her lips, and Caterina tore the fabric of her shirt down both seams below her armpits.

A mile or so farther down the track, and Lucia lost two more buttons. Her shirt was now open down most of its front, and she knotted it as Caterina had done. All three girls had turned up the hems of their trousers, and it was clear they were suffering considerable discomfort.

Helward called a halt in the lee of the ridge, and they set up camp. Once they had eaten the girls took off their tattered clothes and went into the tent. They teased Helward about his own clothes: were they not going to be torn up too? He sat outside the tent on his own, not yet sleepy and not wishing to sit inside the tent with the girls.

The baby started to cry, and Rosario came out of the tent to get it some food. Helward spoke to her, but she did not reply. He watched her as she added water to the dried milk, looked at her naked body in a wholly unsexual way. He had seen her naked only the day before, and he was certain she had not looked like this. She had been almost as tall as he was, yet now she seemed to be more squat, more plump.

'Rosario, is Caterina still awake?'

She nodded wordlessly, and went back into the tent. A few moments later Caterina came out, and Helward stood up.

They faced each other in the light from the camp-fire. Caterina said nothing, and Helward did not know what to say. She too had changed. . . . A moment later Lucia joined them, and she stood at Caterina's side.

Now he was certain. Some time during the day the girls' physical appearance had changed.

He looked at them both. Yesterday, naked beside the stream, their bodies had been long and lithe, their breasts round and full.

Now their arms and legs were shorter, and more thickly built. Their shoulders and hips were broader, their breasts less round and more widely spaced. Their faces were rounder, their necks were shorter.

They came across to him, and stood before him. Lucia took the clasp of his trousers in her hands. Her lips were moist. From the entrance to the tent, Rosario watched.

7

In the morning Helward saw that the girls had changed even further during the course of the night. He estimated now that none of them stood more than five feet high, they talked more quickly than before, and the pitch of their voices was higher.

None of them could get into the clothes. Lucia tried, but could not get her legs into the trousers, and split the sleeves of her shirt. When they left the camp, the girls' clothes were left too, and they continued on their way naked.

Helward could not take his eyes off them. Every hour that passed seemed to reveal a more obvious change in them. Their legs were now so short that they could only take small steps, and he was forced to dawdle so that he would not leave them behind. In addition, he noticed that as they walked their posture was becoming more and more at an angle, so that they appeared to be leaning backwards.

They too were watching him, and when they stopped for water there was an uncanny silence as the strange group passed the canteen from one to the other.

Around them there were outward signs of an inexplicable change in the scenery. The remains of the left outer track, which they still followed, were now indistinct. The last clear impression Helward had seen of one of the sleeper-pits had been more than forty feet in length, and less than an inch in depth. The next set of tracks, the left inner, could not be seen; gradually the strip between the two had widened until it was over to the east by half a mile or more.

The incidence of stay-emplacements had increased. Already that morning they had passed twelve, and by Helward's calculations there were only nine more to go.

But how would he recognise the girls' settlement? The natural scenery of the area was flat and uniform. Where they were resting was like the hardened residue of a lava flow: there was no shade or shelter to be seen. He looked more closely at the ground. If he moved his fingers through it firmly he could still make shallow

130

indentations in the soil, but although it was loose and sandy soil it felt thick and viscous to the touch.

The girls were now no more than three feet tall, and their bodies had distorted even further. Their feet were flat and wide, their legs broad and short, their torsos round and compressed. In this perception of them they became grotesquely ugly, and he found that in spite of his fascination with the physical changes coming over them the sound of their twittering voices was irritating him.

Only the baby had not changed. It was still, as far as Helward could see, much as it had always been. But in relation to its mother it was now disproportionately large, and the squat figure that was Rosario was regarding it with a kind of unspoken horror.

The baby was of the city.

Just as Helward himself had been born of a woman from outside, so was Rosario's baby a child of the city. Whatever transformation was coming over the three girls and the country-side from which they came, neither he nor the baby were affected by it.

Helward had no conception of what he should do, nor what he should make of what he saw.

He felt a growing a fright, for this was beyond any compre-hension he had ever had of the natural order of things. The evidence was manifest; the rationale was without terms of refer-ence.

He looked towards the south, and saw that not too far away was a line of hills. From their shape and overall height he assumed they must be the foothills of some larger range . . . but then he noticed with a surge of alarm that the tops of the hills were white with snow. The sun was as hot as ever, and the air was warm; logic demanded that any snow that could exist in this climate must be on the tops of very high mountains. And yet they were near enough – no more than a mile or two, he thought – for him to judge that at most they were only above five hundred feet in elevation.

He stood up, and suddenly fell.

As he hit the ground he found he was rolling, as if on a steep slope, towards the south. He managed to stop himself and stood up unsteadily, bracing himself against a force that was pulling him towards the south. It was not a new force; he had been feeling its pressure all morning, but the fall had taken him by surprise and the force seemed now far stronger than before. Why had it not affected him until this moment? He thought back. That morning, with the other distractions, he realised he had indeed been aware of it, and he'd felt in the back of his mind that they'd been walking downhill. But that was clearly nonsensical: the land was level as far as the eye could see. He stood by the group of girls, sampling the sensation.

It was not like the pressure of air, nor even like the pull of gravity on a slope. It was somewhere between the two: on level ground, without noticeable air movements, he felt as though he were being pushed or dragged towards the south.

He took a few steps towards the north, and realised he was bracing his legs as if ascending a hill; he turned towards the south, and in conflict with the evidence of his eyes he felt as though he were on a steep slope.

The girls were watching him curiously, and he went back to them.

He saw that in those last few minutes their bodies had distorted still further.

8

Shortly before they moved on, Rosario tried to speak to him. He had difficulty understanding her. Her accent was strong in any case, and now her voice was pitched high and she spoke too quickly.

After many attempts, he got the gist of what she was saying.

She and the other girls were afraid to return to their village. They were of the city now, and would be rejected by their own kind.

Helward said they must go on, as had been their choice, but Rosario said they would not move. She was married to a man in her village, and although at first she had wanted to return to him, she thought now he would kill her. Lucia too was married, and she shared the fear. The people of the villages hated the city, and for their involvement with it the girls would be punished.

Helward gave up trying to answer her. He was having as much difficulty making her understand as he was in comprehending her. He thought she had left it too late for this; after all they had entered the city willingly in the first place as part of the barter. He tried to say this, but she could not understand.

Even while they had been talking the process of change had continued. She was now a little more than twelve inches high, and her body – as the other girls' – was nearly five feet broad. It was impossible to recognise them as having once been human, even though he knew this to be so.

He said: 'Wait here!'

He stood up, and fell again, rolling across the ground. The force on his body was now much greater, and he stopped himself with great difficulty. He crawled back against the force to his pack, and pulled it on. He found the rope, and slung it over his shoulder.

Bracing himself against the pressure, he walked southwards.

It was no longer possible to make out any natural features other than the line of rising ground ahead. The surface on which he walked was now an indistinct blur, and although he stopped to examine it from time to time he could distinguish nothing on it

133

that might once have been grass, or rocks, or soil.

The natural features of the world were distorting: they were spreading laterally to east and west, diminishing in height and depth.

A boulder here might be a strip of dark grey, one hundredth of an inch wide and two hundred yards long. The low, snow-capped ridge ahead might be mountains; the long strip of green a tree.

That narrow strip of off-white, a naked woman.

He reached the higher ground more quickly than he had anticipated. The pull towards the south was intensifying, and when Helward was less than fifty yards from the nearest hill he stumbled ... and was rolling with an ever-increasing speed towards it.

The northern face was almost vertical, like the leeward side of a wind-blown dune, and he collided with it hard. Almost at once the southwards pressure was pulling him up the face, defying the pull of gravity. In desperation, for he knew if he reached the top the pressure on him could never be resisted, he scrambled for a hold somewhere on the rock-hard face. It came in the form of an outjutting spur. Helward grabbed it with both hands, desperately holding himself back against the relentless pressure. His body swung round, so that he was lying vertically against the wall, feet above his head, knowing that if he slipped now he would be taken backwards up the slope and on down towards the south.

He reached behind into his pack, and found the grapple. He lodged it firmly under the spur, attached the rope to it, and wound the other end around his wrist.

The southwards pressure was now so great upon him that the normal downwards pull of gravity was virtually negated.

The substance of the mountain was changing beneath him. The hard, almost vertical wall was slowly widening to east and west, slowly flattening, so that behind him the summit of the ridge appeared to be creeping down towards him. He saw a cleft in the rock beside him which was slowly closing, so he removed the grapple from under the spur and thrust it into the cleft. Moments later, the grapple was securely held.

The summit of the ridge had now distended and was beneath his body. The southward pressure took him, and he was swept over the ridge. The rope held and he was suspended horizontally.

What had been the mountain became a hard protuberance beneath his chest, his stomach lay in what had been the valley beyond, his feet scrambled for a hold against the diminishing ridge of what had once been another mountain.

He was flat along the surface of the world, a giant recumbent across an erstwhile mountain region.

He raised his body, trying to ease his position. Lifting his head he suddenly found he was short of breath. A hard, icy wind blew from the north, but it was thin and short of oxygen. He lowered his head again, resting his chin on the ground. At this level his nose could take air that would sustain him.

It was bitterly cold.

There were clouds, and borne on the wind they skimmed a few inches above the ground like a white unbroken sheet. They surged around his face, flowing around his nose like foam at the bow of a ship.

His mouth was below them, his eyes were above.

Helward looked ahead of him through the thin, rarefied atmosphere above the clouds. He looked towards the north.

He was at the edge of the world; its major bulk lay before him.

He could see the whole world.

North of him the ground was level; flat as the top of a table. But at the centre, due north of him, the ground rose from that flatness in a perfectly symmetrical, rising and curving concave spire. It narrowed and narrowed, reaching up, growing ever more slender, rising so high that it was impossible to see where it ended.

He saw it in a multitude of colours. There were broad areas of brown and yellow, patched with green. Further north, there was a blueness: a pure, sapphire blue, bright on the eyes. Over it all, the white of clouds in long, tenuous whorls, in brilliant swarms, in flaky patterns.

The sun was setting. Red to the north-east, it glowed against the impossible horizon.

The shape of it was the same. A broad flat disk that might be an equator; at its centre and to north and south, its poles existed as rising, concave spires.

Helward had seen the sun so often that he no longer questioned its appearance. But now he knew: the world too was that shape.

9

The sun set, and the world became dark.

The southwards pressure was now so great that his body hardly touched what had once been the mountains beneath him. He was hanging on the rope in the darkness, as if vertically against the wall of a cliff; reason told him that he was still horizontal, but reason was in conflict with sensation.

He could no longer trust the strength of the rope. Helward reached forward, curled his fingertips around two small extrusions (had they once been mountains?), and hauled himself forward.

The surface beyond was smoother, and Helward could hardly find a firm hold. With trouble he discovered he could dig his fingers into the ground sufficiently far to obtain a temporary purchase. He dragged himself forward again: a matter of inches ... but in another sense a matter of miles. The southwards pressure did not perceptibly diminish.

He abandoned his rope and crawled forward by hand. Another few inches and his feet came into contact with the low ridge that had been the mountain. He pressed hard, moved forward again.

Gradually, the pressure on him began to decrease until it was no longer a matter of desperation to hold on. Helward relaxed for a moment, trying to catch his breath. Even as he did so he felt sure that the pressure was increasing again, so he moved forward. Soon, he had gone so far that he could rest on his hands and knees.

He had not looked south. What had been behind him?

He crawled a long way, then felt able to stand. He did so, leaning northwards to counteract the force. He walked forward, feeling the inexplicable drag steadily diminish. He soon felt he was sufficiently far from the worst zone of pressure to sit on the ground, and take a proper rest.

He looked towards the south. All was darkness. Overhead, the clouds which had broken around his face were now some height

136

above him. They occluded the moon, which Helward, in his untutored way, had never questioned. It too was that strange shape; he had seen it many times, always accepted it.

He continued walking northwards, feeling the immense drag weakening still further. The landscape around him was dark and featureless, and he paid no attention to it. Only one thought dominated his mind: that he must move sufficiently far forward before he rested so that he would not be dragged back again to that zone of pressure. He knew now a basic truth of this world, that the ground was indeed moving as Collings had said. Up north, where the city existed, the ground moved with an almost imperceptible slowness: about one mile in a period of ten days. But farther south it moved faster, and its acceleration was exponential. He had seen it in the way the bodies of the girls had changed: in the space of one night the ground had moved sufficiently far for their bodies to be affected by the lateral distortions to which they – and not he – were subjected.

The city could not rest. It was destined to move forever, because if it halted it would start the long slow movement down here – down past – where it would come eventually to the zone where mountains became ridges a few inches high, where an irresistible pressure would sweep it to its destruction.

At that moment, as Helward walked slowly northwards across the strange, dark terrain, he could give no rationale to what he had experienced. Everything conflicted with logic: ground was stable, it could not move. Mountains did not distort as one sprawled across their face. Human beings did not become twelve inches high; chasms did not narrow; babies did not choke on their mothers' milk.

Though the night was well advanced, Helward felt no tiredness beyond the residue of the physical strain he had endured on the side of the mountain. It occurred to him that the day had passed quickly; faster than he could have credited.

He was well beyond the zone of maximum pressure now, but he was still too aware of it to halt. It was not a pleasant thought to sleep while the ground moved beneath him, bearing him ineluctably southwards.

He was a microcosm of the city: he could no more rest than it.

Tiredness came at last and he sprawled on the hard ground, and slept.

137

He was awakened by the sunrise, and his first thought was of the southwards pressure. Alarmed, he sprang to his feet and tested his balance; the pressure was there, but not measurably worse than it had been at his last recollection.

He looked towards the south.

There, incredibly, the mountains stood.

It could not be so. He had seen them, *felt* them reduce to a ridge of hard ground, no more than an inch or two in height. Yet they were clearly there: steep, irregularly shaped, capped with snow.

Helward found his pack, and checked its contents. He had lost the rope and grapple, and much of his equipment had been with the girls when he left them, but he still had one canteen of water, a sleeping-bag, and several packets of the dehydrated food. It would be enough to keep him going for a while.

He ate a little of the food, then strapped his pack in place.

He glanced up at the sun, determined this time to keep his bearings.

He walked south towards the mountains.

The pressure grew about him slowly, dragging him forward. As he watched the mountains they appeared to reduce in height. The substance of the soil on which he walked became thicker, and the terrain once more took on its appearance of fused lateral streaks.

Overhead, the sun moved faster than it had any right to do.

Fighting against the pressure, Helward stopped when he saw that the mountains were once again not much more than an undulating line of low hills.

He was not equipped to go farther. He turned, and moved north. Night fell an hour later.

He walked on through the darkness until he felt the pressure was acceptably low, then rested.

When daylight came again, the mountains were clearly in view . . . and as mountains.

He made no attempt to move, but waited in his place. As the day advanced the pressure grew. He was being borne southwards by the motion of the ground towards the mountains . . . and as he watched and waited he saw them slowly spread laterally.

He moved camp, went northwards before night fell. He had seen enough; it was time to return to the city.

Unaccountably, the thought of this worried him. Would he have to make some kind of report on what had happened?

There was much he felt incapable of even absorbing into his own experience, let alone coalescing what he had seen and felt into a coherent order that he could describe to someone else.

At the centre of it all was the stupefying sight of the world spread before him. Had any man ever been privy to such an experience? How could the mind encompass a concept of which the eye had been incapable of seeing even the entire extent? To left and right – and, for all he knew, to the south of him – the surface of the world had extended seemingly without bound. Only in the north, due north, was there a definition of form: that curving, rising pinnacle of land which stretched to no visible end.

Likewise the sun, likewise the moon. And, for all he knew, likewise every body in the visible universe.

The three girls: how could he report on their safe conduct to their village when they had passed into a state in which he could not communicate with them, nor even see them? They had passed on into their own world, utterly alien to him.

The baby: what had happened to that? Manifestly of the city, for like him it had not been affected by the distortions that were otherwise all about them, presumably it had been abandoned by Rosario . . . and was now presumably dead. Even if it still lived, the motion of the ground would bear it southwards to that zone of pressure where it could not survive.

Lost in such thoughts, Helward walked on, taking little account of his surroundings. Only when he stopped to take a drink of water did he look about, and it was with a start of surprise that he realised that he recognised the terrain.

This was the rocky land to the north of the chasm where the bridge had been built.

He took a few mouthfuls of the water, then retraced his steps. If he was to find his way back to the city he must relocate the tracks, and the site of the bridge would be a better landmark than most.

He encountered a stream which, in his preoccupied state, he must have crossed without noticing. He followed its course, wondering if this could possibly be the same stream, for it appeared to be a tiny rivulet. In due time the banks of the stream became steeper and rougher, but there was no sign of the chasm.

Helward scrambled up the bank, and walked back against the direction of the water-flow. Though naggingly familiar, the appearance of the stream was distended and distorted, and it could be another stream entirely.

Then he noticed a long black oval near the edge of the water. He went down and examined it. There was a faint smell of burn-

139

ing . . . and on closer inspection he realised this was the scar of a fire. His camp-fire.

The stream next to it was no more than a yard wide, and yet when he had been here with the girls it had been at least twelve feet across. He went back to the top of the bank. After a long search he found some marks on the ground which could have been the traces of one of the suspension towers.

From the top of one bank to the next, the distance could have been no more than five or six yards. The drop to the water was a matter of feet.

At this point the city had crossed.

He walked northwards, and in a short while found the trace of a sleeper. It was about seventeen feet long. The one next to it was three inches away.

By the following night the scale of the landscape had assumed proportions that were more familiar to him. Trees looked like trees, not sprawling bushes. Pebbles were round, grass grew in clumps, not spread like a smear of green. The tracks by which he walked were still too widely spread to have any resemblance to the gauge used by the city, but Helward thought that his journey should not be much longer.

He had lost track of the number of days that had passed, but the terrain was becoming increasingly familiar to him, and he knew that so far his time away from the city was still considerably less than that predicted by Clausewitz. Even taking into account the two or three days that had seemed to pass so quickly while he was in the zone of pressure, the city could not have moved more than a mile or two farther to the north while he was away.

This thought encouraged him, for his supplies of food and water were dwindling.

He walked on, and the days passed. There was still no sign of the city, and the tracks by which he walked showed no signs of narrowing to their more normal gauge. By now he was so accustomed to the notion of the lateral distortion of this world in the south, that he took the evidence of it much in his stride.

One morning, he was disturbed by a new thought: for several days the gauge of the tracks had not appeared to change, and could it be that he had encountered a region where the motion of the ground was directly equal to the speed of his own walking? That is, that he was like a mouse on a treadmill, never making any forward progress?

For an hour or two he hastened his walk, but soon reason

prevailed. He had, after all, successfully moved away from the zone of pressure where the southward motion was greater. But more days passed, and the city seemed to be no nearer. Soon he was down to his last two packets of food, and twice he had had to supplement his water-supplies from local sources.

The day he reached the end of his food, he was suddenly taken by a surge of excitement. Potential starvation was no longer a problem . . . he had recognised where he was! This was the region he had been riding through with Barter Collings: at that time, two or three miles north of optimum!

By his estimate of time he had been gone for three miles at the most . . . so the city should be in sight.

Up ahead, the line of track-scars continued until a low ridge . . . and no sign of the city. The sleeper-pits were still distorted, and the next row of scars – the left inner – was some distance away.

All it could mean, Helward reasoned, was that while he was away the city had somehow moved much faster. Perhaps it had even overtaken the optimum, and was in a region where the ground moved more slowly. Already he was beginning to understand why the city moved on; perhaps ahead of optimum there was a zone where the ground did not move at all.

In which case the city could stop . . . the grand treadmill would end.

10

Helward passed a hungry night, and slept badly. In the morning he took a few mouthfuls of water and was soon on his way. The city must be in sight soon. . . .

In the hottest part of the day, Helward was forced to rest. The countryside was barren and open, with little shade. He sat down beside the track.

Staring bleakly ahead, he saw something which gave him fresh hope: three people were walking slowly down the track towards him. They must be from the city, sent out to find him. He waited weakly for them to reach him.

As they approached he tried to stand, but stumbled. He lay still.

'Are you from the city?'

Helward opened his eyes and looked up at the speaker. It was a young man, dressed in a guild-apprentice uniform. He nodded, his jaw slack.

'You're ill . . . what's the matter?'

'I'm O.K. Have you any food?'

'Drink this.'

A canteen of water was offered, and Helward took a mouthful. The water tasted different: it was stale and flat, city water.

'Can you stand?'

With assistance, Helward got to his feet and they walked together away from the track to where a few scrawny bushes grew. Helward sat down on the ground, and the young man opened his pack. With a start of recognition, Helward realised the pack was identical to his own.

'Do I know you?' he said.

'Apprentice Kellen Li-Chen.'

Li-Chen! He remembered him from the crèche. 'I'm Helward Mann.'

Kellen Li-Chen opened a packet of dehydrated food and insinuated some water. Soon a familiar portion of grey porridge was before him, and Helward began to eat it with as near a mood of enthusiasm as he could ever recall.

In the background, some yards away, two girls stood and waited.

'You're going down past,' he said between mouthfuls.

'Yes.'

'I've just been.'

'What's there?'

Suddenly, Helward remembered meeting Torrold Pelham under almost identical circumstances.

'You're down past now,' he said. 'Can't you feel it?'

Kellen shook his head.

'What do you mean?' he said.

Helward meant the southwards pressure, the subtle pull of which he could still feel as he walked. But he understood now that Kellen had probably not yet noticed it. Until it had been experienced in its extremeness, it would not be recognised as a discrete sensation.

'It's impossible to talk about it,' Helward said. 'Go down past and you'll see for yourself.'

Helward glanced over at the girls. They were sitting on the ground, their backs turned quite deliberately on the men. He couldn't help smiling to himself.

'Kellen . . . how far is the city from here?'

'A few miles back. About five.'

Five miles! Then by now it must have easily overtaken the optimum.

'Can you give me some food? Just a little . . . enough to get me back to the city.'

'Of course.'

Kellen took four packets, and handed them over. Helward looked at them for a moment, then handed three of them back.

'One will be enough. You'll need the rest.'

'I haven't got far to go,' said Kellen.

'I know . . . but you'll still need them.' He looked again at the other apprentice. 'How long have you been out of the crèche, Kellen?'

'About fifteen miles.'

But Kellen was much younger than him. He remembered distinctly: Kellen had been two grades below him in the crèche. They must be recruiting apprentices much earlier now. But Kellen looked mature and well filled. His body was not that of an adolescent.

'How old are you?' he said.

'Six hundred and sixty-five.'

143

That couldn't be so . . . he was at least fifty miles younger than Helward, who was by his own reckoning six hundred and seventy.

'Have you been working on the tracks?'

'Yes. Bloody hard work.'

'I know. How has the city been able to move so fast?'

'Fast? It's been a bad period. We had a river to cross, and at the moment the city is held up by hilly country. We've lost a lot of ground. When I left, it was six miles behind optimum.'

'Six miles! Then the optimum's moved faster?'

'Not as far as I know.' Kellen was looking over his shoulder at the girls. 'I think I'd better be moving on now. Are you O.K.?'

'Yes. How are you getting on with them?'

Kellen grinned.

'Not bad,' he said. 'Language barriers, but I think I can find a bit of common vocabulary.'

Helward laughed, and again remembered Pelham.

'Make it soon,' he said. 'It gets difficult later.'

Kellen Li-Chen stared at him for a moment, then stood up.

'The sooner the better, I think,' he said. He went back to the girls, who complained loudly when they realised their break had been only a short one. As they walked past him. Helward saw that one of the girls had unbuttoned her shirt all down the front, and had tied it with a knot.

With the food Kellen had given him, Helward felt certain of reaching the city without any further problems. After the distance he had travelled, another five miles was as nothing, and he anticipated reaching the city by nightfall. The countryside around him was now entirely new to him: in spite of what Kellen had said it certainly seemed that the city had made good progress during his absence.

Evening approached, and still there was no sign of the city.

The only hopeful indication was that now the scars left by the sleepers were of more normal dimensions; the next time Helward stopped for water he measured the nearest pit and estimated that it was about six feet long.

Ahead of him was rising ground, and he could see a ridge over which the track remains ran. He felt sure the city must be lying in the hollow beyond and so he pressed on, hoping for a sight of it before nightfall.

The sun was touching the horizon as he reached the ridge, and looked down into the valley.

A broad river flowed across the floor of the valley. The tracks reached the southern bank . . . and continued on the farther side. As far as he could see they continued up across the valley until lost to sight amongst some woodland. There was no sign of the city.

Angry and confused, Helward stared at the valley until darkness fell, then made his camp for the night.

In the morning he started out soon after daybreak, and within a few minutes was by the bank of the river. On this side there were many signs of human activity: the ground by the side of the water had been churned into a muddy waste, and there was a great deal of discarded timber and broken sleeper-foundations. In the water itself were several timber piles, presumably all that now remained of the bridge the city had had to build.

Helward waded down into the water, holding on to the nearest pile for support. As the water deepened he started to swim, but the current took him and he was swept a long way downstream before he could haul himself on to the northern bank.

Soaked through, he walked back upstream until he reached the track remains. His pack and clothes weighed heavily on him, so he undressed and laid his clothes in the sun, then spread the sleeping-bag and canvas pack. An hour later his clothes were dry, so he pulled them on again and prepared to move off. The sleeping-bag was still not completely dry, but he planned to air it at his next stop.

Just as he was strapping his pack into place, there was a rattling noise and something plucked at his shoulder. Helward turned his head in time to see a crossbow quarrel fall on the ground.

He dived for cover into one of the sleeper foundations.

'Stay right there!'

He looked in the direction of the voice; he couldn't see the speaker, but there was a clump of bushes some fifty yards away.

Helward examined his shoulder: the quarrel had torn away a section of his sleeve, but it had not drawn blood. He was defence-less, having lost his crossbow with the remainder of his possessions.

'I'm coming out . . . don't move.'

A moment later, a man wearing the guild-apprentice uniform stepped out from behind the bush, levelling his crossbow at Helward.

Helward shouted: 'Don't shoot! I'm an apprentice from the city.'

The man said nothing, but continued to advance. He halted about five yards away.

'O.K. . . . stand up.'

Helward did so, seeking the recognition he anticipated.

'Who are you?'

'I'm from the city,' said Helward.

'Which guild?'

'The Futures.'

'What's the last line of the oath?'

Helward shook his head in surprise. 'Listen, what the – ?'

'Come on . . . the oath'

' "All this is sworn in the full knowledge that a betrayal of any one – " '

The man lowered his bow.

'O.K.,' he said. 'I had to be sure. What's your name?'

'Helward Mann.'

The other looked at him closely. 'God, I never recognised you! You've grown a beard!'

'Jase!'

The two young men stared at each other for a few seconds more, then greeted each other affably. Helward realised that they both must have changed out of recognition in the time since they had last met. Then they had both been beardless boys, agonising about the frustrations of life inside the crèche; now they had changed in outlook as well as appearance. In the crèche, Gelman Jase had affected a worldliness and disdain for the order by which they had to exist, and he had mannered himself as a careless and irresponsible leader of the boys who 'matured' less quickly. None of this was apparent to Helward as they stood there beside the river renewing their earlier friendship. His experiences outside the city had weathered Jase, just as they had weathered his appearance. Neither man resembled the pale, undeveloped, and naïve boys who had grown up together: suntanned, bearded, muscular, and hardened, they had both matured quickly.

'What was all that about, shooting at me?' said Helward.

'I thought you were a took.'

'But didn't you see my uniform?'

'Doesn't mean anything any more.'

'But – '

'Listen, Helward, things are changing. How many apprentices have you seen down past?'

'Two. Three, including you.'

'Right. Did you know the city sends an apprentice down past every mile or so? There should be many more down here . . . and as we all take the same route we ought to be meeting each other almost every day. But the tooks are catching on. They're killing

146

the apprentices, and taking their uniforms. Were you attacked?'

'No,' said Helward.

'I was.'

'You could have tried to identify me before you shot at me.'

'I aimed to miss you.'

Helward indicated his torn sleeve. 'Then you're just a lousy shot.'

Jase moved away, and went over to where his quarrel had fallen, he picked it up, examined it for damage, then replaced it in its pouch.

'We ought to be trying to reach the city,' he said when he returned.

'Do you know where it is?'

Jase looked worried.

'I can't work it out,' he said. 'I've been walking for miles. Has the city suddenly accelerated?'

'Not as far as I know. I saw another apprentice yesterday. He said the city had actually been delayed.'

'Then where the hell is it?' said Jase.

'Somewhere up there.' Helward indicated the track-remains leading north.

'Then we go on.'

By the end of the day they still had not sighted the city – though the tracks were now apparently the normal dimensions – and they made a camp in a patch of woodland through which a stream of clean water flowed.

Jase was far better equipped than Helward. In addition to his crossbow, he had a spare sleeping-bag (Helward's wet one had started to smell, and he'd thrown it away), a tent, and plenty of food.

'What do you make of it?' said Jase.

'Down past?'

'Yes.'

'I'm still trying to understand it,' said Helward. 'What about you?'

'I don't know. The same, I suppose. I can't make logic of what I've seen and yet I know I've seen and experienced it, and so it must be so.'

'How can ground possibly move?'

'You noticed it too?' said Jase.

'I think so. That's what happened wasn't it?'

147

Later, each told his own account of what had happened after he left the crèche. Jase's experiences had been remarkably different from Helward's.

He had left the crèche a few miles before Helward, and undergone many of the same experiences working outside the city. An essential difference, though, was that he had not married, and had been invited to meet some of the transferred women. As a result of this, he already knew the two women he was assigned to when he began the journey down past.

He had learned many of the stories told by the local inhabitants about the people of the city. How the city was populated by giants, how they plundered and killed, and raped the women.

As his journey southwards proceeded, Jase had realised that the girls were growing more frightened, and when he asked them why they said that they felt certain they would be killed by their own kind when they returned. They wanted to go back to the city. At this point Jase had been noticing the first effects of the lateral distortions, and was growing curious. He turned the girls back, and told them to make their own way back to the city. He intended to spend one more day on his own, then he too would return northwards.

He travelled south, but did not see much that interested him, then attempted to find the girls. He discovered them three days later. Their throats had been cut, and they were hanging upside down from a tree. Still recoiling from the shock, Jase himself was attacked by a crowd of local men, some of whom were wearing apprentices' uniforms. He had managed to escape, but the men had given chase. There followed three days of nightmare. While making his escape he had fallen and badly twisted his foot, and in his lamed state could do little more than hide. During the chase, he had gone a long way from the tracks, and had moved south by several miles. The hunt had been called off, and Jase was alone. He stayed in hiding . . . but gradually felt a slow build-up of southwards pressure. He realised that he was in a region he could not recognise. He described to Helward the flat, featureless terrain, the tremendous pressure, the way in which physical distortions took place.

He had tried to move back in the direction of the tracks, but his weakened leg made progress difficult. Finally, he had been forced to anchor himself to the ground with the grapple and rope until he could walk again. The build-up of pressure had continued, and fearing the rope would hold no longer he had been forced to crawl northwards. After a long and difficult period he had managed

148

to escape from the zone of worst pressure, and had headed back towards the city.

He had wandered for a long time without finding the tracks. As a consequence his knowledge of the terrain away from the immediate neighbourhood of the tracks was considerably greater than Helward's.

'Did you know there's another city over there?' he said, indicating the land to the west of the tracks.

'*Another* city?' said Helward incredulously.

'Nothing like Earth. This one is built on the ground.'

'But how . . . ?'

'It's immense. Ten times, twenty times as big as Earth. I didn't recognise it for what it was at first . . . I thought it was just another settlement, but one much larger. Helward, listen, it's a city like the cities we learnt about in the crèche . . . the ones on Earth planet. Hundreds, thousands of buildings . . . all built on the ground.'

'Are there any people there?'

'A few . . . not many. There was a lot of damage. I don't know what happened there, but most of it seemed to be abandoned now. I didn't stay long because I didn't want to be seen. But it's a beautiful sight . . . all those buildings.'

'Can we go there?'

'No . . . keep away. Too many tooks. There's something going on out there, the situation is changing. They're organising themselves better, there are lines of communication. In the past, when the city went to a village we were often the first people from outside that the inhabitants had seen for a long time. But from things the girls said to me, I got the impression that that's not likely to be the case any more. Word is spreading about the city . . . and the tooks don't like us. They never have, but in small groups they were weak. Now I think they want to destroy the city.'

'And so they dress as apprentices,' said Helward, still not grasping the seriousness of Jase's tone.

'That's a small part of it. They take the clothes of the apprentices they kill to make further killings easier. But if they decide to attack the city, it'll be when they're well organised and determined.'

'I can't believe that they could ever threaten us.'

'Maybe not . . . but you were lucky.'

In the morning they set out early, and travelled hard. They

149

walked all day, not stopping for more than a few minutes at a time. By their side, the scars left by the tracks had returned to normal dimensions and both were spurred on by the thought that the city could not be more than a few hours' walk ahead.

As the afternoon drew on, the track led in a winding route around the side of a hill, and as they reached the crest of the hill they saw the city ahead of them, stationary in a broad valley.

They stopped, stared down at it.

The city had changed.

Something about it made Helward run forward, hurrying down the side of the hill towards it.

From this elevation they could see the signs of normal activity, about the city: behind it four track-crews tearing up the rails, ahead of it a larger team sinking piles into the river that presently barred the city's way. But the shape of the city had changed. The rear section was misshapen, blackened. . . .

The lines of Militia had been strengthened, and soon Jase and Helward were halted, and their identities checked. Both men fumed at the delay, for it was clear that a major disaster had struck the city. Waiting for clearance from inside the city, Jase learned from the militiaman in charge that there had been two attacks by the tooks. The second one had been more serious than the first. Twenty-three militiaman had been killed; they were still counting bodies inside the city.

The excitement of their return was instantly sobered by what they saw. When the clearance came through, Helward and Jase walked on in silence.

The crèche had been razed: it was the children who had died. Inside the city there was more that had changed. The impact of these changes was severe, but Helward had no time to register any reaction. He could only mark them, then try to push them aside until external pressures eased. There was no time to dwell on his thoughts.

He learnt that his father had died. Only a few hours after Helward had left the city, the angina had stopped his heart. It was Clausewitz who broke the news to him, and Clausewitz who told him that his apprenticeship was now over.

More: Victoria had given birth to a baby – a boy – but it had been one of those that had died in the attack.

More: Victoria had signed a form that pronounced the marriage over. She was living with another man, and was pregnant again.

And more, implicitly tied up with all these events, yet no more

150

conceivable. Helward learnt from the central calendar that while he had been away the city had moved a total of seventy-three miles, and was even so eight miles behind optimum. In his own subjective time-scale, Helward had been gone for less than three miles.

He accepted all these as facts. The reaction of shock would come later; meanwhile another attack was imminent.

Part Three

1

The valley was dark and silent. Across on the northern side of the river I saw a red light flash on twice, then nothing.

Seconds later, I heard from deep within the city the grinding of the winch-drums, and the city began to inch forward. The sound echoed around the valley.

I was lying with about thirty other men in the tangled undergrowth that spread across the face of the hill. I had been drafted temporarily to work with the Militia during this most critical of all the city's crossings. The third attack was anticipated at any moment, and it had been judged that once the city could reach the northern bank of the river it would, by nature of the surrounding terrain, be able to defend itself sufficiently long for the tracks to be extended at least as far as the highest point of the pass through the hills to the north. Once there, it was thought that it could again defend itself for the next phase of track-laying.

Somewhere in the valley we knew that there were about a hundred and fifty tooks, all armed with rifles. They presented a formidable enemy. The city had only twelve rifles taken from the tooks, and the ammunition for them had been spent during the second attack. Our only realistic weapons were the crossbows – at short range, deadly – and an awareness of the value of intelligence work. It was this latter which had enabled us to prepare the reserve counter-attack of which I was a part.

A few hours earlier, as darkness fell, we had taken up this position overlooking the valley. The main force of defence was three ranks of crossbowmen deployed around the city itself. As the city started out across the bridge they would retreat, until they formed a defensive position around the tracks. The tooks would concentrate their fire on these men, and at that moment we could spring our ambush.

With fortune on our side, the counter-attack would not be necessary. Though intelligence work had established that another attack was likely, the bridge-building work had been completed faster than anticipated, and it was hoped that the city would be safely across to the other side under cover of darkness before the tooks realised.

But in the still of the valley, the sound of the winches was unmistakable.

The forward edge of the city had just reached the bridge itself when the first shots were heard. I placed a bolt in the bow, and held my hand over the safety-catch.

It was a cloudy night, and visibility was poor. I had seen the flashes from the rifles, and estimated that the tooks were ranged in a rough semi-circle, approximately one hundred yards from our men. I could not tell if any of their bullets had hit, but so far there were no answering shots.

More rifles fired, and we could tell the tooks were closing in. The city had half its bulk on the bridge . . . and still crept forward.

Down below, a distant shout: '*Lights!*'

Instantly, a battery of eight arc-lamps situated on the rear of the city came on, directed over the heads of the crossbowmen and into the surrounding terrain. The tooks were there, not taking any kind of cover.

The first rank of crossbowmen loosed their bolts, hunched down, and started to reload. The second rank shot, hunched down, and reloaded. The third rank shot, reloaded.

Taken by surprise the tooks had suffered several casualties, but now they threw themselves down against the ground and fired at all they could see of the defenders: the black silhouettes against the arc-lamps.

'*Lights off!*'

Darkness fell at once, and the crossbowmen by the city dispersed. A few seconds later the lights came on again, and the crossbowmen fired from their new positions.

Once again the tooks were taken off aim, and more casualties were inflicted. The lights went off again, and in the sudden darkness the crossbowmen returned to their former position. The manoeuvre was repeated.

There was a shout from below, and as the arc-lamps came on we saw that the tooks were charging. The city was now on the bridge.

Suddenly, there was a loud explosion and a gush of flame against the side of the city. An instant later a second explosion occurred on the bridge itself, and flames spread across the dry timber of the rail-way.

'Reserve force, *ready!*' I stood up, and waited for the order. I was no longer frightened, and the tension of the waiting hours had disappeared. '*Advance!*'

The arc-lamps on the city were still burning, and we could see the tooks clearly. Most of them were engaged in a hand-to-hand battle with the main defence, but several more were crouched on the ground, taking careful aim at the superstructure of the city. Two of the arc-lamps were hit, and they went out.

The flames on the bridge and against the side of the city were spreading.

I saw a took near the bank of the river, swinging his arm back in preparation to throw a metal cylinder. I was no more than twenty yards from him. I aimed, released the bolt . . . and hit the man in his chest. The incendiary bomb fell a few yards away from him, and exploded in a burst of heat and flame.

Our counter-attack had, as anticipated, taken the enemy by surprise. We managed to hit three more of the men . . . but suddenly they broke off and ran towards the east, disappearing into the shadows of the valley.

There was considerable confusion for a minute or two. The city was on fire, and beneath it the bridge was burning fiercely in two separate places. One concentration of flame was directly beneath the city, but the other was a few yards behind it. It was obviously urgent to deal with the fires, but no one was certain that all the tooks had retreated.

The city continued to winch forward, but where the bridge burned large sections of timber were falling away into the river.

Order was restored quickly. A Militia officer shouted orders, and the men formed into two groups. One group renewed the defensive position around the tracks; I joined the second group sent out on to the bridge to fight the fire.

After the second attack – in which incendiaries had been used for the first time – fire-points had been fitted to the outside of the city. The nearest of these had been damaged in one of the explosions, and water was gushing away from it uselessly. We found a second one, and unravelled the short length of hose.

The intensity of the track-fire was too great, and it was almost hopeless to try to fight it. Although the city had now passed over the worst of the damage there were still three of the main runner-wheels to roll over the burning timber . . . and as we fought in the dense smoke and billowing flames I saw the rail beginning to twist under the combined forces of heat and weight.

There was a roar, and another section of timber fell away. The smoke was too thick. Choking, we had to back out from under the city.

The fire in the superstructure was still blazing, but a fire-crew inside the city was attempting to deal with it. The winches turned . . . the city crept slowly towards the comparative safety of the northern bank.

2

In the morning light the damage was assessed. In terms of lost human life, the city had not fared too badly. Three of the militia-men had been killed in the shooting, and fifteen had been injured. Inside the city, one man had been seriously wounded in one of the incendiary explosions, and a dozen more men and women had been overcome by smoke in the ensuing fires.

The physical damage to the city itself was extensive. A whole section of administrative offices had been gutted by the fire, and some of the accommodation section was uninhabitable because of fire or water damage.

Beneath the city there was more damage. Although the main base of the city was steel, much of the construction was timber, and there were whole sections which had been burnt out. The rear runner-wheels on the right outer track had been derailed, and one of the great wheels had sustained a structural crack. It could not be replaced: it would have to be discarded.

After the city had reached the northern bank, the bridge had continued to burn and was now a total loss. With it had gone several hundred yards of our irreplaceable rails, warped and twisted by the heat.

After two days outside the city, working with the track-crews who were salvaging what there was of the rails on the southern bank of the river, I was summoned to see Clausewitz.

Apart from an hour or two spent inside the city when I first returned, I had not reported formally to any of my senior guilds-men. As far as I could determine, the normal protocol of the guilds had been abandoned for the duration of the emergency, and as I myself could see no end to the serious situation – the attacks had caused inevitable delays, and the optimum was ever farther away – I had not expected anyone to call me off my work outside.

There was a disturbing mood amongst those men who were outside – half-way between despair and desperation. The work continued on laying the tracks towards the pass, but the relaxed energy of my early days outside the city seemed to be a long way

159

behind us. Now the tracks were being built in spite of the situation with the tooks, rather than in the way I now understood the motivation of the city to be derived, from an internal need to survive in a strange environment.

The talk among the track-crews, the Militia, the Traction men was all centred in one way or another around the attacks. No longer was there talk of gaining ground on the optimum, or what dangers lay down past. The city was in a crisis, and this was reflected in everyone's attitude.

When I went inside the city the change was apparent here too. Gone was the light, aseptic appearance of the corridors, gone was the general atmosphere of workaday routines.

The elevator was no longer working. Many of the main doors in the corridors were locked, and at one point an entire wall had been torn away – presumably as a result of one of the fires – so that anyone walking through that part of the city could see what was outside. I remembered Victoria's frustrations of old, and reflected that whatever secrecy the guilds might have tried to maintain in the past, no longer was such a system possible.

Thought of Victoria pained me; I still did not realise fully what had happened. In what seemed to me to be the passage of a few days, she had abandoned all the tacit understandings of the marriage between us, and gone to pursue another life without me.

I had not seen her since my return, though I had made sure that she would have known I was back in the city. Under the conditions of the external threat it had not been possible to see her anyway, but that aspect of my life was one I needed time to consider before meeting her. The news of her pregnancy by another man – I was told he was an education administrator named Yung – had not hit me too hard at first, simply because I had just not believed it. Such a situation could not possibly have developed in the time I knew I had been away from the city.

I found my way to the first-order guild area with some difficulty. The interior of the city had changed in many ways.

There seemed to be people, noise, and dirt everywhere. Every spare yard of space had been given over to emergency sleeping-room, and even in some of the corridors lay wounded men from outside. Several walls and partitions had been taken down, and just outside the first-order quarters – where there had been a series of pleasantly appointed recreation rooms for the guildsmen – an emergency kitchen had been placed.

The smell of burnt wood was everywhere.

I knew a fundamental change was coming over the city. I

160

could feel the old structure of the guilds crumbling away. The roles of many people had already changed; working with the track-crews I'd met several men for whom it was the first time outside the city, men who until the attacks had worked on food synthesis, or education, or domestic administration. Took labour was now obviously impossible, and all hands had to be called to move the city. Why at this moment Clausewitz had summoned me I could not imagine.

There was no sign of him in the Futures' room, and so I waited for a while. After half an hour he had still not appeared, so knowing my services could be better employed outside I headed back the way I had come.

I met Future Denton in the corridor.

'You're Future Mann, aren't you?'

'Yes.'

'We're leaving the city. Are you ready now?'

'I was supposed to be seeing Future Clausewitz.'

'That's right. He's sent me instead. Can you ride a horse?'

I had forgotten the horses while I was away from the city. 'Yes.'

'Good. Meet me at the stables in an hour's time.'

He walked on into the Futures' room.

With an hour to spend on my own, I realised that I had nothing to do, no one to see. All my connections with the city were broken; even associative memories of the physical shape and appearance of the city had been disrupted by the damage.

I walked down to the rear of the city to see for myself the extent of the damage to the crèche, but there was not much to see. Almost the whole superstructure had been burnt or latterly demolished, and where the children had been housed was merely the bare steel of the main base of the city. From there I could see back across the river to where the attack had taken place. I wondered whether the tooks would try again. I felt they had been well beaten, but if the city was resented as much as appeared I supposed they would eventually re-form and attack once more.

It came home to me just how vulnerable the city was. Not designed to repel any kind of attack, it was slow-moving, ungainly, built of highly inflammable materials. All its weakest points, the tracks, the cables, the timber superstructure, were easily accessible.

I wondered if the tooks realised how easy it would be to destroy the city: all they needed to do was disable its motive powers permanently, then sit back and watch as the movement of the ground slowly bore it southwards.

I considered this for some time. It seemed to me that the local

161

people did not understand the inherent frailty of the city and its inhabitants, because of the lack of information available to them. As far as I could tell, the strange transformation that had overtaken the three girls down past was subjectively to them no transformation at all.

Here, near optimum, the tooks were not subject to distortion – or only to an indiscernible degree – and so no perception of any difference was possible.

Only if the tooks succeeded, perhaps not even by design, in delaying the city to such a degree that it was borne to a point so far south that it could never haul itself forward again would they see the effect this would have on the city and its occupants.

Under normal conditions, the city would be facing difficult country; the hill to the north of us was probably not the only one in this region. How could it ever again hope to approach the optimum?

For the moment, though, the city was relatively secure. Bounded on one side by the river, and by rising ground which would afford no cover to any aggressor on the other, it was strategically well placed while the tracks were laid.

I wondered whether I had time to find a change of clothes, as I had been working and sleeping in the same ones for many days. This thought inevitably reminded me of Victoria, and how she had objected to my uniform after ten days in it outside the city.

I hoped I should not see her before I left.

I returned to the Futures' room, and made enquiries. There were indeed uniforms available, and I was entitled to one as I was now a full guildsman . . . but there was none available at the moment. I was told that one would be found while I was away.

Future Denton was waiting for me when I arrived at the stables. I was given a horse, and without further delay we rode out from beneath the city and headed north.

3

Denton was not a man who would say much unprompted. He answered any questions I chose to ask, but between there were long periods of silence. I did not find this uncomfortable, because it gave me a much needed opportunity to think.

The early training of the guilds still ran true: I accepted that I would make what I could of what I saw, and not rely on the interpretations of others.

We followed the proposed line of the tracks, up around the side of the hill and through the pass. At the top, the ground ran steadily downwards for a long way, following a small watercourse. There was a small patch of woodland at the end of the valley, and then another line of hills.

'Denton, why have we left the city at this moment?' I said. 'Surely every man is needed.'

'Our work is always important.'

'More important than defending the city?'

'Yes.'

As we rode he explained that during the last few miles the future-surveying work had been neglected. This was partly because of the troubles, and partly because the guild was undermanned.

'We've surveyed as far as these hills,' he said. 'Those trees . . . they're a nuisance to the Track guild, and they could provide cover for the tooks, but we need more timber. The hills have been surveyed for about another mile, but beyond that it's all virgin territory.'

He showed me a map that had been drawn on a long roll of paper, and explained the symbols to me. Our job, as far as I could tell, was to extend the map northwards. Denton had a surveying instrument mounted on a large wooden tripod, and every so often he would take a reading from it and make inscriptions on the map.

The horses were heavily laden with equipment. In addition to large supplies of food and bedding, we were each carrying a crossbow and a good supply of bolts; there was some digging equipment, a chemical-sampling kit, and a miniature video camera and recording equipment. I was given the video kit to use, and Denton showed me how to operate it.

The usual method of the Futures, as he explained it to me, was that over a period of time a different surveyor, or a different team of surveyors, would move north of the city by different routes. By the end of the expedition he would have a detailed map of the terrain through which he had passed, and a video record of its physical appearance. This would then be submitted to the Council of Navigators and they, with the help of other surveyors' reports, would decide which route would be taken.

Towards late afternoon, Denton stopped for about the sixth time and erected his tripod. After he had taken angular readings on the elevation of the surrounding hills, and, by use of a gyroscopically mounted compass, had determined true north, he attached a free-swinging pendulum to the base of the instrument. The weight of the pendulum was pointed, and when its natural momentum was spent and the pointer was stationary, Denton took a graduated scale, marked with concentric circles, and placed it between the legs of the tripod.

The pointer was almost exactly above the central mark.

'We're at optimum,' he said. 'Know what that means?'

'Not exactly.'

'You've been down past, haven't you?' I confirmed this. 'There's always centrifugal force to contend with on this world. The farther south one travels, the greater that force is. It's always present anywhere south of optimum, but it makes no practicable difference to normal operations for about twelve miles south of optimum. Anything farther than that, and the city would have real problems. You know that anyway, if you've felt the centrifugal force.'

He took further readings from his instrument.

'Eight and a half miles,' he said. 'That's the distance between here and the city . . . or how much ground the city has to make up.'

I said: 'How is the optimum measured?'

'By its null gravitational distortions. It serves as the standard by which we measure the city's progress. In physical terms, imagine it as a line drawn around the world.'

'And the optimum is always moving?'

'No. The optimum is stationary . . . but the ground moves away from it.'

'Oh yes.'

We packed our gear and continued northwards. Just before sunset we made camp for the night.

4

The surveying work was undemanding mentally, and as we moved slowly northwards I found that my only external preoccupation was a need to be everwatchful for signs of hostile inhabitants. Denton told me that an attack on us was unlikely. but nevertheless we were on our guard.

I was still thinking about the awesome experience of seeing the whole world lying before me. As an event, it was enough; understanding it was something else.

On our third day out from the city I suddenly started to think about the education I had been given as a child. I'm not sure what started the train of thought; it was possibly a number of things, not least the shock of seeing how utterly the crèche had been destroyed.

I had thought little of my education since leaving the crèche. At the time I had felt, in common with most of the children in the crèche, that the teaching we were given was not much more than a penance, in which time was served as of necessity. But looking back, much of the education pushed into our unwilling heads took on a new dimension in the context of the city.

For instance, one of the subjects which had inspired in us the most boredom was what the teachers referred to as 'geography.' Most of these lessons had been concerned with the techniques of cartography and surveying; in the enclosed environment of the crèche, such exercises had been almost wholly theoretical. Now, though, those hours of tedium took on their relevance at long last. With a little concentration and a certain amount of digging into my often faulty memory, I grasped quickly the principles of the work Denton was showing me.

We had had many other subjects taught to us theoretically, and I saw now how those too had practical relevance. Any new guild apprentice would already have a background knowledge of the work his own guild would expect him to do, and in addition would have similar information about many of the other functions of the city.

Nothing could have prepared me for the sheer physical grind

of working on the tracks, but I'd had an almost instinctive understanding of the actual machinery used to haul the city along those tracks.

I cared not at all for the compulsory training with the Militia, but the puzzling – at the time – emphasis placed on military strategy during our education would clearly help those men who later took arms for the security of the city.

This process of thought led me to wonder whether there had been anything in my education that could possibly have prepared me for the sight of a world which was shaped the way this one appeared to be.

The lessons we had been given which specifically referred to astrophysics and astronomy had always spoken of planets as spheres. Earth – the planet, not our city – was described as an oblate spheroid, and we had been shown maps of some of its land surface area. This aspect of physical science was not dwelt upon; I'd grown up to assume that the world on which Earth city existed was a sphere like Earth planet, and nothing I had been taught had contradicted this assumption. Indeed, the nature of the world was never discussed openly at all.

I knew that Earth planet was part of a system of planets, which were orbiting a spherical sun. Earth planet itself was circled by a spherical satellite. Again, this information seemed always to be theoretical . . . and this lack of practical application had not concerned me even when I left the city, for it was always clear that a different circumstance obtained. The sun and moon were not spherical, and neither was the world on which we lived.

The question remained: where were we?

The solution lay perhaps in the past.

This too had been covered comprehensively, although the histories we were taught were exclusively about Earth planet. Much of what we learned concerned military manoeuvres, the transference of power and government from one state to another. We knew that time was measured in terms of years and centuries on Earth planet, that recorded history existed for about twenty centuries. Perhaps unfairly, I formed an impression that I should not care to live on Earth planet, as most of its existence seemed to be a series of disputes, wars, territorial claims, economic pressures. The concept of civilisation was far advanced, and explained to us as the state in which mankind congregated within cities. By definition, we of Earth city were civilised, but there seemed to be no resemblance between our existence and theirs. Civilisation on Earth planet was equated with selfishness and greed; those people who lived in a civilised state exploited those who did not. There were shortages of vital commodities on Earth planet, and the people in the civilised nations were able to monopolise those commodities by reason of their greater economic strength. This imbalance appeared to be at the root of the disputes.

I suddenly saw parallels between our civilisation and theirs. The city was undoubtedly on a war footing as a result of the situation with the tooks, and that in its turn was a product of our barter system. We did not exploit them through wealth, but we had a surplus of the commodities in short supply on Earth planet: food, fuel energy, raw materials. Our shortage was man-power, and we paid for that with our surplus commodities.

The process was inverted, but the product was the same.

Following my line of reasoning, I saw that the examination of the history of Earth planet prepared the way for those who would become Barter guildsmen, but it took me no further along my own search for understanding. The histories began and ended on Earth planet, with no mention of how the city came to be on this world, nor how the city had been built, nor about who its founders were and where they came from.

A deliberate omission? Or forgotten knowledge?

I imagined that many guildsmen had tried to construct their own patterns of logic, and for all I knew either the answers were available somewhere in the city, or there was a commonly accepted hypothesis which I had not yet encountered. But I had fallen naturally into the ways of the guildsmen. Survival on this world was a matter of initiative: on the grand scale, by hauling the city northwards away from that zone of amazing distortion behind us, and on the personal scale by deriving for oneself a pattern of life that was self-determined. Future Denton was a self-sufficient man, and so had been most of those I had met. I wanted to be one with them, and comprehend things on my own account. I supposed that I could discuss my thoughts with Denton, but I chose not to.

The journey northwards was slow and meandering. We did not take a route due north, but followed many diversions to east and west. Periodically Denton would measure our position against optimum, and never at any time were we farther north than about fifteen miles.

I asked him if there were any reason why we should not strike even farther north of optimum.

'Normally, we would go as far north as we can,' he said. 'But the city's in a special circumstance. As well as seeking the easiest

167

northwards route, we need terrain that will allow us to defend ourselves best.'

The map we were compiling was becoming more complete and detailed every day. Denton allowed me to operate the equipment whenever I wished, and soon I was as adept as he. I learned how to triangulate the land with the surveying instrument, how to estimate the elevation of hills, and how to calculate the distance we were north or south of optimum. I was growing to like working the camera, in spite of the fact I was forced to curb my enthusiasm to conserve the energy in the batteries.

It was peaceful and agreeable away from the tensions of the city, and I discovered that Denton, in spite of his long silences, was an amiable and intelligent man.

I had lost track of the days we had been away, but it was certainly at least twenty. Denton showed no sign of wanting to return.

We encountered a small settlement, nestling in a shallow valley. We made no attempt to approach it. Denton merely marked it on the map, with a rough estimate of the population.

The countryside was greener and fresher than that to which I had grown accustomed, although the sun was no cooler. It rained more often here, usually during the night, and there were many different sizes of streams and rivers.

All the features of the region, natural or man-made, difficult for the city to pass through or suitable to its peculiar needs, Denton marked without comment on his map. It was not the job of the Future Surveyors to decide which route the city should take; we worked simply to establish the actual nature of future terrain.

The atmosphere was restful and soporific, the natural beauty of our surroundings seductive. I knew the city would travel through this region in the miles to come, and pass it without registering appreciation. For the city's aesthetics, this verdant and gentle countryside might equally be a windswept desert.

During the hours when I was not actually engaged in any of our routine tasks, I was still lost in speculative thought. I could not get out of my mind that spectacle of the manifest appearance of the world on which we existed. There must have been something, somewhere in those long years of tedious education that would, subconsciously, have prepared me for that sight. We live by our assumptions; if one took for granted that the world we travelled across was like any other, could any education ever prepare one for a total reversal of that assumption?

The preparation for that sight had begun the day Future Denton had taken me outside the city for the first time, to see for myself a

168

sun that revealed itself to be any shape but that of a sphere.

But I still felt there must have been an earlier clue.

I waited for a few more days, still worrying at the problem when I found time, then had an idea. Denton and I had camped one evening in open country beside a broad, shallow river, and as sunset approached I took the video camera and recorder and walked alone up the side of a low hill about half a mile away. At the top there was a clear view towards the north-eastern horizon.

As the sun neared the horizon, the atmospheric haze dimmed its glare and its shape became visible: as ever, a broad disk spiked top and bottom. I switched on the camera, and took a long shot of it. Later I replayed the tape, checking that the picture was clear and steady.

I never tired of the spectacle. The sky was reddening, and after the main disk had passed beneath the horizon, the upright pinnacle of light slid quickly down. For a few minutes after its passing there was an impression of a bright focus of orange-white at the centre of the red glow . . . but soon this passed and night came on quickly.

I played the tape again, watching the image of the sun on the recorder's tiny monitor. I froze the picture, then adjusted the brightness control, dimming the image until only the white shape remained.

There in miniature was an image of the world. My world. I had seen that shape before . . . long before leaving the confines of the crèche. Those weird symmetrical curves made an overall pattern that someone had once shown me.

I stared at the monitor screen for a long time, then conscience struck me and I switched off to conserve the batteries. I did not return to Denton straight away: I was straining my memory for some key to that faint recollection of the time when someone had drawn four lines on a sheet of card, and held up for all to see the place where Earth city struggled to survive.

The map that Denton and I were compiling was taking on a definite shape.

Drawn on the long roll of stiff paper he had brought, the plan took the form of a long, narrow funnel, with its narrowest point at the patch of woodland a mile or so to the north of where the city had been when we left it. Our travels had all been within the funnel, enabling us to make measurements of large features from all sides, to ensure that we compiled information as nearly accurate as possible.

Soon the work was finished, and Denton said that we would return at once to the city.

I had, in the video recorder, a complete and cross-referenced visual record of all the terrain we had covered. In the city, the Council of Navigators would examine as much as they felt necessary to plan the city's next route. Denton told me that other Futures would go north soon, draw another funnel map of the terrain. Perhaps it too would start at the patch of woodland, and take a course five or ten degrees to east or west, or, if the Navigators felt that a safe route could be found in the terrain we had surveyed, the new map would start farther up the known territory, and push forward again the frontier of the future we had surveyed.

We headed back towards the city. I had expected, in some melodramatic way, that now we had the information we had been despatched to obtain, we would ride through day and night with no regard to safety or comfort; instead, the leisurely ride through the countryside continued.

'Shouldn't we hurry?' I said in the end, thinking that perhaps Denton was idling for some reason connected with me; I wished to show that I was willing to move with speed.

'There's never any hurry up future,' he said.

I didn't argue with him, but it had occurred to me that we had been away from the city for at least thirty days. In that time, the movement of the ground would have taken the city another three miles away from the optimum, and consequently the city would have to travel at least that distance to stay within safety limits.

I knew that the unsurveyed territory began only a mile or so beyond the city's last position.

In short, the city would need the information we had.

The return journey took three days. On the third day, as we loaded the horses and continued on south, the memory I had been seeking came to me. It came unbidden, as is often the case when trying for something buried in the subconscious.

I felt I had exhausted all my conscious memories of the lessons I'd had, and sorting through the memory of the long academic courses had been as fruitless as the sessions had been tedious at the time.

Then, from a subject I had not even considered, the answer came.

I remembered a period in my last few miles inside the crèche, when our teacher had taken us into the realms of calculus. All aspects of mathematics had induced the same response in me –

170

I showed neither interest nor success – and this further development of abstract concepts had seemed no different.

The teaching had covered a kind of calculus known as functions, and we were taught how to draw graphs representing these functions. It was the graphs that had provided the memory key: I had always had a moderate talent for drawing, and for a few days my interest had flickered into life. It died almost immediately, for I discovered that the graphs were not an end in themselves but were drawn to provide a means of finding out more about the function . . . and I didn't know what a function was.

One graph in particular had been discussed in great and onerous detail.

It showed the curve of an equation where one value was represented as a reciprocal – or an inverse – of the other. The graph for this was a hyperbola. One part of the graph was drawn in the positive quadrant, one in the negative. Each end of the curve had an infinite value, both positive and negative.

The teacher had discussed what would happen if that graph were to be rotated about one of its axes. I had neither understood why graphs should be drawn, nor that one might rotate them, and I'd suffered another attack of daydreaming. But I did notice that the teacher had drawn on a piece of large card what the solid body would look like should this rotation be performed.

The product was an impossible object: a solid with a disk of infinite radius, and two hyperbolic spires above and below the disk, each of which narrowed towards an infinitely distant point.

It was a mathematical abstraction, and held for me then as much interest as such an item should.

But that mathematical impossibility was not taught to us for no reason, and the teacher had not without reason attempted to draw it for us. In the indirect manner of all our education, that day I had seen the shape of the world on which I lived.

171

5

Denton and I rode through the woodland at the bottom of the range of hills . . . and there ahead of us was the pass.

Involuntarily, I drew back on the reins and halted the horse.

'The city!' I said. 'Where is it?'

'Still by the river I should imagine.'

'Then it must have been destroyed!'

There could be no other explanation. Had the city not moved in all those thirty days, only another attack could have delayed it. By now the city should at least be in its new position in the pass.

Denton was watching me, an amused expression on his face.

'Is this the first time you've been so far north of optimum?' he said.

'Yes it is.'

'But you've been down past. What happened when you came back to the city?'

'There was an attack on,' I said.

'Yes. . . . but how much time had elapsed?'

'More than seventy miles.'

'Was that more than you expected?'

'Yes. I thought . . . I'd been gone only a few days, a mile or two in time.'

'O.K.' Denton moved forward again, and I followed. 'The opposite is true if you go north of optimum.'

'What do you mean?'

'Hasn't anyone told you about the subjective time values?' My blank expression gave him the answer. 'If you go anywhere south of optimum, subjective time is slowed. The farther south you go, the more that occurs. In the city, the time scale is more or less normal while it is near the optimum, so that when you return from down past, it seems that the city has moved far farther than possible.'

'But we've been north.'

'Yes, and the effect is opposite. While we ride north, our subjective time scale is speeded, so that the city appears not to have moved at all. From experience, I think you'll find that about four

172

days have elapsed in the city while we've been gone. It's more difficult to estimate at the moment, as the city itself is farther south of optimum than normal.'

I said nothing for a few minutes, trying to understand the idea.

Then: 'So if the city itself could move north of optimum, it wouldn't have so many miles to travel. It could stop.'

'No. It always has to move.'

'But if where we've been slows down time, the city would benefit from being there.'

'No,' he said again. 'The differential in subjective time is relative.'

'I don't understand,' I said honestly.

We were now riding up the valley towards the pass. In a few minutes we would be able to see the city, if it was indeed where Denton had predicted.

'There are two factors. One is the movement of the ground, the other is how one's values of time are changed subjectively. Both are absolute, but not necessarily connected as far as we know.'

'Then why – ?'

'Listen. The ground moves, physically. In the north it moves slowly – and the farther north one travels the slower it moves – in the south it moves faster. If it was possible to reach the most northern point we believe the ground would not move at all. On the other hand, we believe that in the south the movement of the ground accelerates to an infinite speed at the farthest extremity of the world.'

I said: 'I've been there . . . to the farthest extremity.'

'You went . . . what? Forty miles? Perhaps more by accident? That was far enough for you to feel the effects . . . but only the beginning. We're talking in terms of millions of miles. Literally . . . millions. Much more, some would say. The city's founder, Destaine, thought the world was of infinite size.'

I said: 'But the city has only to travel a few miles farther, and it would be north of optimum.'

'That's right . . . and it would make life a lot easier. We would still have to move the city, but not so often and not so far. But the problem is that it's as much as we can do to stay abreast of optimum.'

'What is special about the optimum?'

'It's where conditions on this world are nearest to those on Earth planet. At the optimum point our subjective values for time are normal. In addition, a day lasts for twenty-four hours.

Anywhere else on this world one's subjective time produces slightly longer or shorter days. The velocity of the ground at optimum is about one mile in every ten days. The optimum is important because in a world like this, where there are so many variables, we need a standard. Don't confuse miles-distance with miles-time. We say the city has moved so many miles when we really mean that ten times that number of twenty-four hour days have elapsed. So we would gain nothing in real terms by being north of optimum.'

We had now ridden to the highest point of the pass. Cable-stays had been erected, and the city was in the process of being winched. The militiamen were much in evidence, standing guard not only around the city itself but also at both sides of the tracks. We decided not to ride down to the city, but to wait by the stays until the winching was completed.

Denton said suddenly: 'Have you read Destaine's Directive?'

'No. I've heard of it. In the oath.'

'That's right. Clausewitz has a copy. You ought to read it if you're a guildsman. Destaine laid down the rules for survival in this world, and no one's ever seen any reason to change them. You'd understand the world a little better, I think.'

'Did Destaine understand it?'

'I think so.'

It took another hour for the winching to be completed. There was no intervention by the tooks, and, in fact, there was no sign of them. I saw that several of the militiamen were now armed with rifles, presumably taken from the tooks killed in the last engagement.

When we went inside the city I went straight to the central calendar, and discovered that while we had been north three and a half days had elapsed.

There was a brief discussion with Clausewitz, then we were taken to see Navigator McMahon. In some detail, Denton and I described the terrain we had travelled through, pointing out the major physical features on our map. Denton outlined our suggestions for a route that the city could take, indicating the kinds of feature that might create a problem, and alternative routes around them. In fact, the terrain was in general suited to the city. The hills would mean several deviations from true north, but there were very few steep inclines, and overall the ground was some hundred feet lower at its northern point than the city's present elevation.

'We'll have two more surveys immediately,' the Navigator said to Clausewitz. 'One five degrees to east, and one five degrees to west. Do you have men available?'

'Yes, sir.'

'I'll convene Council today, and we'll set your provisional route for the time being. If better terrain appears from these two new surveys, we'll reconsider later. How soon will you be able to conduct a normal surveying pattern?'

'As soon as we can release men from Militia and Tracks,' said Clausewitz.

'They're priorities. For the moment, these surveys will have to suffice. If the situation eases, re-apply.'

'Yes, sir.'

The navigator took our map and my video tape, and we left the Navigation chambers.

Outside, I said to Clausewitz: 'Sir, I'd like to volunteer for one of the new surveys.'

He shook his head. 'No. You get three days' leave, and then you go back to the Track guild.'

'But – '

'Guild rules.'

Clausewitz turned away, and he and Denton walked towards the Futures' room. Technically that area was mine too, but suddenly I felt excluded. Quite literally, I had nowhere to go. While I had been working outside the city I had been sleeping in one of the Militia dormitories; now, officially on leave, I wasn't even sure where I lived. There were bunks in the Futures' room, and I could sleep there for the moment, but I knew that I should see Victoria as soon as possible. I had been putting this off; being away from the city conveniently prevented it. I was still wondering how I could deal with the new situation with her, and the answer to that lay in meeting her. I changed my clothes, and had a shower.

6

Nothing much had changed inside the city while I'd been north, and the domestic and medical administrators were wholly pre-occupied with looking after the wounded and reorganising the sleeping accommodation. There was less sense of desperation in the faces of the people I saw, and some efforts had been made to keep the corridors clear, but even so I realised that this was probably a bad moment to try to settle a domestic issue.

Victoria was difficult to trace. After enquiring of several of the domestic administrators I was sent to a makeshift dormitory on the lowest level, but she was not there. I spoke to the woman in charge.

'You're her ex-husband, aren't you?'

'That's right. Where is she?'

'She doesn't want to see you. She's very busy. She'll contact you later.'

'I want to see her,' I said.

'You can't. Now, if you'll excuse me we're very busy.'

She turned her back on me and continued her work. I glanced around the crowded dormitory: off-shift workers slept at one end, and there were several wounded lying in rough beds at the other. Although there were a few people moving between the beds, Victoria was not among them.

I walked back up to the Futures' room. During the time I had been looking for Victoria I had made a decision. There was no point in my hanging around the city aimlessly; I might as well go back to work on the tracks. But first, I had decided to read Clausewitz's copy of Destaine's Directive.

The Futures' room was empty but for one guildsman. He introduced himself to me as Future Blayne.

'You're Mann's son, aren't you?'

'Yes.'

'Glad to see you. Have you been up future yet?'

'Yes,' I said. I liked the look of Blayne. He was not much older than myself, and he had a fresh, open face. He seemed glad to have someone to talk to; he was, he said, due to go north on one of the surveys later in the day, and would be on his own for the next few miles.

'Do we normally go north alone?' I said.

'Normally, yes. We can work in pairs if Clausewitz gives his approval, but most Futures prefer to work alone. I like company myself, find it a bit lonely up there. How about you?'

'I've only been up future once. That was with Future Denton.'

'How did you get on with him?'

And so we talked, amiably and without the usual guards that seemed to show up whenever I had talked to other guildsmen. I had unconsciously adopted this manner myself, and at first I suppose I might have seemed diffident in his company. Within a few minutes, though, I found his forthright manner relaxing, and soon I felt as if we were old friends.

I told him I had made a video recording of the sun.

'Did you wipe it?'

'What do you mean?'

'Erase it from the tape.'

'No . . . should I have?'

He laughed. 'You'll have the Navigators down on you if they see it. You're not supposed to use the tapes for anything except cross-referenced images of the terrain.'

'Will they see it?'

'They might. If they're satisfied with the map, they'll probably check a few cross-references. They're not likely to go through the whole tape. But if they do . . . '

'What's wrong with it?' I said.

'Guild rules. Tape is valuable, and shouldn't be wasted. But don't worry about it. Why did you record the sun, anyway?'

'An idea I had. I wanted to try and analyse it. It's such an interesting shape.'

He looked at me with new interest.

'What do you make of it?' he said.

'Inverse values.'

'That's right. How did you work it out? Did someone tell you?'

'I remembered something from the crèche. A hyperbola.'

'Have you thought it through yet? There's more to it than that. Have you thought about the surface area?'

'Future Denton was explaining. He said it was very large.'

Blayne said: 'Not very large . . . *infinitely* large. North of the city the surface curves up until it is almost, but never quite, vertical. South of the city it becomes almost but not quite horizontal. The world is spinning on its axis, and so with an infinite radius it is spinning at infinite speed.'

He delivered this flatly and without expression.

'You're joking,' I said.

'No I'm not. I'm perfectly serious. Where we are, near optimum, the effects of the spin are the same as they would be on Earth planet. Farther south, although the angular velocity is identical, the speed increases. When you were down past, did you feel the centrifugal force?'

'Yes.'

'If you'd gone any farther, you wouldn't be here now to remember it. That force is bloody real.'

'I was told,' I said, 'that nothing could travel faster than the speed of light.'

'That's true. Nothing does. In theory the world's circumference is infinitely long and moves at infinite speed. But there is, or there is considered to be, a point where matter ceases to exist, and serves as an effective circumference. That point is where the spinning of the world imparts a velocity on the matter equivalent to the speed of light.'

'So it's not infinite.'

'Not quite. But bloody big. Look at the sun.'

'I have,' I said. 'Often.'

'That's the same. If it wasn't spinning it would be, literally, infinitely large.'

I said: 'Even so, in theory it is that large. How can there be room for more than one object of infinite size?'

'There's an answer to that. You won't like it.'

'Try me.'

'Go to the library, and find one of the astronomical books. It doesn't matter which. They're all Earth planet books, so they all have the same assumptions. If we were now on Earth planet we would be living in a universe of infinite size, which would be occupied by a number of large, but finite, bodies. Here the inverse is the rule: we live in a large but finite universe, occupied by a number of bodies of infinite size.'

'It doesn't make sense.'

'I know,' said Blayne. 'I said you wouldn't like it.'

'Where are we?'

'No one knows.'

'Where is Earth planet?'

'No one knows that either.'

178

I said: 'Down past something strange happened. I was with three girls. As we went south, their bodies changed. They –'

'Did you see anyone up future?'

'No, we . . . we kept away from the villages.'

'North of optimum the local people change physically. They become very tall and thin. The farther north we travel, the more the physical factors change.'

'I've only been about fifteen miles north.'

'Then you probably wouldn't have noticed anything peculiar. Farther than thirty-five miles north of optimum, it's very strange.'

Later, I said: 'Why does the ground move?'

'I'm not sure,' said Blayne.

'Is anyone?'

'No.'

'Where is it moving to?'

'More to the point,' said Blayne, 'where is it moving *from*?'

'Do you know?'

'Destaine said that the movement of the ground was cyclic. He says in his Directive that the ground is actually stationary at the north pole. Farther south, it is moving very slowly towards the equator. The nearer it approaches to the equator the faster it moves, both angularly, because of the rotation, and linearly. At the farthest extreme it is moving in two directions at once at infinite speed.'

I stared at him. 'But –'

'Wait . . . it's not finished. The world has a southern part too. If the world was a sphere it would be called a hemisphere, but Destaine adopted it for convenience. In the southern hemisphere, the opposite is true. That is, the ground moves from the equator towards the south pole, steadily decelerating. At the south pole it is stationary again.'

'You still haven't said where the ground moves from.'

'Destaine suggested that north and south poles were identical. In other words, once any point on the ground reaches the south pole it reappears at the north pole.'

'That's impossible!'

'Not according to Destaine. He says that the world is shaped like a solid hyperbola; that is, all limits are infinite. If you can imagine that, the limits adopt the characteristics of their opposite value. An infinite negative becomes an infinite positive, and vice versa.'

'Are you quoting him verbatim?'

179

'I think so. But you should read the original.'

'I intend to,' I said.

Before Blayne left the city to go north, we agreed that when the crisis outside the city was settled we would ride together.

Alone once more, I read through the copy of Destaine's Directive that Blayne obtained for me from Clausewitz.

It consisted of several pages of closely printed text, much of which would have been incomprehensible to me had I read it when I had first ventured outside the city. Now, with my own ideas and experiences, and with what Blayne had said, it served only to confirm. I saw some of the sense of the guild system: the experience had laid the way to understanding.

There was a lot of theoretical mathematics, interspersed with profuse calculations, at which I glanced only briefly. Of more interest was what appeared to be a hurried journal, and some sections caught my eye:

We are a long way from Earth. Our home planet is one I doubt we shall ever see again, but if we are to survive here we must maintain ourselves as a microcosm of Earth. We are in desolation and isolation. All around us is a hostile world that daily threatens our survival. As long as our buildings remain, so long shall man survive in this place. Protection and preservation of our home is paramount.

Later he wrote:

I have measured the rate of regression at one tenth of a statute mile in a period of twenty-three hours and forty-seven minutes. Although this southwards drift is slow it is relentless; the establishment shall therefore be moved at least one mile in every ten day period.

Nothing must stand in the way. We have already encountered one river, and it was crossed at great hazard. Doubtless we shall encounter further obstacles in the days and miles ahead, and by then we must be ready. We must concentrate on finding some indigenous materials that can be stored permanently within the buildings for later use as construction materials. A bridge should not be too difficult to build if we have enough warning.

Sturner has been forward and warns of a marshy region some miles ahead. Already we have sent other teams to north-east and north-west to determine the extent of this marsh. If it is not too wide we can deviate from due north for a time, and make up the difference later.

Following this entry were two pages of the theory Blayne had tried to explain to me. I read it through twice, and each time it made slightly better sense. I left it and read on. Destaine wrote:

Chen has provided the inventory of fissionable materials I requested. All of it waste! With the translat generator, no more need! Said nothing to L. I enjoy the arguments with him . . . why curtail them now? Future generations will be warm!

Today's outside temperature: -23°C. Still we move north.

Later:

Trouble with one of the caterpillar tracks. T. has advised me to authorise stripping them. Says that Sturner reports from the north that he has found what appears to be the remains of a railway line. Some incredible scheme to run the establishment along the tracks somehow. T. says it would work O.K.

Later:

Decided to create a guild system. Pleasant archaism that everyone approves. A way of structuring the organisation without drastically changing the way the place is run, but I think it might impose a form to the establishment that will survive us all.

Caterpillar-track stripping proceeding well. Has caused a long delay. Hope we can catch up.

Natasha gave birth today: boy.

Doctor S. gave me some more pills. Says I'm working too hard, and have to rest. Later, maybe.

Towards the end of the Directive, a more didactic tone emerged:

What I have written here shall be privy only to those who venture outside; no need for those inside the establishment to be reminded of our dreadful prospects. We are organised enough: we have sufficient mechanical power and human initiative to maintain us safely in this world for ever more. Those who follow must learn the hard way of what will happen if we fail to exploit either our power or our initiative, and this knowledge will suffice to keep both working to the maximum.

Someone from Earth must find us one day, God willing. Until then our maxim is survival, *at any cost*.

From now, it has been agreed and is hereby directed:

That the ultimate responsibility lies in the hands of the Council. These men shall navigate the establishment, and be known as Navigators. Their number, which shall at no time fall below twelve, shall be elected from the senior members of the following guilds:

Track Guild: who shall be responsible for the maintenance of the rail-way along which the establishment runs;

Traction Guild: who shall be responsible for the maintenance of the motive power of the establishment;

Future Guild: who shall be responsible for surveying the lands that lie in future time of our establishment;

Bridge-Builders Guild: who shall be responsible for safe conduit over physical obstacles, should no other way be available.

181

Further, should it be necessary to create other guilds in the future, no guild might be created except by unanimous vote of the Council.

(signed)
Francis Destaine

The major bulk of the Directive consisted of short entries, dated in a sequence that ran from 23 February 1987 to 19 August 2023. The final signed statement was dated 24 August 2023.

There were two further sheets. One was a codicil, marking the formation of the Barter Guild and the Militia Guild. These were undated. The other sheet was a graph drawn by hand. It showed the hyperbola produced by the equation $y = \frac{1}{x}$ and beneath it were some mathematical signs which I could not understand.

Such was Destaine's Directive.

7

Outside the city, work on the tracks was proceeding well.

When I joined the track-crews, most of the rail now behind the city had been taken up, and already more crews were relaying them from the head of the pass down the long shallow valley towards the woodland at the bottom. The atmosphere had improved; helped, I think, by the successful and undisturbed winching of the city away from the river. Additionally, the gradient for the next section was in our favour. The cables and stays would have to be used, because the gradient was not sufficiently steep to overcome the effects of the centrifugal force that could be felt even here.

It was a strange sensation to stand on the ground by the city, and see it stretching out in each direction in an overall horizontal way. I knew now that this apparent levelness was no such thing; at optimum, which on the vast scale of this world was not substantially distant, the ground was actually tilted at a full forty-five degree gradient towards north. Was this, though, any different from living on the surface of a spherical world like Earth planet? I remembered a book I had read in the crèche, a book written in and about a place called England. The book was written for young children, and described the life of a family who were planning to emigrate to a place called Australia. The children in the book had believed that where they were going they would be upside-down, and the author had gone to some pains to describe how all points on a sphere appeared to be upright because of gravitational effects. So it was on this world. I had been both north and south of optimum, and always the ground appeared to be level.

I enjoyed the labours on the tracks. It was good once more to be using my body, and not give myself time to think about the other distractions.

One loose end remained stubbornly untied: Victoria.

I needed to see her, however distasteful such an interview might be, and I wanted to settle the situation soon. Until I had spoken to her, whatever the outcome, I would not feel at ease in the city.

I was now settled in my acceptance of the physical environment of the city. Very few questions remained to be answered. I understood how and why the city was moved, I was aware of the many subtle dangers that lay in wait should the city ever cease its northwards journey. I knew that the city was vulnerable and, at this very time, in imminent danger from renewed attacks, but that I felt would be resolved soon.

But none of these could settle the personal crisis of becoming alienated from a girl I had loved in the space of what seemed to me to be a few days.

As a guildsman I discovered I was allowed to attend meetings of the Council of Navigators. I could not take an active part, but no aspect of the session was closed to me as a spectator.

I was told that a meeting was to be held, and decided to attend it.

The Navigators met in a small hall set just behind the main Navigation quarters. It was disarmingly informal; I had anticipated much ceremony and air of occasion, but the fact was that the meetings were crucial to the efficient operation of the whole city, and there was a businesslike air as the Navigators came into the chamber and took their seats round a table.

Two Navigators I knew by name, Olsson and McMahon, were present, and thirteen others.

The first matter to be discussed was the military situation outside. One of the Navigators stood up, introduced himself as Navigator Thorens, and gave a succinct report of the current situation.

The Militia had established that there were still at least a hundred men in the neighbourhood of the city, and most of them were armed. According to military intelligence, their morale was low as many losses had been suffered; this contrasted sharply, the Navigator said, with the morale of our troops, who felt they could contain any further development. They were now in possession of twenty-one rifles captured from the tooks, and although there was not much ammunition, some had been captured and the Traction guild had devised a method of manufacturing small quantities.

A second Navigator confirmed that this was so.

The next report was on the condition of the city's structure.

There was considerable discussion about how much re-building should be carried out, and how soon. It was stated that there was considerable pressure on the domestic administrators, and sleeping-accommodation was at a premium. The Navigators agreed that a new dormitory block should be given priority.

This discussion led naturally into wider issues, and these were of great interest to me.

As far as I could tell, the opinions of the Navigators present were divided. There was one school of thought of the opinion that the previous 'closed city' policy should be re-introduced as soon as possible. The others thought that this had outlived its purpose, and should be permanently abandoned.

It seemed to me that this was a crucial issue, one which could radically alter the social structure of the city . . . and indeed, this was the undercurrent of the discussion. If the 'closed' system were abandoned, it would mean that anyone growing up in the city would learn gradually the truth of the situation in which the city existed. It would mean a new way of education, and it would bring subtle changes in the powers of the guilds themselves.

In the end, after many calls for votes, and several amendments, there was a show of hands. By a majority of one it was decided not to re-introduce the 'closed city' system for the time being.

More revelations followed. It transpired from the next item that there were seventeen transferred women inside the city, who had been there since before the first attack by the tooks. There was some discussion about what should be done with them. The meeting was informed that the women had said they wished to stay inside the city; it was immediately clear that it was possible that the attacks had been made in an attempt to free the women.

Another vote: the women should be allowed to stay within the city for as long as they wished.

It was also decided not to re-introduce the down past initiative test for apprentices. I understood that this has been suspended after the first attack, and several Navigators were in favour of now bringing it back. The meeting was told that twelve apprentices were known to have been killed down past, and a further five were still unaccounted for. The suspension remained for the time being.

I was fascinated by what I heard. I hadn't realised before the extent to which the Navigators were in touch with the practicalities of the system. Nothing specific had been said, but there was a general feeling amongst some of the guildsmen that the Navigators were a group of ageing fuddy-duddies out of touch with reality. Advanced in years some of them certainly were, but their perceptions had not faded. Looking round at the mostly

185

empty guild seats, I reflected that perhaps more guildsmen should attend the Navigators' meetings.

There was more business to deal with. The report that Denton and I had made of the terrain to the north was presented by Navigator McMahon, with the added information that two further five-degree surveys were presently being conducted and that the results would be known within a day or two.

The meeting agreed that the city should follow the provisional route marked by Denton and myself until any better route was devised.

Finally, the subject of the city's traction was raised by Navigator Lucan. He said that the Traction guild had come up with a scheme for moving the city slightly faster. Re-gaining ground on optimum would be a major step towards returning the city to a normal situation, he argued, and there was agreement to this.

The proposal, he said, was for the city to be put on to a continuous traction schedule. This would involve a greater liaison with the Track guild, and perhaps a greater risk of cables breaking. But he argued that as we were now short of much valuable rail stock after the burning of the bridge, the city would have to make shorter hauls. The Traction guild's suggestion was to maintain a shorter length of track actually laid to the north of the city, and to keep the winches running permanently. They would be phased out for periodic overhaul, and as the gradients of future territory were largely in our favour we could keep the city running at a speed sufficient to bring us back to optimum within twenty or twenty-five miles of elapsed time.

There were few objections to this scheme, although the chairman called for a detailed report. When the vote was cast the result was nine in favour, six against. When the report was produced, the city would transfer to continuous running as soon as could be managed.

8

I was due to leave the city for a survey mission to the north. In the morning I had been called away from my work on the tracks, and Clausewitz had given me my briefing. I would leave the city the next day, and travel twenty-five miles to the north of optimum, reporting back on the nature of the terrain and the positions of various settlements. I was given the choice of working alone or with another Future guildsman. Recalling the new and welcome acquaintanceship with Blayne, I requested that he and I work together, and this was granted.

I was eager to leave. I felt no obligation to remain on the manual work of the tracks. Men who had never been outside the city were working well as teams, and more progress was made than at any time we had employed local labour.

The last attack by the tooks now seemed a long way behind us, and morale was good. We had made it to the pass in safety, ahead was the long slope down through the valley. The weather was fine, and hopes were high.

In the evening I returned to the inside of the city. I had decided to talk over the survey mission with Blayne, and spend the night in the Futures' quarters. We would be ready to leave at first light.

Walking through the corridors, I saw Victoria.

She was working alone in a tiny office, checking through a large batch of papers. I went inside, and closed the door.

'Oh, it's you,' she said.

'You don't mind?'

'I'm very busy.'

'So am I.'

'Then leave me alone, and get on with whatever it is.'

'No,' I said. 'I want to talk to you.'

'Some other time.'

'You can't avoid me for ever.'

'I don't have to talk to you now,' she said.

I grabbed at her pen, knocking it from her hand. Papers fell on the floor, and she gasped.

'What happened, Victoria? Why didn't you wait for me?'

She stared down at the scattered papers, and made no answer.

'Come on . . . answer me.'

'It's a long time ago. Does it still matter to you?'

'Yes.'

She was looking at me now, and I stared back at her. She had changed a lot, seemed older. She was more assured, more her own woman . . . but I could recognise the familiar way she held her head, the way her hands were clenched: half a fist, two fingers erect and interfolded.

'Helward, I'm sorry if you were hurt, but I've been through a lot too. Will that do?'

'You know it won't. What about all the things we talked about?'

'Such as?'

'The private things, the intimacies.'

'Your oath is safe . . . you needn't worry about that.'

'I wasn't even thinking of it,' I said. 'What about the other things, about you and me?'

'The whispered exchanges in bed?'

I winced. 'Yes.'

'They were a long time ago.' Perhaps my reaction showed, for suddenly her manner softened. 'I'm sorry, I didn't mean to be callous.'

'O.K. Say what you like.'

'No . . . it's just that, I wasn't expecting to see you. You were gone so long! You could have been dead, and no one would tell me anything.'

'Who did you ask?'

'Your boss. Clausewitz. All he'd say was that you'd left the city.'

'But I told you where I was going. I said I had to go south of the city.'

'And you said you'd be back in a few miles' time.'

'I know,' I said. 'I was wrong.'

'What happened?'

'I . . . was delayed.' I couldn't even begin to explain.

'That's all. You were delayed?'

'It was a lot farther than I thought.'

Aimlessly, she began shuffling the papers, making them into a semblance of a tidy pile. But she was just working her hands; I'd broken through.

'You never saw David, did you?'

'David? Is that what you called him?'

'He was – ' She looked up at me again, and her eyes were

brimming with tears. 'I had to put him in the crèche, there was so much work to do. I saw him every day, and then the first attack came. I had to be on a fire point, and couldn't – Later we went down to the –'

I closed my eyes, turned away. She put her face in her hands, started to cry. I leant against the wall, resting my face against my forearm. A few seconds later I started to cry too.

A woman came through the door quickly, saw what was happening. She closed the door again. This time I leant my weight against it to prevent further interruptions.

Later, Victoria said: 'I thought you would never come back. There was a lot of confusion in the city, but I managed to find someone from your guild. He said that a lot of apprentices had been killed when they were in the south. I told him how long you had been gone. He wouldn't commit himself. All I knew was how long you'd been gone and when you said you'd be back. It was nearly two years, Helward.'

'I was warned,' I said. 'But I didn't believe it.'

'Why not?'

'I had to walk a distance of about eighty miles, there and back. I thought I could do it in a few days. No one in the guild told me why I couldn't.'

'But they knew?'

'Undoubtedly.'

'They could have at least waited until we'd had the child.'

'I had to go when I was told. It was part of the guild training.'

Victoria was now more composed than before; the emotional reaction had completely destroyed the antipathy that was there, and we were able to talk more rationally. She picked up the fallen papers, arranged them into a pile, then put them away into a drawer. There was a chair by the opposite wall, and I sat on it.

'You know the guild system is going to have to change,' she said.

'Not drastically.'

'It's going to break down completely. It has to. In effect it's happened already. Anyone can go outside the city now. The Navigators will cling to the old system for as long as they can, because they're living in the past, but –'

'They're not as hidebound as you think,' I said.

'They'll try to bring back the secrecy and the suppression as soon as they can.'

'You're wrong,' I said flatly. 'I know you're wrong.'

'All right . . . but certain things will have to change. There's no one in the city now who doesn't know the danger we're in. We've been cheating and stealing our way across this land, and it's that which has created the danger. It's time for it to stop.'

'Victoria, you don't – '

'You only have to look at the damage! There were thirty-nine children killed! God knows how much destruction. Do you think we can survive if the people outside keep on attacking us?'

'It's quieter now. It's under control.'

She shook her head. 'I don't care what the current situation looks like. I'm thinking about the long term. All our troubles are ultimately created by the city being moved. That one condition produces the danger. We move across other people's land, we bargain for manpower to move the city, we take women into the city to have sex with men they hardly know . . . and all in order to keep the city moving.'

'The city can never stop,' I said.

'You see . . . already you are a part of the guild system. Always this flat statement, without looking at it in a wider light. The city must move, the city must move. Don't accept it as an absolute.'

'It is an absolute. I know what would happen if it stopped.'

'Well?'

'The city would be destroyed, and everyone would be killed.'

'You can't prove that.'

'No . . . but I know it would be so.'

'I think you're wrong,' said Victoria. 'And I'm not alone. Even in the last few days I've heard it said by others. People can think for themselves. They've been outside, seen what it's like. There's no danger apart from the danger we create for ourselves.'

I said: 'Look, this isn't our conflict. I wanted to see you to talk about us.'

'But it's all the same. What happened to us is implicitly bound up in the ways of the city. If you hadn't been a guildsman, we might still be living together.'

'Is there any chance . . . ?'

'Do you want it?'

'I'm not sure,' I said.

'It's impossible. For me, at least. I couldn't reconcile what I believe with accepting your way of life. We've tried it, and it separated us. Anyway, I'm living with – '

'I know.'

She looked at me, and I felt at second hand the alienation she had experienced.

'Don't you have any beliefs, Helward?' she said.

'Only that the guild system, for all its imperfections, is sound.'

'And you want us to live together again, living out two separate beliefs. It couldn't work.'

We had both changed a lot; she was right. It was no good speculating about what might have been in other circumstances. There was no way of making a personal relationship distinct from the overall scheme of the city.

Even so, I tried again, attempting to explain the apparent suddenness of what had happened, attempting to find a formula that could somehow revive the early feelings we had had for each other. To be fair, Victoria responded in kind, but I think we had both arrived at the same conclusion by our separate routes. I felt better for seeing her, and when I left her and went on towards the Futures' quarters I was aware that we had succeeded in resolving the worst of the remaining issue.

9

The following day, when I rode north with Blayne to start the future survey, marked the beginning of a long period which produced for the city a state of both regained security and radical change.

I saw this process develop gradually, for my own sense of actual city-time was distorted by my journeys to the north. I learnt by experience that at a distance roughly twenty miles to the north of optimum, a day spent was equivalent to an hour of elapsed time in the city. As far as possible, I kept in touch with what happened in the city by attending as many Navigators' meetings as I could.

The placidity of the city's existence that I had experienced when I first left to work outside returned more quickly than most people had expected.

There were no more attacks by the tooks, although one of the militiamen, engaged in an intelligence mission, was captured and killed. Soon after this, the leaders of the Militia announced that the tooks were dispersing, and heading for their settlements in the south.

Although military vigilance was maintained for a long time – and never in fact wholly abandoned – gradually men from the Militia were freed to work on other projects.

As I had learnt at that first Navigators' meeting, the method of hauling the city was changed. After several initial difficulties, the city was successfully launched into a system of continuous traction, using a complicated arrangement of alternating cables and phased track-laying. One tenth of a mile in a twenty-four hour period was not, after all, a considerable distance to move, and within a short time the city had reached optimum.

It was discovered that this actually gave the city greater freedom of movement. It was possible, for instance, to take quite considerable detours from a bearing of true north if a sufficiently large obstacle were to appear.

In fact the terrain was good. As our surveys showed, the overall elevation of the terrain was falling, and there were more gradients in our favour than were against us.

There were more rivers in this region than the Navigators would have liked, and the Bridge-Builders were kept busy. But with the city at optimum, and with its greater capacity for speed relative to the movement of the ground, there was more time available for decision-making, and more time in which to build a safe bridge.

With some hesitation at first, the barter system was reintroduced.

There was the benefit of hindsight in the city's favour, and barter negotiations were conducted more scrupulously than before. The city paid more generously for manpower – which was still needed – and tried for a long time to avoid the necessity of bartering for transferred women.

Through a long series of Navigators' meetings I followed the debate on this subject. We still had the seventeen transferred women inside the city who had been with us since before the first attack, and they had expressed no desire to return. But the predominance of male births continued, and there was a strong lobby for the return of the transfer system. No one knew why there should be such an imbalance in the distribution of the sexes, but it was undoubtedly so. Further, three of the transferred women had given birth within the last few miles, and each of these babies had been males. It was suggested that the longer women from outside remained in the city, the more chance there was that they too would produce male children. Again, no one understood why this should be so.

At the last count, there were now a total of seventy-six male and fourteen female children below the age of one hundred and fifty miles.

As the percentage continued to mount the lobby strengthened, and soon the Barter guild was authorised to commence negotiations.

It was actually this decision which emphasised the changes in the society of the city which were taking place.

The 'open city' system had remained, and non-guildsmen were allowed to attend Navigators' meetings as spectators. Within a few hours of the announcement about the barter for women being renewed, everyone in the city knew, and there were many voices raised in protest. Nevertheless, the decision was implemented.

Although hired labour was again being used, it was to a far lesser extent than before, and there was always a considerable number of people from the city working on the tracks and cables. There was not much that wasn't known about the city's operations.

But general education about the real nature of the world on which we lived was poor.

During one debate, I heard the word 'Terminator' used for the first time. It was explained that the Terminators were a group of people who actively opposed the continued movement of the city, and were committed to halting it. As far as was known, the Terminators were not militant and would take no direct action, but they were gaining a considerable amount of support within the city.

It was decided that a programme of re-education should begin, to dramatise the necessity of moving the city northwards.

At the next meeting there was a violent disruption.

A group of people burst into the chamber during the session, and tried to take the chair.

I was not surprised to see that Victoria was among them.

After a noisy argument, the Navigators summoned the assistance of the Militia and the meeting was closed.

This disruption, perversely, had the effect desired by the Terminator movement. The Navigators' meetings were once again closed to general session. The dichotomy in the opinions of the ordinary people of the city widened. The Terminators had a considerable amount of support, but no real authority.

A few incidents followed. A cable was found cut in mysterious circumstances, and one of the Terminators tried one day to speak to the hired labour in an attempt to get them to return to their villages . . . but by and large the Terminator movement was no more than a thorn in the side of the Navigators.

Re-education went well. A series of lectures was mounted, attempting to explain the peculiar dangers of this world, and they were well attended. The design of the hyperbola was adopted as the city's motif, and it was worn as an ornament on the guildsmen's cloaks, stitched inside the circle on their breasts.

I don't know how much of this was understood by the ordinary people of the city; I overheard some discussion of it, but the influence of the Terminators perhaps weakened its credibility. For too long the people of the city had been allowed by omission to assume that the city existed on a world like Earth planet, if not Earth planet itself. Perhaps the real situation was one too outrageous to be given credence: they would listen to what they were told, and perhaps understand it, but I think the Terminators held a greater emotional appeal.

In spite of everything, the city continued to move slowly northwards. Sometimes I would take time off from other matters, and try to view it in my mind's eye as a tiny speck of matter on an alien world; I would see it as an object of one universe trying to survive in another; as a city full of people, holding on to the side of a forty-five degree slope, pulling its way against a tide of ground on a few thin strands of cable.

With the return to a more stable environment for the city, the task of future surveying became more routine.

For our purposes the ground to the north of the city was divided into a series of segments, radiating from optimum at five degree intervals. Under normal circumstances the city would not seek a route that was more than fifteen degrees away from due north, but the city's extra capability to deviate did allow considerable flexibility from this for short periods.

Our procedure was simple. Surveyors would ride north from the city – either alone or, if they chose, in pairs – and conduct a comprehensive survey of the segment allotted to them. There was plenty of time available to us.

On many occasions I would find myself seduced by the feeling of freedom in the north, and it was one which Blayne once told me was common to most Futures. Where was the urgency to return if a day spent lazily on the bank of a river wasted only a few minutes of the city's time?

There was a price to pay for the time spent in the north, and it was one that did not seem real to me until I saw its effects for myself. A day spent idling in the north was a day in my life. In fifty days I aged the equivalent of five miles in the city, but the city people had aged only four days. It did not matter at first: our return visits to the city were so comparatively frequent that I saw and felt no difference. But in time, the people I had known – Victoria, Jase, Malchuskin – seemed not to have aged at all, and catching a sight of myself in a mirror one day I saw the effect of the differential.

I did not want to settle down permanently with another girl; Victoria's notion that the ways of the city would disrupt any relationship took greater meaning every time I considered it.

The first of the transferred women were coming to the city, and as an unmarried man I was told that I was eligible to mate with one of them temporarily. At first I resisted the idea because, to be frank, the idea repelled me. It seemed to me that even a purely physical affair should have some complement in shared emotional feelings, but the manner in which the selection of the partners was

195

arranged was as subtle as it could be under the circumstances. Whenever I was in the city I and other eligible men were encouraged to mix socially with the girls in a recreation-room set aside for this purpose. It was embarrassing and humiliating at first, but I grew used to these occasions and eventually my inhibitions waned.

In time, I formed a mutual liking with a girl named Dorita, and soon she and I were allocated a cabin we could share. We did not have much in common, but her attempts to speak English were delightful, and she seemed to enjoy my company. Soon she was pregnant, and between my surveying missions I watched her pregnancy proceed.

Slowly, so unbelievably slowly.

I began to grow increasingly frustrated with the apparently sluggish progress of the city. By my own subjective time scale, a hundred and fifty, perhaps two hundred miles had elasped since I had become a Future guildsman, and yet the city was still in sight of those hills we had been passing through at the time of the attacks.

I applied to transfer temporarily to another guild; much as I enjoyed the leisured life in the future I felt that time was passing me by.

For a few miles I worked with the Traction guild, and it was during this period that Dorita gave birth. She produced twins: a boy and a girl. Much celebration . . . but I found that the city life discontented me in another way. I had been working with Jase, someone who had once been several miles older than me. Now he was clearly younger than me, and we had little in common.

Shortly after she had given birth, Dorita left the city and I returned to my own guild.

Like the Future guildsmen I had seen as an apprentice, I was becoming a misfit in the city. I enjoyed my own company, relished those stolen hours in the north, was uncomfortable when in the city. I had developed an interest in drawing, but told almost no one about it. I did my guild work as quickly and efficiently as possible, then rode off alone through the future countryside, sketching what I saw, trying to find in line drawings some expression of a terrain where time could almost standstill.

I watched the city from a distance, seeing it as alien as it was; not of this world, no longer even of me. Mile by mile it hauled itself forward, never finding, nor even seeking, a final resting place.

Part Four

1

She waited in the doorway of the church while the discussion continued on the far side of the square. Behind her, in the temporary workshop, the priest and two assistants were working patiently on the job of restoring the plaster image of the Virgin Mary. It was cool in the church, and in spite of the part of the roof that had caved in, it was clean and restful. She knew she shouldn't be here, but some instinct had sent her inside when the two men had arrived.

She watched them now, talking earnestly to Luiz Carvalho, the self-appointed leader of the village, and a handful of other men. In other times, perhaps the priest would have assumed responsibility for the community, but Father dos Santos was, like herself, a newcomer to the village.

The men had ridden into the village along the dried-up bed of the stream, and now their horses grazed while the discussion continued. She was too far away to hear the actual words, but it seemed that some deal was being struck. The men from the village talked volubly, feigning no interest, but she knew that if their attention had not been caught they would not still be talking.

It was the horsemen who held her interest. That they were not from any of the nearby villages was self-evident. In contrast with the villagers, their appearance was striking: each wore a black cape, well-fitting trousers, and leather boots. Their horses were saddled and apparently groomed, and although each of the horses was bearing large saddle-bags well loaded with equipment they stood without apparent fatigue. None of the horses she had seen locally was in anything like such good condition.

Her curiosity began to override her instinct, and she stepped forward to learn for herself what was going on. As she did so, the negotiations appeared to be completed, for the village men turned away and the other two returned to their horses.

They mounted immediately, and headed back the way they had come. She stood and watched them, debating whether or not to go after them.

When they were out of sight amongst the trees that grew along-side the stream, she hurried out of the square, ran between two of the houses and scrambled up the rise of ground behind. After a few moments she saw the men emerging from the trees. They rode a short distance farther, then drew up the reins, and halted.

They conferred for about five minutes, several times looking back in the general direction of the village.

She kept out of sight, standing in the dense scrub that grew all over the hill. Suddenly, one of the men raised his hand to the other, and swung his horse round. He set off at a gallop in the direction of some distant hills; the other man turned his horse in the opposite direction and walked it at a leisured pace.

She returned to the village, and found Luiz.

'What did they want?' she said.

'They need men for some work.'

'Did you agree to this?'

He looked evasive. 'They're coming back tomorrow.'

'Are they going to pay?'

'With food. Look.'

He held out a handful of bread, and she took it from him. It was brown and fresh, smelt good.

'Where did they get this?'

Luiz shrugged. 'And they have special food.'

'Did they give you any of that?'

'No.'

She frowned, wondering again who the men might be.

'Anything else?'

'Only this.' He showed her a small bag, and she opened it. Inside was a coarse white powder, and she sniffed at it.

'They said it would make fruit grow.'

'They have more of this?'

'As much as we need.'

She put the bag down, and went back to the church workshop. After a word with Father dos Santos she walked quickly to the stables, and saddled up her own horse.

She rode out of the village by way of the dried-up stream, and followed in the direction of the second man.

2

Beyond the village was a wide area of scrubland, dotted with trees. She soon saw the man some distance ahead of her, heading towards a larger patch of woodland. On the far side of this, she already knew, a river flowed. Beyond that were some low hills.

She kept her distance from the man, not wishing to be seen until she found out where he was heading.

When he entered the woods she lost sight of him, and she dismounted. She led the horse by its reins, keeping a wary eye open for any sign of him. Soon she could hear the sound of the river; shallow at this season, its bed littered with pebbles.

She saw his horse first, tethered to a tree. She tied up her own horse, and walked on alone. It was warm and still under the trees, and she felt dusty from the ride. She wondered again what had prompted her to follow this man, when reason warned of any number of potential risks. But the presence of the two men in the village had been unthreatening enough, their motives peaceable if mysterious.

She moved more cautiously as she approached the edge of the wood. Here she halted, looking down the shallow bank towards the water.

The man was there, and she looked at him with interest.

He had discarded his cloak, and it lay with his boots beside a small pile of equipment. He had waded down into the river, and was clearly relishing the cool sensation. Completely oblivious of her presence, he kicked his feet in the water, sending up showers of glittering spray. In a moment, he bent down, scooped up some water in his hands and splashed it over his face and neck.

He turned, waded out of the water and went over to the equipment. From a black leather case he took a small video camera, then suspended the case by its strap over his shoulder, and connected it to the camera with a short, plastic-coated lead. This done, he adjusted a small ferruled knob on the side.

He put down the camera for a moment, and unfurled a long paper roll, wound like a scroll. He laid this on the ground, looked at it thoughtfully for a few seconds, then picked up the camera and returned to the water's edge.

Deliberately, he pointed the camera upstream for a second or two, then lowered the camera and turned. He pointed it at the opposite bank, then, startling her, he pointed it in her direction. She ducked down out of sight, and by his lack of reaction she guessed he had not seen her. When she next looked, he was pointing the camera downstream.

He returned to the length of paper, and with great care inscribed a few symbols.

Still moving deliberately, he put the camera back in its case, rolled up the paper and stowed it with the rest of the equipment.

He stretched elaborately, then scratched the back of his head. Listlessly, he returned to the water's edge, sat down, and dangled his feet in the water. In a moment, he sighed and lay back, his eyes closed.

She regarded him closely. He certainly looked harmless enough. He was a big, well-muscled man, and his face and arms were deeply tanned. His hair was long and shaggy: a great mane of light auburn hair. He wore a beard. She estimated his age somewhere in the middle thirties. In spite of the beard he had a clean-cut, youthful face, grinning at the simple animal bliss of cold wet feet on a hot dry day.

Flies hovered around his face, and from time to time he would swipe at them lazily.

After a few more moments of hesitation she started forward, and half-walked, half-skidded down the bank, pushing a minor avalanche of soil before her.

The man's reaction was immediate. He sat up, looked round sharply, and scrambled to his feet. In so doing he turned awkwardly, and slipped down on his stomach, his feet thrashing in the water.

She started to laugh.

He recovered his foothold, and dived for his equipment. A few seconds later he had a rifle in his hands.

She stopped laughing . . . but he did not raise the rifle.

Instead, he said something in Spanish so bad that she could not understand it.

She spoke only a little Spanish herself, so instead she said in the language of the villagers: 'I didn't mean to laugh. . . . '

He shook his head, then looked at her carefully. She spread her hands to prove that she carried no kind of weapon, and gave him what she hoped was a reassuring smile. He seemed satisfied

202

that she presented no threat to him, and put down the rifle.

Again, he said something in atrocious Spanish, then muttered something in English.

'You speak English?' she said.

'Yes. Do you?'

'Like a native.' She laughed again, and said: 'Do you mind if I join you?'

She nodded towards the river, but he continued to stare dumbly at her. She slipped off her shoes, and walked down to the bank. She waded in, hitching up her skirt. The water was freezing cold; it made her toes curl with pain, but the sensation was delightful. In a moment, she sat on the ground, keeping her feet in the water.

He came and sat beside her.

'Sorry about the gun. You startled me.'

'I'm sorry too,' she said. 'But you looked so blissful.'

'It's the best thing to do on a day like this.'

Together they stared down at the water flowing over their feet. Beneath the rippling surface, the white flesh appeared to distort like a flame flickering in a draught.

'What's your name?' she said.

'Helward.'

'Helward.' She tried the sound of the word. 'Is that a surname?'

'No. My full name is Helward Mann. What's yours?'

'Elizabeth. Elizabeth Khan. I don't like being called Elizabeth.'

'I'm sorry.'

She glanced at him. He looked very serious.

She was a little confused by his accent. She had realised he was not a native of this region, and he spoke English naturally and without effort, but he had a strange way of pronouncing his vowels.

'Where do you come from?' she said.

'Round here.' He stood up suddenly. 'I'd better water the animal.'

He stumbled again as he climbed the bank, but this time Elizabeth did not laugh. He walked straight into the trees, did not pick up his equipment. The rifle was still there. He looked over his shoulder at her once, and she turned away.

When he returned he was leading both horses. She got up, and led her own down to the water.

Standing between the horses, Elizabeth stroked the neck of Helward's.

'She's beautiful,' she said. 'Is she yours?'

'Not really. I just ride her more often than any of the others.'

'What do you call her?'

'I . . . haven't given her a name. Should I?'

'Only if you want to. Mine hasn't got a name either.'

'I enjoy riding,' Helward said suddenly. 'It's the best part of my work.'

'That and paddling in rivers. What do you do?'

'I'm a . . . I mean, it hasn't really got a label. What about you?'

'I'm a nurse. Officially, that is. I do lots of things.'

'We have nurses,' he said. 'In the . . . where I come from.'

She looked at him with new interest. 'Where's that?'

'A city. In the south.'

'What's it called?'

'Earth. Although most of the time we just call it the city.'

Elizabeth smiled uncertainly, not sure she had heard correctly. 'Tell me about it.'

He shook his head. The horses had finished drinking, and were nuzzling each other.

'I think I'd better be on my way,' he said.

He walked quickly towards his equipment, scooped it up, and stuffed it hurriedly in the saddle-bags. Elizabeth watched curiously. When he had finished he took the rein, turned the horse round and led her up the bank. At the fringe of the trees he looked back.

'I'm sorry. You must think me very rude. It's just . . . you're not like the others.'

'The others?'

'The people round here.'

'Is that so bad?'

'No.' He looked around the riverside as if seeking some further excuse to stay with her. Abruptly, he seemed to change his mind about leaving. He tethered the horse to the nearest tree. 'Can I ask you something?'

'Of course.'

'I wonder . . . do you think I could draw you?'

'Draw me?'

'Yes . . . just a sketch. I'm not very good, I haven't been doing it very long. While I'm up here I spend a lot of time drawing what I see.'

'Was that what you were doing when I met you?'

'No. That was just a map. I mean proper drawings.'

'O.K. Do you want me to pose for you?'

He fumbled in his saddle-bag, then brought out a wad of paper of assorted sizes. He flicked through them nervously, and she saw that there were line-drawings on them.

'Just stand there,' he said. 'No . . . by your horse.'

He sat down on the edge of the bank, balancing the papers on his knees. She watched him, still disconcerted by this sudden development, and felt a growing self-consciousness that was generally alien to her personality. He stared over the paper at her.

She stood by the horse, her arm running underneath its neck so that she could pat the other side, and the horse responded by pressing its nose against her.

'You're standing wrong,' he said. 'Turn towards me more.'

The self-consciousness grew, and she realised she was standing in an unnatural, awkward position.

He worked away, slipping through one sheet of paper after the next, and she began to relax more. She decided to pay no attention to him, and petted the horse again. After a while he asked her to sit in the saddle, but she was growing tired.

'Can I see what you've done?'

'I never show this to anyone.'

'Please, Helward. I've never been drawn before.'

He sifted through the papers, and selected two or three. 'I don't know what you'll think.'

She took them from him.

'God, am I as skinny as that?' she said, without thinking.

He tried to take them away from her. 'Give them back.'

She turned away from him, and flicked through the others. It was possible to see that they were of her, but his sense of proportion was . . . unusual. Both she and the horse were drawn too tall and thin. The effect was not unpleasing, but rather weird.

'Please . . . I'd like them back.'

She gave them to him, and he put them at the bottom of the pile. Abruptly he turned his back on her, and walked towards his horse.

'Have I offended you?' she said.

'It's O.K. I knew I shouldn't have shown them to you.'

'I think they're excellent. It's just . . . it's a bit of a shock to see yourself through someone else's eyes. I told you I had never been drawn.'

'You're difficult to draw.'

'Could I see some of your others?'

'You wouldn't be interested.'

'Look, I'm not just trying to smooth your ruffled feathers. I really am interested.'

'O.K.'

He gave her the whole pile, and continued on his way towards his horse. While she sat down again and began to go through the drawings, she was aware of him in the background pretending to adjust the horse's harness, but in fact trying to anticipate her response.

There were a variety of subjects. There were several of his horse: grazing, standing, throwing its head back. These were amazingly naturalistic; with a few lines he had caught the very essence of the animal, proud yet docile, tamed yet still its own master. Curiously, the proportions were exactly right. There were several drawings of a man . . . self-portraits, or the man she had seen him with earlier? He was drawn in his cloak, without his cloak, standing by a horse, using the video camera she had seen earlier. Again, the proportions were almost exactly right.

There were a few sketches of scenery: trees, a river, a curious structure being dragged by ropes, a distant range of hills. He wasn't as adept with views; sometimes his proportions were good, at other times there was a disturbing distortion that she could not quite identify. Something wrong with the perspective? She couldn't tell, not having a sufficient artistic vocabulary.

At the bottom of the pile she found the drawings he had made of her. The first few were not very good, clearly his first attempts. The three he had shown her were by far the best, but there was still this elongation of her and the horse that puzzled her.

'Well?' he said.

'I –' She couldn't find the right words. 'I think they're good. Very unusual. You've got an excellent eye.'

'You're a difficult subject.'

'I particularly like this one.' She searched through the pile, found one of the horse with its mane flying wild. 'It's so lifelike.'

He grinned then. 'That's my own favourite.'

She glanced again through the drawings. There was something about them she hadn't understood . . . there, in one of the drawings of the man. High in the background, a weird, four-pointed shape. There was one in each of the sketches he had done of her.

'What's this?' she said, pointing to it.

'The sun.'

She frowned a little, but decided not to pursue it. She felt she had done enough damage to his artistic ego for the moment.

She selected what she thought was the best of the three.

'Could I have this one?'

'I thought you didn't like it.'

'I do. I think it's marvellous.'

He looked at her carefully, as if trying to divine whether she was being truthful, then took the pile from her again.

'Would you like this one too?'

He handed her the one of the horse.

'I couldn't. Not that one.'

'I'd like you to have it,' he said. 'You're the first person to have seen it.'

'I – thank you.'

He placed the papers carefully into the saddle-bag, and buckled the cover.

'Did you say your name was Elizabeth?'

'I prefer to be called Liz.'

He nodded gravely. 'Goodbye, Liz.'

'Are you going?.'

He didn't answer, but untethered the horse and swung into the saddle. He rode down the bank, splashed through the shallow water of the river, and spurred his horse on up the opposite bank. In a few seconds he was lost to sight in the trees beyond.

3

Back at the village Elizabeth found she had no appetite for more work. She was still waiting for a consignment of proper medical supplies, and a doctor had been promised for more than a month. She had done what she could to see that the villagers were getting a balanced diet – but food supplies were limited – and she had been able to deal with the more obvious ailments such as sores, rashes, and so forth. Last week she had helped deliver a baby for one of the women, and it wasn't until this that she had felt she was doing any good at all.

Now, with the strange encounter by the river still fresh in her mind, she decided to return to headquarters early.

She found Luiz before she left.

'If those men come back,' she said, 'try to find out what it is they want. I'll be back in the morning. If they come before I arrive, try to keep them here. Find out where they're from.'

It was nearly seven miles to the headquarters, and it was evening when she arrived. The place was almost deserted: many of the field operatives stayed out for several nights on end. Tony Chappell was there, though, and he intercepted her as she headed for her room.

'Are you free this evening, Liz? I thought we might –'

'I'm very tired. I thought I'd have an early night.'

When she had first arrived, Elizabeth had felt the first stirrings of attraction towards Chappell, and made the mistake of showing them. There were only a few women at the station, and he had responded with great eagerness. Since then he had hardly left her alone, and although she now found him very dull and self-centred she hadn't yet discovered a polite way of cooling his unwelcome ardour.

He tried to persuade her to do whatever it was he wanted, but after a few minutes she managed to escape to her room.

She dumped her bag on the bed, undressed, and took a long shower.

Later, she went to find something to eat, and inevitably, Tony joined her.

During the meal, she remembered she'd been meaning to ask him something.

'Do you know any towns around here, called Earth?'

'Earth? Like the planet?'

'That's what it sounded like. I might have misheard.'

'I don't know any. Whereabouts?'

'Somewhere round here. Not far.'

He shook his head. 'Urf? Or Mirth?' He laughed loudly, and dropped his fork. 'Are you sure?'

'No . . . not really. I think I must have got it wrong.'

In his own inimitable way, Tony continued to make bad puns until once again she found an excuse to get away.

There was a large map of the region in one of the offices, but she couldn't see anything that might be where Helward said he lived. He had described it as a city lying in the south, but there was no large settlement for nearly sixty miles.

She was genuinely exhausted, and returned to her room.

She undressed, and took the two sketches Helward had given her and taped them to the wall by the bed. The one he had drawn of her was so strange . . . .

She looked at it more closely. The paper it was drawn on was evidently quite old, for its edges were yellowed. Looking at the edges, she realised that the top and bottom were slightly burred where they had been torn, but the line was quite straight.

Experimentally, she ran the tip of her finger along it. The sensation was a quite regular vibration: the paper had been perforated. . . .

Careful not to damage the drawing, she separated the tape from the wall, and took the sketch down.

On the back she discovered that a column of numbers had been printed down one side. One or two of them were asterisked.

Printed in pale blue ink along the side were the words: IBM Multifold ™.

She taped the sketch back on the wall . . . and stared at it uncomprehendingly for a long time.

4

In the morning Elizabeth put in another teleprinted request for a doctor, then set off for the village.

The daytime heat was flooding the village when she arrived, and already the listless mood of lethargy that had so infuriated her at first had set in. She sought out Luiz, who was sitting in the shadow of the church with two other men.

'Well . . . have they been back?'

'Not today, Menina Khan.'

'When did they say they'd come again?'

He shrugged idly. 'Sometime. Today, tomorrow.'

'Have you tried that – ?'

She stopped, irritated with herself. She had meant to take the purported fertiliser to headquarters to have it analysed, and in her preoccupation had forgotten it.

'Let me know if they come.'

She went to see Maria and her new baby, but her mind was not fully on her work. Later she supervised a meal, which was served to all comers, then talked to Father dos Santos in the workshop. All this time she was aware that she had one ear cocked for any sounds of horses.

No longer trying to make any excuse for herself, she went down to the stable and saddled up the horse. She rode away from the village, towards the river.

She was trying not to dwell on her own thoughts, trying not to examine her own motives, but it was inevitable. The last twenty-four hours had been momentous in their own way. She had come out here to work in the field because of a feeling that her life at home was wasted, only to find a new kind of frustration here. In spite of intents and appearances, all the voluntary workers could offer was a sight of recovery to the impoverished people here. It was too little, too late. A few government handouts of grain, or a few inoculations, or a repaired church were all right, and better than nothing. But the root of the problem remained unsolved in practice: the central economy had failed. There was nothing on this land but what the people themselves could take.

The intrusion of Helward into her life was the first event of interest she had experienced since she arrived. She knew, as she rode the horse across the scrubland towards the trees, that her motives were mixed. Perhaps there was simple curiosity there, but it ran deeper.

The men on the station were obsessed with themselves and what they imagined their roles to be; they spoke in abstracts about group psychology, social readjustment, patterns of behaviour . . . and in her more cynical moods she found such an outlook simply pathetic. Apart from the unfortunate Tony Chappell, she had formed no kind of interest in any of the men, which was not as she had anticipated at all before she arrived.

Helward was different. She refrained from spelling it out to herself, but she knew why she was riding out to find him.

She found the place on the river-bank, and allowed her horse to drink. Later, she tethered it in the shade, and sat down by the water to wait. Again she tried to blank out the turmoil of mental activity: thoughts, desires, questions. Concentrating hard on the physical environment, she lay back on the bank in the sunshine and closed her eyes. She listened to the sound of the water as it ran across the pebbles of the river-bed, the sound of the gentle wind in the trees, the humming of insects, the smell of dry undergrowth, hot soil, warmth.

A long time passed. Behind her, the horse whisked its tail every few seconds, patiently flicking away the swarm of flies.

She opened her eyes as soon as she heard the sound of the other horse, and sat up.

Helward was there on the opposite bank. He raised his hand in greeting, and she waved back.

He dismounted immediately, and walked quickly along the bank until he was opposite her. She smiled to herself: he was evidently in high spirits because he was fooling around, trying to amuse her. When he stood opposite her, he leaned forward for some reason and tried to stand on his hands. After two attempts he made it, then toppled right over and landed with a shout and a splash in the river.

Elizabeth jumped up, and ran through the shallow water towards him.

'Are you all right?' she said.

He grinned at her. 'I could do that when I was a kid.'

'So could I.'

He stood up, looking down ruefully at his soaked clothes.

'They'll soon dry,' she said.

'I'll get my horse.'

They splashed back through the river to the other side, and Helward stood his horse next to Elizabeth's. She sat down on the bank again, and Helward sat close beside her, stretching out his legs in the sun so that his clothes might dry.

Behind them the horses stood nose to tail, whisking away the flies from each other's face.

Questions, questions . . . but she suppressed them all. She enjoyed the intrigue, didn't want to destroy it with understanding. The rational account was that he was an operative from a station similar to hers, and that he was enjoying an elaborate and somewhat pointless joke at her expense. If that was so, she didn't care: his presence was enough, and she was herself sufficiently emotionally suppressed to relish the break with routine he was unwittingly bringing her.

The only common bond she knew of was his sketches, and she asked to see them again. For a while they talked about the drawings, and he expressed his various enthusiasms; she was interested to see that all the sketches were on the back of old computer print-out paper.

Eventually, he said: 'I thought you were a took.'

He pronounced it with a long vowel, like *shoot*.

'What's that?'

'One of the people who live round here. But they don't speak English.'

'A few do. Not very well. Only when we teach them.'

'Who is "we"?'

'The people I work for.'

'You're not from the city?' he said suddenly, then looked away.

Elizabeth felt a glimmer of alarm; he had looked and acted like this the day before, and then he had suddenly left. She didn't want that, not now.

'Do you mean your city?'

'No . . . of course you're not. Who are you?'

'You know my name,' she said.

'Yes, but where are you from?'

'England. I came here about two months ago.'

'England . . . that's on Earth isn't it?' He was staring at her intently, the drawings forgotten now.

She laughed, a nervous reaction to the strangeness of the question.

212

'It was the last time I was there,' she said, trying to make a joke of it.

'My God! Then – '

'What?'

He stood up abruptly, and turned away from her. He took a few steps, then turned again and stood over her, staring down.

'You've come from Earth?'

'What do you mean?'

'Are you from Earth . . . the planet?'

'Of course . . . I don't understand.'

'You're looking for us,' he said.

'No! I mean . . . I'm not sure.'

'You've found us!'

She stood up, backed away from him.

She waited by the horses. The aura of strangeness had become one of madness, and she knew she should leave. The next move must come from him.

'Elizabeth . . . don't go.'

'Liz,' she said.

'Liz . . . do you know who I am? I'm from the city of Earth. You must know what that means!'

'No, I don't.'

'You haven't heard about us?'

'No.'

'We've been here for thousands of miles . . . many years. Nearly two hundred.'

'Where is the city?'

He waved his arm in the direction of the north-east. 'Down there. About twenty-five miles to the south.'

She didn't react to the contradiction of direction, assumed he had made a mistake.

'Can I see the city?' she said.

'Of course!' He took her hand excitedly, and placed it on the rein of her horse. 'We'll go now!'

'Wait . . . How do you spell the name of your city?'

He spelt it for her.

'Why is it called that?'

'I don't know. Because we are from the planet Earth. I suppose.'

'Why do you differentiate between the two?'

'Because . . . isn't it obvious?'

'No.'

She realised she was humouring him as if he were a maniac,

213

but it was only excitement that shone in his eyes, not mania. Her instinct, though, on which she had been so dependent recently, warned her to be careful. She could not be sure of anything now.

'But this is not Earth!'

She said: 'Helward . . . meet me here tomorrow. By the stream.'

'I thought you wanted to see our city.'

'Yes . . . but not today. If it is twenty-five miles away, I would have to get a fresh horse, tell my superiors.' She was making excuses.

He looked at her uncertainly.

'You think I'm making it up,' he said.

'No.'

'Then what's wrong? I tell you, as long as I can remember, and for many years before I was born, the city has survived in the hope that help would come from Earth. Now you are here and you think I am mad!'

'You are on Earth.'

He opened his mouth, closed it again.

'Why do you say that?' he said.

'Why should I say otherwise?'

He took her arm again, and whirled her round. He pointed upwards.

'What do you see?'

She shielded her eyes against the glare. 'The sun.'

'The sun! The sun! What about the sun?'

'Nothing. Let go of my arm . . . you're hurting me!'

He released her, and scrambled over to the discarded drawings. He took the top one, held it out for her to see.

'That is the sun!' he shouted, pointing at the weird shape that was drawn at the top right of the picture, a few inches away from the spindly figure that he said was her. 'There is the sun!'

Heart beating furiously, she tore the rein away from the tree around which it was tied, climbed up into the saddle, and kicked in her heels. The horse wheeled round, and she galloped it away from the river.

Behind her, Helward stood, still holding out his drawing.

5

It was evening by the time Elizabeth reached the village, and she judged it already too late to set out for headquarters. She had no will to return there anyway, and there was somewhere she could sleep in the village.

The main street was empty of people; unusual, for this time of day was a popular one with the people for sitting in the dust outside their houses and talking idly while they drank the strong, resinous wine that was all they could ferment round here.

There was a noise coming from the church, and she headed that way. Inside, most of the men of the village were gathered, and a few of the women. One or two of these were crying.

'What's going on?' Elizabeth said to Father dos Santos.

'Those men came back,' he said. 'They've offered a deal.'

He was standing well to one side, obviously incapable of influencing the people in any way.

Elizabeth tried to catch the gist of the discussion, but there was much shouting, and even Luiz, who stood prominently near the wrecked altar, could not make himself heard over the hubbub. Elizabeth caught his eye, and at once he came over.

'Well?'

'The men came today, Menina Khan. We are agreeing to their terms.'

'It doesn't sound like there's much agreement. What are their terms?'

'Fair.'

He started to head back towards the altar, but Elizabeth caught his arm.

'What did they want?' she said.

'They will give us many medicines, and a lot of food. There is more of the fertiliser, and they say they will help repair the church, though that is not wished by us.'

He was looking at her evasively, his gaze flickering up to her eyes, then away, then back again.

'And in return?'

'Only a little.'

215

'Come on, Luiz. What did they want?'

'Ten of our women. Is nothing.'

She stared at him in amazement. 'What did you – ?'

'They will be well looked after. They will make them healthy. and when they return to us they will bring more food.'

'And what do the women say to that?'

He glanced over his shoulder. 'They are not happy.'

'I'll bet they're not.' She looked over at the six women who were present. They stood in a small group, and the men nearest to them were already looking sheepish. 'What do they want them for?'

'We do not ask.'

'Because you think you know.' She turned to dos Santos. 'What's going to happen?'

'They've already made up their minds,' he said.

'But why? Surely they can't seriously consider trading their wives and daughters for a few sacks of grain?'

Luiz said: 'We need what they offer.'

'But we have already promised you food. There is a doctor on his way now.'

'Yes . . . and so you have promised. Two months you have been here and very little food, no doctor. These men are honourable, because we can tell.'

He turned his back on her, and returned to the front of the crowd. In a moment he called for a vote by show of hands. The deal was confirmed, and none of the women voted.

Elizabeth passed a restless night, although by the time she rose in the morning she knew what she was going to do.

The day had produced a volume of unexpected developments. Ironically, the one development of which she had felt instinctively confident had not materialised. Now that the encounter with Helward had taken on a new perspective, she could put words to what she had expected: the stirring inside her had been a physical restlessness, and she had ridden down to the river in full expectation of being seduced by him. It could still have happened until that moment the fanatical expression had taken his eyes; even now she still experienced stirrings of that sensation – not fear, not amazement, somewhere between – whenever she recalled the shouted conversation under the trees.

'What about the sun?' still echoed.

Undoubtedly there was more to the scene than had appeared. Helward's behaviour the day before had been different; she had tapped then a hidden sensitivity, and he had responded the way any man would. There was no sign of the presumed mania then. And not until she talked to him about his life, or her life, had he reacted that way.

And there was the mystery about the computer paper. There was only one computer within a thousand miles of here, and she knew where it was and what it was used for. It didn't use paper print-outs, and it certainly wasn't an IBM. She knew of IBMs; anyone who was trained in the basics of computers had heard of them, but no machine had been made by them since the Crash. Certainly the only ones intact, if not working, were in museums.

Finally, the deal proposed by the men who had visited the village had been wholly unanticipated, at least by her, although when she remembered Luiz's expression after he had first spoken to the men she felt sure that he had had at least an inkling of what had been expected by way of payment.

Somehow, all must be connected. She knew the men who had come to the village were from the same place as Helward, and that his behaviour was linked in some way with this deal.

There remained the question of her own involvement in this.

Technically, the village and its people were the responsibility of her and dos Santos. There had been a visit from one of the supervisors from headquarters in the early days, but much of the attention of the hierarchy was directed towards overseeing the repair of a big harbour on the coast. In theory, she was in the charge of dos Santos, but he was a local man who had been one of the several hundred students who had been crammed through the government theological college in an effort to take religion back to the outlying regions. Religion was the traditional opiate here, and the missionary work was given a high priority. But the facts of the situation spoke for themselves: dos Santos's work would take years, and for most of the first few years he would be working uphill towards re-establishing the church as the social and spiritual leadership of the community. The villagers tolerated him, but it was of Luiz they took notice, and, to a certain extent, herself.

It would be equally useless to look to headquarters for guidance. Although the establishment was run by good and sincere men, their work was still so new that they had not yet taken their heads out of the clouds of theory; a plain, human problem like women bartered for food would not be in their scope.

If any action were to be taken, it would have to be on her own initiative.

The decision did not come quickly; throughout that long, warm night she did what she could to separate the pros and cons, the risks and the benefits, and however she looked at it her chosen course of action seemed to be the only one.

She rose early, and went down to Maria's house. She had to be quick: the men had said they would be coming soon after sunrise.

Maria was awake, her baby was crying. She knew of the decision taken the night before, and she questioned Elizabeth about it as soon as she arrived.

'No time for that,' Elizabeth said brusquely. 'I want some clothes.'

'But yours are so beautiful.'

'I want something of yours . . . anything will do.'

Grumbling speculatively, Maria found a selection of rough garments, and laid them out for Elizabeth's inspection. They were all well-used, and probably none had ever seen soap and water. For Elizabeth's purpose they were ideal. She selected a ragged, loose-fitting skirt and an off-white shirt that had presumably once belonged to one of the men.

She slipped off her own clothes, including her underwear, and pulled on Maria's. She folded her own clothes into a neat pile, and gave them to Maria to look after for her until she returned.

'But you look no better than a village girl!'

'Right.'

She looked at the baby to make sure it was not ill, then went through with Maria the daily routines she should follow. Maria, as ever, pretended to listen, although Elizabeth knew she would forget everything as soon as she was not there to watch her. Had she not reared three children already?

Walking barefoot up the dusty street, Elizabeth wondered if she would pass for one of the village women. Her hair was long and brown, and her body had become tanned in the weeks here, but she knew her skin lacked the lustrous quality of the local women. She ran her fingers through her hair, changing the parting, and hoping it would become more straggly.

There was already a small group of people in the square in front of the church, and more were arriving every minute. Luiz was at the centre of everything, trying to persuade the women who were watching out of curiosity to return to their homes.

Beside him was a small group of girls; the youngest and the most attractive in the village, Elizabeth realised with a feeling

218

of appalled horror. Soon, all ten were standing beside Luiz, and she pushed forward through the crowd.

Luiz recognised her at once.

'Menina Khan – '

'Luiz, who is the youngest of these?'

Before he could answer she had picked out the girl for herself: Lea, who was no more than about fourteen. She went over to her.

'Lea, go back to your mother. I will go instead.'

Unsurprised and uncomplaining, the girl walked mutely away. Luiz stared at Elizabeth for a moment, then shrugged.

They did not have long to wait. In a few minutes three men appeared, each riding a horse and each leading another. All six horses were laden with packages, and without ceremony the three riders dismounted and unloaded the materials they had brought.

Luiz watched keenly. Elizabeth heard one of the men say to him: 'We'll be back in two days with the rest. Do you want the work done on the church?

'No . . . we do not need that.'

'As you wish. Do you want to change any of the terms of the barter?'

'No. We are satisfied.'

'Good.' The man turned and faced the rest of the people who were watching the transaction. He spoke to them as he had spoken to Luiz, in their own language, but with a heavy accent. 'We have tried to be men of good will and good word. Some of you may not be in favour of the terms we have proposed, but we ask your understanding. The women you have loaned to us will be cared for and will not be treated badly in any way. Their health and happiness is in our interests as much as yours. We shall see that they return to you as soon as possible. Thank you.'

The ceremony, for what it was, was over. The men offered the horses to the women to ride. Two of the girls climbed on to one horse, and five more took a horse each. Elizabeth and the two others elected to walk, and soon the small party left the village, walking the horses up the dried-up river bed to the wide scrubland beyond.

6

Throughout the journey Elizabeth maintained the same silence as the other girls. As far as possible she was trying to remain anonymous.

The three men spoke to each other in English, assuming that none of the girls would be able to understand them. At first, Elizabeth was listening intently, hoping to learn something of interest, but to her disappointment discovered that most of what the men said was concerned with complaints about the heat, the lack of shade, and how long the journey would take.

Their concern for the women seemed genuine enough, and they made repeated enquiries about their condition. Speaking occasionally to the other girls in their own language, Elizabeth discovered their preoccupations were much the same: they were hot, thirsty, tired, anxious that the journey be completed.

Every hour or so they took a brief rest, and took it in turns to ride on the horses. None of the men rode for any of the way, and in time Elizabeth began to sympathise with their complaints. If their destination was, as Helward had said, twenty-five miles away, it was a long walk on a hot day.

Later in the day, perhaps inhibitions had become relaxed by tiredness, or the general lack of reaction from any of their companions had re-affirmed their lack of understanding of the language, but the men somehow turned the topic of conversation to less immediate concerns. It started with grumbles about the unrelenting heat, but shifted to another topic almost at once.

'Do you think all this is still necessary?'

'The barters?'

'Yes . . . I mean, it's caused trouble in the past.'

'There's no other way.'

'It's too damned hot.'

'What would you do instead?'

'I don't know. Not my decision. If I had my way I wouldn't be out here now.'

'It still makes sense to me. The last lot haven't moved out yet, and there's no sign of them doing so. Maybe we won't have to barter any more.'

'We will.'

'You sound as if you don't approve.'

'Frankly, I don't. Sometimes I think the whole system's crazy.'

'You've been listening to the Terminators.'

'Maybe I have. If you listen to them they make a bit of sense. Not completely, but they're not as bad as the Navigators make out.'

'You're out of your mind.'

'O.K. Who wouldn't be in this heat?'

'You'd better not repeat that in the city.'

'Why not? Enough people are saying it already.'

'Not guildsmen. You've been down past. You know what's what.'

'I'm just being realistic. You've got to listen to people's opinions. There are more people in the city who want to stop than there are guildsmen. That's all.'

'Shut up, Norris,' said the man who had so far not spoken, the one who had addressed the crowd.

They continued on their way.

The city had been in sight for some time before Elizabeth recognised it for what it was. As they came nearer she looked at it with great interest, not comprehending the system of tracks and cables that stretched away from it. Her first assumption was that it was some kind of marshalling yard, but there was no sign of any rolling-stock and anyway the length of track was too short for any practical use.

Later she noticed several men apparently patrolling the tracks, each of whom carried a rifle or what appeared to be a crossbow. More than this she could not absorb, since most of her attention was on the structure itself.

She had heard the men refer to it as a city, and Helward too, but to her eyes it was not much more than a large and misshapen office block. It did not look too safe, constructed mainly of timber. It had the ugliness of functionalism, and yet there was a simplicity to its design which was not altogether unattractive. She was reminded of pictures she had seen of pre-Crash buildings, and although most of those had been steel and reinforced concrete they shared the squareness, the plainness, and lack of exterior decoration. Those old buildings had been tall, though, and this strange structure was nowhere more than seven storeys high. The timber showed varying stages of weathering; most of what she could see had been well bleached by the elements, but there were newer parts visible.

The men took them right up to the base of the building, and then into a dark passageway. Here they dismounted, and several young men came forward to lead away the horses.

The men took them to a door in the passageway, up a staircase, and through another doorway. They emerged into a brightly lit corridor.

At the end of this there was another door, and here they parted company with the men. There was a printed sign on the door, which said: TRANSFERENCE QUARTERS.

Inside they were greeted by two women, who spoke to them in the badly accented language of the people.

Once Elizabeth had adopted her pose, there was no way of abandoning it.

In the next few days she was subjected to a series of examinations and treatments which, had she not suspected the reason, she would have found humiliating. She was bathed, and her hair was washed. She was medically examined, her eyes were tested, her teeth were checked. Her hair and scalp were inspected for infestation, and she was given a test which she could only imagine was to determine whether or not she had VD.

Without surprise, the woman supervising the examination passed her with a clean bill of health – of the ten girls, Elizabeth was the only one who was so passed – and she was then given over to two more women who began to instruct her in the rudiments of speaking English. This caused her some considerable private amusement, and in spite of her best efforts to delay the learning process she was soon considered fit and educated enough to be released from this initial period of habilitation.

The first few nights she had slept in a communal dormitory in the transference centre, but now she was given a tiny room of her own. This was scrupulously clean and furnished minimally. It contained a narrow bed, a space to hang her clothes – she had been given two identical sets of clothes to wear – a chair, and about four square feet of floor space.

Eight days had passed since coming to the city, and Elizabeth was beginning to wonder what she had hoped to achieve. Now she had been cleared by the transference section she was assigned to the kitchens, where the work she was given was straightforward drudgery. The evenings were free, but she was told that she was

222

expected to spend at least an hour or two in a certain reception-room where, she was told, she was supposed to mix socially with the people she met there.

This room was situated next to the transference section. It had a small bar at one end with, Elizabeth noted, a distinct shortage of choice, and next to this an ancient video set. When she switched it on a tape device attached to it showed a comedy programme that she frankly couldn't understand at all, although an invisible audience laughed all the way through. The comic allusions were evidently contemporary, and thus meaningless to her. She watched the programme through, and from a copyright notice at the end learnt that it had been taped in 1985. More than two hundred years old!

There were usually only a few people in this room when she was there. A woman from the transference section worked behind the bar, maintaining a fixed grin, but Elizabeth could not work up much interest in the other people there. A few men came in occasionally – dressed, as Helward had been, in the dark uniform – and there were two or three local girls.

One day, working in the kitchen, she accidentally solved a problem that had continued to nag at her.

She was stacking away some of the clean crockery in a metal cupboard used for this purpose, when something about it caught her attention. It had been changed almost out of recognition – its components had been removed, and it had been fitted with wooden shelves – but the IBM motif on one of the doors still showed through the covering layer of paint.

When she could, Elizabeth walked around the rest of the city, curious about almost everything she saw. Before entering the city she had expected to find herself a virtual prisoner, but beyond the bounds of the duties she had to perform she was free to go wherever she liked, do whatever she wished. She talked to people, she saw, she registered, and she thought.

One day she came across a small room set aside for use by the ordinary people of the city in their leisure hours. Lying on a table she found a few sheets of printed paper, neatly stapled together. She glanced at them without much interest, saw the title on the first page: Destaine's Directive.

Later, as she walked through the city she saw many more of these printed sheets, and in due time, with her curiosity piqued, she read one set through. Having seen its contents, she immediately concealed a copy in the bedclothes of her bunk, meaning to take it with her when she left the city.

223

She was beginning to understand. . . . She returned again to Destaine, read his words so often they became almost photographically recorded. And she thought about Helward, and his apparently wild behaviour and words, and she tried to remember what he had said.

In time, a kind of logical pattern appeared . . . but there was one ineradicable flaw in everything.

The hypothesis by which the city and its people existed was that the world on which they lived was somehow inverted. Not only the world, but all the physical objects in the universe in which that world was supposed to exist. The shape that Destaine drew – a solid world, curved north and south in the shape of hyperbolas – was the approximation they used, and it correlated indeed with the strange shape that Helward had drawn to depict the sun.

One day Elizabeth saw the flaw, as she walked through one of the parts of the city presently being re-built.

She glanced up at the sun, shielding her eyes with her hand. The sun was as she had ever known it: a brilliant white ball of light high in the sky.

7

Elizabeth planned to leave the city the following morning, taking one of the horses and riding across country to the village. From there she could get back to headquarters and take some leave. She was due for some leave in a few weeks' time, and she knew she could have it brought forward without much difficulty. With the four weeks then available, she would have plenty of time to get back to England and try to find some authority somewhere who could be made interested in what she had discovered.

She did not wish to draw attention to herself once she had formed this plan, and so spent the day working in the kitchens as normal. In the evening she went to the reception room.

When she walked through the door, the first man she saw was Helward. He was standing with his back to her, talking to one of the transferred girls.

She went and stood behind him.

'Hello, Helward,' she said quietly.

He turned round to acknowledge her, then looked at her in amazement.

'You!' he said. 'What are you doing here?'

'Ssh! I'm not supposed to be able to speak English very well. I'm one of your transferred women.'

She walked over to a deserted part of the room. The woman at the bar nodded her head in patronising approval as Helward followed.

'Look,' Elizabeth said at once, 'I'm sorry about the last time we met. I understand better now.'

'And I'm sorry if I frightened you.'

'Have you said anything to any of the others?'

'About you being from Earth? No.'

'Good. Don't say anything.'

He said: 'Are you really from Earth planet?'

'Yes, but I wish you wouldn't refer to it as that. I'm from Earth, and so are you. There's a misunderstanding.'

'God, you can say that again.' He looked down at her from the nine inches advantage he had in height. 'You look different here . . . but what are you doing as a transfer?'

'It was the only way of getting into the city I could think of.'

'I would have taken you.' He glanced around the room. 'Have you paired up with any of the men yet?'

'No.'

'Don't.' As he talked, he kept looking over his shoulder. 'Have you got a room to yourself? We could talk better.'

'Yes. Shall we go?'

She closed the door when they were inside the room; the walls were thin, but at least it had the appearance of privacy. She wondered why he needed to be guarded in speaking to her.

She sat on the chair, and Helward sat on the edge of the bed.

'I've read Destaine,' she said. 'It was fascinating. I've heard of him somehow. Who was he?'

'The founder of the city.'

'Yes, I'd gathered that. But he was known for something else.'

Helward looked blank. 'Did what he write make any sense to you?'

'A little. He was a very lost man. But he was wrong.'

'Wrong about what?'

'The city, and the danger it was in. He writes as if he and the others had somehow been transported to another world.'

'That's so.'

Elizabeth shook her head. 'You've never left Earth, Helward. As I sit here and talk to you now, we're both on Earth.'

He shook his head in despair. 'You're wrong, I know you're wrong. Whatever you say, Destaine knew the true situation. We are on another world.'

Elizabeth said: 'The other day . . . you drew me with the sun behind me. You drew it like a hyperbola. Is that how you see it? You drew me too tall. Is that how you see me?'

'That's not how I see the sun, that's how it *is*. And it is how the world is. You I drew tall, because . . . that's how I saw you then. We were a long way north of the city. Now . . . It's too difficult to explain.'

'Try it.'

'No.'

'O.K. Do you know how I see the sun? It's normal . . . round, spherical, whatever the correct description is. Can't you see that it's a question of what we ourselves perceive? Your perceptions inform you incorrectly . . . I don't know why, but Destaine's perception was wrong too.'

226

'Liz, it's more than perception. I've seen, felt, *lived* in this world. Whatever you say, it's real to me. I'm not alone. Most of the people in the city carry the same knowledge. It started with Destaine because he was there at the beginning. We've survived here a long time, simply because of that knowledge. It's been the root of everything, and it's kept us alive because without it we would not keep the city moving.'

Elizabeth started to say something, but he carried on. 'Liz, after I saw you the other day I needed time to think. I rode north, a long way north. I saw something there that is going to test the city's capacity for survival like it has never been tested before. Meeting you was . . . I don't know. More than I had expected. But it led indirectly to a much bigger thing.'

'What is it?'

'I can't tell you.'

'Why not?'

'I can't tell anyone, except the Navigators. They've declared it restricted for the moment. It would be a bad time for the news to get out.'

'What do you mean?'

'Have you heard of the Terminators?'

'Yes . . . but I don't know who they are.'

'They're a . . . political group in the city. They've been trying to get the city to stop. If this news leaked out at the moment, there'd be a lot of trouble. We've just survived a major crisis, and the Navigators don't want another.'

Elizabeth stared at him without saying anything. She had suddenly seen herself in a new light.

She was at an interface of two realities: one was hers, one was his. However close they came together there would never be any contact between them. Like the graph line Destaine had drawn to approximate the reality he perceived, the nearer she came to him in one sense the further she moved away in another. Somehow, she had drawn herself into this drama, where one logic failed in the face of another, and she knew she was incapable of dealing with it.

Persuaded as she was by Helward's sincerity, and the manifest existence of the city and its people, and further by the apparently strange concepts around which they had planned their survival, she could not eradicate from her mind the basic contradiction. The city and its people existed on Earth, the Earth she knew, and whatever she saw, whatever Helward said, there was no way around this. Evidence to the contrary made no sense.

227

But when the interface was challenged, there was an impasse.

Elizabeth said: 'I'm going to leave the city tomorrow.'
'Come with me. I'm going north again.'
'No . . . I've got to get back to the village.'
'Is that the one where they bartered for the women?'
'Yes.'
'I'm going that way. We'll ride together.'
Another impasse: the village lay to the south-west of the city.
'Why did you come to the city, Liz? You aren't one of the local women.'
'I wanted to see you.'
'Why?'
'I don't know. You frightened me, but I was seeing the other men who were like you, trading with the village people. I wanted to find out what was going on. Now I wish I hadn't, because you still frighten me.'
'I'm not raving at you again, am I?' he said.
She laughed . . . and she realised that it was for the first time since she came to the city.
'No, of course not,' she said. 'It's more . . . I can't say. Everything I take for granted is different here in the city. Not everyday things, but the bigger things, like the reason for being. There's a great concentration of determination here, as if the city itself is the only focus of all human existence. I know that's not so. There are a million other things to do in the world, and survival is undoubtedly a drive, but not the primary one. Here the emphasis is on your concept of survival, at any cost. I've been outside the city, Helward, a long way outside the city. Whatever else you may think, this place is not the centre of the universe.'
'It is,' he said. 'Because if we ever stopped believing that, we would all die.'

8

Leaving the city presented Elizabeth with no problems. She went down to the stables with Helward and another man, whom he introduced as Future Blayne, collected three horses, and rode in a direction which Helward declared was northwards. Again, she questioned his sense of direction as by her reckoning of the position of the sun the true direction was towards the south-west, but she made nothing of it. By this time she was so accustomed to the straightforward affronts to what she considered logic that she saw no point in remarking on them to him. She was content to accept the ways of the city, if not to understand them.

As they rode out from under the city, Helward pointed out the great wheels on which the city was mounted, and explained that the motion forwards was so slow as to be almost undetectable. However, he assured her, the city moved about one mile every ten days. Northwards, or towards the south-west, whichever way she cared to think of it.

The journey took two days. The men talked a lot, both to each other and to her, although not much of it made sense to her.

She felt that she had suffered an overload of new information, and could absorb no more.

One the evening of the first day they passed within a mile or so of her village, and she told Helward she was going there.

'No . . . come with us. You can go back later.'

She said: 'I want to go back to England. I think I can help you.'

'You ought to see this.'

'What is it?'

'We're not sure,' said Blayne. 'Helward thinks you might be able to tell us.'

She resisted for a few more minutes, but in the end went on with them.

It was curious how she succumbed so readily to the various involvements of these people. Perhaps it was because she could identify with some of them, and perhaps it was because the society within the city was a curiously civilised existence – for all its strange ways – in a countryside that had been wasted by anarchy for generations. Even in the few weeks she had been in the village the peasant outlook, the unquestioning lethargy, the inability to cope with even the most minor of problems had sapped her will to meet the challenge of her work. But the people of Helward's city were of a different order. Evidently they were some offshoot community that had somehow managed to preserve themselves during the Crash, and now lived on past that time. Even so, the makings of a regulated society were there: the evident discipline, the sense of purpose, and a real and vital understanding of their own identity, however much of a dichotomy existed between inner similarities and outer differences.

So when Helward requested her to go with them, and Blayne supported him, she could put up no opposition. She had by her own actions involved herself in the affairs of their community. The consequences of her abandoning the village would have to be faced later – she could justify her absence by saying she wanted to know where the women were being taken – but she felt now that she must follow this through. Ultimately, there would be some official body who would have to rehabilitate the people of the city, but until then she was personally involved.

They spent the night under canvas. There were only two tents, and the men gallantly offered her one of them for her own use . . . but before that they spent a long time talking.

Helward had evidently told Blayne about her, and how she was different, as he saw her, from both the people of the city and the people of the villages.

Blayne now spoke directly to her, and Helward stayed in the background. He spoke only rarely, and then to confirm things that Blayne said. She liked the other man, and found him direct in his manner: he tried not to evade any of her questions.

By and large he affirmed what she had learned. He spoke of Destaine and his Directive, he spoke of the city and its need to move forward, and he talked of the shape of the world. She had learnt not to argue with the city outlook, and she listened to what they said.

When she eventually crawled into her sleeping-bag she was exhausted from the long ride through the day, but sleep came slowly. The interface had hardened.

Though the confidence in her own logic had not been shaken, her understanding of the city people's had been deepened. They lived, they said, on a world where the laws of nature were not the same. She was prepared to believe that . . . or rather, prepared to believe that they were sincere, but mistaken.

It was not the exterior world that was different, but their perception of it. By what manner could she change that?

Emerging from woodland they encountered a region of coarse scrubland, where tall grasses and scrawny bushes grew wildly. There were no tracks here and progress was slow. There was a cool, steady wind blowing now, and an exhilarating freshness sharpened their senses.

Gradually, the vegetation gave way to a hard, tough grass, growing in sandy soil. Neither of the men said anything; Helward in particular stared ahead of him as he rode, letting his horse find its own route.

Elizabeth saw that ahead of them the vegetation gave way altogether, and as they breasted a ridge of loose sand and gravel, only a few yards of low sand-dunes lay between them and the beach. Her horse, who had already sensed the salt in the air, responded readily to the kick of her heels and they cantered down across the sand. For a few heady minutes she gave the horse its head, and exulted in the freedom and joy of galloping along a beach, its surface unlittered, unbroken, untouched by anything but waves for decades.

Helward and Blayne had ridden down to the beach behind her, and now stood close together by their horses, looking out across the water.

She trotted her horse over to them, and dismounted.

'Does it extend east and west?' said Blayne.

'As far as I explored. There's no way round I could see.'

Blayne took a video camera from one of his packs, connected it to the case, and panned it slowly across the view.

'We'll have to survey east and west,' he said. 'It would be impossible to cross.'

'There's no sign of an opposite bank.'

Blayne frowned at the beach. 'I don't like the soil. We'll have to get a Bridge-Builder up here. I don't think this would take the weight of the city.'

'There must be some way.'

The two men entirely ignored her. Helward erected a small instrument, a tripodal device with a concentric chart suspended by three catches below the fulcrum. He hung a plumb-line over the chart, and took some kind of reading from it.

'We're a long way from optimum,' he said eventually. 'We've got plenty of time. Thirty miles . . . almost a year city-time. Do you think it could be done?'

231

'A bridge? It'd take some doing. We'd need more men than we've got at the moment. What did the Navigators say?'

'Check what I reported. Do you check?'

'Yes. I can't see that I can add anything.'

Helward stared for a few seconds longer at the expanse of water, then seemed to remember Elizabeth. He turned to her. 'What do you say?'

'About this? What do you expect me to say?'

'Tell us about our perceptions,' said Helward. 'Tell us there's no river here.'

She said: 'It's not a river.'

Helward glanced at Blayne.

'You heard her,' he said. 'We're imagining it.'

Elizabeth closed her eyes, turned away. She could no longer confront the interface.

The breeze was chilling her, so she took a blanket from her horse and moved back to the sandy ridge. When she faced them again they were paying no more attention to her. Helward had erected another instrument, and was taking several readings from it. He called them out to Blayne, his voice whipped thin by the wind.

They worked slowly and painstakingly, each checking the other's reading at every step. After an hour, Blayne packed some of the equipment on his horse, then mounted and rode along the coast in a northerly direction. Helward stood and watched him go, his posture revealing a deep and overwhelming despair.

Elizabeth interpreted it as a tiny weakness in the barrier of logic that lay between them. Clutching the blanket around her, she walked down across the dunes towards him.

She said: 'Do you know where you are?'

He didn't turn.

'No,' he said. 'We never will.'

'Portugal. This country is called Portugal. It's in Europe.'

She moved round so that she could see his face. For a moment his gaze rested on her, but his expression was blank. He just shook his head, and walked past her towards his horse. The barrier was absolute.

Elizabeth went over to her own horse, and mounted it. She walked it along the beach and soon moved inland, heading back in the general direction of the headquarters. In a few minutes the troubled blue of the Atlantic was out of sight.

Part Five

1

The storm raged all night and none of us got much sleep. Our camp was half a mile from the bridge, and as the waves came crashing in the sound reached us as a dull, muted roar, almost obliterated by the howling gale. In our imaginations, at least, we heard the splintering of timber in every temporary lull.

Towards dawn the wind abated, and we were able to sleep. Not for long, for soon after sunrise the kitchen was manned and we were given our food. No one talked as we ate; there would be only one topic of conversation, and none wished to speak of that.

We set off towards the bridge. We had gone only fifty yards when someone pointed to a piece of broken timber lying washed up on the river-bank. It was a grim foreboding and, as it turned out, an accurate one. There was nothing left of the bridge beyond the four main piles that were planted in the solid ground nearest to the water's edge.

I glanced at Lerouex who, for this shift, was in charge of all operations.

'We need more timber,' he said. 'Barter Norris . . . take thirty men, and start felling trees.'

I waited for Norris's reaction; of all the guildsmen on the site he had been the most reluctant to work, and had complained loud and long during the early stages of the work. Now he showed no rebellion; we were all past that. He simply nodded to Lerouex, picked a body of men and headed back towards the camp to collect the tree-felling saws.

'So we start again,' I said to Lerouex.

'Of course.'

'Will this one be strong enough?'

'If we build it properly.'

He turned away, and started to organise the clearing up of the site. In the background the waves, still huge in the aftermath of the storm, crashed against the river-bank.

We worked all day, and by evening the site had been cleared and Norris and his men had hauled fourteen tree-trunks over to the site. The next morning we could start work yet again.

Before then, during the evening, I sought out Lerouex. He was sitting alone in his tent, apparently checking through his designs of the bridge, but in fact I realised his stare was vacant.

He did not seem pleased to see me, but he and I were the two senior men on the site and he knew I would not come without purpose. We were now of roughly equal age: by the nature of my work in the north I had passed many subjective years. It was a matter of some discomfort between us that he was the father of my former wife, and yet we were now contemporaries. Neither of us had ever referred directly to it. Victoria herself was still only comparatively few miles older than she had been when we were married, and the gulf between us was now so wide that everything we knew of each other was totally irretrievable.

'I know what you've come to say,' he said. 'You're going to tell me that we can never build a bridge.'

'It's going to be difficult,' I said.

'No . . . impossible is what you mean.'

'What do you think?'

'I'm a Bridge-Builder, Helward. I'm not supposed to think.'

'That's as much crap as you know it is.'

'All right . . . but a bridge is needed, I build it. No questions.'

I said: 'You've always had an opposite bank.'

'That makes no difference. We can build a pontoon.'

'And when we're mid-river, where do we get the timber? Where do we plant the cable-stays?' I sat down unbidden, opposite him. 'You were wrong, incidentally. I didn't come to see you about this.'

'Well?'

'The opposite bank,' I said. 'Where is it?'

'Out there somewhere.'

'Where?'

'I don't know.'

'How do you know there is one?'

'There must be.'

'Then why can't we see it?' I said. 'We're striking away from this bank a few degrees from perpendicular, but even so we should be able to see the bank. The curvature – '

'Is concave. I know. Don't you think I haven't thought about that? In theory we can see forever. What about atmospheric haze? Twenty or thirty miles is all we can see, even on a clear day.'

'You're going to build a bridge thirty miles long?'

'I don't think we'll have to,' he said. 'I think we're going to be O.K. Why else do you think I persevere?'

appreciated by the Navigators, was the erosion of traditional political power within the city.

Victoria, and presumably the other overt Terminators, still carried out nominal tasks on behalf of the city, but perhaps it was a sign of their influence that much of the day-to-day routines of the city were falling behind. Officially, the Navigators put this down to the re-deployment of so many men to the bridge, but few were in doubt as to the real causes.

Within guild circles, the resolution was almost complete. There was much complaining and some dissent with decisions, but in general there was complete acceptance that the bridge must be built. Halting the city would be unthinkable.

'Are you going to accept the Navigatorship?' I said.

'I think so. I don't want to retire, but – '

'Retire? There's no question of that.'

'It means retirement from active guild work,' he said. 'It's new Navigator policy. They believe that by bringing on to the Council men who have been playing an active role they will acquire a more forceful voice. That, incidentally, is why they want you on the Council.'

'My work's up north,' I said.

'So is mine. But we reach an age – '

'You shouldn't think of retiring,' I said. 'You're the best Bridge man in the city.'

'So they say. No one has the tactlessness to point out that my last three bridges have been unsuccessful.'

'You mean the ones that were damaged at this river?'

'Yes. And the new one will go as soon as there's another storm.'

'You said yourself – '

'Helward . . . I'm not the man to build that bridge. It needs young blood. A new approach. Perhaps a ship is the answer.'

Lerouex and I both understood what that admission meant to him. The Bridge-Builders guild was the proudest in the city. No bridge had ever failed.

We walked on.

Almost as soon as I arrived in the city I was fretting to return to the north. I did not like the present atmosphere; it was now as if the people had replaced the old system of guild suppression with a self-inflicted blindness to reality. Terminator slogans were everywhere, and crudely printed leaflets littered the corridors. People talked of the bridge, and they talked fearfully. Men returning from a work shift told of the failures, spoke of building a bridge towards a farther bank that could not be seen. Rumours, presumably orginated by the Terminators, told of dozens of men being killed, more took attacks.

In the Futures' room I was approached by Clausewitz, who was himself now a Navigator. He presented me with a formal letter from the Council of Navigators, naming a proposer (Clausewitz) and a seconder (McMahon) who requested me to join them.

'I'm sorry,' I said. 'I can't accept this.'

'We need you, Helward. You're one of our most experienced men.'

'Maybe. I'm needed on the bridge.'

'You could do better work here.'

'I don't think so.'

Clausewitz took me aside, and spoke confidentially.

'The Council is setting up a working party to deal with the Terminators,' he said. 'We want you on that.'

'How can you deal with them? Suppress their voices?'

'No . . . we're going to have to compromise with them. They want to abandon the city for good. We're going to meet them half-way, abandon the bridge.'

I stared at him incredulously.

'I can't be a party to that,' I said.

'Instead we build a ship. Not a big one, not nearly as complex as the city. Just large enough to get us to the opposite bank, when we'll rebuild the city.'

I handed back the letter and turned away.

'No,' I said. 'That's my final word.'

3

I prepared to leave the city forthwith, determined to return to the north and carry out yet another survey of the river. Our survey reports had confirmed that the river was indeed such, that the banks were not circular and that it was not a lake. Lakes can be circled, rivers have to be crossed. I remembered Lerouex's one optimistic remark, that the opposite bank might come into view as the river neared optimum. It was a desperate hope, but if I could locate that opposite bank there could be no further argument against the bridge.

I walked down through the city realising that by my words and intents I had made certain my actions. I had committed myself to the bridge, even though I had alienated myself from the instrument of its construction: the Council. In a sense I was on my own, in spirit and in fact. If a compromise was planned with the Terminators, I would have to subscribe to it eventually, but for the moment the bridge was the only tangible reality, however improbable.

I remembered something Blayne had once said. He described the city as a fanatical society, and I questioned this. He said that one definition of a fanatic was a man who continued to struggle against the odds when all hope was lost. The city had been struggling against the odds since Destaine's day, and there were seven thousand miles of recorded history, none of which had been easily won. It was impossible for mankind to survive in this environment, Blayne had said, and yet the city continued to do so.

Perhaps I had inherited that fanaticism, for now I felt that only I maintained the city's sense of survival. For me it was given substance in the building of the bridge, however hopeless that task might seem.

In one of the corridors I met Gelman Jase. He was now many subjective miles younger than me, because he had been north only infrequently.

'Where are you going?' he said.

'Up north. There's nothing for me in the city at the moment.'

'Aren't you going to the meeting?'

'Which meeting?'

'The Terminators'.'

'Are you going?' I said.

My voice had obviously reflected the disapproval I felt, for he said defensively: 'Yes. Why not? It's the first time they've come into the open.'

'Are you with them?' I said.

'No . . . but I want to hear what they say.'

'And what if they persuade you?'

'That's not likely,' said Jase.

'Then why go?'

Jase said: 'Is your mind totally closed, Helward?'

I opened my mouth to deny it . . . but said nothing. The fact was that my mind was closed.

'Don't you believe in another point of view?' he said.

'Yes . . . but there's no debate on this issue. They're in the wrong, and you know it as well as I do.'

'Just because a man's wrong doesn't mean he's a fool.'

I said: 'Gelman, you've been down past. You know what happens there. You know the city would be taken there by the movement of the ground. Surely there's no question about what the city should do.'

'I know. But they have the ear of a large percentage of the people. We should hear them out.'

'They're enemies of the city's security.'

'O.K. . . . but to defeat an enemy one should know him. I'm going to the meeting because this is the first time their views are being publicly expressed. I want to know what I'm up against. If we're going to go across that bridge, it's going to be people like me who will see us across. If the Terminators have got an alternative, I want to hear it. If not, I want to know it.'

'I'm going up north,' I said.

Jase shook his head. We argued a while longer, and then we went to the meeting.

Some miles before, the work on rebuilding the crèche had been abandoned. The damage had long since been cleared leaving bare the broad metal base of the city, open on three sides to the countryside. At the northern side of this area, against the bulk of the rest of the city, some reconstruction work had been done, and the timber facings afforded the speakers a suitable background and a slightly raised platform from which to address the crowd.

As Jase and I came out of the last building and walked across the space there were already a considerable number of people there. I was surprised that so many were here; the resident population of the city had already been considerably depleted by the men drafted to work on the bridge, but at a rough estimate it seemed to me that there were at least three or four hundred people present. Surely there could be few people who were not here? The workers on the bridge, the Navigators, and a few proud guildsmen?

A speech was already in progress, and the crowd was listening without much response. The main text of the speech – made by a man I recognised as one of the food synthesists – was a description of the physical environment through which the city was currently passing.

'. . . the soil is rich, and there is a good chance that we could grow our own crops. We have abundant water, both locally and to the north of us.' Laughter. 'The climate is agreeable. The local people are not hostile, nor need we make them so – '

After a few minutes, he stood down to a ripple of applause. Without preamble, the next speaker came forward. It was Victoria.

'People of the city, we face another crisis brought upon us by the Council of Navigators. For thousands of miles we have been making our way across this land, indulging ourselves in all that is inhuman to stay alive. Our way of staying alive has been to move forward, towards the north. Behind us – ' and she waved her hand to encompass the broad stretch of countryside that lay beyond the southern edge of the platform '– is that period of our existence. Ahead of us they tell us there is a river. One we must cross to further ensure our survival. What is beyond that river they do not tell us, because they do not know.'

Victoria talked for a long time, and I confess I was prejudiced against her from her first words. It sounded to me like cheap rhetoric, but the crowd seemed to appreciate it. Perhaps I was not as indifferent as I supposed, for when she described the building of the bridge and threw in the accusation that many men had died, I started forward to protest. Jase caught my arm.

'Helward . . . don't.'

'She's talking rubbish!' I said, but already a few voices in the crowd shouted that that was rumour. Victoria conceded it neatly, but added that there was probably more going on at the bridge site than was generally known; this was greeted with some approval.

Victoria brought her speech to an unexpected conclusion.

'I say that not only is this bridge unnecessary, but that it is dangerous too. In this I have an expert opinion. As many of you know, my father is Chief Guildsman of the Bridge-Builders. He it is who designed the bridge. I ask you now to listen to what he has to say.'

'God . . . she couldn't do that!' I said.

Jase said: 'Lerouex is not a Terminator.'

'I know. But he's lost faith.'

Bridges Lerouex was already on the platform. He stood by the side of his daughter, waiting for the applause to die down. He did not look directly at the crowd, but stared down at the floor. He looked tired, old, and beaten.

'Come on, Jase. I'm not going to watch him be humiliated.'

Jase looked at me uncertainly. Lerouex was preparing to speak.

I pushed forward through the crowd, wanting to be away before he said anything. I had learned to respect Lerouex, and did not wish to be present in his moment of defeat.

A few yards forward, I stopped again.

Standing behind Victoria and her father, I had recognised someone else. For a moment I couldn't place either the name or the face . . . then it came. It was Elizabeth Khan.

I was shocked to see her again. It had been many miles since she had left: at least eighteen miles in city-time, many more in my own subjective time. After she had left I had tried to put her from my mind.

Lerouex had started to address the crowd. He spoke softly, and his words did not carry.

I was staring at Elizabeth. I knew why she was there. When Lerouex had finished humiliating himself, she was going to speak. I knew already what she would say.

I started forward again, but suddenly my arm was caught. It was Jase.

'What are you doing?' he said.

'That girl,' I said. 'I know her. She's from outside the city. We mustn't let her speak.'

People around us were telling us to be quiet. I struggled to release myself from Jase but he held me back.

Suddenly, there was a burst of applause, and I realised that Lerouex had finished.

I said to Jase: 'Look . . . you've got to help me. You don't know who that girl is!'

Out of the corner of my eye I saw Blayne coming towards us.

'Helward . . . have you seen who's here?'

'Blayne! For God's sake help me!'

I struggled again, and Jase fought to hold me. Blayne moved over quickly, took my other arm. Together they pulled me backwards, out of the crowd to the very edge of the city's metal base.

'Listen, Helward,' said Jase. 'Stay here and listen to her.'

'I know what she's going to say!'

'Then allow the others to hear.'

Victoria stepped forward to the edge of the platform.

'People of the city, we have one more person to speak to you. She is not known to many of us, because she is not of our city. But what she has to say is of great importance, and afterwards there will no longer be any doubt in your minds as to what we must do.'

She raised her hand, and Elizabeth stepped forward.

Elizabeth spoke softly, but her voice carried clearly to all present.

'I am a stranger to you here,' she said, 'because I was not born as you were within the walls of the city. However, you and I are of one kind: we are human, and we are of a planet called Earth. You have survived in this city for nearly two hundred years, or seven thousand miles by your way of measuring time. About you has been a world in anarchy and ruins. The people are ignorant, uneducated, stricken with poverty. But not all people of this world are in this state. I am from England, a country where we are beginning to reconstruct a kind of civilisation. There are other countries too, bigger and more powerful than England. So your stable and organised existence is not unique.'

She paused, testing the reaction of the crowd so far. There was silence.

'I came across your city by accident, and lived here for a while within your transference section.' There was some surprised reaction to this. 'I have talked with some of you, I know how you live. Then I left the city, and returned to England. I've spent nearly six months there, trying to understand your city and its history. I know much more now than I did on my first visit.'

She paused again. Somewhere in the crowd a man shouted: 'England is on Earth!'

Elizabeth did not respond. Instead she said: 'I have a question. Is there anyone here responsible for the city's engines?'

There was a short silence, then Jase said: 'I am a Traction guildsman.'

Heads turned in our direction.

'Then you can tell us what powers the engines.'

'A nuclear reactor.'

'Describe how the fuel is inserted.'

Jase released me and moved to one side. I felt Blayne's hold on me loosen, and I could have escaped him. But like everyone else listening, my attention had been caught by the curious questions.

Jase said: 'I don't know. I have never seen it done.'

'Then before you can stop your city, you must find out.'

Elizabeth moved back, and spoke quietly to Victoria. A moment later she came forward again.

'Your reactor is no such thing. Unwittingly, the men you call your Traction guildsmen have been misleading you. The reactor is not functioning, and has not done so for thousands of miles.'

Blayne said to Jase: 'Well?'

'She's talking nonsense.'

'*Do* you know what fuels it?'

'No,' said Jase quietly, although many of the people around us were listening. 'Our guild believes that it will run indefinitely without attention.'

'Your reactor is no such thing,' Elizabeth said again.

I said: 'Don't listen to her. The fact that we have electrical power means the reactor is working. Where else do we get the power?'

From the platform, Elizabeth said: 'Listen to me.'

Elizabeth said she was going to tell us about Destaine. I listened with the others.

Francis Destaine was a particle physicist who lived and worked in Britain, on Earth planet. He lived at a time when Earth was running critically short of electrical energy. Elizabeth recited the reasons, which were essentially that fossil fuels were burnt to provide heat, which was converted into energy. When the fuel deposits ran out there would be no more energy.

Destaine, Elizabeth said, claimed to have devised a process whereby apparently unlimited amounts of energy could be produced without any kind of fuel. His work had been discredited by most scientists. In due course the energy that was derived from fossil fuels had run out, and there followed on Earth planet a long period now known as the Crash. It has brought to an end the advanced technological civilisation that had dominated Earth.

She said that the people on Earth were now beginning to rebuild, and Destaine's work was instrumental in this. His process as originally outlined was crude and dangerous, but a more sophisticated development was manageable and successful.

'What has this to do with halting the city?' someone shouted.

Elizabeth said: 'Listen.'

Destaine had discovered a generator which created an artificial field of energy which, when existing in close proximity to another similar field, caused a flow of electricity. His discreditors based their criticisms on the fact that this had no practical use as the two generators consumed more electricity than they produced.

Destaine was unable to obtain either financial or intellectual support for his work. Even when he claimed to have discovered a natural field – a translateration window, as he called it – and could thus produce his effect without the need of a second generator, he was still ignored.

He claimed that this natural window of potential energy was moving slowly across the surface of the Earth, following a line which Elizabeth described as the great circle.

Destaine eventually managed to raise money from private sponsors, had a mobile research station built, and with a large team of hired assistants set off for the Kuantung province of southern China where, he claimed, the natural translateration window existed.

Elizabeth said: 'Destaine was never heard from again.'

Elizabeth said that we were on Earth planet, that we had never left Earth.

She said that the world on which we existed was Earth planet, that our perception of it was distorted by the translateration generator which, self-powering as long as it was running, continued to produce the field about us.

She said that Destaine had ignored the side-effects that other scientists had warned him of: that it could permanently affect perception, that it could have genetic and hereditary effects.

She said that the translateration window still existed on Earth, that many others had been found.

She said that the window Destaine had discovered in China was the one our own generator was still tapping.

That following the great circle it had travelled through Asia, through Europe.

That we were now at the edge of Europe and that before us lay an ocean several thousand miles wide.

She said . . . and the people listened. . . .

Elizabeth finished speaking. Jase walked slowly through the crowd towards her.

I headed back towards the entrance to the rest of the city. I passed within a few feet of the platform, and Elizabeth noticed me.

She called out: 'Helward!'

I took no notice, pushed on through the crowd and into the interior of the city. I went down a flight of steps, walked through the passageway beneath the city and out again into the daylight.

I headed north, moving between the tracks and cables.

4

Half an hour later I heard the sound of a horse, and I turned. Elizabeth caught up with me.

'Where are you going?' she said.

'Back to the bridge.'

'Don't. There's no need. The Traction guild have disconnected the generator.'

I pointed up at the sun. 'And that is now a sphere.'

'Yes.'

I walked on.

Elizabeth repeated what she had said before. She pleaded with me to see reason. She said again and again that it was only my perception of the world that was distorted.

I kept my silence.

She had not been down past. She had never been farther away from the city than a few miles north or south. She hadn't been with me when I saw the realities of this world.

Was it perception that changed the physical dimensions of Lucia, Rosario, and Caterina? Our bodies had been locked in sexual embrace: I knew the real effects of that perception. Was it the baby's perception that had made it reject Rosario's milk? Was it only my perception that caused the girls' city-made clothes to tear as their bodies distorted inside them?

'Why didn't you tell me what you've just said when you were in the city before?' I said.

'Because I didn't know then. I had to go back to England. And you know something? No one cared in England. I tried to find someone, anyone, who could be made to find some concern for you and your city . . . but no one was interested. There's a lot going on in this world, big and exciting changes are taking place. No one cares about the city and its people.'

'You came back,' I said.

'I had seen your city myself. I knew what you and the others were planning to do. I had to find out about Destaine . . . someone had to explain translateration to me. It's a dull, everyday technology now, but I didn't know how it worked.'

'That's self-evident,' I said.

'What do you mean?'

'If the generator's off, as you say, then there's no further problem. I just have to keep looking at the sun and telling myself that it's a sphere, whatever else it might look like.'

'But it's only your perception,' she said.

'And I perceive that you are wrong. I know what I see.'

'But you don't.'

A few minutes later a large crowd of men passed us, heading south towards the city. Most of them were carrying the possessions they had taken with them to the bridge site. None of them acknowledged us.

I walked faster, trying to leave her behind. She followed, leading her horse by its harness.

The bridge site was deserted. I walked down the river-bank to the soft, yellow soil and walked out along the surface of the bridge. Beneath me the water was calm and clear, although waves still broke on the bank behind me.

I turned and looked back. Elizabeth was standing on the bank with her horse, watching me. I stared at her for a few seconds, then reached down and took off my boots. I moved away from her, to the very end of the bridge.

I looked over at the sun. It was dipping down towards the north-eastern horizon. It was beautiful in its own way. A graceful, enigmatic shape, far more aesthetically satisfying than a simple sphere. My only regret was that I had never been able to draw it successfully.

I dived from the bridge head first. The water was cold, but not unpleasantly so. As soon as I surfaced an incoming wave pushed me back against the nearest bridge pile, and I kicked myself away from it. With strong, steady strokes I swam northwards.

I was curious to know if Elizabeth was still watching, so I turned on my back and floated. She had moved away from the ridge and was now riding her horse slowly along the uneven surface of the bridge. When she reached the end she stopped.

She sat in the saddle and looked in my direction.

I continued to tread water, waiting to see if she would make any gesture towards me. The sun was bathing her in a rich yellow light, stark against the deep blue of the sky behind her.

I turned, and looked towards the north. The sun was setting, and already most of its broad disk was out of sight. I waited until its northern spire of light had slipped down below the horizon. As darkness fell I swam back through the surf to the beach.

FUGUE FOR A
DARKENING ISLAND

to friends

I have white skin. Light brown hair. Blue eyes. I am tall: five feet, eleven inches. My mode of dress tends to the conservative: sports jackets, corduroy trousers, knitted ties. I wear spectacles for reading, though they are more an affectation than a necessity. I smoke cigarettes to a moderate amount. Sometimes I drink alcohol. I do not believe in God; I do not go to church; I do not have any objections to other people doing so. When I married my wife, I was in love with her. I am very fond of my daughter Sally. I have no political ambitions. My name is Alan Whitman.

* * *

My skin is smudged with dirt. My hair is dry, salt-encrusted and itchy. I have blue eyes. I am tall: five feet, eleven inches. I am wearing now what I was wearing six months ago, and I smell abominably. I have lost my spectacles, and learned to live without them. I do not smoke at all most of the time, though when cigarettes are available I smoke them continually. I am able to get drunk about once a month. I do not believe in God; I do not go to church. When I last saw my wife, I was cursing her, though I have learned to regret it. I am very fond of my daughter Sally. I do not think I have political ambitions. My name is Alan Whitman.

* * *

I met Lateef in a village ruined by an artillery bombardment. I disliked him the moment I saw him, and it was evidently reciprocated. After the first moments of caution, we ignored each other. I was looking for food in the village, knowing that as the bombardment had finished only recently it would not yet be in a totally plundered state. There were several houses still intact and I ignored these, knowing from experience that the ground-troops habitually ransacked these first. It was more fruitful to

5

sift through the rubble of partially destroyed buildings.

Working methodically, I had filled two haversacks with canned food by midday, and had stolen for future barter three road-maps from abandoned cars. I did not see the other man again during the morning.

On the outskirts of the village I found a field which had evidently been cultivated at one time. In one corner I discovered a row of freshly-dug graves, each marked with a simple piece of wood upon which were stapled metal dog-tags bearing the name of the soldier. I looked at each of the names, and deduced that they were African troops.

As that part of the field was the most secluded I sat down near the graves, and opened one of the cans. The food was odious: half-cooked and greasy. I ate it hungrily.

Afterwards, I walked out to the wreck of the helicopter that had crashed near by. It was not likely to contain food, though if any instruments were recoverable they would be suitable for future exchanges. I needed a compass most of all, though it was not likely that the helicopter would have carried one that would be either easily detachable or portable. When I reached the wreck I saw that the man I had seen earlier was inside the smashed cockpit, working at the dashboard with a long-bladed knife in an attempt to remove an altimeter. When he became aware of my presence he straightened slowly, his hand moving towards a pocket. He turned to face me, and for several minutes we regarded each other carefully, each seeing in the other a man who responded to a situation in the same way as himself.

*   *   *

We decided we would have to abandon our house in Southgate the day the barricade was erected at the end of our road. The decision was not implemented at once; for several days we thought we would be able to adjust to the new mode of life.

I do not know who took the decision to erect the barricade. As we lived at the far end of the road, near to the edge of the playing-fields, we did not hear the noises in the night, but when Isobel took the car down the road to take Sally to school she returned almost at once with the news.

It was the first concrete sign in our lives that irrevocable change was taking place in the country. Ours was not the first of such barricades, but there were few others in our particular neighbourhood.

6

When Isobel told me about it I walked down to see it for myself. It did not appear to be very strongly constructed—made mostly of wooden supports and barbed-wire loops—but its symbolism was unmistakable. There were a few men standing around, and I nodded cautiously to them.

The following day, we were at home when the noise of the eviction of the Martins disturbed us. The Martins lived almost opposite us. We had not had much to do with them, and since the Afrim landings had allowed them to keep to themselves. Vincent Martin worked as a research technician at an aircraft-components factory in Hatfield. His wife stayed at home, looking after their three children. They were West Indians.

At the time of their eviction I had nothing to do with the Street Patrol which was responsible for it. Within a week, though, all men in the street had been enrolled, and every member of their families was given a pass-ticket which had to be carried at all times as identification. We saw the pass-tickets as potentially the most valuable possessions we had, as by this time we were no longer blind to the developments around us.

Cars were allowed in and out of the street only at certain times, and the barricade-patrols enforced this rule with absolute inflexibility. As the street opened on to a main road which government regulations kept clear of all parked traffic after six in the evening, it meant that if you arrived home after the barricade had closed, you were required to find somewhere else to park the car. As most streets quickly followed our example and closed their entrances, the effect of this was that you were obliged to leave your car at some considerable distance from home, and walking the rest of the way at such a time was hazardous in the extreme.

The normal strength of a street patrol was two men, though on a few occasions this was doubled, and on the night before we finally decided to leave there were fourteen men. I was part of a patrol three times; sharing the duty with a different man each time. Our function was simple. While one man stayed at the barricade with the shotgun, the other walked up and down the street four times. The positions were then reversed, and so on through the night.

While I was at the barricade, I was always most frightened of a police-car coming along. Although I did see their cars on many occasions, none of them ever stopped. During meetings of the Patrol committee, the question of what to do in such an event was often raised, but no satisfactory answer, at least to my mind, was ever given.

In practice, we and the police would leave each other alone, though one did hear stories of battles between the occupants of barricaded streets and riot-shielded police. No news of these ever appeared in the newspapers or on television, and the absence was more noticeable than the news itself would have been.

The true purpose of the shotgun was to deter illegal squatters from attempting to enter our street, and secondarily to show as a form of protest that if the government and the armed forces were unable or unwilling to protect our homes then we would take the matter into our own hands. Such was the essence of what was printed on the backs of our pass-tickets, and was the unspoken creed of the men on the street patrol.

For my own part, I was uneasy. The burnt-out shell of the Martins' house opposite ours was a constant reminder of the violence inherent in the patrols, and the never-ending parade of homeless shambling through the night past the barricades was disturbing in the extreme.

The night the barricade on the next street fell, I was asleep. I had heard that the patrol was to be enlarged, but it was not my turn of duty.

Our first awareness of the fighting was the firing of a shot near by; while Isobel took Sally downstairs to shelter in the space beneath the staircase, I dressed hurriedly and went to join the patrol at the barricade. Here, the men of the street stared sullenly at the army lorries and police vans parked across the main road. About thirty armed soldiers faced us, evidently nervous and trigger-happy.

Three water-cannons rumbled past, and disappeared through the jumble of parked vehicles towards the next street. From time to time we heard more shots, and the sound of voices raised angrily. Ocasionally, the explosions were deeper and more powerful, and slowly a red glow brightened near by. More army lorries and police vans arrived, and the men inside ran towards the street. We at our barricade said nothing, only too aware of the flagrant provocation and absolute inadequacy that our solitary shotgun represented. It was kept fully loaded, but out of sight. At that time, I would not have liked to be the man in possession of it.

We waited at the barricade all night, listening to the sounds of the battle only fifty yards away. As dawn came, the noise gradually lessened. We saw the bodies of several soldiers and

8

policemen carried away, and many more wounded driven off in ambulances.

As the full light of day came, nearly two hundred white people, some dressed in only their nightclothes, were escorted by the police towards a fleet of ambulances and lorries a mile away. As they passed our barricade, some of them tried to argue with us, but were herded on by the soldiers. While they passed, I looked at the men on our side of the barricade and wondered whether the hard lack of expression was also on my own face.

We waited for the activity outside to die down, but the sound of gunfire continued spasmodically for many hours. We saw no normal traffic on the road, and assumed that it had of necessity been diverted. One of the men at our barricade was carrying a transistor radio, and we listened anxiously to each of the BBC's news-bulletins hoping to hear some word of reassurance.

By ten o'clock it was apparent that events had levelled off. Most of the police vehicles had driven away, but the army was still around us. About once every five minutes there was a gun-shot. A few houses in the next street were still burning, but there was no sign of the fires spreading.

As soon as I could manage it I slipped away from the barricade, and walked back to my house.

I found Isobel and Sally still sheltering under the stairs. Isobel had withdrawn almost entirely; she had lost all her colour, the pupils of her eyes were dilated and she slurred her speech when she spoke. Sally was no better. Their story was a garbled and incomplete recounting of a series of events they had experienced at second-hand: explosions, shouting voices, gunfire and the spreading crackle of burning wood . . . all heard as they lay in the dark. While I made them some tea and warmed up some food, I inspected the damage to the house.

A petrol-bomb had exploded in the garden, setting fire to our shed. All the windows at the back had been broken, and lodged in the walls I found several bullets. Even as I stood in the back room a bullet flew through the window and missed me by a few inches.

I crawled on my hands and knees to the window, and peered through.

Our house normally commanded a view across the intervening gardens to the houses in the next street. As I knelt there, I saw that of them only about a half were still intact. Through the windows of some of these I could see several people moving. One man, a short Negro in filthy clothes, stood in the garden sheltering behind a part of a fence. It was he who had fired his gun at me. As I watched he fired again, this time at the house next to mine.

When Isobel and Sally had dressed, we took the three suit-cases we had packed the previous week and I put them in the car. When Isobel went through the house and systematically locked all interconnecting doors and cupboards, I collected our cash.

Shortly afterwards, we drove down to the barricade. Here we were stopped by the other men.

'Where do you think you're going, Whitman?' one of them asked me. It was Johnson, one of the men with whom I had shared a patrol three nights before.

'We're leaving,' I said. 'We're going to Isobel's parents.'

Johnson reached in through the open window, turned off the ignition before I could stop him, and took the key.

'Sorry,' he said. 'No one leaves. If we all ran out, the niggers'd be in like a flash.'

Several of the men had crowded round. By my side, I felt Isobel tense. Sally was in the back. I didn't care to think how this may be affecting her.

'We can't stay here. Our house overlooks those others. It's only a matter of time before they come through the gardens.'

I saw several of the men glance at one another.

Johnson, whose house wasn't on the same side as ours, said stubbornly: 'We've got to stick together. It's our only hope.'

Isobel leaned over me and looked up at Johnson imploringly.

'Please,' she said. 'Have you thought of us? What about your own wife? Does she want to stay?'

'It's only a matter of time,' I said again. 'You've seen the pattern in other places. Once the Afrims have got a street to themselves, they spread through the rest of the district in a few nights.'

'But we've got the law on our side,' one of the other men said, nodding his head in the direction of the soldiers outside the barricade.

'They're not on anyone's side. You might as well pull down the barricade. It's useless now.'

Johnson moved away from the car-window and went to speak to one of the other men. It was Nicholson, one of the leaders of the patrol committee. After a few seconds, Nicholson himself came over.

'You're not leaving,' he said finally. 'No one's leaving. Get the car away from here and come back on barricade duty. It's all we can do.'

He tossed the ignition-key in, and it fell on Isobel's lap. She picked it up. I wound the window-handle and closed the window tightly.

As I started the engine, I said to Isobel: 'Do you want to chance it?'

She looked at the men in front of us, and at the barbed-wire barricade, and at the armed soldiers beyond it. She said nothing.

Behind us, Sally was crying. 'I want to go home, Daddy,' she said.

I turned the car round and drove back slowly to our house. As we passed one of the other houses on the same side of the street as our own, we heard the sound of a woman screaming inside. I glanced at Isobel, and saw her close her eyes.

I stopped the car by the house. It looked strangely normal. We sat in the car and made no move to get out. I left the engine running. To turn it off would have been too final.

After a while I put the car into forward gear and drove down to the end of the street, towards the recreation-field. When the barricade had been erected at the main-road end, only two strands of wire had been put across here, and it was normally unmanned. So it was now. There was no one around; like the rest of the street it was at once unnervingly normal and abnormal. I stopped the car, jumped out and pulled down the wire. Beyond it was a wooden fence, held in place by a row of stakes. I tried it with my hands, and found that it was firm but not immovable.

I drove the car over the wire and stopped with the bumper-bar touching the wooden fence. In first gear I pushed the fence, until it snapped and fell. In front of us the recreation-field was deserted. I drove across it, feeling the car lurch in and out of the ruts of the previous year's sport.

*　*　*

I pulled myself out of the water and lay gasping for breath on the bank of the river. The physical shock of the cold water had exhausted me. Every part of my body ached and throbbed. I lay still.

Five minutes later I stood up, then looked back across the water to where Isobel and Sally were waiting for me. I walked upstream, carrying the end of the rope I had towed behind me, until I was directly opposite them. Isobel was sitting on the soil of the bank, not watching me but staring blankly downstream. By her side, Sally stood attentively.

I shouted instructions to them across the water. I saw Sally saying something to Isobel, and Isobel shaking her head. I stood impatiently, feeling my muscles shivering into the beginnings of cramp. I shouted again and Isobel stood up. Sally and she tied the end of the rope around their waists and across their chests in the manner I had shown them, then walked nervously to the edge of the water. In my impatience I may have pulled the rope too hard. In any event, just as they had reached the edge of the water they fell forward and began floundering in the shallows. Isobel could not swim and was afraid of drowning. I could see Sally struggling with her, trying to prevent her mother from crawling back on to the bank.

Taking the initiative from both of them, I pulled the rope, towing them out into the centre of the river. Whenever Isobel's face came above the surface, she shouted and screamed in a mixture of fear and anger.

In just under a minute I had them on my side. Sally lay on the muddy bank, staring at me wordlessly. I wanted her to criticise me for what I had done, but she said nothing. Isobel lay on her side, doubled over. She retched up water for several minutes, then swore at me. I ignored her.

Although the river was cold from the hills, the air was warm. We took stock of our possession. Nothing had been lost in the crossing, but everything we carried had become soaked. It had been part of the original plan that Isobel should hold our main haversack up out of the water, while Sally supported her. Now, all our clothes and food were wet, and our matches for lighting a fire were unusable. We decided it would be best if we removed all our clothes, and hung them in the bushes and trees in the hope that they would be wearably dry by morning.

We lay together on the ground, shivering miserably, and cuddling each other for warmth. Within half an hour Isobel was asleep, but Sally lay in my arms with her eyes open.

We each knew the other was awake and stayed so for most of the night.

*   *   *

I was to spend the night with a woman named Louise. She had taken a room for the purpose in an hotel in Goodge Street, and as I had told Isobel that I was taking part in an all-night demonstration at the college I was able to get away from home for a whole night.

Louise and I dined at a small Greek restaurant in Charlotte Street, then, not wishing to spend the entire evening in her hotel room, we went to a cinema in Tottenham Court Road. I do not recall the title of the film. All I can remember is that it was foreign, that its dialogue was sub-titled in English and that it concerned a violently-resolved love-affair between a coloured man and a white woman. The film contained several scenes of complete sexual frankness, and although it had not been banned, few cinemas were willing to show films which depicted the various forms of the sex act in detail because of several instances of police action. However, at the time we saw the film it had been showing unmolested for more than a year.

Louise and I had bought seats at the rear of the cinema, and when the police came in by way of the entrances along each side, we were able to see the precision with which it was done, indicating that the raid had been planned carefully. One policeman stood at each door and the others moved in a loose cordon around the audience.

For a minute or two there seemed to be no further action, and we continued to watch the film until the house-lights went up. The film still showed and went on doing so for several more minutes. Finally it stopped abruptly.

We sat in the auditorium for twenty minutes without knowing what was happening. One of the policemen forming part of the cordon was near me and I asked him what was going on. He made no answer.

We were ordered to leave the auditorium row by row and to divulge our names and addresses. By a stroke of good fortune I did not have with me any form of self-identification, and was thus unable to prove who I was. Under the circumstances I gave the police a false name and address, and although my pockets were searched in an attempt to find authentication for my story, I was allowed to go free after Louise vouched for my identity.

We returned to her hotel immediately and went to bed. After the events of the evening I was rendered impotent, and in spite of Louise's best efforts we were unable to have intercourse.

John Tregarth's government had been in power for three months.

*   *   *

As adversaries we detested the Afrim troops. We continually heard rumours of their cowardice in battle; and of their arrogance in victory, however small or relative it may be.

One day we encountered a member of the Royal Nationalist Air Force who had been captured by an Afrim patrol. This man, who had been a pilot until crippled by the Africans' torture, told us of brutalities and atrocities in their military interrogation centres that made our own experience as civilians appear to be trivial and perfunctory. The pilot had lost one leg below the knee, and had suffered lacerated tendons in the other, and he counted himself as among the more fortunate. He asked us for assistance.

We were reluctant to become involved and Lateef called a meeting to decide what to do. In the end we voted to transport the crippled man to within a mile of the R.N.A.F. station, and to allow him to find his own way from there.

Shortly after this incident, we were rounded up by a large Afrim patrol and taken to one of their civilian interrogation centres.

We said nothing to them about the pilot, nor about their military methods in general. On this occasion we made no attempt to resist arrest. For my own part it was because I felt it might be connected in some way with the recent abduction of the women, but on the part of the group as a whole our lack of resistance was an outcome of the overall lethargy being experienced at the time.

We were taken to a large building on the outskirts of one of the Afrim-held towns, and in a large marquee in the grounds told to strip and pass through a delousing section. This was a part of the tent which had been partitioned off and filled with a dense steam. Coming out a few minutes later, we were told to dress again. Our clothes lay untouched where we had left them.

We were then divided into groups of one, two or three men. I was one of those on my own. We were taken to rooms inside the main building and interrogated briefly. My own interrogator was a tall West African, who, in spite of the central-heating system, wore a brown greatcoat. I had noticed on entering the room that the two uniformed guards in the corridor had been holding Russian rifles.

The interrogation was sketchy. Identification-papers, certificate of state and origin and Afrim-stamped photograph shown and checked.

'Your destination, Whitman?'

'Dorchester,' I said, giving him the answer we had agreed

14

upon in the event of arrest.

'You have relatives there?'

'Yes.' I gave him the name and address of fictitious parents.

'You have a family?'

'Yes.'

'But they are not with you.'

'No.'

'Who is the leader of your group?'

'We are self-directed.'

There was a long silence while he rescrutinised my papers. After this I was returned to the marquee where I waited with the others as the remainder of the interrogation-sessions were completed. Then two Afrims dressed as civilians went through our possessions. The search was superficial in the extreme, turning up only a fork for eating that one of the men had left near the top of his haversack. The two knives I had secreted in the lining of my own bag went undetected.

After this search there was another long period of waiting, until a lorry bearing a large red cross on a white background was driven up alongside the marquee. The agreed Red Cross hand-out to refugees had been established for some time as being five pounds of protein, but since the Afrims had been handling their own side of the arrangement, provisions had decreased steadily. I received two small cans of processed meat and a packet of forty cigarettes.

Later, we were driven away from the town in three lorries and dumped in the countryside seventeen miles from where we had been arrested. It took us the whole of the next day and part of the day after to find the cache of supplies we had made at the first warning that we were about to be arrested.

At no time during our involuntary visit to Afrim-occupied territory had we seen or heard any sign or hint of the women. That night, I lay awake despairing of seeing Sally and Isobel again.

*　　*　　*

It had been announced on the early news that the unidentified ship which had been sailing up the English Channel for the last two days had entered the Thames Estuary.

During the morning I followed the regular bulletins. The ship had neither answered nor made any radio signals since first being sighted. It was not flying any flag. A pilot cutter had gone out to it from Tilbury, but the men had not been able to board it. From the name on her bows, the ship had been identified as a medium-sized cargo tramp, registered in Liberia and according to Lloyd's was at present chartered to a shipping firm in Lagos.

It happened that from twelve-thirty I was free to leave the college, and not having any appointments or lectures in the afternoon I decided to go down to the river. I caught a bus to Cannon Street and walked out on to London Bridge. Several hundred other people, mainly workers from near-by offices, had had the same notion, and the east side of the bridge was crowded.

As time passed several people moved away, evidently in order to return to their offices, and as a result I was able to move forward to the parapet of the bridge.

At just after two-thirty we were able to make out the ship, coming upriver towards the Tower Bridge. We saw that there were several craft in attendance around it, and that many of them were launches of the river police. A wave of speculation passed through the crowd.

The ship approached the bridge, which kept its road down. A man standing near to me had a small pair of field-glasses, and he told us that the pedestrians on the bridge were being moved off, and the road was being closed to traffic. A few seconds later the bridge opened just in time for the ship to pass through.

I was aware of sirens near by. Turning, I saw that four or five police-cars had driven on to London Bridge. The men remained inside, but left the blue lights flashing on the roofs. The ship came on towards us.

We observed that several men on the small launches around the ship were speaking to those on board through loud-hailers. We could not make out what was said, but the sound came to us across the water in tinny resonances. It became unnaturally quiet on the bridge, as the police sealed off each end to traffic. A mounted policeman rode up and down telling us to leave the bridge. Only a few of us obeyed.

The ship was now less than fifty yards from us, and it was possible to see that its decks were crowded with people, many of whom were lying down. Two of the police-launches had reached London Bridge, and were turned towards the ship. From one of them, a policeman with a loud-hailer shouted to the captain of the ship to stop his engines and to submit to a boarding party.

There was no acknowledgement from the ship, which sailed on slowly towards the bridge, though many of the people on the decks of the ship were shouting back at the police, unable to make themselves understood.

The bows of the ship passed underneath an arch of the bridge about fifteen yards from where I stood. I looked down at it. The decks were crowded to the rails with people. I had no more time to observe their condition, because the superstructure amidships crashed into the parapet of the bridge. It was a slow, grinding collision, making an ugly scraping noise of metal on stone. I saw that the paintwork of the ship and its superstructure was filthy and rusty, with many panes of broken glass in the ports.

I looked down at the river and saw that the police-launches and two river-authority tugs had gone in against the hull of the old ship, and were trying to push her stern towards the concrete bank of the New Fresh Wharf. I saw from the black smoke still issuing from her funnel and from the white-cream froth at the stern, that the ship's engines were still running. As the tugs made headway in pushing her towards the bank the metal super-structure scraped and crashed repeatedly against the bridge.

I saw movement on the ship, on the decks and inside. The people on board were moving towards the stern. Many of them fell as they ran. As the stern rammed into the concrete quay the first men jumped ashore.

The ship was wedged firmly between the bank and the bridge, her bows still under the arch, her superstructure against the parapet and her stern overhanging the quay. A tug moved round to the bridge, to make sure that until the engines were stopped the ship wouldn't turn somehow and move back into the river. Four police-launches were now against her port side, and ropes and rope-ladders were thrown with grappling-irons on to the decks. The fleeing passengers made no efforts to remove them. When the first ladder was secured the police and customs officials began to climb it.

On the bridge, our interest was directed to the people leaving the ship: the Africans were coming ashore.

We watched them with a mixture of horror and fascination. There were men, women and children. Most if not all were in an advanced state of starvation. Skeletal arms and legs, dis-tended stomachs, skull-like heads holding staring eyes; flat, paper-like breasts on the women, accusing faces on them all. Most were naked or nearly so. Many of the children could not walk. Those whom no one would carry were left on the ship.

A metal door in the side of the ship was opened from within and a gangplank pushed across the strip of water to the quay. From below-decks more Africans came out on to the shore.

Some fell to the concrete as they stepped on the land, others moved towards the wharf-building and disappeared either into it or around its sides. None of them looked up at us on the bridge, or back at their fellows who were in the process of leaving the ship.

We waited and watched. There seemed to be no end to the number of people on board.

In time, the upper decks were cleared, though people still poured ashore from below. I tried to count the number of people lying, dead or unconscious, on the deck. When I had reached one hundred, I stopped counting.

The men who had gone aboard finally managed to stop the engines, and the ship was made fast to the quay. Many ambulances had arrived at the wharf, and those people suffering most were put inside and driven away.

But hundreds more just wandered from the wharf, away from the river, and up into the streets of the City, whose occupants knew nothing as yet of the events on the river.

I learned later that the police and the river authorities had found more than seven hundred corpses on the ship, most of them children. The welfare authorities accounted for another four and a half thousand survivors, who were taken to hospitals or emergency centres. There was no way of counting the remainder, though I heard once an estimate of three thousand people who had wandered away from the ship and tried to survive alone.

Shortly after the ship had been secured, we were moved off the bridge by the police, who told us that its structure was considered to be unsafe. The following day, however, it was open again to traffic.

The event I had witnessed became known in time as the first of the Afrim landings.

*　　*　　*

We were signalled down by a prowling police-car and questioned at some length as to our destination, and the circumstances surrounding our departure. Isobel tried to explain about the invasion of the next street and the imminent danger in which our home had been.

While we waited for permission to continue, Sally tried to soothe Isobel, who was taken by a flood of tears. I did not want to be affected by it. While being in full sympathy with her feelings, and realising that it is no small upset to be dispossessed in such a manner, I had experienced Isobel's lack of fortitude for the last few months. It had been understandably awkward while I was working at the cloth factory, but in comparison with some of my other former colleagues at the college, our situation was relatively settled. I had made every attempt to be sympathetic and patient with her, but had succeeded only in reviving old differences.

In a few moments the policeman returned to our car and informed us that we could proceed, on condition we headed for the U.N. camp at Horsenden Hill in Middlesex. Our original destination had been Isobel's parents, who now lived in Bristol.

The policeman told us that civilians were not advised to make long-distance journeys across country after dark. We had spent a large part of the afternoon cruising about the London suburbs in an attempt to find a garage that would sell us enough petrol to fill not only the tank of the car, but also the three five-gallon cans I carried in the boot, and consequently it was now beginning to get dark. All three of us were hungry.

I drove along the Western Avenue towards Alperton, after having made a wide detour through Kensington, Fulham and Hammersmith to avoid the barricaded Afrim enclaves at Notting Hill and North Kensington. The main road itself was clear of obstructions, though we saw that every side-road and one or two of the subsidiary main-roads that crossed it at intervals were barricaded and manned by armed civilians. At Hanger Lane we turned off the Western Avenue and up through Alperton, along the route we had been directed. At several points we saw parked police vehicles, several dozen uniformed police and many U.N. militiamen.

At the gates of the camp we were again detained and interrogated, but this was only to be expected. In particular, we were questioned closely about the reasons we had left our home, and what precautions had been made to protect it while we were away.

I told them that the street in which we lived had been barricaded, that we had closed and locked every door in the house, for which we had keys, and that troops and police were in the neighbourhood. While I spoke, one of the questioners wrote in a small notebook. We were obliged to give our full address and the names of the men at the barricades. We waited in the car while the information was relayed by telephone. In the end, we were told to park the car in a space just inside the gates and to take our belongings on foot to the main reception centre.

The buildings were farther from the gates than we had anticipated, and when we found them we were somewhat surprised to find that they consisted mainly of light prefabricated huts. On the front of one of them was a painted board, written in several different languages, and which was illuminated by a floodlight. It directed us to separate; men to go towards a hut known as D Central, and women and children to enter this one.

I said to Isobel: 'We'll see each other later, I suppose.'

She leaned over and kissed me lightly. I kissed Sally. They went into the hut, leaving me on my own with the suitcase.

I followed the directions and found D Central. Inside, I was told to surrender the suitcase for search, and to take off my clothes. These I did, and my clothes and suitcase were taken away together. I was then instructed to pass through a shower of hot water and to scrub myself clean. Understanding that this was to minimize health risks I complied, even though I had bathed only the night before.

When I came out, I was given a towel and some rough clothing. I asked if I could have my own clothes back. This was refused, but I was told that I could have my night-clothes later.

When I had dressed, I was ushered into a plain hall which was full of men. The ratio of whites to blacks was about one to one. I tried not to show my surprise.

The men were sitting at several benches, eating, smoking and talking. I was instructed to take a bowl of food from the serving-hatch, and although this did not satisfy my hunger, I was told I might have more if I requested it. At the same time, I learned that cigarettes could be obtained at the hatch, and I collected a packet of twenty.

I was wondering about Isobel and Sally, and assumed that they were receiving similar treatment somewhere else. I could only hope that we would be reunited before going to bed.

While I was consuming the second bowl of food, I noticed that several more men came into the hall from time to time and that they were given the same treatment irrespective of race. At my own table there were more Negroes than whites, and although I felt uncomfortable at first, I rationalised that being in the same position as myself, they represented no threat to me.

Two hours later we were ushered to other huts near by, where we were to sleep on narrow beds equipped with only one blanket, and without a pillow. I did not see Isobel and Sally.

In the morning I was allowed an hour with them.

They told me how badly they were treated in the women's

quarters, and that they had not been able to sleep. While discussing this, we heard a report that the government had reached a negotiated settlement with the leaders of the militant Afrims and that everything would be back to normal in a matter of days.

It was this that made us decide to return home, arguing that if our house was still in danger we would return to the refugee camp that night.

After a great deal of difficulty, we contacted a U.N. official in the camp and told him we wished to leave. For some reason he was reluctant to agree to this, saying that far too many people were wanting to leave, and that it would not be wise until the situation had stabilised. We told him that we considered our home to be safe, and he warned us that the camp was nearly full, and that if we left now he would not be able to guarantee us a place should we return.

In spite of this, we left the camp after retrieving our clothes and our car. Although our suitcases had obviously been searched, none of our belongings was missing.

* * *

At the time of the second Afrim landing I was in a small spa town in the north of England, attending a symposium of academics. I remember little of the proceedings. I can recall, though, that the event was well organised and that the formal programme was adhered to rigidly.

On two consecutive occasions I happened to share my lunch-table with a young woman from Norwich, and in time we became friendly. During the second of our lunches together I was spoken to by an acquaintance from my days at the university. We exchanged greetings and he joined us at the table. I did not wish to see him, but I was polite to him. Shortly after this the young woman left us.

I found my thoughts turning to her during the afternoon, and though I made several attempts to find her I was unsuccessful. She did not appear for dinner and I assumed she had left the conference early.

I spent the evening in the company of my university friend, exchanging reminiscences of our student activities there.

That night, as I was undressing in my hotel room, there was a knock at my door. It was the young woman. She came in and we shared the remainder of a half-bottle of Scotch I had. Our conversation was of little consequence. She told me her name, though I have since forgotten it. We seemed to make intellectual contact, even as our subject-matter was trivial. It was as if the ponderous content of the day's formal proceedings had exhausted us both of the capacity for thought, though not of the ability to establish a rapport.

Later, we made love together on my bed, and she stayed in my room for the rest of the night.

The following day was the last one of the conference, and apart from a small ceremony in the main hall there were to be no formal events. The young woman and I shared a table for breakfast, aware that this was probably the last time we would spend together. It was during breakfast that the news came through of the second Afrim landing, and we spoke for several minutes about the significance of this.

*　　*　　*

Following a confused discussion with Lateef, I found myself working alone in a small town on the south-coast. It had been clear to me that Lateef had not formed any plan, and that my present mission was as ill-defined as his instructions had been. As far as I knew he wanted to have some kind of defensive weapons against future attacks, and we who had been sent foraging were to attempt to provide some.

I had little or no idea where to start, or what would constitute an effective defence.

I felt uneasy because the town was within Afrim-held territory, and although I was not impeded in any way I felt my movements were being observed.

All shops had been looted. The main parade was a desolate line of ruined stores, their racks emptied by repeated pillagings, but in one store I discovered a domestic-sized glass-cutting instrument, and pocketed it in lieu of there being anything else of worth.

I moved on down to the shore.

There was a large group of white refugees here, living in a crude encampment of old beach-huts and tents. Though I approached them, they shouted at me to go away. I walked along what had once been the beach promenade in a westerly direction until out of their sight.

I encountered a long row of bungalows which, judging by their affluent appearance, at one time would have been occupied by the wealthy retired. I wondered if the Africans had any plans

22

to use them and why the refugees I had seen were not camping there. Most of the bungalows were unlocked and there appeared to be nothing to prevent entry. I walked along the row, glancing into them all. There was no food to be had from any of them, nor anything that could be conceivably used as a weapon. Though most of them were still furnished, removable commodities, such as sheets and blankets, had been taken.

About two-thirds of the way along the line I encountered a bungalow that was empty of all furniture. Its doors were locked securely.

Intrigued, I broke in through a window, and searched it. In one of the back rooms I noticed that some of the floorboards had been removed and replaced. I levered them up with my knife.

In the space below there was a large crate full of empty bottles. Someone had gouged a diagonal line across each of them with a file, thus weakening them. Near by was a neatly folded pile of linen, torn into squares about fifteen inches across. In another room, also under the floorboards, I discovered ten five-gallon drums of petrol.

I considered the use of petrol-bombs to us and whether it would be worth telling Lateef of their presence. It was obviously impossible for me to move them single-handed, and it would be necessary for several men to come here to take them.

In the time I had been with Lateef and the other refugees, there had been some considerable discussion concerning the kinds of weapons which would be of use to us. Rifles and guns were obviously the prime necessity, but they were at a premium. It was unlikely we would ever obtain them except by stealing. Then there was the problem of ammunition. We all carried knives, though they were of assorted qualities. My own had formerly been a carving-knife, which I had honed down to a usable size and sharpness.

The kind of use to which a petrol-bomb is best put is as an anti-personnel device in enclosed spaces. Operating as we were in the countryside, we would have little use for incendiaries.

In the end I returned the bottles, linen and petrol to their hiding-places, reasoning that if Lateef disagreed with me, we could always return for them.

The lavatory was in working condition and I used it. Afterwards I noticed that a bathroom cabinet on the wall still had its mirror intact, and this gave me an idea. I prised it away and, using the glass-cutter, I sliced it up into long triangular strips.

I managed to cut seven such strips from the thick glass. I fashioned the ends to as sharp a tine as possible, twice drawing my blood in the process. With a chamois leather I took from my bag I made handles for the daggers, wrapping it in strips around the thicker ends.

I tried out one of the new daggers, swinging it experimentally in the air. It made a lethal but difficult weapon. I would have to devise some method by which the daggers could be carried conveniently so that their users would not be endangered by them if they fell. I packed the seven new daggers into a heap, and prepared to roll them up into a piece of sacking so that I might carry them back to the others. As I did so, I noticed that one of the shards had a minute fault in the glass, near the handle. I saw that it might shatter easily, perhaps lacerating the hand of whoever used it. I discarded it.

I was ready to return to Lateef and the others. Night was falling, so I waited for the dark to come. The twilight was shorter than normal, because of the atmospheric murk and low clouds. When I felt it would be safe to move, I collected my possessions and started back towards the encampment.

The time I had spent by the shore had had a strangely soothing effect on me, and I felt it might be good future policy to spend more time there. I resolved to suggest it to Lateef.

*   *   *

I was hiding at the top of a barn because my elder brother had told me that the bogey would get me. I was about seven years old. Had I been older I would have been able to rationalise the fears that took me. They were formless, but for the clear image of some monstrous being with black skin that was out to get me.

Instead, I cowered at the top of the barn, lying in my own private hidey-hole which no one knew was there. Where the farmer had stacked the bales of straw, a small cavity had been left between three of them and the roof.

The comforting subjective security of the hide-out restored my confidence, and some time later my fears had receded and I was involved in a juvenile fantasy involving airplanes and guns. When I heard rustling in the straw below, my first panicky thoughts were of the bogey, and I lay in a state of frozen terror while the rustling continued. Finally, I summoned courage to creep as silently as possible to the edge of my hide-out and peer downwards.

In the loose straw on the ground, at the back of the bales, a young man and a girl were lying with their arms around one another. The man was on top of the girl and the girl had her eyes closed. I did not know what they were doing. After a few minutes, the young man moved slightly and helped the girl to take off her clothes. It seemed to me that she did not really want him to take them off, but she resisted only a little. They lay down again and within a very short period of time she helped him remove his own clothes. Not wishing to change my position, I lay very still and quiet. When they were both naked he lay on top of her again and they began to make noises with their throats. The girl's eyes were still closed, though the lids fluttered from time to time. I can recall very little of my impressions during this; I know I was curious to see a girl who could open her legs so wide – all the women with whom I had come into contact (my mother and my aunts) had seemed incapable of opening their knees more than a few inches. After a few more minutes the couple stopped moving around and lay together in silence. It was only then that the girl's eyes opened properly and looked up at me.

Many years later my elder brother was among the first British National soldiers to be killed in action against the Afrims.

*　　*　　*

The words of the official at the U.N. camp came to mind as I drove along the North Circular Road. The radio had confirmed that an amnesty had been offered by Tregarth's emergency cabinet, but had implied also that the leaders of the Afrims were not responding in a wholly favourable way.

One possibility was that they did not trust Tregarth. On several occasions in the past he had initiated social reforms that had acted against the Afrims, and there was no reason that now they had an upper hand in a military sense Tregarth would compromise with them in a way prejudicial to his own administration. With a rift established in the armed forces, and another threatened within the police forces, any policy of appeasement which was at all suspect would not work.

It was estimated that already more than 25 per cent of the army had seceded, and had placed itself at the disposal of the Afrim leaders in Yorkshire, and three ground-attack squadrons of the Royal Air Force had so far similarly changed allegiances.

In a later programme we heard a group of political pundits speculating that public opinion in favour of the Afrims was diminishing, and that Tregarth and his cabinet would take more militant action.

The only outward sign of the events taking place that we could discern was that traffic was unusually light. We were stopped several times by police patrols, but we had grown accustomed to this in the last few months and thought little of it. We had learned the appropriate responses to make to questioning, and maintained a consistent story.

I was disturbed to notice that many of the police we encountered were from the civilian-reserve special force. Stories describing various atrocities had been circulating continuously; in particular, one heard of coloured people being arrested without warrant, and released only after experiences of personal violence. On the other hand, white people were subjected to harassment if known or suspected to be involved with anti-Afrim activities. The entire situation regarding the police was confused and inconsistent at this time, and I for one felt that it would not be an entirely bad thing if the force were to divide formally.

Just to the west of Finchley, I was obliged to stop the car and refill the tank with petrol. I had intended to use some of the petrol I had put by as a reserve, but discovered that during the night two of the cans had been emptied. Consequently, I was forced to use up the whole of my reserve. I said nothing of this to Isobel or Sally, as I anticipated being able to restock sooner or later, even though none of the garages we had passed that day was open.

While I was pouring the petrol into the tank a man came out of a near-by building carrying a pistol and accused me of being an Afrim sympathiser. I asked him on what evidence he formed this suspicion, and he told me that no one could be driving a car at this time without the support of one political faction or another.

At the next police road-block I reported this incident and was told to ignore it.

As we approached our house all three of us reflected by our behaviour the apprehensions we felt. Sally became restless and asked to go to the toilet. Isobel smoked one cigarette after another and snapped irritably at me. I found myself continually pushing up the speed of the car unconsciously, although I knew that it was generally better to stay at lower speeds.

To relieve the tension between us, I responded to Sally's requests by stopping the car at a public lavatory about a mile and a half from where we lived, and while Isobel took her inside

26

I took the opportunity to turn on the car radio and listen to a news bulletin.

Isobel said, when they had got back into the car: 'What shall we do if we can't get into the street?'

She had voiced the fear none of us had liked to express.

'I'm sure Nicholson will listen to reason,' I said.

'And if he doesn't?'

I didn't know. I said: 'I just listened to the radio. They said that the Afrims were accepting the terms of the amnesty, but that occupation of empty houses was continuing.'

'What do they mean by empty?'

'I don't like to think.'

Behind us, Sally said: 'Daddy, are we nearly home?'

'Yes, dear,' Isobel said.

I started the engine and moved off. We reached the end of our street a few minutes later. The police and army trucks had moved off, but the barbed-wire barricade was still there. On the other side of the road, mounted on the top of a dark-blue van, was a television camera operated by two men. It was protected in front and at the sides by heavy plates of glass.

I stopped the car five yards from the barricade, but left the engine running. No one appeared to be near the barricade. I blew the horn and regretted the action an instant later. Five men appeared from the house nearest to the barricade and walked towards us carrying rifles. They were Afrims.

'Oh God,' I said under my breath.

'Alan, go and talk to them. Perhaps our house is not being used by them!'

There was an edge of hysteria in her voice. Undecided, I sat in my seat and watched the men. They lined up at the barricade and stared at us without expression.

Isobel urged me again, and I got out of the car and walked over to them.

I said: 'I live at number 47. Can we get through to our house, please?' They said nothing, but continued to stare. 'My daughter is ill. We must get her to bed.'

They stared.

I turned towards the camera-crew and shouted: 'Can you tell me if anyone has been allowed in here today?'

Neither of them responded, though the man pointing the microphone in our direction looked down at his equipment and adjusted the setting of a knob.

I turned back to the Africans.

27

'Do you speak English?' I said. 'We must get to our house.'

There was a long silence, and then one of the men said in a thick accent: 'Go away!'

He lifted his rifle.

I got back into the car, put it into gear and accelerated away, swinging across the deserted road in a wide U-turn. As we passed the camera the Afrim fired his rifle and our windscreen shattered into opacity. I banged my forearm against it and a shower of glass fragments blew in. Isobel screamed and fell to the side, covering her head with her arms. Sally reached over from the back seat and put her arms around my neck and shouted incoherently into my ear.

When we were about a hundred yards away I slowed a little and leaned forward in my seat, pulling myself from Sally's grip. I looked in the rear-view mirror and saw that the camera-operator had turned the instrument to follow our flight down the road.

*   *   *

I stood with many others on the beach at Brighton. We were watching the old ship that was drifting in the Channel, listing to port at an angle of what the newspapers told us was twenty degrees. It was about a mile from the shore, riding the rough seas uneasily. The lifeboats from Hove, Brighton and Shoreham stood by, awaiting radio confirmation that they might take it in tow. Meanwhile, we on the shore were watching for it to sink, some of us having come many miles to see the spectacle.

*   *   *

I reached the main group without meeting any patrols, and as soon as I considered it prudent I approached Lateef and gave him the mirror-daggers.

He said nothing about the other men who had been foraging, nor whether they had been successful.

He looked critically at the daggers, but was unable to conceal his grudging admiration for my initiative. He took one in his right hand, balanced it, held it up, tried holstering it in his belt. His habitual frown deepened. I wanted to make excuses for the crudity of the weapons, explain about the shortage of materials suitable for the manufacture of armaments, but held my silence as I knew he was aware of this.

His criticism of my handiwork was political, not practical.

28

Later, I saw him throwing away my daggers, and I decided against mentioning the petrol-bombs.

* * *

As I passed through my adolescence I underwent, as is common to most boys, many puzzling stages of development towards full sexuality.

Near where I lived with my parents and brothers was a large area of waste ground which was cluttered with many piles of building materials, and torn into moulds of bare earth by bull-dozers. I understood that at one time it had been scheduled for development, but for reasons unknown to me the scheme had been delayed. Consequently, the area provided an ideal playing-ground for myself and my friends. Though officially we were forbidden to play there, the many hundreds of hiding-places made it possible for us to evade the various forms of authority as manifested by parents, neighbours and the local police-constable.

During this period I was undergoing doubts as to whether or or not I should be indulging in such childish activities. My elder brother had obtained a place at a good university and was half-way through his first year there. My younger brother was at the same school as I, and by all accounts was more academically successful than I had been at his age. I knew that if I wished to emulate my elder brother's achievement I should apply myself more purposefully to my studies, but my mind and my body were occupied with an uncontrollable restlessness and many times I found myself on the building-site with boys not only a year or two younger than I, but who attended a different school.

It had always appeared to me that the other boys were more advanced in their thinking than I was.

It was always they who made the suggestions about what we should do, and I who followed. Any move to a new activity came from someone else, and I was often amongst the last to take it up. In this way, such pastimes that I had at that time were secondhand to me and did not provide me with any real involvement.

In a limbo between what I was doing and what I should be doing, neither was effected well.

Accordingly, when two or three local girls joined us on occasional evenings, I was slow to appreciate the subtlety of how

29

their presence was affecting the behaviour of the others.

By chance, I knew one of these girls already. Her parents and mine were on friendly terms, and we had passed several evenings in each other's company. My relationship with her to this point, however, had been platonic and superficial: I had not reacted to her presence in any sexual way. When she and her friends appeared for the first time on the waste ground I did not exploit this small advantage I had over the other boys. On the contrary, I became embarrassed at her presence, imagining in some obscure way that word of my activities would get back to my parents.

The first evening they were with us was awkward and unsettling. The conversation became an aimless and banal banter, with the girls feigning disinterest in us, and myself and the other boys pretending to ignore them. This set the pattern for the next few encounters.

It happened that I went away with my parents for a short holiday, and on my return I discovered that the relationship with the girls had entered a more physical phase. Some of the boys had air-rifles, and they used these to impress the girls with their marksmanship. There was a lot of fake hostility and sometimes we would become involved in wrestling matches with them.

Even through this I failed to observe the sexual aspects of what was happening.

One evening a pack of cards was produced by one of the boys. For a while we played childish games with them, but became bored quickly. Then one of the girls said she knew a variety of the game Consequences which could be played with cards. She took the pack and dealt out cards to us all, explaining as she went. The idea was very simple: everyone was dealt cards from the top of the pack, and the first boy and the first girl to receive a card of the same value – say two Queens or two Sevens – were matched up for Consequences.

I did not fully understand, but took the first card as it was given to me. It was a Three. On the first deal, no two people had similar cards, though one of the other boys also had a Three. This provoked ribald comments, which I laughed at without properly appreciating the humour. On the next deal, the girl I knew through my parents was given a Three.

A short discussion ensued, the outcome of which was that I was adjudged to be the winner as I had drawn the Three before the other boy. I was willing to let him take my turn, as I was uncertain of what was expected of me.

The girl who had started the game explained that it was usually played strictly to the rules, and that I had to take my turn. I was to go, she said, to the far side of some near-by earthworks with the other girl and that we would be allowed ten minutes.

The girl and I stood up, and amid many catcalls did as directed.

When we reached the other side of the earthworks, I felt I could not admit to her that I did not know what to do. Alone with a girl for the first time in my life I stood in miserable silence.

Then she said: 'Are you going to?'

I said: 'No.'

She sat down on the earth and I stood before her. I kept glancing at my watch.

I asked the girl several questions. I found out how old she was, and what her middle name was. She told me the school she went to and what she was going to do when she left. In answer to my question, she told me that she had lots of boyfriends. When she asked me how many girlfriends I had I told her that there were a few.

As soon as the ten minutes were up we went back to the others.

I was handed the cards, which I shuffled and then dealt for the second round. This time there was no question as to who the winners were, as two Tens came up on the first deal. The boy and the girl left us and went to the other side of the earthworks. While we waited for them to return, several dirty jokes were told. The atmosphere amongst those of us waiting was tense and strained, and though I joined in with the others I found myself wondering what was going on behind the mound of bare earth.

At the end of the ten minutes they had not returned. The girl who had started the game was the one with the boy and we assumed she would play by the rules. One of the boys suggested that we go and get them, and this we did, running towards the earthworks shouting and whistling. Before we reached them they came out and we went back to the cards. I noticed that neither of them looked at each other, nor at any of us.

On the third deal, the girl I had been with drew a number with one of the other boys, and they went off to the mound. I found myself disturbed by this. After a moment or two I declared I was sick of the game and walked off in the direction of my house.

As soon as I was out of sight of the others, I worked round

through the waste ground and approached the earthworks from the side. I was able to get close up to the couple without being observed, as a pile of unpainted window-frames was stacked near by. From this cover I watched them.

They were standing up. The girl was wearing her school blazer and dress. The boy was standing close to her, with his back to me. They were talking quietly.

Suddenly, he threw his arms around her neck and dragged her to the floor. They wrestled together for a moment, in the way we had often done before. At first she fought back, but after a minute or so she rolled away from him and lay passively. He reached over to her and laid his hand very tentatively on her stomach. Her head lolled away from him, facing towards my hiding-place, and I saw that her eyes were tightly closed. The boy pushed aside her blazer and I could see the gentle swell of her breasts by his hand. Because she was lying down, they were not as protuberant as normal. The boy was staring at them rigidly, and I discovered that I was beginning to have an erection. With my hand in my trouser pocket I moved my penis so that it was less uncomfortable, and as I did so the boy's hand slid up and cupped one of her breasts. He slid the hand backwards and forwards with increasing speed. In a while, the girl cried out as if it were hurting her, and she rolled back towards him. Though she then had her back to me, I could see that she had put her hand at the top of his legs and was caressing him.

I was becoming intolerably excited by this, and though I wanted to stay where I was I felt very unsettled by what I was witnessing. I backed away and walked in the direction I had come. As I did so my hand was still in my pocket holding my penis, and in a moment I ejaculated. I mopped myself clean with a handkerchief, then went back to the others, explaining that I had returned home but that my parents were out.

A few minutes later the girl and boy came back. Like the others, they did not meet our eyes.

We were prepared for a fourth hand, but the girls said they were fed up and wanted to go home. We tried to persuade them to stay, but in a few moments they left. As they walked away we could hear them giggling. When he was sure they were gone, the boy who had just come back undid the fly of his trousers and showed us his penis. It was still erect and looked a dark red colour. He masturbated in front of us and we watched enviously.

The girls came back to the waste ground the following evening, by which time I had devised a method of ensuring I dealt myself the right cards. I rubbed the breasts of each of the three girls, and one of them allowed me to put my hand inside her dress and brassière and feel her nipples. After this the cards were no longer used and we took it in turns. By the end of the following week I had had sexual intercourse with the girl I had known through my parents, and was proud that I was the only one of us she would do it with.

I took my examinations in the weeks following and was not successful. I was obliged to reapply myself to my work and in course of time I lost contact with the group. I entered university two years later.

* * *

If anything, the wind had increased in the time I had been on the beach, and as the waves broke on the shingle about twenty-five yards from where I stood, a fine spray was driven across our faces. I was wearing my spectacles, and within a few minutes the lenses were misted with a thin deposit of salt. I removed them and placed them inside my pocket in their case.

The sea was now very rough, white breakers flickering across its surface as far as the horizon. As yet the sun still shone, though there was a bank of dark cloud in the south-west. I stood in a large crowd of people, and we were watching the drifting ship.

The transistor radio carried by someone near by announced the news that the ship was not to be assisted by rescue craft, and that the lifeboats were being ordered to return to their stations. Not a mile away from us we could see the very boats circling, obviously undecided whether to obey the orders from the shore or their own consciences. Some distance behind the drifting ship we could see the Royal Navy frigate which had been detailed to follow. So far, it had not interfered.

At one point I turned round to make an estimate of the number of people watching from the shore and saw that every available access point was crowded along the side of the King's Road that overlooked the beach, in addition to the hundreds of people that stood on the Central Pier.

At just after four minutes past two o'clock the lifeboats turned away from the ship and headed back to their respective stations. I estimated that in less than a quarter of an hour the ship would have drifted past the end of the pier and be invisible from where I was standing. I debated whether or not to move, but decided to stay.

33

The ship sank at just before ten past. Its angle of list had increased markedly in the last few minutes, and many of the people on board could be seen jumping over the side. The ship sank quickly and unspectacularly.

Within fifteen minutes of its sinking the majority of the crowd had dispersed. I stayed on, enthralled in some primeval way by the feel of the wind, the sound and the sight of the great surf and by what I had just witnessed. I left the shore an hour or so later, distressed by the appearance of the few Africans who managed to swim to the shore. Less than fifty of them made it to the beach alive, though I understand from my acquaintances in Brighton that in the next few days the sea threw up hundreds of dead with every tide. Human flotsam, made buoyant by its distended, gas-filled belly.

*　*　*

As night fell I pulled the car into the side of the road and stopped. It was too cold to continue driving with the glass of the windscreen knocked away, and in any case I was reaching the end of our supply of petrol and did not wish to discuss this with Isobel in front of Sally.

For security we had driven north from London and were in the countryside around Cuffley. I had debated mentally whether to try to reach the U.N. camp again, but after two long and extremely tiring journeys to and from there in the last twenty-four hours, neither I nor the others were anxious to repeat it if an alternative could be found. In addition, the twin factors of a dwindling supply of petrol and the discouragement of the official that morning combined to indicate that we should at least find an alternative.

We took our warmest clothing from the suitcases and put it on. Sally lay down on the back seat of the car and we covered her with as much warm material as we could find. Isobel and I waited in silence, smoking the last of our cigarettes, until we felt reasonably sure she had drifted off into sleep. None of us had eaten a proper meal during the day, the only food we had consumed being some chocolate we found in an automatic machine outside a row of closed shops. While we sat there it began to rain, and in a few minutes a trickle of water came in through the empty rubber frame, and ran over the dashboard on to the floor.

'We'd better make for Bristol,' I said.

'What about the house?'

I shook my head. 'We've no hope of going back.'

'I don't think we should go to Bristol.'

'Where else can we go?'

'Back to the U.N. camp. At least, for the next few days.'

'And after that?'

'I don't know. Things *must* get better. We can't be kicked out of our house just like that. There must be a law . . .'

I said: 'That won't be the answer. Things have gone too far now. The Afrim situation has grown out of the housing shortage. I can't see them agreeing to a compromise where they will have to give up the house they've already taken over.'

Isobel said: 'Why not?'

I didn't answer. In the few weeks preceding the recent events Isobel had shown an increasing disinterest in the progress of the Afrim situation, and this had only widened the distance between us. Whereas I had been continually faced with the breakdown of the society that we knew, Isobel appeared to withdraw from the reality as if she could survive by ignoring events. Even now, with our home inaccessible to us, she was content to allow me to take the decisions.

Before we settled for the night, I walked from the car in the direction of a near-by house, from whose windows showed warm amber light. Less than a hundred yards away, an unaccountable fear came into my mind, and I turned away. The house was of the upper middle-class variety, and there were two expensive cars and a trailer in the drive.

I considered my own appearance: unshaven and in need of a change of clothing. It was difficult to say what would have been the reaction of the occupiers of the house had I knocked at the door. The anarchy of the situation in London bore no relation to this area, which had as yet had no contact with the homeless and militant African people.

I returned to the car.

'We're going to an hotel for the night,' I said.

Isobel made no answer, but stared out of her side-window into the dark.

'Well, don't you care?'

'No.'

'What do you want to do?'

'We'll be all right here.'

The rain still dribbled into the car through the gaping hole that had been our windscreen. In the few minutes I had been

35

outside, the drizzle had soaked my outer clothes. I wanted Isobel to touch me, share to some measure the experience of my walk . . . yet I shrank mentally from the thought of her hand on my arm.

'What about Sally?' I said.

'She's asleep. If you want to find an hotel, I won't object. Can we afford it?'

'Yes.'

I thought about it for a bit longer. We could stay here, or we could drive on. I glanced at my watch. It was just after eight o'clock. If we slept in the car, in what kind of condition would we be by morning?

I started the engine and drove slowly back to the centre of Cuffley. I knew of no hotels in the neighbourhood, but was confident of finding somewhere. The first place we found was full, and so was the second. We were following directions to a third when the petrol-tank finally ran dry. I coasted the car into the side and stopped.

I was relieved in a way that the decision had been made for us; I'd held out no real hopes of finding accommodation in an hotel. Isobel said nothing, but sat with her eyes closed. Her face and clothes were damp from the rain which had blown in through the screen.

I ran the heater until the water inside the mechanism had cooled to a point where there was no more benefit to be had. Isobel said she was tired.

We agreed to take it in turns to lie across one another; I said she could have the first period. She tucked her knees up and lay across from her seat with her head in my lap. I put my arms around her to keep her warm, then tried to find a comfortable position myself.

Within a few minutes Isobel had passed into a semblance of sleep. I spent the night uneasily, unable to pass into complete sleep because of my uncomfortable position.

Behind us Sally stirred from time to time; of the three of us she was probably the only one rested fully in the night.

*   *   *

Lateef showed me a leaflet he had found. It was printed by the Royal Secessionist Air Force, and it stated that ten minutes' warning, in the form of three low traverses, would always be

36

given to civilian occupants of villages before a raid was to take place.

*　　*　　*

There was a road through the New Forest. I drove along it in the twilight of the evening, knowing that we had stayed away too long. It had not been wise to do what we had done in any event, and with the present police situation it had been fool-hardy.

I had a girl in the car with me. Her name was Patti. She and I had been at an hotel in Lymington and we were hurrying to get back to London before nine o'clock. She was asleep next to me, her head resting lightly on my shoulder.

She was awakened by my stopping the car at a road-block on the outskirts of Southampton. There were several men standing by the block, which was a makeshift arrangement of two old cars and an assortment of heavy building materials. Each of the men carried a weapon, though only one had a rifle. It occurred to me that for the last few miles we had not seen any traffic going in the same direction as us, and guessed that most local people would have known about the block and have found an alternative route.

As a result of the road-block we were obliged to turn round and follow a long diversion through the countryside to Win-chester, and thence to the main road to London. We had been warned by the people at the hotel to expect similar obstructions at Basingstoke and Camberley, and as it turned out we were required to make lengthy detours around these also.

The road into south-west London was unobstructed by civilian defence groups, but we saw many police vehicles and spot-checks on motorists. We were fortunate in passing through without delay. I had not been out of London for several months and had had no idea that access and movement had been cur-tailed to this degree.

I dropped Patti near the flat she shared in Barons Court and carried on towards my home in Southgate. Again, none of the major roads was blocked by civilian resistance groups, but I was stopped by the police near King's Cross and my possessions were searched.

It wan't until nearly one in the morning that I arrived home. Isobel had not waited up for me.

*　　*　　*

37

The next morning I went to a near-by house and managed to persuade the occupier to let me have a gallon of petrol siphoned from out of his car's tank. I paid him two pounds for it. He informed me that there was a garage less than three miles away which had been selling petrol up until the night before. He gave me directions to find it.

I returned to the car and told Isobel and Sally that with any luck we would be able to make Bristol during the day.

Isobel said nothing, though I knew she did not want to go to her parents. From my point of view it was the only solution. As it was equally obvious that we could no longer return to our house, the prospect of moving to the relatively distant town was one sufficiently familiar to reassure us.

I filled the tank with the gallon of petrol and started the engine. As we drove towards the garage as directed, we listened to a news broadcast on the radio which announced the first break in the police. About a quarter of the force had seceded in favour of the Afrims. There was to be a meeting of chief constables with both the Afrim command and Tregarth's Home Office, and a statement would be issued from Whitehall later in the day.

We found the garage with difficulty and were allowed what the proprietor informed us was the standard quota: three gallons. With what we had, this gave us a maximum potential mileage of around one hundred and thirty miles. This should be just sufficient for us to reach Bristol, provided we were not forced to make too many detours from the shortest route.

I told Isobel and Sally, and they expressed relief. We agreed to set off as soon as we had had something to eat.

At Potters Bar we found a small café which gave us a good breakfast at normal prices. No mention was made of the Afrim situation, and the radio that was playing carried only light music. At Isobel's request we were sold a vacuum-flask which was filled for us with hot coffee, and after we had washed in the toilets of the café we set out.

The day was not warm, but there was no rain. Driving with the windscreen missing was unpleasant, but not impossible. I decided not to listen to the radio, seeing for once some wisdom in Isobel's attitude of not allowing the events around us to affect us. Although it was of course essential to keep abreast of the developing situation, I was won over to her passivity.

A new worry materialised in the form of a continual vibration from the engine. I had been unable to maintain regular servicing on it, and I knew that one of the valves was in need of replace-

38

ment. I trusted to it lasting at least until we reached Bristol and did not mention it to the others.

As far as I could see, the worst part of the journey would be in avoiding barricaded sections of the suburbs around London. I therefore skirted the north-western edge of the city, driving first to Watford (unbarricaded), then to Rickmansworth (barricaded, but open to through traffic on the by-pass), and then across-country to Amersham, High Wycombe and south towards Henley-on-Thames. As we went farther from London we saw fewer and fewer overt signs of the trouble, and a mood of tranquillity came over us. We were even able to purchase more petrol and fill our reserve cans.

At another small café on the way into Reading we ate a lunch and made our way towards the main road to Bristol, confident of arriving there well before nightfall.

Five miles to the west of Reading the engine-vibrations increased suddenly, and the power faded. I kept the car going as long as possible, but at the first incline it stopped. I did what I could to investigate, but the fuel- and ignition-systems were not faulty, and I could only assume that the valve had finally blown.

I was on the point of discussing this with Isobel and Sally when a police-car pulled up alongside.

*   *   *

I worked for some months as part-time barman in a public-house in the East End of London. It had become necessary to earn some extra money. I was then studying for my Finals and my grant had been spent.

It came as something of a surprise for me to learn that the East End was a series of loosely connected ghettos, containing Jews, Negroes, Chinese, Greeks, Cypriots, Italians and English. Until this work I had always assumed that this part of London was primarily white. The pub reflected this cosmopolitan aspect to some degree, although it was clear that the publican did not encourage it. Arguments in the bar often arose, and we had been instructed to remove bottles and glasses from the counters if a fracas developed. It was part of my duties as barman to assist in breaking up any fight that started.

When I had been at the pub for three months the publican decided to hire a pop-group for the week-ends, and within a matter of weeks the trouble had passed. The type of customer changed noticeably.

Instead of the older drinker, set in his ways and dogmatically opinionated, the pub began to attract a younger element. Members of the minority groups no longer came, and within a couple of months almost every customer at the pub was aged less than thirty.

The clothing fashions at the time tended to be colourful and casual, but these were not common at the pub. I learned in time that this was an outward manifestation of an innate conservatism that is widespread in this part of London.

The publican's first name was Harry; I never learned his surname. He had once been an all-in wrestler, and on the wall of the bar behind the counter there were several photographs of him in satin dressing-gowns and with a long pigtail. I never heard Harry talk about his experience in the ring, though his wife once told me that he had earned enough money from it to enable him to buy the pub outright.

Towards the end of the evenings several of Harry's friends, who were in general around his own age, would come into the bar. Often after closing-time, Harry would invite them to stay behind and have a few drinks with him. On these occasions he would offer me a few extra shillings to stay later and serve them. As a result of this I overheard many of their conversations and came to learn that their prejudices and information on subjects such as race and politics were as conservative as those attitudes implied by the dress of the other customers.

Several years later, John Tregarth and his party were to gain a substantial electroal backing from areas in which different races were mixed freely.

*   *   *

We stayed a few more days at the encampment. Each of us was undecided what should be done. Most of the men had lost a wife or a sleeping-partner in the abduction, and though we knew from what had happened to Willen that it would serve no purpose to approach the Afrims directly, it was instinctive to stay in the place from where they had been taken. I felt restless, and worried continually for the safety of Sally. Isobel I was less concerned for. It was with relief, then, that I heard at the end of the week the rumour that we were to go to Augustin's.

Though I had no personal wish to visit the place, it did at least mean that we were to move and with apparent purpose.

As we loaded our possessions on to the handcarts and preparations were made for the move, Lateef came over to me and confirmed that we were going to Augustin's. It would, he said, be good for the morale of the men.

He appeared to be right, as within a couple of hours the mood had changed, and in spite of a sharp fall in temperature we walked the first few miles in a spirit of cavalier good humour.

* * *

'You do have a name?' I said.
    'Yes.'
    'Are you going to tell me?'
    'No.'
    'Do you have a reason for withholding this information?'
    'Yes. That is, no.'
    'Well, tell it to me then.'
    'No.'
That is the first conversation I had with my wife. Her name was Isobel.

* * *

As the full scale of the forthcoming disaster made itself apparent to the British public, there descended on the country the kind of stalwart resolution and directed confusion that my parents had sometimes told me about when recounting their experience of the early months of the second world war.

In line with a major part of the intellectual element of the country, our college formed a society which professed to be sympathetic to the plight of the Africans. Our motives were principally humanitarian, though there were a few members – mainly those who had earlier reflected a more conservative view, and who joined the society for policy reasons – who adopted a more academic attitude. It was people such as these who first discredited the movement, as they were unable to answer the charges in the press and other media that the pro-Afrim groups were left-wing revolutionaries.

It was undeniably true that the African immigrants were forming themselves into armed groups, that they were being supplied with weapons from abroad and that they were moving into cities on a large scale and occupying houses and displacing the former white inhabitants.

Most people had seen for themselves that these charges were

true, but the belief of our college society was that the fault lay with the government. If a more charitable attitude had been adopted from the outset, the Africans' plight would have been lessened, and political opportunities would not have been able to exploit the situation. But extreme policies induce extreme reactions, and the tight conservatism of Tregarth and his government – approved of by a sizeable percentage of the country – allowed for little liberalism towards the illegal coloured immigrants.

In the remaining weeks of the college term my colleagues and I did what we could to pass our beliefs on to our students. When the end of term arrived, the period of our influence passed. I felt apprehensive as I delivered the last of my own lectures, and even before I left the college grounds I was censuring myself for not having expended more energy in this direction.

In the weeks that followed, as industrial unrest spread and public demonstrations in the streets became an everyday event, I saw that we had been wrong to believe that our attempts to arouse sympathy for the Afrims would do much good. There was a small and vociferous section of the community which adhered to its moral principles, but more and more ordinary people were coming into direct conflict with the Afrims as the armed insurgence went on.

At one of the largest demonstrations in London I saw some of the students from the college carrying a large banner emblazoned with the name of our society. I had not intended to join the march, but I abandoned my intended errand and followed the demonstration to its noisy and violent conclusion.

In the event, the doors of the college were never opened for the following term.

*   *   *

We were told by the two police-officers that we were in restricted territory and that we must move at once. There were reports, they said, that there had been a mutiny in a near-by army-camp, and that the entire neighbourhood was being sealed off by government forces.

I told the police that our car had broken down and that though we were not disputing what they told us, we had come into the vicinity without any warning from the authorities.

The policemen appeared to be incapable of listening to reason.

Their instructions were repeated and we were told to leave the area immediately. Sally began to cry at this point, as one of the policemen had opened the door of the car and dragged her out. I protested at once and was hit hard across my face with the back of a hand.

I was pressed up against the side of the car and my pockets were searched. When they looked in my wallet and saw that I had once been a lecturer at the college, my identity-card was confiscated. Again I protested, but was ignored.

Isobel and Sally were similarly searched.

When this was completed our belongings were taken from the car and put in the road. Our reserve petrol cans were taken from the boot and placed inside the police-car. I remembered what I had heard on the radio earlier, and asked to see the warrant-cards of the police. I was again ignored.

We were told that the police-car would be returning along this road in half an hour. We were to be gone by then. Otherwise, they said, we would be responsible for the consequences.

As they turned to get back into their car, I moved forward quickly and kicked the man who had hit me. I got my shoe hard against his coccyx, throwing him forward on to the ground. The other man turned round and dived at me. I swung my fist at his face, but missed. He threw an arm around my neck, pulled me to the ground and held me there with my arm twisted up against my back and my face pressed painfully into the dirt. The man I had attacked had climbed to his feet, and now he came over and placed three hard kicks into my side.

When they had gone Isobel helped me on to the front passenger-seat of the car, and with a paper tissue wiped away some of the blood that was coming out of my mouth.

As soon as I had recovered sufficiently to walk we set off across a field in a direction opposite to the one in which the police had waved vaguely when telling us about the army mutiny.

There was a severe pain in my side, and although I could walk with some difficulty I was unable to carry anything heavy. Isobel was therefore obliged to take our two large suitcases, and Sally had to carry the small one. I held our transistor radio under my arm. As we walked I switched it on, but was able to raise only one channel of the BBC, and that was the one playing continuous light music.

All three of us were at the point of despair. Neither Isobel nor Sally asked me what we should do next . . . for the first time since leaving our house, we were wholly aware how far beyond our control events had moved. Later, the rain returned and we sat under a tree on the edge of a field, frightened, directionless, and utterly involved in a sequence of events that no one had expected and that no one now seemed capable of stopping.

*   *   *

I learned from the newspaper I read regularly that the mood of the country had polarised into three general groups.

Firstly, those people who had come into contact with the Afrims and suffered accordingly, or those people who were colour-prejudiced in any case, who followed the government's policy and who felt the Afrims should be deported. According to several polls this feeling was prevalent.

Secondly, those people to whom there was no question but that the Afrims should be allowed to stay in Britain and be afforded as much charity as possible until they were capable of integrating with our society in a normal way.

Thirdly, those people who did not care whether or not the Africans landed, so long as they themselves were not directly affected.

The apparent apathy of this third group displeased me, until I realised that for my general lack of involvement I should probably be counted a member.

I questioned my own moral stand. Although my instinct was to remain uncommitted – at this time I was conducting an affair with a woman and she was occupying a major part of my thoughts – it was this awareness of my insularity which convinced me I should join the pro-Afrim society at the college.

The political and social climates were not responsive to the kind of moral judgements that had to be made.

Soon after the second election Tregarth's government introduced much of the new legislation it had promised in its manifesto. The police had wider powers of entry and detention, and the elements that some of Tregarth's ministers described as subversive were more effectively dealt with. Public demonstrations on any political issue were controlled tightly by the police, and the armed forces were empowered to assist in the keeping of the peace.

As the boats from Africa continued to land on British shores, the problem could no longer be ignored.

After the first wave of landings the government issued the warning that illegal immigrants would be prevented from landing, forcibly if necessary. This led directly to the incident in Dorset, where the army confronted two shiploads of Africans. Thousands of people had come to Dorset from all over the country to witness the landing, and the result was a confrontation between army and public. The Afrims got ashore.

After this, the government's warning was modified to the effect that as illegal immigrants were captured they would be given suitable treatment in hospital, then deported.

In the meantime, polarisation of attitudes was accelerated by the illegal supply of arms to the Afrims. As their presence developed into a military threat, so there grew deeper schisms in the country.

The private life of everyone in the regions directly affected – and of many in areas away from the insurgence – became oriented entirely around the immediate problem. The police force divided, and so did the Army and Air Force. The Navy remained loyal to the government. When a detachment of American Marines was landed to act in an advisory capacity to what had become known as the Nationalist side, and when the United Nations drafted a peace-keeping force, the military aspect of the situation became resolved.

By this time, no one could be said to be uninvolved.

* * *

'I hear we're going to Augustin's.'

The man marching next to me stared straight ahead. 'About bloody time.'

'You been missing it then?'

'Piss off, will you?'

I said nothing, but let them drag out the interplay of ideas to their logical conclusion. I'd heard this or a similar conversation a dozen times in the last week.

'It was Lateef that decided. The others wanted to stay put.'

'I know. Good old Lat.'

'He's missing it, too.'

'They got one of his? He never mentions it.'

'Yeah. They say he was screwing Olderton's wife on the quiet.'

'I don't believe it.'

'It's a fact.'

'What about Olderton, then?'

'Never knew a thing.'

45

The other man laughed. 'You're right. I have been missing it.'

'Haven't we all.'

They both laughed then, cackling like two old women in the uncanny cold silence of the countryside.

*   *   *

We slept that night in the open, and in the morning were fortunate in finding a shop still open that sold us, at normal prices, a good deal of camping equipment. At this stage we still had not formulated a serious plan, beyond a recognition of the fact that we must get to Bristol at the earliest opportunity.

We walked all that day, sleeping again in the open, but this time with the equipment. It rained during the course of the night and we were adequately protected. In spite of what at first seemed to be great difficulties, our spirits stayed high, though when I overheard Isobel talking with Sally shortly before the girl fell asleep I thought I detected a considerable strain of false optimism in their tone.

As far as I was concerned, I was passing through what I was to learn later was a temporary phase of genuine high spirits. Paradoxical as this may seem, the comparative freedom we now enjoyed, at a time when the martial law in the cities was imposing impossible restrictions on most of the population, served to compensate for all the other facts such as that we had lost virtually all our possessions, were now homeless and that the possibility of our reaching Bristol was remote.

We encountered a stretch of woodland and for a few days made our encampment there. It was during this time that our mood became depressed.

For food, we visited a near-by village where we were sold all we required without question. But later in the week, when a detachment of the Afrim forces raided the village and as a result the inhabitants erected barricades, this supply was cut off from us.

We decided to move on, and travelled across country in a southerly direction. I became increasingly aware of Isobel's unspoken resentment about what was happening to us, and I found myself competing with her for Sally's approval. In this way, Sally became the instrument of our conflict (as in fact she had always been) and suffered considerably.

The day after the soaking of our equipment and possessions

46

in the crossing of the river, the conflict came to a head.

By this time we were out of touch with the rest of the world. The batteries of the radio had been growing weaker, and now the water had damaged it beyond our repair. While Isobel and Sally laid out our clothes and equipment to dry in the sun, I went off by myself and tried to condense my knowledge into something from which I could plan our next moves.

We knew only that we were in grave difficulty and that our personal problems were aggravated by the situation around us. Though we knew only too well the extent of our own difficulties, we would have been better placed to cope with them had we been able to know the current state of the political situation.

(Much later, I learned that at this time there was a large-scale welfare scheme being initiated by the Red Cross and the United Nations, which was attempting to rehabilitate all those people like ourselves who had been dispossessed by the fighting. As it turned out, this effort was fated, as with the worsening state of the conflict, both organisations became discredited in the mind of the public, and their work was used by all participating sides as a tactical, political or social weapon against the others. The result of this was a massive distrust of all welfare organisations, and in time their function became the superficial one of maintaining a presence.)

It was difficult to reconcile ourselves to the standards of existence we were now having to accept.

I found myself looking at the situation as being a predetermined one. That my attitude to Isobel, the way in which our marriage had become nothing more than a social convenience, had resolved itself. While we were living at our house we were able to disregard both the fact that our relationship was hypocritical and that the political situation of that period had an effect on us.

But now that the latter had so changed our mode of existence we could no longer pretend about ourselves.

In those few minutes alone, I saw with penetrating clarity that our marriage had reached its conclusion and that the moment had arrived when the pretence must be abandoned. Practical considerations tried to intrude, but I ignored them. Isobel could fend for himself, or surrender herself to the police. Sally could come with me. We would return to London, and from there decide what next to do.

For one of the few times in my life I had reached a positive decision by myself, and it was not one I liked. Memories of what had gone before – good memories – pulled at me. But I still had the bruises from the policeman's boot in my side and these served to remind me of the true nature of our lives.

The past had moved away from us and so had the present. Those moments with Isobel when I had thought we might once again work out a way to live with each other, presented themselves to me as falsehoods. Regret did not exist.

* * *

We were due to arrive at Augustin's the following day, but of necessity we slept that night in a field. None of us liked sleeping in the open, preferring to find abandoned houses or farm-buildings. I had never found it easy to settle when on hard ground and exposed to the cold. In addition, we discovered around midnight that by chance we had camped less than a mile from an anti-aircraft emplacement. Several times the guns opened fire, and although searchlights were used twice we were unable to see at what it was they were firing.

We moved on at first light, every one of us cold, irritable and tired. Five miles from Augustin's we were stopped by a patrol of U.S. Marines, and searched. It was routine, perfunctory, and it was over in ten minutes.

Sobered from garrulous irritability to our habitual watchful silence, we arrived in the vicinity of Augustin's around midday.

Lateef detailed myself and two others to move on ahead and establish that the camp was still there. All we had by way of directions was an Ordnance Survey grid-reference which had been passed on to us along the refugee network. Although we had no reason to doubt this information – the network was the only reliable form of news-dissemination – it was possible that one or another of the military groups had moved it on. In any case, it was essential to ensure that at the time we were there we would not interrupt anyone or be interrupted.

While Lateef organised the preparation of a meal we moved forward.

The grid-reference turned out to be a field which had carried crop-growth. It had evidently lain fallow for more than a year, as it was overgrown with rank grass and weeds. Although there were several signs of human habitation – a soil latrine in one corner, many bare patches in the grass, a refuse tip, the burnt ulcers where open fires had been – the field was empty.

We searched it in silence for a few minutes, until one of the other men found a piece of white card inside a polythene bag resting under a tiny cairn of stones. It said: *Augustin's*, and was followed by another grid-reference. We consulted the map and found that it was less than three-quarters of a mile farther on.

The new site was inside a wood and we found it with comparative ease. It consisted of several tents of various sizes, ranging from crude sheets of canvas large enough to shelter only one or two persons, up to a medium-sized marquee of the sort once found at circuses. The whole encampment was roped off, except at one part where a large tent had been erected. Anyone wishing to enter the encampment was thus obliged to pass through this tent.

Over the entrance was tacked a crudely painted sign on what had once been a sheet or tablecloth: AUGUSTIN. Underneath that was written: SCREW A BLACK FOR PIECE. We went inside.

A young boy sat behind a trestle table.

I said to him: 'Is Augustin here?'

'He's busy.'

'Too busy to see us?'

'How many?'

I told the boy the number of men there were in our group. He left the tent and walked through into the encampment. A few minutes later Augustin himself joined us. Few refugees know what nationality Augustin is. He is not British.

He said to me: 'You got men?'

'Yes.'

'When they coming?'

I told him in about an hour. He looked at his watch.

'O.K. But out by six?'

We agreed to this.

He added: 'We got more in evening. O.K.?'

We agreed again, then returned to our own temporary camp where Lateef and the others were waiting for us. It occurred to me that if we told them where Augustin's was the others would not wait for us, and our own choices would be correspondingly restricted. Accordingly, we refused to divulge the exact location, and said that the camp had moved. When it was clear we intended to say no more, we were given food. After we had eaten we led the others to Augustin's.

Lateef went into the tent with myself and the other two men. The remainder crushed in behind us, or waited outside. I observed that in the time we had been away, Augustin had tidied up his own appearance and had placed a wooden barrier across the inner flap of the tent to prevent us from passing straight through.

He was sitting behind the testle table. At his side was a tall white woman, with long black hair and remarkable blue eyes. She glared at us with what I took to be contempt.

Augustin said: 'How much you offer?'

'How much do you want?' Lateef said.

'No food.'

'Food is the best we can offer you.'

'No food. We want rifles. Or women.'

Lateef said: 'We have fresh meat. And chocolate. And plenty of tinned fruit.'

Augustin tried to look displeased, but I could tell he was unable to resist accepting our offers.

'O.K. Rifles?'

'No.'

'Women?'

Lateef told him, without mentioning the abduction, that we had no women. Augustin spat on to the surface of the table.

'How many nigger-slaves?'

'We haven't got any.'

I had expected Augustin not to believe this. Lateef had once told me that at his last visit, when Augustin was in a more expansive mood, he had confided to him that he 'knew' every refugee-group had several Negroes along as slaves or hostages. Notwithstanding the moral issue, the sheer practical fact of the constant searches and interrogations would have precluded this. In any case, Augustin appeared to take our word for it at the present moment.

'O.K. What food?'

Lateef passed him a sheet of paper, containing a list of provisions with which we would be willing to part. The woman read it out to him.

'No meat. We have enough. It stink too quick. More chocolate.'

Finally, the barter was agreed. Knowing what had had to be paid in the past, I realised that Lateef had struck a fair bargain. I had expected him to be forced to pay much higher. Perhaps for all Augustin's bluff manner, his surplus of food was not as great as he pretended and was experiencing hardship in other respects. It occurred to me to wonder at his insistence on weapons.

We moved outside the tent to where our handcarts were and off-loaded the agreed amounts of food. The business side accomplished, we were conducted through the tent and into a small clearing. Augustin paraded us proudly past his wares.

There were approximately three times as many men as there were available girls. We agreed to behave in a reasonable fashion, and divided ourselves into three groups. We then drew lots as to the order in which we would go to the girls. I was in the group which selected the lot for the first of the three. While the others waited we walked up to the line of girls, who stood waiting for us as if they were troops on inspection.

All of the girls were Negroes. It appeared they had been chosen by Augustin personally, as they were similar in appearance: tall, full-breasted and wide-hipped. Their ages ranged from youthful middle-aged to one girl who was obviously in her early teens.

I selected a young woman of about twenty-five. As I spoke to her she bared her teeth as if I were to inspect those, too.

After a few words she led me away from the clearing to a small tent at the very edge of the encampment. There was little room inside the tent, so she took off her clothes outside. As she did so, I looked round at the other tents I could see and observed that outside each one the other women were similarly disrobing.

When she was naked she went inside. I took off my trousers and laid them on the ground next to where she had put her clothes. I followed her inside.

She was lying on a rough bed made out of several old blankets thrown on the ground. There were no flaps at either end of the tent, and had she been a few inches taller, both her head and her feet would have protruded.

As I entered the tent, the sight of her naked, outstretched body aroused me. I crawled in between her legs and lay down on top of her. I ran my left hand down between our bodies, caressing first her right breast, and then reaching down and holding tightly the tuft of brittle black hair.

I supported myself with my right arm at first, then as she put her arms around me, allowed it to rest down by her side. As I entered her I felt the cold hardness of metal by her side. Taking pains not to show my awareness of this, I explored as far as I dared with my fingers, and at length decided what I could feel was the trigger and guard of a rifle.

As we copulated, I managed to push the rifle away from us and towards the edge of the tent. I am satisfied that my movements were sufficiently unobtrusive, as she showed no sign of awareness. Finally, the rifle was about twelve inches away from us, yet still covered in part by the blankets.

My preoccupation with the presence of the weapon had lessened my sexual desire and I found that my erection had diminished, even though I had continued to make movements against her. I returned my attention to the girl and her body. Because of what had happened I took much longer than normal to come to a climax, and by the time I finished we were both perspiring freely.

Afterwards we dressed and returned to the clearing. From the ribald comments of the other men I gathered we had been away longer than anyone else. My girl lined up with the others and the second group of men went over and made their selections.

As they moved in pairs towards the outlying tents, I stepped past the others, through the tent with the trestle-table where Augustin and his woman sat in earnest conversation, and out to where we had left the handcarts.

I walked past them into the trees.

Twenty yards away I turned and looked back. Augustin was watching me suspiciously from his tent. I made a lewd gesture towards my crutch, indicating that I was about to urinate, and he waved to me. I walked on.

When I was out of sight of the encampment I turned and walked in a broad circle, keeping the camp on my left. After a while I turned in towards it again, and approached it cautiously. I came to the camp from the side. No one saw me.

Using every available tree and bush as cover, I moved around until I was opposite the tent where I had been. Again making sure that I was not observed, I crawled up to it on my hands and knees. I lay beside it on my stomach, the boundary rope directly above me.

Inside, the man was insulting the girl, cursing and blaspheming and insulting her race, pouring out verbal excrement about the colour of her skin. She replied with groans of passion.

I slid my hand under the flap of the tent, found the rifle, and gripped it. With a slowness that nearly panicked me, I slid it out, then made for the cover of the trees. I secreted the rifle in the wildly growing brambles of a hawthorn bush, then returned to the camp.

As I went past Augustin he made a vulgar comment about urine. He was eating the chocolate and had brown smears on his chin.

*   *   *

52

With the closing of the college I found myself in the second major financial crisis of my life. For a while we existed on our savings, but within a month it was clear I would have to find an alternative occupation. Though I telephoned the administrative section of the college on several occasions, I was rarely able even to obtain an answer, let alone a satisfactory resolution to the predicament. In the meantime, I applied myself to the task of obtaining employment.

It should be understood that at this time the country was passing through a phase of extreme economic difficulty. The balance of payments policy on which John Tregarth and his government had first come to power was seen to be working badly, if at all. As a result, prices continued to rise, and an increasing number of men were made to be unemployed. At first confident of myself and my Master's Degree in English History, I toured the offices of publishers intending to pick up some temporary position as an editor or adviser. I was soon disillusioned, finding that the world of books, like virtually everything else, was cutting back on expense and staff at every opportunity. With a similarly universal sequence of sadly shaking heads, I found that the way into some form of clerical work was also barred. Manual labour was, by and large, out of the question: since the middle seventies the industrial labour-pool had been directed by the unions.

At this stage I grew extremely depressed and went to my father for assistance. Though he was now retired he had been managing director of a small chain of companies and still had some influence. Neither of us cared for the brief contact into which this brought us, as we had not communicated except formally and politely for several years. Though he managed to obtain for me an insignificant position in a cloth-cutting factory, I never found a way to express fully my gratitude. When he died a few months later I tried unsuccessfully to feel more than a few minutes of regret.

With the more immediate aspects of the personal financial crisis solved, I turned my attention to developments on the national scene. There was no sign of a halt to the progress of events which were taking away the state of affairs I chose to think of as normal. It was of great significance to me that the government had closed the college. Though at first there had been a public outcry about the seemingly arbitrary way in which the universities were being dealt with, popular interest soon passed to other things.

53

I shall not attempt to describe the details of my work in the cloth factory. In brief, my labours entailed cutting certain types and colours of cloth to determined lengths, ensuring that they were labelled and packed corectly, and following through each consignment to the despatch point.

Within a week I had memorised all relevant details and from there the work degenerated into a meaningless routine which I acted out for the sole purpose of the money it brought me.

* * *

I said to Isobel: 'I want to talk to you. Come over here for a minute.'

'I want to talk to you too.'

We left Sally by the tents and walked back to where I had been before. We stood facing each other, uncomfortable in each other's presence. I realised that this was the first time I had been really alone with her for several days, if not weeks. That thought led me to remembering that we had not had intercourse for over three months.

I tried not to look at her.

'Alan, we've got to do something,' she said. 'We can't go on like this. I'm terrified of what's going to happen. We ought to go back to London. It isn't fair on Sally.'

'I don't know what to do,' I said. 'We can't go back, we can't reach Bristol. All we can do is wait.'

'But wait for *what*?'

'How do I know? Until things settle down again. You know the position as well as I do.'

'Have you thought what this is doing to Sally? Have you *looked* at her recently? Have you thought about what this is doing to me?'

'I know what it's doing to all of us.'

'And you do damn-all about it!'

'If you've got any positive suggestions . . .'

'Steal a car from someone. Shoot someone. Do *anything*, but get us out of this damned field and back to decent living! There must be somewhere we can go. Things would be all right in Bristol. Or we could go back to that camp. I'm sure they'd have us if they saw Sally.'

'What's wrong with Sally?'

'Nothing you'd ever notice.'

'What do you mean?'

She didn't answer, but I thought I caught her intention. This

54

was her way of using Sally against me.

I said: 'Be reasonable. You can't expect me to solve everything. There's nothing I or you can do. If there was, we'd do it.'

'There must be *something*. We can't live in a tent in somebody's field for ever.'

'Look, the country's in one hell of a state, I don't know what's going on, and I doubt if we would if we were in London. There are police on all the main roads, troops in most of the towns. There're no newspapers and nothing on the radio. All I'm suggesting is that we stay as we are as long as we have to, until things get better. Even if we had a car we probably wouldn't be allowed to drive it. How long is it since we saw one on the road?'

Isobel burst into tears. I tried to comfort her, but she pushed me away. I stood by her, waiting for her to calm down. I was becoming confused. When I had thought about what I was going to say to her, it had seemed to be so simple.

As she wept, Isobel stepped away from me, shouldering me aside as I tried to pull her back. Across the field I could see Sally staring in our direction.

When Isobel had stopped crying, I said to her: 'What do you want most of all?'

'There's no point in telling you.'

'Yes, there is.'

She shrugged hopelessly. 'I think I want us to be as we were before this started.'

'Living in Southgate? With all those rows going on?'

She said: 'And you out till all hours of the night, sleeping with some little whore.'

Isobel had known about my affairs for two or more years. She no longer possessed the ability to sting me with them.

'You'd prefer that to this? Would you really? Think about it, will you?'

'I've thought about it,' she said.

'And about the rest of the marriage. Would you honestly want any of that back again?' I had already considered the question, knew my own answer to it. Our marriage had finished before it began.

'Anything . . . rather than this.'

'That's no answer, Isobel.'

I debated again whether or not to say to her what I had decided. As callous as it seemed to me in the face of her present state of mind, it presented an alternative to a situation we both detested.

55

Though she wanted to retrogress and I was going to move on. Was there, I wondered, any real significance?

'All right,' she said. 'How about this? We'll split up. You go back to London and try to find somewhere for us to live. I'll take Sally and we'll try to reach Bristol. We'll stay there until we hear from you.'

I said at once: 'No. Absolutely not. I'm not letting you take Sally. I don't trust you with her.'

'What do you mean? I'm her mother, aren't I?'

'That doesn't embrace every capability.'

For a second or two I saw genuine hatred in Isobel's face and I looked away. My unfaithfulness to Isobel in the past had been a negative reaction away from her, rather than some distinct movement to someone else in seeking something that she could not provide. It had come about through my inadequacy to confront the reality of our marriage, instead of out of a constructive awareness of some shortcomings in the relationship. Though I knew that our generally unsuccessful sex-life, which had initiated in some psychological difficulty in Isobel, was one of the first causes, it was no longer the whole reason and it was the complexity of our failure that made me unable to deal with it. My own motives were suspect. Thus, in provoking Isobel's overt hatred, I was rendered discomfited.

She said: 'That's what I want. You're obviously incapable of supplying an alternative.'

'I do have a suggestion.'

'What is it?'

And so I told her. I said I was taking Sally and that she was to go on to Bristol by herself. I offered her most of our remaining cash and as much equipment as she wanted. When she asked me why I wished to do this, I told her without compromising my earlier conception. I said as bluntly as I could that our marriage as such was over, that the social disruption had only resolved the situation into a more recognisable form. I told her that if she persisted in thinking that we could pick up again she was deluding herself and, in the long run, jeopardising Sally's future. The break had been forced on us, but nevertheless it was a natural one. I considered that Sally would be safer with me, and that when things settled down again we could obtain a divorce and Sally would get legal protection.

Isobel just said: 'I don't know,' and walked away.

*　　*　　*

I examined the rifle at the earliest opportunity and discovered that it was of a sort for which we carried ammunition. Lateef had this, so I was obliged to reveal to him that I had come into possession of a rifle.

Lateef had had the ammunition when I first joined his group, and I had no idea from where it had come.

Speaking to me in private, he told me that he had twelve rounds of ammunition that would suit my rifle, but warned me that it was in the interests of us all to dispose of the weapon at once. When I asked him why, he told me that he had heard that the death-penalty had been invoked for the unlicensed use of firearms.

From what he said, I drew the conclusion that he was envious of my having found the rifle.

I argued the need for protection, that had we been armed earlier we might have been able to protect the women. I made the observation that atrocities against refugees were on the increase, and that there was now no organised force which we could trust.

Lateef countered my arguments by pointing out the increased frequency of interrogations, and that so far we had managed to avoid personal violence against ourselves, whereas other refugee groups had suffered beatings, imprisonment and rape at the hands of military bodies.

His contention was that this was because we were manifestly defenceless.

I told him that I was prepared to accept any and all consequences of my being found in possession of the rifle; that if we were taken for interrogation I would hide it at once, and that if I was caught actually holding or using the rifle I would absolve the rest of the group from any knowledge or complicity.

Lateef seemed satisfied that this undertaking of mine effectively disposed of any disadvantage to him or the others, and in due course gave me the ammunition.

I took the weapon to pieces, cleaned and lubricated it, and learned how to sight it. Unwilling to waste any of the ammunition, or to draw attention to ourselves by the sound of its explosion, I did not fire it. A man in our group who knew something of rifles told me that it was powerful and accurate, and should be used with discretion.

In the days that followed I appreciated that there had been a subtle shift of emphasis in the way in which the group organised itself.

*   *   *

I came to town in the early afternoon, while arrangements for the day's festivities were in their last stages. The square in the centre of the town had been emptied of cars, and people walked across the open space as if unaware that on normal days the town was jammed tight with the traffic passing through towards the coast.

Most of the shops which opened on to the square had laid out wooden stands in front of their windows and laden them with goods. Several men worked on the tops of ladders, attaching coloured bunting across the streets. Nearly every window ledge was decorated with a handful of flowers.

At the wide end of the square, in front of the council offices, there was a small fairground, consisting of a children's round-about, a helter-skelter, a row of swing-boats and several prize-booths.

As I waited outside my hotel, a large coach stopped in a near-by sidestreet and about fifty or sixty passengers climbed out and trooped into a mock-Tudor restaurant on the far side of the square. I waited until the last one was inside, then walked in the opposite direction until I was out of the town centre and in residential sidestreets.

When I returned the festivities were in full swing.

I caught my first sight of the girl as she stood by a display of handbags outside a leather store. It was the fashion at that time for girls to wear clothes made of very light material and with skirts several inches above the knee. She was dressed in pale blue and wore her hair straight and long. To me she was very beauti-ful. As I crossed the square towards her she moved on and was lost in the crowds. I waited by the leather shop, hoping to catch another glimpse of her, but was not able to. After a few minutes I changed my position and stood in the narrow alley that ran between the shooting-gallery and coconut-shy.

I returned to my hotel after an hour and ordered some coffee. Later, I went back into the square and saw her profile against the side of one of the lorries that transported the fairground equipment. She was walking at right angles to my line of sight, staring thoughtfully at the ground. She reached the steps outside the council offices and walked up them. At the top she turned

58

and faced me. Across the square we gazed at one another. I walked towards her.

I reached the bottom of the steps and she turned and went into the building. Not liking to follow her, I went up to where she had been standing and stood facing into the building. Behind me, I heard an abrupt explosion and a scream, and the sound of several people shouting. I did not turn. For about two minutes the square was noisy with the sound of shouting and music. Finally, someone thought to turn off the music that was being relayed by tannoy into the square, and silence fell. Somewhere a woman was sobbing.

Only as the ambulance arrived did I turn to face the square and saw that an accident had happened on the roundabout. A small child was trapped by its legs between the platform and the motor in the centre.

I waited for the child to be released. The ambulance men did not appear to know how to go about it. Finally, a fire-appliance drove up and three men using an electric saw cut through the wood of the platform and freed the child's legs. The child was unconscious. As the ambulance drove away, and the music started up again, I realised that the girl stood beside me. I took her hand and led her away from the centre into the streets along which I had walked earlier.

Her beauty took away from me my ability for glib conversation. I wanted to flatter her and impress her, but the appropriate words would not flow.

We returned to my hotel in the evening and I bought her dinner. When we had finished eating she became distracted and told me she had to leave. I saw her to the door of the hotel but she would not allow me to escort her any farther. I went into the hotel lounge and watched television for the rest of the evening.

The following morning I purchased a newspaper and learned that the child had died on the way to hospital. I threw away the newspaper.

I had arranged to meet Isobel in the afternoon and had until then in which to pass the time. For most of the morning I watched the men dismantling the pieces of the fairground and loading them on to the lorries. By midday the square had been emptied of equipment and the police were allowing normal traffic to pass through.

After luncheon in the hotel I borrowed a friend's motor-cycle and took it out on to the main road. Half an hour later in a buoyant mood, I met Isobel. She was wearing the pale-blue dress again, as I had requested. Again we walked, this time leaving the town and finding several paths through the countryside. I wanted to make love to her, but she would not allow me to.

On our way back to the town we were caught unexpectedly in a summer shower, which soaked us thoroughly. I had planned to entertain her with another dinner at the hotel, but instead we hitched a ride back to her house. She would not let me go inside with her. Instead, I promised to return to the town during the following week. She agreed to see me then.

As I went into the foyer of the hotel one of the porters told me that the mother of the child had committed suicide in the afternoon. It had been she, according to the porter, who had encouraged the child to stand on the roundabout as it was moving. For a while we discussed the tragedy, then I had a meal in the hotel restaurant. Afterwards I went to the local cinema and watched a double-feature horror programme. In the interval I noticed Isobel sitting a few rows in front of me, kissing with a young man approximately her own age. She didn't see me. I left at once and in the morning I returned to London.

*   *   *

In one village I discovered a transistor radio. Its batteries were flat. I took them out of the back of the radio and warmed them slowly the next time I was near a fire. While they were still warm I put them back into the radio and switched it on.

At that time the BBC was broadcasting on one wavelength only, interspersing long sessions of light music with news-reports. Though I listened until the batteries went flat two hours later, I heard no bulletin about the fighting, nor about the plight of the refugees, nor about any political subject whatsoever. I gathered that there had been a plane-crash in South America.

The next time I had batteries for the radio, the only channel I could find was Radio Peace . . . broadcast from a converted iron-ore ship moored off the Isle of Wight. The output of that was limited to prolonged prayer-sessions, Bible-readings and hymns.

*   *   *

We were running short of food again and Lateef made the decision to approach a near-by village and arrange a barter. We consulted our maps.

From experience we had learned that it was good general policy to avoid any village or town with more than about a thousand inhabitants, or situated anywhere near a major road. We had found that a high percentage of such places were either occupied by one faction or another and were subject to martial law in practice as well as theory, or else that a small garrison or camp would be maintained. As this effectively took from our sphere of operations most towns and villages, we were obliged to obtain the bulk of our supplies from isolated hamlets and solitary farms and houses. If we were fortunate enough to find somewhere that would provide us readily with what we needed, then we would either make an encampment near by, or keep on the move in the immediate neighbourhood.

Looking at the map, Lateef made a decision to go towards a village about two miles to the west of us. One of the other men dissented, saying that he had heard that in the town three miles beyond this village was a Nationalist Forces headquarters. He said he would be happier if we detoured around the town either through villages to the north or to the south.

For a while we discussed it, but finally Lateef overruled us. He said that our primary concern was food and that because of the number of farms near the village we would stand the best chance there.

As we approached the village we saw two or three farms securely barricaded and defended.

By an unwritten law of the countryside, refugees were allowed to traverse or camp in fields lying fallow, on condition they stole no food nor attempted to enter the farmhouses. In all my time on the road, I was subconsciously aware of this rule, and like everyone else I tried to work within it.

For a short time some refugees from East Anglia had joined Lateef's group, but they clearly adopted the attitude of each man for himself, and Lateef had separated us from them.

We passed the farmhouses, therefore, and headed for the village.

As was our custom, Lateef walked at the head of our column with three other men, immediately behind them came the handcarts containing our possessions, camping equipment and goods for barter, and the rest of the group followed on behind.

Because of my rifle, Lateef told me to walk alongside the leading cart, secreting the weapon in the false bottom in which we normally concealed unacceptable materials during searches or interrogations.

By this I could detect a slight reversal in Lateef's attitude towards the rifle. Whereas before he had maintained that it was better to be unarmed as a form of self-protection, I saw now that he acknowledged the need to defend ourselves even if that defence was not itself apparent to potential aggressors.

We came to the village along a minor road that ran across country from the town on the far side of this village until where it joined a major road some eight miles to the east of us. Again, it was from experience that we knew it was better to come to a strange village along a road rather than across the fields. Though we felt immediately more exposed, we believed we were establishing a better basis for the coming barter by doing so.

According to the map the village had no actual nucleus, but was more a straggling collection of houses along two narrow roads: the one we were on and one that crossed it at right angles. From one end to another it was probably more than a mile long – typical of the villages in this region.

We passed the first house in silence. It had been abandoned and its windows were all broken. The same was true of the next house, and the one after, and of all the houses for the first two hundred yards leading into the centre.

As we rounded the bend, there was an explosion in front of us, and one of the men at Lateef's side was thrown backwards.

We stopped. Those near the handcarts crouched down behind them, the others took what cover they could find at the side of the road. I looked down at the man who had fallen. He was on the ground five yards from where I crouched. The bullet had struck him in the throat, tearing away a large chunk of his neck. Blood spurted fitfully from his jugular vein, and though his eyes stared skywards with the dull glaze of death, he continued to make faint rasping noises from what was left of his throat. In seconds, he quietened.

Ahead of us a barricade had been erected across the road. It wasn't the kind of barricade to which we had grown accustomed – an untidy barrier of paving-stones, old cars or masonry – but had been designed purposively and built with bricks and cement. In the centre was a narrow gate through which pedestrians could pass, and on either side of this were two protective raised sections behind which I could just make out the figures of men. As I watched one of them fired again, and the bullet smashed into the wood of the front of the handcart not two feet from where I was. I crouched down even lower.

'Whitman! You've got the rifle. Shoot back.'

I looked over at Lateef. He was lying on the ground with two other men, trying to shelter behind a low mound of earth.

I said: 'They're too well protected.'

I saw that the houses to each side of the barricade had been similarly defended with a wall of concrete. I wondered whether it would be possible to enter the village by going across the fields and coming to it from the side, but the inhabitants were so obviously hostile that there would be little point.

Reaching into the false bottom of the handcart I slid out the rifle and loaded it. I was aware that every member of our group was watching me. Still attempting to keep as close to the side of the cart as possible, I aimed the rifle towards the barricade, trying to find a target I would be reasonably certain of striking.

I waited for a movement.

In the next few seconds a variety of thoughts passed through my mind. This wasn't the first occasion on which I had been in possession of a lethal weapon, but it was the first time I had ever taken deliberate aim with the knowledge that if I was successful I would kill or injure somebody. It is at times like this that one would try to rationalise all one's actions if it were not for the immediate need for direct participation.

Lateef said quietly: 'What are you waiting for?'

'I can't see anyone to aim at.'

'Put a shot over their heads. No . . . wait. Let me think.'

I let the barrel sink. I had not wanted to fire. As the next few seconds passed I knew I would not be able to fire it in this premeditated way. Thus, when Lateef told me to return it to its hiding-place, I was relieved. A direct order from him to shoot would have created a situation almost impossible for me to resolve.

'It's no good,' he said, not just to me, but to everyone in earshot. 'We'll never get in there. We'll have to retreat.'

I think I had known that from the moment of the first shot. I realised that to Lateef this decision meant a lot as it was in some ways an abrogation of his authority. The man who had told Lateef about the Nationalist garrison was near him, but he said nothing.

There was a white sheet over the top of the handcart. We had used it on several occasions in the past when wishing to underline our neutrality. Lateef asked me to pass it to him. He stood up, unfolding the cloth as he did so. No one at the barricade fired. I had to admire his bravery; under the same circumstances of leadership I would have risked anyone's life but my own.

63

When I am in danger I have found that my capacity for self-honesty overrules all my thoughts.

After several seconds Lateef told us to get back in the road and to move away slowly. I stood up myself, crouching down behind the bulk of the handcart. Our little convoy began to move back the way we had come.

Lateef stood between us and the hostile village. He held the white sheet at arm's length, as if to provide cover for the rest of us. Slowly, carefully, he stepped backwards, obviously uncertain what would happen if he turned and walked with the rest of us.

The handcart was half-way round the bend that would take us out of the line of fire, when the last shot sounded. Although some of the men not actually hauling on a handcart scattered to the sides of the road, the rest of us broke into a sprint until we were round the curve in the road. When we were all out of the line of gunfire we stopped.

Lateef rejoined us a few seconds later. He was swearing violently. The bullet had passed through the white sheet and scuffed his sleeve. A piece of cloth about four inches square had been torn away from near his elbow. We judged that had the bullet been even a quarter of an inch higher it would have smashed his bone.

When I was in my sleeping-bag that night it occurred to me that Lateef had come out of the day's events in a stronger position. I was glad that my own thoughts were private, for they revealed me to be a greater coward than I had feared. For the first time since she had been taken by the Afrims I felt a strong sexual urge for Isobel, missing and wanting her, tormented by false memories of happiness together.

*   *   *

In the afternoon I spent about an hour with Sally, while Isobel walked into a near-by village to try to obtain food. Money was the greatest problem in this respect, as we had only a pound or two left out of all that we had brought with us.

In talking to Sally I found myself treating her as an adult for the first time. She had no way of knowing what Isobel and I had discussed, but her bearing had the manner of a suddenly increased sense of responsibility. This pleased me immensely.

The evening passed in silence for the large part; certainly, Isobel and I exchanged only a couple of sentences. When night

64

came we laid out in our tents in the manner we had done since the start: Isobel and Sally in one tent and myself in the other.

I found myself regretting that the conversation with Isobel had not come to a more determined conclusion. As it was, I felt we had not achieved anything.

I lay awake for an hour, then drifted into sleep. Almost at once, it seemed, I was awoken by Isobel.

I reached out and touched her; she was naked.

I said: 'What . . . ?'

'Sshh. You'll wake Sally.'

She undid the zip of my sleeping-bag and lay down with her body against me. I put my arms around her and, still half-asleep and unthinking of what had gone between us during the day, I began to caress her sexually.

Our love-making was not well matched. My mind made indistinct by sleep, I was unable to concentrate and achieved orgasm only after a long time, Isobel, though, was voracious in a way I had never known her before, the noise of her gasps almost deafening me. She came to orgasm twice, disconcertingly violently the first time.

We lay together linked for several minutes afterwards, then Isobel murmured something and attempted to wriggle out from under me. I rolled to one side and she pulled away. I tried to restrain her, placing an arm around her shoulders. She said nothing, but got to her feet and went out of the tent. I lay back in the residual warmth of our bodies and fell asleep again.

In the morning Sally and I found we were on our own.

*   *   *

There was a policy discussion the next day, stemming mainly from our lack of food. After checking our stores carefully we established that there was now sufficient food to last us only another two days. After that, we would be able to manage on biscuits, chocolate and so forth for another week.

This was our first encounter with a real prospect of starvation, and none of us liked it.

Lateef outlined the alternatives open to us.

He said that we could continue as we had been doing so far: moving from village to village, bartering for food as necessary, and pilfering exchangeable goods from abandoned buildings and cars as we came across them. He pointed out that the military activity around us was on the increase, and though we were not involved in it because of our vagrancy, we could not afford to ignore it. People still living in towns and villages were taking defensive precautions accordingly.

Lateef recounted to us a story he had not previously told us, about a village in the north which had been taken over by a group of Negroes claiming to be a part of the regular Afrim forces. Although the blacks had not established a proper garrison, and appeared to have no military discipline, the suspicions of the villagers had not been aroused. After a week, when units of the Nationalist Army were reported to be in the neighbourhood, the blacks had run amok, killing several hundred civilians before the Nationalist forces had arrived.

This, Lateef said, was not an isolated incident. Similar outrages had been recorded all over the country and had been committed by members of the armed forces on all three sides of the conflict. From the point of view of the private citizens, all outsiders should be treated as enemies. This attitude was spreading, he said, and made more hazardous our attempts to trade with civilians.

Another alternative would be to surrender ourselves formally to one side or another and enrol into the military. The arguments for this were strong: a rationalisation of our existence, the fact we were all reasonably healthy men capable of military duty, a commitment to a situation that had a deep effect on us all.

We could join the Nationalists, the so-called 'legal' army that defended the policies of Tregarth's government, but one that was now committed to an overt policy of genocide. We could join the Royal Secessionists, the white supporters of the Afrim cause who although officially non-legal and under continuous sentence of death, had a great deal of public support. If Tregarth's government were overthrown, either from within by a military victory or by effective diplomatic action from the U.N., it was likely that the Secessionists would take or sponsor office. We could join the United Nations peace-keeping force, which although technically non-participating, in effect had had to intervene on many occasions. Or we could align ourselves with one of the outside participants, such as the U.S. Marines (which had taken over civilian police responsibility) or the theoretically uncommitted Commonwealth forces, who had little effect on the progress of the war beyond further confusing the situation.

A third choice open to us, Lateef said, was to surrender ourselves to a civilian welfare organisation and return eventually to a quasi-legal situation. Though this was ideally the most attractive alternative, it was doubtful if any of the refugees would be prepared to take it in practice. Until the military situation quietened down, and the social effects of the Afrim uprising were absorbed, such a recourse would be hazardous. In any event, it would mean ultimately that we would have to live under Tregarth's government, which would automatically involve us in the crisis.

Lateef said that it was our present lack of effective involvement which was the best argument for continuing to stay as we were. In any event, the main preoccupation of most of the men was to be reunited with their women and to surrender ourselves to a participating faction would reduce our chances of this.

A vote was taken and we elected to do as Lateef suggested. We moved on towards a village five miles to the north of us.

Again I detected a feeling amongst the other men that Lateef's position had been strengthened both by the shooting at the barricade the day before, and by his reasoned arguing of the alternatives. I myself had no wish to become involved with him in a struggle for power, but nevertheless my possession of the rifle could not be entirely ignored by him.

As we moved northwards I walked at his side.

*   *   *

By this time I had bought my own motor-cycle and used it those week-ends I went to see Isobel.

My early days of recklessness had passed and though I still enjoyed the sensation of speed, I kept to within the legal limits for much of the time. It was rare for me, when by myself, to open up the cycle and take it to its maximum speed, though when Isobel was on the back she encouraged me to do it often.

Our relationship was developing more slowly than I would have liked.

Before I had met her I had enjoyed several physical affairs with other girls, and though Isobel could present me with no moral, religious or physical reason why we should not sleep together, she had never allowed me to go further than superficial contact. For some reason I persevered.

One afternoon, in particular, we had ridden on the motor-cycle up to a near-by hill where there was a gliding club. We had watched the sailplanes for some time before growing bored.

On our way back to town, Isobel directed me away from the

road and into a copse of trees. This time, she took the initiative in our preliminary kissing and did not stop me when I removed part of her clothing. The moment, though, my hand went inside her brassière and touched her nipple, she pulled away from me. On this occasion I was not willing to stop and persisted. She tried again to prevent me, and in the ensuing struggle I pulled off her brassière and skirt, tearing the latter in the process.

From this point there was no reason to continue, and after she had dressed we returned to her parents' house. I went back to my room at the hall of residence that evening and did not see Isobel again for three weeks.

*　　*　　*

As the news reached us, there was much speculation about the implications of the war. The main danger was that it would spread from continental Africa to the rest of the world. Though the bombing was over in a matter of days, no one really knew or cared to reveal how many nuclear devices there had been in Africa.

The two main powers were in the process of formal disarmament at the time, with teams of observers in both continents. The main danger, as far as both powers were concerned, was China, which had been stockpiling devices since the end of the nineteen-sixties. Territorial interests of China in Africa were not known, and it was not possible to predict how much of an influence there had been. Fissionable ores were not, by and large, readily available in Africa, nor was the necessary technology to assemble the weapons. Under these circumstances, it appeared that one or both of the powers had been supplying various countries illegally.

In effect, the source of the weapons was irrelevant; they were present in Africa and they were used.

There was one wave of bombing, then four days later another. The rest of the world waited uneasily, but that was the last of it. Things began to move: welfare organisations launched huge relief-schemes for what survivors there may be, the main powers argued, threatened, but quietened. In Britain, the news was taken calmly: the holocaust in Africa was the embodiment of something awful, but not something that seemed to threaten us directly. And, anyway, we were in the last stages of a General Election; the one declared by John Tregarth six months after he had come to power, and the one in which he consolidated his majority.

Meanwhile, reports came back from Africa describing the horrors of the thermonuclear aftermath. Most major cities had been partially or wholly destroyed, some were still intact. But Africa is large; a majority of the population survived the bombing. Many died later from the results of flash-burns, radiation-sickness and the residual radioactivity . . . but millions survived.

The relief workers were almost entirely incapable of dealing with the survivors. Many died; perhaps five millions, and not all of these as an outcome of the bombing.

But for all the deaths, millions still survived, and as hunger grew so did desperation. And as it seemed that continental Africa was no longer capable of supporting human life, so there developed a drift away from it.

It started slowly, but within three months it had built up into an exodus. Any boat or aircraft that could be found and made to operate was used. The emigrants headed for nowhere in particular . . . only away from Africa.

They landed in due course in countries all over the world: India, France, Turkey, the Middle East, America, Greece. In the period of evacuation, it was estimated that between seven and eight million people left Africa. In the course of about a year, just over two millions of them landed in Britain.

The Africans, the Afrims, were welcome nowhere. But where they landed, they stayed. Everywhere they caused social upheaval; but in Britain, where a neo-racist government had come to power on an economic-reform ticket, they did much more.

*　*　*

I reported to the recruiting-station at the appointed time of one-thirty in the afternoon.

For several days there had been a saturation of advertisements on television and in the press, stating that entry into the armed forces was still voluntary, but that conscription was to be introduced in the next few weeks. This statement was underlined with an implication that men who volunteered at this time would be given preferential treatment over those who were eventually drafted.

I learned through friends of mine that certain categories of men would be the first to be selected. My job at the cloth factory qualified me for one of these categories.

During this period, my working life at the factory was not happy and the pay in the army would be slightly higher than what I was then receiving. I therefore had a variety of motives when I reported for the medical examination.

I had applied for officer training, learning from the advertisements that a degree was sufficient to establish suitability. I was directed to a specific room in the building where a sergeant-major in dress uniform told me what to do, adding the word 'sir' to the end of every sentence.

I was given an IQ test, which was marked in my presence. The errors I made were carefully explained to me. Then I was questioned sketchily on my background and political standing, and finally I was instructed to remove my clothes and to go into the next room.

The lighting was very bright. There was a wooden bench along one wall and I was told to sit on it while waiting for the doctor. I was not sure where the doctor was, for apart from myself the room was deserted.

I had been waiting for ten minutes when a young nurse came in and sat at a desk opposite to where I was sitting. I found I was embarrassed to be naked in her presence. My arms were folded across my chest, and not liking to attract her attention I did not move them. I crossed my legs in an attempt to preserve modesty.

I felt myself to be in a position of exceptional sexual vulnerability, and although she paid little attention to me, and I told myself that she was accustomed to seeing men in the nude, I was constantly aware of her presence. In a few moments I felt a tightening in my groin, and to my consternation realised that my penis was beginning to erect.

Awareness of the tumescence did nothing to reduce the condition. I tried to restrain the organ by gripping it tightly between my thighs, but this soon became painful. It was at this point that the nurse glanced up from her work and looked at me. As she did so, the penis swung out of the restraint of my legs and assumed its fully erect position. I covered it at once with my hands. The nurse looked back at her work.

'The doctor will see you in a few moments,' she said.

I sat motionlessly, concealing my penis with my hands. By the clock on the wall opposite I saw that ten minutes passed. I was still in possession of a full erection when a man in a white coat appeared at the far end of the room and asked me to step inside. As it would have appeared unnatural to walk across the room with my hands at my crutch, I reluctantly allowed my arms to swing at my side. I was aware of the girl's gaze on my body as I walked past her desk.

Once inside the main examination room the erection began to dwindle and in less than a minute had gone altogether.

I was given a routine medical examination, had my chest X-rayed and samples of my blood and urine taken. I was presented with a form to sign which stated that subject only to medical suitability I would be commissioned into the British Nationalist Army as a trainee 2nd Lieutenant, and that I would report for duty at the time and place indicated on my mobilisation certificate. I signed it and was given my clothes again.

There followed an interview with a man in civilian clothing, who questioned me at great length on subjects central to my overall character and personality. It was a distasteful interview and I was glad when it was over. I recall that in its course I revealed my former membership in the pro-Afrim society at the college.

A week later I received a duplicated letter which stated that my medical examination had revealed a liver complaint and that my temporary commission was accordingly terminated.

The day before this letter arrived I had seen conscription reintroduced by the Ministry of Internal Security and a corresponding increase in militant Afrim activities. A month later, with the massacre of the Nationalist troops at Colchester barracks and the arrival of the first American aircraft-carrier in the Irish Sea, I saw that the military situation was more serious than I had imagined. Though relieved at my own lack of personal involvement, day-to-day life became less easy and my own experiences as a civilian were not better than anyone else's.

After receiving the letter from the military I visited my own doctor and had the complaint in my liver investigated. After a few days of deliberation I was informed that there was nothing wrong with it.

* * *

We encountered a large band of Negroes and were at once uncertain of what was to happen. We had the choice of three courses of action: run from them, show our defensive ability with the rifle or meet them.

What disconcerted us most was that they were not wearing Afrim uniforms, but were clad in the same sort of clothes as ourselves. It was possible that they were a group of civilian refugees, but we had heard that Nationalist troops treated such people with extreme callousness. The result of this was that most Negro civilians had surrendered themselves to the welfare organisations, and those few who remained had integrated themselves with white groups.

The men we met were friendly, well-fed and appeared to be unarmed. They did have three large handcarts near to which we were not allowed to approach, and it is possible that these contained weapons.

We spoke for several minutes, exchanging the usual pieces of news which were the only real currency on the refugee network. The blacks showed no signs of nerves, nor any awareness that we had a guarded attitude towards them.

They did however reveal certain signs of excitement, a cause for which we were unable to determine. Our main concern during the encounter was for our own sakes, and as such we were not judging their behaviour as much as we might at another time. But it seemed to me that they behaved as if jubilant, or as if anticipating something.

In the end we moved on, leaving the blacks near a wood. We crossed a field, then passed out of sight. Lateef called me over to him.

'They were Afrim guerrillas,' he said. 'Did you notice their identity-bracelets?'

*　　*　　*

Sally and I waited for a few hours to see whether Isobel was going to return. I felt in no need to explain to Sally why she had left us; on the contrary, I deduced from the child's manner that she had anticipated some such act. I think that she regretted that it had had to come, but that she was capable of accepting the new situation.

Isobel had taken with her exactly half of our remaining money, in addition to a suitcase of her own clothes and some of the food. All the camping and sleeping equipment she had left with us.

By midday it was clear that Isobel was not coming back. I began to make preparations for a meal, but Sally said she would do it. I allowed her to take over and meanwhile packed our gear. At this point I had made no decision about what we were to do, but I felt that it was time to leave this particular location.

When we had eaten, I explained to Sally as best I could what we could do.

My predominant feeling at this time was a sense of inadequacy. This extended to my ability to make the right decision regarding our movements, as well as giving me severe doubts as to the real reasons for the breakdown of my marriage. I felt that Sally was in potential danger as I could, through my inadequacy, make more mistakes. In consulting her on the next move we should take, I felt I was not only giving Sally some participation, but was assisting myself to come to terms with my own weaknesses.

I explained to Sally that her mother and I had agreed that we were to return to London, while she went on to Bristol. We were not going to return to our house, but we were going to find somewhere new to live. Sally told me that she understood.

I then went into some detail about the difficulties confronting us: that we were out of touch with the political situation, that we had very little money, that it would not be possible to go back by car, that we would probably have to hike for the major part of the way.

Sally said: 'But couldn't we go on a train, Daddy?'

Children have a facility for cutting sideways across a problem and seeing possible solutions that have not occurred to their parents. In the time we had been living in the countryside I had completely overlooked the existence of the railway system. I wondered if Isobel had similarly not thought of it, or whether she was intending to reach Bristol that way.

'It's a question of money,' I replied. 'We probably haven't got enough. We'll have to find out. Is that what you'd like to do?'

'Yes. I don't want to live in the tent any more.'

I had learned that it was not possible to plan too far ahead. But I couldn't avoid returning to the question of what we would do if the situation in London was as bad as when we had left. If the occupation by militant Afrims of houses was continuing, and the law-enforcement agencies were divided, then we would not be the only people looking for accommodation. If the situation was as bad as I feared, we might well be obliged to leave London once more. If that happened, then the only place I could think of going to was my younger brother's house in Carlisle. Even if we were able to go there, the practical difficulty of travelling three hundred miles was still to be faced. Unfortunately, I could see no alternative – he was the only remaining member of my family after the death of my parents four years before, and of Clive, my elder brother, in the confrontation at Bradford.

As far as Sally was concerned, though, the matter was settled, and we collected the remainder of our belongings and packed them. I carried our remaining suitcase and the rucksack, and Sally carried the other bag containing our clothes. We walked eastwards, not knowing the location of the nearest railway station, but moving in that direction as we felt it was the right one.

We came, after about a mile and a half, to a macadamed road. We followed this in a northerly direction until we encountered a telephone-box. As a matter of course, I lifted the receiver to find out whether it was working. In the past we had found that although the receivers had not been damaged in any way, the lines were dead.

On this occasion there was a short series of clicks, and then a woman's voice answered.

'Exchange. Which number do you require?'

I hesitated. I had not expected a reply and was thus unprepared.

'I'd like to make a call . . . to Carlisle, please.'

'I'm sorry, caller. All trunk lines are engaged.'

There was a note of finality to her voice, as if she were about to close the connection.

'Er – could you get me a London number then, please?'

'I'm sorry, caller. All lines to London are engaged.'

'Would you ring me back when they are free?'

'This exchange is open for local calls only.' That final tone again.

I said quickly: 'Look, I wonder if you can help me. I'm trying to get to the railway station. Could you direct me to it, please?'

'Where are you speaking from?'

I gave her the address of the telephone-box as printed on the plaque in front of me.

'Hold the line a moment.' She closed the connection and I waited. After about three minutes she came back on. 'The station nearest to you is in Warnham, about three miles to the south of you. Thank you, caller.'

The line cleared.

Sally was waiting for me outside the box and I related to her the substance of the conversation. As I did so, we both became aware of the sound of heavy diesel-lorries, and a few seconds later seven troop-carriers passed us. An officer was standing in the rear of one of them and he shouted something to us as they passed. We were not able to hear him. I recall a feeling of vague reassurance at that moment, even though it was the first time

I had witnessed actual troop-movements.

When the lorries had passed I was able to identify the state which had caused my earlier disquiet. It was that we were the only people around.

While living in the tent, our only contact with other people had been on those occasions when we had visited shops to purchase food. Even then, we had all observed a slackness which had not been noticeable before the trouble began. But now Sally and I were as if alone.

We began our walk to Warnham, and within a few minutes saw more signs of military activity and civilian inactivity that caused us both alarm.

A mile from the telephone-box we passed through a village. We walked the length of the street without meeting anyone, but in the windows of the last house we saw the shape of a man. I waved and called out to him, but either he did not see me or did not choose to, and he moved out of sight.

Outside the village we encountered an emplacement of heavy artillery manned by several hundred soldiers. There was a rough, but guarded, barbed-wire barrier between them and the road, and as we approached it were warned to move on. I tried to speak with the soldier, and an N.C.O. was called. He repeated the injunction, adding that unless we were out of the neighbourhood by nightfall we would find our lives in danger. I asked him whether they were Nationalist troops and received no reply.

Sally said: 'Daddy, I don't like guns.'

We moved on towards Warnham. Several times jet aircraft flew overhead, sometimes in formation, sometimes alone. I discovered the remains of an old newspaper and tried to read it to learn what I could about what was going on.

It was a privately printed tabloid and one which I felt sure was illegal. We had heard on the radio two weeks before that the operations of the press had been suspended temporarily. I found the tabloid to be virtually unintelligible; badly printed, abominably written, disgustingly slanted towards an overt racist xenophobia. It spoke of knives and leprosy, guns and venereal disease, rape, cannibalism and plague. It contained detailed instructions for the manufacture of such home-made weapons as petrol-bombs, coshes and garrottes. There were items of 'news', such as mass rape by Afrim militants, and raids by loyal military forces on Afrim strongholds. On the back page, at the bottom, I learned that the paper was published weekly for civilian consumption by the British Nationalist Army (Home Division).

I burned it.

The approach to Warnham Station was guarded by more soldiers. As we came into their view Sally's hand took hold of mine and gripped it tightly.

I said to her: 'It's nothing to worry about, Sally. They're just here to make sure no one tries to prevent the trains running.'

She didn't reply, perhaps detecting that I was as alarmed as she at their presence. It meant, in effect, that the trains were still running, but that they were under military control. We walked up to the barricade and I spoke to a lieutenant. He was polite and helpful. I noticed that on his sleeve he had a strip of cloth on which was stitched: *Loyal Secessionists*. I did not refer to it.

'Is it possible to get a train to London from here?' I said.

'It's possible,' he said. 'But they don't run very often. You'll have to inquire, sir.'

'May we pass through?'

'Of course.'

He nodded to the two soldiers with him and they pulled back a section of their barricade. I gave the officer my thanks and we walked up to the booking office.

It was manned by a civilian wearing the normal uniform of British Rail.

'We want to go to London,' I said. 'Could you tell me when the next train's due?'

He leaned forward across the counter, put his face close up to the glass panel and looked through at us.

'You'll have to wait till tomorrow,' he said. 'There's only one way to get a train here and that's to ring through the day before.'

'Are you saying that no trains stop here?'

'That's right. Not unless someone wants 'em to. You have to ring through to the terminal.'

'But suppose it's urgent.'

'You have to ring through to the terminal.'

I said: 'Is it too late to get a train to stop here today?'

He nodded slowly. 'The last one went through an hour ago. But if you'd like to buy your tickets now, I'll ring through to the terminal for you.'

'Just a minute.'

I turned to Sally. 'Listen, love, we'll have to sleep tonight in the tent again. You don't mind, do you? You heard what the man said.'

'O.K., Daddy. But can we definitely go home tomorrow?'

'Yes, of course.'

I said to the clerk: 'How much are the tickets?'

'Ninety pence each, please.'

I pulled out of my pocket what remained of our money and counted it. We had less than a pound.

'Can I pay for them tomorrow?' I asked the clerk.

He shook his head. 'Got to be paid in advance. If you haven't got enough now, though, I'll take a deposit and you can pay the rest tomorrow.'

'Will this be enough?'

'Should be.' He dropped the change into a drawer, reckoned the amount on to a register and passed me a slip of printed paper. 'Bring this and the rest of the money tomorrow. The train'll be here about eleven in the morning.'

I glanced at the slip. It was just a receipt for the money, not a ticket. I thanked the man and we went back outside. It had started to drizzle. I wasn't sure how I was going to obtain the rest of the money by morning, but already a half-formed determination to steal it if necessary had come to mind.

At the barricade, the young lieutenant nodded to us.

'Tomorrow, eh?' he said. 'That's happened to a lot of people here. Are you refugees?'

I told him we were, though I had not previously applied the word to our predicament.

'You should be all right in London,' he said. 'Our lot are getting things organised there.'

He gave me the name and address of a group in London who were trying to find accommodation for the homeless. I wrote it down and thanked him. He expressed concern about what we were to do tonight.

'I could have offered to find you a billet,' he said. 'We've done it before. But there's something on. We might be moving out tonight. What will you do?'

'We've got camping-equipment,' I said.

'Oh, that's all right then. But if I were you, I'd get as far away from here as you can. We're being mobilised. The Nationalists are only a couple of miles away.'

Again I thanked him and we moved on. Both Sally and I had been comforted by his outgoing nature, by his apparent willingness to assist us. But what he had said had given us cause for alarm and I decided to heed his warning. We walked another three or four miles to the south before trying to find somewhere to camp. In the end, we came across a suitable place on the side of a low hill, screened on three sides by woodland.

That night while we lay in the dark together we heard the sound of artillery, and jet aircraft roared overhead. The night was lit by brilliant flashes from explosions to the north of us. We heard troops marching along the road a quarter of a mile from us, and a stray shell exploded in the woods behind us. Sally clung to me and tried to comfort her. The noise of the artillery itself remained constant, but the explosions from the shells varied considerably between being very close and very distant. We heard small-arms fire from time to time and the sounds of men's voices.

In the morning it drizzled again, and the countryside was still. Reluctant to move, as if the act of doing so would reinitiate the violence, Sally and I stayed in our bivouac until the last possible moment. Then at ten o'clock we packed our gear hastily and set off towards the station. We arrived at just before eleven. This time there were no soldiers. The station had been bombed, and the railway track itself had been blown up in several places. We looked at the ruin in desolate horror. Later, I threw away the receipt.

That evening we were captured by a detachment of the Afrim forces and taken in for our first session of interrogation.

* * *

Isobel and I lay together in the dark. We were on the floor. In the room above us her parents were asleep in bed. They did not know I was there. Though they liked me, and encouraged Isobel to see more of me, they would not have been pleased if they were aware of what we had been trying to do in their sitting-room.

It was after three in the morning and therefore essential we made no noise.

I had removed my jacket and shirt.

Isobel had taken off her dress, her slip and her brassière. At this time our relationship had developed to the point where she allowed me to remove most of her clothing while we kissed, and to fondle her breasts. She had never allowed me to touch her in the region of her pubes. In the past, most of the girls I had known had shown a liberal attitude towards sex, and I was puzzled at Isobel's apparent lack of interest. Her reticence had been alluring at first – and continued to be so – but now I was beginning to see that she was genuinely frightened of sex. Although my interest in her had been initially almost entirely sexual, as we grew to know one another I had developed a deep liking for her and had made my sexual advances to her more and more gently. The combination of her physical beauty and her gaucherie was a continual delight to me.

After a prolonged session of kissing and petting I lay back on the floor and allowed Isobel to run her hand lightly over my chest and stomach. While she did this I found myself willing her to slide her hand into the top of my trousers and caress my penis.

Gradually her hand moved down until it was rubbing lightly against the cloth of the waistband. When her fingers did eventually explore the cloth, they came into contact with the end of my penis almost at once. Evidently unaware to that moment of my tumescence, she snatched her hand away at once and lay at my side, facing away from me, trembling.

'What's the matter?' I whispered to her after a minute or two, knowing both that I would get no reply and that I already knew what had happened. 'What's the matter?'

She said nothing. After a while I put my hand on her shoulder and found her skin to be cold.

'What's the matter?' I whispered again.

She still made no reply. In spite of what had happened, I remained erect, unaffected by the trauma she experienced.

In a while she rolled back towards me and, laying on her back, took my hand and placed it on her breast. Like her shoulder, it was cold. The nipple was shrunken and lumpy.

She said: 'Go on. Do it.'

'Do what?'

'You know. What you want.'

I didn't move, but lay there with my hand on her breast, not wishing to create a positive movement by either doing as she said or taking my hand away altogether.

When I made no response, she took my hand again and thrust it down roughly to her crutch. With her other hand she dragged down her pants and laid my hand on her pubes. I felt warm, soft down. She started shaking.

I made love to her at once. It was painful for both of us. Pleasureless. We made a lot of noise; so much so that I was scared her parents would hear us and come to investigate. As I climaxed, my penis slipped from its place and my semen went half inside her, half on to the floor.

I pulled away from her as soon as I could and lay away from her. Part of me remained detached, seeing wryly my experienced sexual artistry reduced to fumbling adolescence by the encounter with frigid innocence; part of me lay curled up on the floor, unwilling to move. . . .

In the end it was Isobel who moved first. She stood up and switched on the low-powered table-lamp. I looked up at her, seeing her slim young body nude for the first time, denuded for the first time of sexual mystery. She pulled on her clothes, kicked mine across to me. I put them on. Our eyes didn't meet.

On the carpet where we had laid there was a small patch of damp. We tried to remove it with paper tissues, but a faint stain remained.

I was ready to leave. Isobel came over to me, whispered in my ear that I was to push my motor-cycle to the end of the road before starting it up. Then she kissed me. We agreed to see each other again the following week-end. As we walked out into the hall we were holding hands.

Her father was sitting on the bottom step of the stairs dressed in his pyjamas. He looked tired. As I walked past him he said nothing to me, but stood up and held Isobel tightly by her wrist. I left, starting the engine outside the house.

We had not used any form of contraceptive. Though Isobel did not become pregnant from that intercourse she did conceive a few weeks before we were married. From that time we had sex together very occasionally, and to my knowledge she attained orgasm only rarely. After Sally was born, what sexual dependence on one another that we had ever had grew less, and in due course I found myself turning to other women who were able to give me what Isobel couldn't.

In the good times, I would gaze at Isobel across a distance, seeing again the pale blue dress and the youthful beauty of her face, and a bitter regret would well inside me.

*   *   *

As the days passed since the abduction of the women by the Afrim soldiers, it seemed to me that while my own quest grew stronger that of the other men diminished. I found myself questioning whether we were moving on in the eternal search for a safe place to camp and somewhere that we may obtain food, or whether we were still pursuing our search for the women.

They were mentioned less and less frequently, and since the visit to Augustin's brothel it was sometimes as if they had never been with us. But we were reminded forcibly of what might have happened to them on the day after we met the African guerrillas.

We came to a group of houses that were marked on the map as being a hamlet called Stowefield. At first sight it appeared to be no different from any one of a hundred others we had come across in the past.

We approached it with our customary caution, determined that if the hamlet were barricaded we would retreat immediately.

That there had at one time been barricades became apparent at once. Across the road at the side of the first house there was a pile of rubble, which had been pushed aside to make a gap wide enough for a lorry to pass through.

With Lateef, I inspected the ground behind where the barricade had been and we discovered several dozen empty shotgun cartridges.

We investigated every house in the hamlet and within half an hour had established that it had been evacuated. We were fortunate in finding canned food in several of the houses and were thus able to replenish our supplies.

We speculated as to the identity of the men who had raided the village. It was probably prejudice which prompted the majority of us to assume it was the Afrims, but it had been our experience that this was the kind of action they would take against small settlements that they found barricaded.

What had become of the inhabitants we had no way of telling. Later, as we searched the houses for suitable billets, one of the men discovered something and shouted for the rest of us to come.

I arrived with Lateef. As soon as we saw what was there, he shouted at everyone, telling them to wait downstairs. He indicated that I was to stay.

There were the bodies of four young white women in the upstairs room. Each was naked and each had been assaulted sexually. My heart had begun to beat faster at my first sight of them, as the fates that could have befallen Sally and Isobel had been prominent in my imagination for some time. It took only two or three seconds to establish that these women were unknown to me, but even so my heart continued at an accelerated pace for some minutes afterwards.

My early alarm soon turned to shock and then to anger. Each of the women was young and had been physically attractive. Their deaths had come after a long period of helpless agony: the torment was embedded in their expressions. Each one was tied hand and foot, and had evidently struggled to escape from the bonds in her last few minutes of life.

81

The men who assaulted them had disfigured their bodies with either bayonets or knives, slashing them many times in the region of their genitals. There was blood all over the floor.

Lateef and I discussed what we should do. I suggested that we bury them, but neither of us relished the task of carrying the bodies downstairs. The alternative that Lateef suggested was to burn the house. It was set apart from the ones nearest to it, and it did not seem likely that the blaze would spread to others.

We went downstairs and spoke with the others. Two of the men had been sick, the rest of us felt nauseated in the extreme. Lateef's suggestion was adopted, and a few minutes later the house was fired.

We moved away to the other end of the village and set up a camp for the night.

* * *

For a variety of reasons I was one of the few men who worked in the cutting-shop of the factory. In spite of the equal-pay legislation that had gone through in the last months of the government immediately prior to Tregarth taking office, there were still many different kinds of work which were exclusively or nearly exclusively the domain of women. In the bulk-cloth industry cutting is one of these.

My own colleagues of my own sex were old Dave Harman, a pensioner who came in mornings to sweep the floor and make tea, and a youngster named Tony who tried to flirt with the younger women but who was treated by them all as a cheeky young urchin. I never discovered his true age, but he couldn't have been less than twenty. How he came to be working at the factory I never asked, and there built up between us a kind of male understanding that unified us against the vulgarity of the women.

My own relationship with the women was acceptable once we had overcome the initial problems.

It was thought, for instance, by a sizeable number of the women that I had been brought in as some form of supervisor or inspector, and whenever I attempted to speak to them I was treated with cold politeness. In this, my college-rounded vowels did little to help. Once I had established in my mind what was the probable cause of the friction, I went to great pains to let them know my position in the cutting-shop. When this was clear the atmosphere lightened considerably, though there were still one or two women who could not but retain a slightly distant air. Within a few weeks things had relaxed to the point where I felt as if my presence was taken for granted.

With this relaxation came a growing vulgarity of behaviour. In my relatively sheltered life to this point – sheltered in the sense that I had not mixed with large numbers of working people – I had lived by the assumption that women were the more socially restrained sex. It may of course have been the developing national situation which encouraged a slackening of morality as a reaction against the new repressive laws, or simply that this group of women had known each other for years and were of a similar background. In any event, a typical working day was punctuated with obscenities, disgusting jokes and various direct and indirect references to either my or Tony's sexual organs. Tony told me once that shortly before I had come to the cutting-shop, one of the women, in a mock-serious kind of way, had unzipped the front of his trousers and tried to grab him. He told me this off-handedly, though I could tell he had been upset by the incident.

There were several coloured women in the cutting-shop, and as the Afrim situation intensified I watched them when I could to see how they reacted. There were five Indians or Pakistanis, and seven of Negro stock. On the face of it, their behaviour showed no change, though during some of the more offensive sessions of banter, I noticed how they would remain silent.

It was my custom during this period to eat for lunch the sandwiches that Isobel made for me. This was partly in order to save a little of our money, and partly because the quality of food available in public restaurants deteriorated considerably.

I understood that the company was not receiving as many orders as it had once done, and consequently the work-load upon us was light. Following government restrictions it was not possible to make staff redundant, except at the cost of high financial penalty, and our labour-force was not reduced in any way. Shortly after I joined the firm the length of our break for lunch was increased from one and a half to two hours, and at the time of the first secessions in the armed forces it was increased by a further half-hour. Sick-leave was encouraged by our employers, though after the government's temporary withdrawal of National Health benefits absenteeism was rare.

It became necessary to find ways of passing the surplus time in the social company of each other.

Board games were brought in from home, and packs of playing-cards. Several women brought in such things as needlework or knitting, and others wrote letters. For my own part I used the free time for reading, but found that if I did too much of it in the dimly lit room, my eyes would begin to hurt. Very few of us ventured out during the lunch-break. Once or twice, some of the women went out shopping together, but on the whole it was considered too hazardous to be done habitually.

I don't know how it began, but several of the women used the time to get together around the top of a bench and play on an improvised ouija board. The first I was aware of it was one day when I was walking through the adjoining warehouse with the intention of stretching my muscles. The women were in a corner of the warehouse. Seven of them actually sat at the table and another ten or twenty stood around watching. The pointer they were using was an inverted plastic tumbler, and the letters of the alphabet were scribbled on scraps of paper around the edge.

One of the older women was asking questions into the air, while the tumbler spelled out the answers from under the fingertips of the seven participants. I watched fascinated for a while, unable to determine whether the women were actually moving the tumbler voluntarily or not. Annoyed that I was unable to understand it, I walked away.

At the far side of the warehouse, behind a stacked pile of rolls of cloth, I came across Tony and one of the girls who worked with him. Although they were both fully clothed, they were lying in the normal position for intercourse, and he had his hand inside the top of her dress, holding one of her breasts. Neither of them saw me.

As I turned away there was the sound of several voices from the ouija table. One of the women, a Negress, broke away from the group and ran into the cutting-room. A few seconds later I heard her talking loudly to her friends, and then the sound of someone crying.

By the end of the following week all the coloured women had left the firm.

*　　*　　*

As night fell the house was still burning; a glow of orange a hundred yards away.

The mood of the group had altered subtly. For me, and I presumed for the other men, the assault on the four young women represented a physical manifestation of our fears about our own abducted women. It is one thing to imagine an atrocity; it is

84

something else again to witness it.

Individually, I think we were all horrified and numbed . . . but working as a group our reaction was one of more directed determination not to become further involved in the civil war. The search for the abducted women was not mentioned; for my own part what I had seen in the house had only hardened my resolution in this respect. It was Sally I was worried about, for she was innocent. My daughter, not my wife, was uppermost in my mind.

As darkness came on, I moved away from the main group of men and went into a house about twenty yards from the one we had fired. Behind me there was a glow of smouldering wood. The blaze had finished now, but it would go on smouldering for hours. There was a sweet smell of smoke in the air, obstinately pleasant.

I sat by myself in an old armchair in a downstairs room of the house I had occupied and brooded about what I would do in the morning.

Time passed. I became aware of the sound of engines, but I ignored them. They grew louder, drowning my thoughts. I leaped out of my chair and ran through the house and into the small garden at the rear.

The sky was clear of clouds and a quarter-moon threw enough light to mark the ground. I had been sitting in the dark in the house (as was our custom when temporarily occupying evacuated property) and my eyes adapted at once.

It took me only a couple of seconds to locate the source of the sound: it was a formation of helicopters travelling at a low height and speed from the south in a direction that would carry them over the village. As they approached, I dropped to the ground, my hand tightening over the rifle. I counted them as they passed overhead: there were twelve. They slowed even more in the next few seconds, and landed in one of the fields beyond the village.

From where I was lying I was not able to see them. I climbed to my feet and peered over the hedge. I heard the engines ticking over together in a low, muted grumbling sound.

I waited.

For another ten minutes I stood still, debating whether to rejoin the others. There was no way of telling why the helicopters were here, or whether they knew of our presence. It was unlikely that they had not seen the smouldering remains of the house.

With an abruptness that startled me, there was a burst of gunfire in the near distance, and two or three loud explosions. From the direction of the flashes I guessed that they were coming from the far side of a large wood that I had seen earlier, running alongside the main road about a mile from the hamlet. There was more gunfire, more explosions. I saw one spout of white flame then a red verey-light shot up into the sky from the direction of the wood.

Almost immediately the helicopters took off again still holding their formation. They swooped into the air and swung away towards the wood. They became lost to sight though the sound of their engines remained clear.

I heard a movement behind me: the house door opening, closing.

'Is that you, Whitman?'

I made out the dim shape of another man. As he came up to me I saw that it was Olderton, a man with whom I had had only superficial contact so far.

'Yes. What's going on?'

'No one knows. Lateef sent me to find you. What the devil are you doing?'

I told him I had been looking for food and that I was going back to the main camp in a few minutes.

'You'd better come back now,' Olderton said. 'Lateef's talking of moving on. He thinks we're too close to the main road.'

'I think we ought to know what's happening before we move.'

'That's up to Lateef.'

'Is it?' For no reason I could determine at that moment I felt a taint of rebellion in being told what to do. In any event, I didn't want to discuss it with Olderton.

The sound of the helicopters in the distance took on a new note, and we went back to where I had been standing before, looking across the fields in the direction of the wood.

'Where are they?' Olderton said.

'I can't see.'

There was a renewed burst of gunfire, then a shrill, high-pitched whistling sound followed immediately by four explosions coming almost together. A brilliant ball of flame rose up inside the wood, then dwindled. I heard more gunfire, then a helicopter roared over the village. There was another whistling sound, and four more explosions. As the second helicopter passed overhead the sequence was repeated again.

'Rockets,' Olderton muttered. 'They're after something on the main road.'

'Who are they?'

86

'Lateef thought they were Afrims. He said the helicopters looked as if they were Russian.'

Over at the main road the barrage went on. The helicopters were timed exactly right. As the explosion from one set of rockets died down, another gunship came in and followed up. Meanwhile, small-arms fire rattled from the ground.

'I think it's those guerrillas,' I said suddenly. 'The ones we met yesterday They've ambushed something on the main road.'

Olderton said nothing. As I thought about it, the more likely it became. The Negroes had been concealing something, on that we had all agreed. If, as Lateef had guessed, the helicopter gunships were Russina-supplied and manned by Afrims, then everything made sense.

For a few more minutes the battle went on. Olderton and I watched as well as we could, seeing only the flame of the explosions and the gunships as they came by overhead after their pass. I found myself counting the number of attacks made. After the twelfth, there was a slight pause, and we could hear the helicopters re-grouping in the distance. Then one of the machines flew over the wood again, this time without firing any of its rockets. It zoomed overhead, then went to join the others. We waited again. From the direction of the wood there was now a steady glow of orange and the occasional sound of a small explosion. There did not appear to be any more gunfire.

'I think it's over,' I said.

Olderton said: 'There's still one of them around.'

To my ears it seemed as if the formation of gunships was moving away, but there was no uniformity in the sound of the engines. I kept looking around, but could see no sign of any of the helicopters.

'There it is!' Olderton said. He pointed over to our right.

I could just make out its shape. It was moving slowly and near the ground. It had no navigation lights. It came towards us steadily, and irrationally I felt it was looking for us. My heart began to beat rapidly.

The aircraft moved across the field in front of us, then turned, and climbing slightly flew directly over us. When it reached the smouldering remains of the house on the other side of the road it hovered.

Olderton and I went back into our house, climbed the stairs and watched the helicopter. It was about twenty feet above the burnt-out ruin, and the draught from its vanes sent cinders scudding over the ground. Flames took again in some of the timbers, and smoke swirled up and across to us.

In the glow from the ground I could see the helicopter's cabin clearly. I lifted my rifle, took careful aim and fired.

Olderton leaped over to me and knocked the barrel aside.

'You stupid bastard!' he said. 'They'll know we're here.'

'I don't care,' I said. I was watching the helicopter.

For a moment I thought my shot had had no effect. Then the engine of the machine accelerated abruptly and it lifted away. Its tail spun round, stopped, then spun again. The helicopter continued to climb, but it was moving to one side, away from us. The engine was screaming. I saw the helicopter check its sideways motion, but then it flipped again. It skidded down over the burnt-out house, disappeared from sight. Two seconds later there was a loud crash.

'You cunt, you stupid bastard,' Olderton said again. 'The others will be back to find out what happened.'

I said nothing. We waited.

* * *

During the period in which Isobel left us, Sally and I were in a state of continual fear and disorientation. I think it was because this was the first manifestation in personal terms of the real crisis: the breakdown of all aspects of life we had known before the start of the fighting. I knew Sally would not see it in this way; like all children her grief stemmed mainly from personal considerations.

Isobel's absence induced in me some unexpected reactions. In the first place, I experienced quite distinct pangs of sexual jealousy. In the time we had been married, I knew that Isobel had had both the opportunity and the motivation to take a lover. Yet at no time had I suspected her of doing so. With the present uncertainty, however, I found my thoughts turning to her often.

Secondly, for all the conflict we had endured, I found I missed her company, negative though I had often felt it to be.

Both Isobel and I had been aware of the future, of what would have happened to us when Sally grew up and left us. In practice, our marriage would have ended at that time, though in fact it had never started.

Alone with Sally in the countryside it felt as if the predictable course of our life had ended abruptly, that from this point nothing more could be planned, that life had ended, that the future was the past.

*   *   *

An hour passed, during which Lateef and the others joined us. The night was quiet, with only the faint flicker of light from the wood to show that for a few minutes the war had been conducted around us.

I found myself in an ambivalent position. Though I detected an aura of grudging respect over the shooting down of the helicopter, Lateef and one or two others stated unequivocally that it had been an unintelligent action. Fear of reprisals was always great, and had the other gunships learned of my action at the time, it was likely that they would have attacked the village.

Now that the moment of action, and the subsequent period of greatest danger, had passed, I was able to think objectively about what I had done.

In the first place, I was convinced that the pilots of the gunships had been either Afrims or their sympathisers. And while it was generally conceded that, regardless of racial or nationalistic prejudices, participating Afrims were the one common enemy, in my particular case the firing of the rifle had represented to me a gesture of my individual reaction to the abduction of the women. In this I still felt I differed from the other men, though it was arguable that as I possessed the only rifle I was the only one placed to make such a gesture. In any event, I had derived a curious pleasure from the incident, as it had signalled my first positive participation in the war. From here I had committed myself.

There was some discussion over our next move. I was tired and would have been pleased to get some sleep. But the others were debating whether to visit the wrecked helicopter or to trek across to the wood and examine whatever it was that had been attacked by the Afrims.

I said: 'I'm against either. Let's get some sleep, then move before dawn.'

'No, we can't risk sleeping here,' said Lateef. 'It's too dangerous. We've got to move, but we need barter for food. We'll have to take what we can from the helicopter, then get as far away as possible.'

It was suggested by a man called Collins that there might be more of value in the wood, and several of the men agreed with him. Anything that was considered a worthy target by the military forces represented to us a potential source of exchangeable commodities. In the end it was agreed that we would break with our normal policy, and separate. Lateef, myself and two others would approach the wrecked helicopter; Collins and Olderton would take the rest of the men over to the wood. Whichever group finished first was to join the other.

We returned to the camp at the other end of the village, repacked our gear, and separated as planned.

The helicopter had crashed in a field behind the burnt-out house. There had been no explosion when it hit the ground, nor had it caught fire. In that respect at least it would be safe to approach it. The condition of whatever crew there had been aboard was the main hazard. If they had been killed in the crash, from our point of view all would be well. On the other hand, if any of them were still alive we could be in an extremely precarious position.

We said nothing as we moved towards it. When we reached the edge of the field we could see the shape of the wreck, like a huge smashed insect. There appeared to be no movement, but we watched for several minutes in case.

Then Lateef muttered: 'Come on,' and we crept forward. I had my rifle ready, but still doubted privately whether I would have the guts to fire it again. Lateef's use of me as an armed assistant reminded me uncomfortably of the incident at the barricade.

The last thirty or forty yards we moved on our stomachs, crawling forward slowly, prepared for anything. As we neared the wreck we realised that if anybody were still inside he would not be in a condition to present a threat to us. The main structure had collapsed and one of the vanes had bitten into the cockpit.

We reached the wreck unchallenged, and stood up.

We walked round it cautiously, trying to see if there were anything that we could liberate from the wreckage. It was difficult to tell in the dark.

I said to Lateef: 'There's nothing here for us. If it were daylight –'

As soon as I spoke we heard a movement inside and we backed away at once, crouching warily in the grass. A man's voice came from inside, speaking breathlessly and haltingly.

'What's he saying?' one of the other men said.

We listened again, but could not understand. Then I recognised the language as Swahili – though I had no knowledge of the language, the sound of it was familiar to me as most radio broadcasts that I had heard in the last few months had been duplicated in Swahili. It is an indistinct language, not easy on European ears.

None of us needed to speak the language to know instinctively what the man was saying. He was trapped and in pain.

Lateef took out his torch and shone it on the wreckage, keeping the beam low in an attempt to prevent from seeing it anyone else who may be in the vicinity.

For a moment we were unable to make out coherent shapes, though on one patch of relatively undamaged metal we made out an instruction printed in the Cyrillic alphabet. We moved in closer and Lateef shone the torch inside. After a moment we saw a Negro lying in the broken metal. His face, which was towards us, was wet with blood. He said something again and Lateef shut off the beam.

'We'll have to leave it,' he said. 'We can't get inside.'

'But what about the man?' I said.

'I don't know. There's not much we can do.'

'Can't we try to get him out?'

Lateef switched on his torch again and flashed it over the wreck. Where the man was lying was almost totally surrounded by large pieces of broken cockpit and fuselage. It would take heavy lifting-gear to move.

'Not a hope,' said Lateef.

'We can't just leave him.'

'I'm afraid we'll have to.' Lateef returned the torch to his pocket. 'Come on, we can't stay here. We're too exposed.'

I said: 'Lateef, we've got to do something for that man!'

He turned to me and came and stood very close.

'Listen, Whitman,' he said. 'You can see there's nothing we can do. If you don't like blood, you shouldn't have shot the fucking thing down. O.K.?'

To foreshorten the exchange, as I did not like the new tone in his voice, I said: 'O.K.'

'You've got the rifle,' he went on. 'Use it, if that's what you want.'

He and the other two men started back across the field in the direction of the houses.

'I'll catch you up,' I said. 'I'm going to see what I can do.'

No one replied.

It took only a matter of seconds to establish that what Lateef had said was substantially true. There was no way of freeing the

Afrim. Inside, his voice kept lifting and dropping, interrupted by sudden intakes of breath. If I'd had a torch I would have been tempted to shine it inside and look again at him. As it was, I was relieved not to be in the position to do so. Instead, I ran the barrel of the rifle into the space, and aimed it in the approximate direction the man's face had been.

And paused. . . .

I had no wish to shoot him, any emotion in me having been expended by the act of shooting at the helicopter in the first place. The fact that I was confronted with an Afrim – and that it was barely conceivable that this man may be connected indirectly with those men who had abducted Sally and Isobel – was irrelevant. Practical considerations, such as that I might attract the attention of other troops in the area with the sound of the shot, were similarly unconsidered. The fact was that the physical act of pulling the trigger and killing the man was too positive an act . . . one in which my commitment would be affirmed.

And yet the humane instinct in me, which had kept me here originally, argued that to kill the man quickly would be marginally better than to leave him here to die.

A final thought was that I had no way of knowing how badly he may be injured. He would be discovered in the morning, and if still alive then would perhaps have his life saved. If this were a possibility, any arbitrary act I made here would be inappropriate.

I pulled the rifle out, stood up, and stepped back two paces. Then I lifted the barrel and fired two shots into the air.

The voice inside the wreckage stopped.

* * *

Within two years of Sally's birth my relationship with Isobel had virtually disintegrated. We learned to suffer one another; growing to dislike the sound of each other's voice, the sight of each other's face, the touch of our backs against each other as we lay in bed.

* * *

My friend explained that the purpose of the new laws was not to persecute the African immigrants but to protect them. He said that the government took the view that they were essentially at our mercy, and that we should treat them as temporary dependants rather than as unwelcome intruders. The population of the country should not be panicked into unconsidered actions by the sight of one or two aliens who may be armed. As illegal immigrants they could only act outside the law for as long as it took the law to apprehend them. This was the whole purpose of the new Order Act.

I argued that I had heard many stories of persecution, of rape, murder and abduction. There was the well-publicised Gorton torture case, in which ten African women had been systematically degraded, raped, mutilated and finally murdered.

My friend agreed with me and said that this was precisely the kind of atrocity which the new Act was intended to prevent. By restricting the rights and movements of the aliens, they would be afforded a greater degree of official protection provided they themselves submitted to the various regulations. The fact that so far the majority of the Afrims had rejected this protection was only a further indication of their essential alienness.

My friend went on to remind me of John Tregarth's early political career, when, even as an Independent back-bencher, he had made a name for himself by his commendable policies of patriotism, nationalism and racial purity. It was a measure of his sincerity that he had held to his views even during the temporary phase of neo-liberal xenophilia before the beginning of the emergency. Now he had risen to high office, the nation would see that its far-sightedness in electing his party into government would be rewarded.

I said that I was under the impression that Tregarth had come to power through the sponsorship of various business interests which had undertaken the expense of the campaign.

Again my friend agreed with me, pointing out that it is an expensive business to create an entirely new political party. The fact that they had been defeated at only one general election before taking office was further evidence of their immense popularity.

I argued that it was only through creating a rift in the existing Opposition that Tregarth had acquired any following at all.

We lapsed into silence for a while, knowing that political differences can damage friendship if not discussed amicably. I did not care for the way in which the present situation was affecting my own life. I had thought my days of political participation ended when I finished my studies, but now I was able to see with my own eyes the human effects of political extremism.

My friend reminded me that Tregarth had come to power several months before the Afrim situation began, and that there was no question of racial discrimination in the way the emergency was now being handled. A difficult set of circumstances must be dealt with firmly, and for all the declared humanitarian motives expressed from some quarters, the fact remained that the Afrims were hostile and dangerous aliens and must be treated as such.

*   *   *

I caught up with Lateef and the other two in the village, and we moved on in the direction of the wood. Lateef said nothing about the man inside the helicopter. I had evidently overrated the importance of the incident.

As we came out of the village and joined the main road that ran through the wood, one of the older men who had gone with Collins came up to us excitedly.

'In the wood! Collins says it's there!'

'What is?' said Lateef.

'He sent me to get you. We've found them.'

Lateef pushed past him and walked quickly in the direction of the flames. As I followed, I glanced at my wristwatch, holding up the face to catch what little light I could from the moon. It was barely possible to make out the time: it was half past three. I was getting more tired with every minute and could not see us setting up another camp within the next hour. We had found that it was hazardous to try to sleep during the day, unless we were able to find somewhere well concealed.

As we came to the edge of the wood I found my lungs filling with smoke. The flavour of it was not one I was familiar with and appeared to be a composite of many fires. Overriding it all, though, was the stench of cordite; the flavour of war, the stink of a spent cartridge.

We approached the scene of the ambush. A heavy agricultural lorry had been parked broadside across the road. Twenty yards from it was the wreck of the leading truck of the convoy. It had received at least one direct hit from the rockets of the gunships, and it was scarcely recognisable as having once been a vehicle. Behind it were the wrecks of several more: I counted only seven, though afterwards I heard Lateef say that there had been twelve. How he had access to this information, I do not know. At any rate, there were four trucks still burning. To each side of the road, shrubbery had been ignited by the explosions and the smoke from this joined with that of the vehicles. There was

94

not much wind, and in the region of the trucks the air was virtually unbreathable.

I stood with Lateef. We were trying to discern on which side the trucks had been; in this undeclared civil war, the opposing forces rarely displayed colours and it was unusual to see any kind of vehicle bearing identification-marks. Logically, the trucks had been driven by Nationalist or Loayalist troops, as the helicopters had been shown to be piloted by the Afrims, but there was no way of telling for certain. I thought the trucks looked as if they had been American, but neither of us was sure.

A man came out of the smoke and stood before us. In the orange light from the blaze we could see that it was Collins. He had tied a piece of cloth over his nose and mouth, and was breathing heavily.

'I think it was a Nationalist supplies-convoy, Lat,' he shouted to us.

'Is there anything for us?' Lateef said.

'No food. Not much else. But come and see what we've found.'

Lateef took a rag from his pocket and tied it around his face. I followed suit. When we were ready, Collins led us past the remains of the first two trucks and up to the third. This one was not alight.

A rocket had evidently landed directly in front of it, wrecking the driver's cab, but not setting fire to the main part of it. The truck had then collided with the one in front of it, which had burned earlier but without affecting the other. The truck immediately behind it had been victim of a direct hit and its remains were smouldering. Eight or nine of our men stood around, looking expectantly at Lateef.

Collins gestured towards a crate lying on the ground. 'We found that on the truck.'

Lateef knelt before it, reached inside, and pulled out a rifle. He laid it on the ground.

'Are there any more of these?'

'It's full of them.'

Just then, a truck about fifty yards away from us exploded, and we all crouched defensively. I was holding my own rifle and instinctively I backed away towards the nearest trees. I watched Lateef.

He looked round. I heard him say: 'Is there any ammunition?'

'Yes.'

'Get it off quickly. As much as we can carry. Kelk!' One of the men ran forward. 'Get a handcart. Empty everything off it. We'll carry the rifles on that.'

I stepped back into the trees, suddenly an observer.

It occurred to me that if the ammunition truck were to explode, then all of the men around it would probably be killed. I noticed how much of the grass and shrubbery around the truck was blackened with heat, and how sparks from other trucks drifted near by. I wondered if there was much diesel-oil on the truck, or if there were any unexploded rocket-shells in the vicinity. It was possible that rifles and the ammunition for them were not the only explosives on the truck, and that some of it might explode simply by being manhandled. Though my fears were based on logical grounds, there was an element of irrationality too . . . a feeling, superstitious perhaps, that if I moved to assist the others I would somehow provoke disaster.

I stood amongst the trees, the rifle redundant in my hand.

Once, Lateef left the others and stood with his back to the truck, staring towards me in the trees. He called my name.

I waited until the loading was finished to Lateef's satisfaction. Then as they pushed the handcart away, I followed at a discreet distance until a camp-site was selected at a distance of about half a mile from the ambushed convoy. I made an excuse to Lateef that I had thought I saw a figure lurking in the woods, and had investigated. Lateef was displeased, and to appease him I offered to stand first guard on the liberated weapons. Another man, Pardoe, was told to share the watch with me, which lasted for two hours.

In the morning each man was issued with a rifle and ammunition. The remainder were stowed on the handcart.

*   *   *

In the weeks following, Sally and I were on our own. For some time we continued to live in our tent, but were fortunate finally in finding a farm where we were allowed to live in one of the labourers' cottages. The couple who lived in the farm itself were elderly and took little interest in us. We paid no rent, and in return for assisting with work around the property we were given food.

In this period we had a semblance of security, though we were never allowed to forget the growing military activity in the countryside.

The area was under the control of the Nationalist forces and the farm itself was considered to be strategic. Men from the army came in occasionally to help with the work, and an anti-aircraft battery was built in one of the outer fields, though it was never, to my knowledge, used.

At first, I had an overwhelming interest in the progress of the civil war but soon learned to curb this. I spoke only once with the farmer about the political situation and learned that he was either unwilling or unable to discuss it. He told me that he had once had a television and radio, but that they had been removed by the army. His telephone did not work. His only access to information about the outside world was through the army tabloid that was distributed free to all civilians. His occasional meetings with other farmers were uninformative, since they were all in a similar position.

I spoke several times with the men from the army who worked on the farm. Here, too, I was not able to learn much. They had evidently been ordered not to speak with civilians about the progress of the war, and though this was not strictly adhered to it was plain that the major part of their knowledge consisted of the propaganda put out by their superiors.

One night, in early October, the farm was the target of a raid by enemy forces. At the first pass of the reconnaissance plane, I took Sally to the best available cover – a disused pigsty, which had the advantage of being constructed with stout brick walls – and we laid there until the attack was over.

Our cottage was not damaged, but the farmer's house had been destroyed. The couple were missing.

In the morning the commander of the Nationalist troops visited the farm and took away what remained of the equipment that had been dumped there. The anti-aircraft battery was abandoned.

For no better reason than an unwillingness to uproot ourselves, Sally and I remained in the cottage. Though we felt we were in a precarious situation, the prospect of living once more under canvas was not attractive. Later in the day, the farm was occupied by a detachment of integrated Afrim and Secessionist soldiers, and we were questioned closely by the African lieutenant in charge.

We observed the soldiers with great interest, as the sight of white men actually fighting alongside the Africans was new to us.

There were forty men in all. Of these, about fifteen were white. Both officers were Africans, but one of the N.C.O.s was

97

white. The discipline appeared to be good, and we were treated well. We were allowed to stay temporarily in the cottage.

During the next day the farm was visited by a high-ranking Secessionist officer. As soon as I saw him I recognised him from the photographs which had been published regularly in the Nationalist tabloid. His name was Lionel Coulsden, and before the war he had been a prominent campaigner for civil rights. During the period of Afrim infiltration of private property in the towns, he had renewed the commission he held earlier in the army and at the outbreak of overt military hostilities had been one of the leaders of the secession to the African cause. He was now a colonel in the rebel army, and was currently under sentence of death.

He spoke personally to Sally and me, and explained that we would have to leave. A Nationalist counter-attack was anticipated shortly and our lives would be in danger. He offered me an immediate commission into the Secessionist forces, but I turned it down, explaining that I had to consider Sally.

Before we left, he handed me a sheet of paper which explained in simple language the long-term aims of the Secessionist cause.

These were a restoration of law and order; an immediate amnesty for all Nationalist participants; a return to the parliamentary monarchy that had existed before the civil war; the restitution of the judiciary; an emergency housing-programme for displaced civilians; and full British citizenship for all contemporary African immigrants.

We were transported by lorry to a village eight miles from the farm. This, we were told, was in liberated territory. We noticed that there was a small Afrim army-camp situated near by, and we approached them for assistance in finding somewhere to stay temporarily. We were not greeted with the affability displayed by the Secessionist colonel, and were threatened with imprisonment. We left at once.

The village was a singularly unfriendly place and we experienced distrust and hostility from the few people we encountered. That night we slept under canvas in a field on the side of a hill three miles to the west of the village. I heard Sally crying.

A week later we found a house standing in small grounds of its own. It was near a main road, but screened from it by a wood. We approached it warily, but though we were met with some initial caution we were not turned away. The house was occupied by a young married couple, who offered to allow us to shelter with them until we could find alternative accommodation. We stayed for three weeks.

* * *

It was the first time I had seen Lateef frightened.

We were all tired after the events of the night and our nerves were stretched accordingly. Lateef, in particular, betrayed the stress he was feeling; unable to decide whether or not we should move on, he prowled to and fro clutching his new rifle, as if by releasing it he would have his authority undermined. The rest of us watched him uneasily, not liking the personality that had been revealed by this latest development.

I was occupied with my own doubts, for I found growing in me a feeling of alarm generated by our acquisition of the weapons. Already I had overheard one remark about forming an effective guerrilla organisation against the Afrims. I had heard the phrase 'black bastards' used on more occasions recently than at any other time, including the vengeful hours after the women had been abducted.

Lateef was at the focus of my fears, as well as the mood of the rest of the men. Now, as never before, there was a sense that our actions would be determined solely by him.

What it was in Lateef that occasioned my apprehension was the man's apparent indecision. He was frightened himself: frightened to stay here in the camp we had made less than half a mile from the ambushed convoy, and yet not able to summon the courage to move on.

Both fears were understandable. To stay so close to the scene of the attack was to court discovery by any party sent out to investigate. But to move, laden down as we were with so many rifles, would be disastrous if we were seen by any of the participating military forces. It was the nature of Lateef's position to direct us, and though we were at this moment looking to him for instructions, it was tacit that if he failed in his leadership we would replace him.

For the moment we stayed where we were, as by non-action we did at least have the semblance of decision.

With three of the other men I made an inventory of the rifles we now possessed. In addition to the ones carried by each of us, we had twelve crates. In each crate there were six rifles. There were also several boxes of ammunition. In all, the pile of weaponry was almost more than we could handle. We had loaded most of it on to our handcarts, but it was apparent that this could not be a permanent arrangement.

I glanced at the other men sitting in a ragged group among the trees, their new-found rifles close at their sides. I looked beyond them to where Lateef stood, lost in his own thoughts.

* * *

I felt that of all the men, I had come nearest to Lateef in recent weeks. In a while, I went over to him. He was not pleased to be interrupted, especially by me. I saw at once I had made a basic error of judgement, and realised I should have stayed with the other men.

He said: 'Where the hell were you last night?'

'I told you what happened. I thought I saw someone.'

'You should have told me. If it had been the Afrims they'd have shot you.'

I said: 'I thought we were in danger. I had my rifle and I was the only one able to defend us.' I did not wish to tell him the truth.

'We've all got rifles now. You don't have to undertake hazardous missions for our benefit. We can look after ourselves, thanks very much, Whitman.'

The tone of his voice was not only bitter. It was impatient, irritated, distracted. His mind was on something else; my crossing to speak to him had only reminded him of the night before, it was not uppermost in his mind.

'You've got all the rifles you need,' I said. 'What are you going to do with them?'

'What would *you* like to do with them?'

'I think we should throw them away. They'll bring us more problems than they'll solve.'

'No . . . I'm not throwing them away. I have other ideas.'

I said: 'What are they?'

He shook his head slowly, grinning at me. 'You tell me something. What would you use them for, assuming you could get away with it?'

'I've already told you.'

'Wouldn't you barter them to other refugees? Or try to shoot down more helicopters?'

I saw what he was getting at. I said: 'It's not just the fact of having weapons. It's that if everyone has them, instead of one or two people, the effectiveness is lost.'

'So while you were number one with the rifle, it was all right. Now that distinction no longer exists, it isn't.'

I said: 'I gave you my arguments for having a rifle when I first discovered it. One rifle represents a form of defence; complete arming constitutes aggression.'

Lateef looked at me thoughtfully. 'Perhaps we agree more than I had thought. But you still haven't told me what practical use you would put them to.'

I considered for a moment. I still had only one real motivation, however impracticable it might appear to be.

'I would try to do something about finding my daughter,' I said.

'I thought that's what you'd say. It wouldn't do any good, you know.'

'As far as I'm concerned, anything would be better than what we've done so far.'

'Don't you understand?' Lateef said. 'There's nothing we can do about that. The best you can hope for is that they're in an internment camp. More likely they've been raped or murdered, probably both. You saw yesterday what they do to white women.'

'And you can just accept that?' I said. 'It isn't the same for you, Lateef. That was my wife and my daughter that they took. My daughter!'

'It didn't only happen to you. There were seventeen women taken.'

'But none of them were yours.'

Lateef said: 'Why can't you accept it like the other men have, Alan? There is nothing we can do to find them. We're outside the law. Approach any of the authorities and we'll be imprisoned immediately. We can't go to the Afrims because first of all we don't know where they are, and anyway we couldn't expect them to admit that they've abducted our women. We'll get no sympathy from the U.N. people. All we can do is continue to survive.'

I looked round angrily. 'You call this survival? We're living like animals.'

'You want to give yourself up?' Lateef's tone had changed; he was trying to be persuasive now. 'Listen, do you know how many refugees there are like us?'

'No one knows.'

'That's because there are so many. Thousands of them . . . perhaps millions. We're just operating in a small stretch of the country. All over England there are homeless people like ourselves. You said we shouldn't be aggressive. But why not?

Every single one of those refugees has an excellent reason for wanting to participate. But circumstances are against him. He's weak. He has little food, no resources. He has no legal position. Err to one side and he is a potential danger to the military forces because he is mobile, because he sees the war being conducted; too far the other way and he becomes politically involved. You know how the government treats refugees? As secessionist fraternisers. Do you want to see the inside of a concentration camp? So the refugee does just what we've been doing: he lives and sleeps rough, he congregates in small groups, he barters, steals and keeps out of the way of everyone else.'

'And has his women taken from him,' I said.

'If that's the way it has to be, yes. It's not an attractive state, but there's no ready alternative.'

I said nothing to him, aware that he was probably right. I had long felt that had there been an alternative to the wretched vagrant life we had been leading we would have discovered it. But what we saw of the various organised bodies during the brief periods of interrogation to which we had been subjected, made clear to us that there was no place for the displaced civilian. The major towns and cities were under martial law, smaller towns and villages were either under military control or had defended themselves with civilian militia. The countryside was ours.

After a minute or two I said: 'But it can't stay this way for ever. It's not a stable situation.'

Lateef grinned. 'Not now it isn't.'

'Now?'

'We're armed. That's what the difference is. The refugees can unite, defend themselves. With rifles we can take back what is ours . . . freedom!'

I said: 'That's insane. You've only got to leave this wood and the first detachment of regular troops will slay you.'

'A guerrilla army. Thousands of us, all over the country. We can occupy villages, ambush supplies-convoys. But we'll have to be careful, have to stay hidden.'

'Then what would be the difference?'

'We'll be organised, armed, *participating*.'

'No,' I said. 'We mustn't become involved in the war. There's too much already.'

'Come on,' he said. 'We'll put it to the others. It'll be demo-cratic, it can only work if we're all in favour.'

We walked back through the trees to where the others were

waiting for us. I sat on the ground a little distance from Lateef, and looked at the handcarts laden with crates. I was only half listening to Lateef; my mind was preoccupied with the image of a disorganised band of men, thousands of them in every rural area of the country, hungering for revenge against the impersonal military forces and civilian organisations on every side.

I saw that where once the refugees had represented a desperate but ineffectual neutral presence in the fighting, their organisation into a fighting guerrilla force – if such a task could be accomplished – would only add to the chaos which tore at the country.

I stood up and backed away from the others. As I stumbled through the trees, with an ever-growing desperation to be away from them, I heard the men shout their approval in unison. I headed south.

*　　*　　*

I noticed the girl on a table a few feet away from mine. As soon as I recognised her I stood up and walked over to her.

'Laura!' I said.

The girl stared at me in surprise. Then she recognised me, too.

'Alan!'

I am not generally motivated by nostalgia, but for some reason I had come back to the restaurant in the park, automatically associating it with the times I had spent with Laura Mackin. Even though I was dwelling on the memory of her, it took me by surprise to see her; I had not known she still came here.

She moved to my table.

'Why are you here?'

'Isn't that obvious?'

We stared at each other across the table. 'Yes.'

We ordered some wine to celebrate with, but it was oversweet. Neither of us wanted to drink it, but we could not be bothered to complain to the waiter. We toasted each other, and the rest didn't matter. While we ate I was trying to work out why I had come here. It could not have been only a seeking for the past. What had I been thinking during the morning? I tried to remember, but memory was inconveniently blank.

'How is your wife?'

The question that had been so far unspoken. I had not expected her to ask it.

'Isobel? The same.'

'And you are still the same.'

'No one changes much in two years.'

'I don't know.'

'What about you? Are you still sharing a flat?'

'No. I've moved.'

We finished our meal, drank coffee. The silences between our conversations were an embarrassment. I began to regret meeting her.

'Why don't you leave her?'

'You know why not. Because of Sally.'

'That's what you said before.'

'It's true.'

Another silence.

'You haven't changed, have you? I know damn well that Sally's just an excuse. This is what went wrong before. You're too weak to disentangle yourself from her.'

'You don't understand.'

We ordered more coffee. I wanted to end the conversation, leave her here. Instead, it was easier to carry on. I had to acknowledge that what she said about me was true.

'Anyway, I can't say anything that will change you.'

'No.'

'I've tried too often in the past. You realise that this is why I wouldn't see you any more?'

'Yes.'

'And nothing's changed.'

I said, as plainly as I could: 'I am in love with you still, Laura.'

'I know. That is what is so difficult. And I love you for your weakness.'

'I don't like you saying that.'

'It doesn't matter. I only mean it.'

She was hurting me in the way she had done before. I had forgotten this about Laura: her capacity to give pain. Yet what I said to her was true, in spite of everything I continued to love her even though I had not been able to admit this to myself until I met her here. Of the women I had known outside my marriage, Laura was the only one for whom I had deeper feelings than those of physical desire. And the reason for this was because she saw me and understood me for what I was. Though it pained me, Laura's appraisal of my inability to confront my relationship with Isobel was for me an attractive quality. I don't know why she was in love with me, though she said she was. I had never been able to come to understand her fully. She existed in a kind of personal vacuum . . . living in but not belonging to our society. Her mother had been an Irish immigrant, had died giving birth. Her father had been a coloured seaman, and she had never met him. Her skin was pale, but her features were negroid. She was one of the first victims of the Afrim situation, killed in the second London riot. That day in the park restaurant was the last time I saw her.

*   *   *

I recognised the leader of the group as the man I had met in the ruined village when we were plundering the remains of the helicopter. At that time he had told me his name was Lateef, but it had given me no clue as to his origin. Because of the events of the time, I had grown to distrust anyone with coloured skin, however faint it may be.

The group he was leading consisted of about forty individuals, including several children. They were not well organised.

I watched them from the upper floor of the old house, hoping they would not make enough noise to awaken Sally. We had had a long and distressing day and were both hungry. The house was a temporary refuge only; as the winter approached we knew we ought to find more permanent quarters.

The problem I faced was whether or not we should make our presence known.

I considered that Sally and I had not been wholly unsuccessful on our own. We had only moved from the couple's house when we heard that unregistered civilians, and those sheltering them, would be sent to internment camps if captured. Though this ruling was withdrawn soon after, we judged it best that we should move on. That is how we came to this house.

I watched the group indecisively.

If we continued to operate on our own there would be less danger of being captured, but to join an established group would mean that food supplies would be more regular. Neither prospect appealed, but in the time we had been with the young couple we had listened to the bulletins from continental radio-stations, and learned of the true nature and extent of the civil war. Sally and I were among the main casualties so far: the two million displaced civilians who were forced to live as vagrants.

Most of the refugees were in the Midlands and the North, and up there conditions were supposed to be worse. There were fewer in the south, and it was supposed to be easier, but nevertheless there were estimated to be around one hundred and fifty thousand civilians living off the countryside.

In a while the group of refugees below me started to organise themselves better, and I saw two or three tents being pitched. A man came into the ground floor of the house and filled two buckets with water. A fire was lit in the garden and food was laid out.

Then I noticed one of the women who was looking after two young boys. She was trying to get them to wash themselves, though without much success. She looked dirty and tired, her hair tied untidily into a rough bun behind her head. It was Isobel.

If anything this should have made my indecisiveness greater, but instead I went downstairs and asked Lateef if Sally and I could join his group.

*   *   *

I was heading south. Alone, I felt more secure than I had done with Lateef and the others. I had no rifle, nor any other form of weapon. I carried only my bag containing a few personal possessions, a sleeping-bag and a little food. I was able to avoid unwanted encounters with military forces, and found that my treatment at barricaded villages or defended houses was easier than if I had been with a group. The first night I slept under a hedge, the second in a barn, the third I was given a room in a house.

On the fourth day I came into contact with another group of refugees. Once initial reservations about each other had been overcome, I spoke for some time with their leader.

He asked me why I had left Lateef and the others. I told him about the rifles and what Lateef intended to do with them. I gave him my reasons for fearing the outcome of participation by refugees. I also told him about my search for my wife and daughter.

We were speaking to each other in what had once been a car-park for a pub. The rest of his group were preparing a meal and taking it in turns to wash in the kitchen of the abandoned building.

'Was your group as large as ours?'

'It was larger originally,' I said. 'Before the raid there were twenty-nine men and seventeen women.'

'Who were the women? Were they your wives?'

'Mostly. I had my daughter with me, and there were three single girls.'

'There are thirty-five of us. And we've got more women than men.'

He told me about an incident when they had been rounded up by some Nationalist forces. Those men of suitable age had been given two alternatives: internment in concentration-camps, or mobilisation into the army. Though the remainder of the group had been freed when a United Nations inspection team had arrived at the camp, many of the men had stayed behind to fight with the Nationalists.

I made a wry remark to the effect that one side wanted the men, and the other wanted the women.

The man said: 'Are you sure it was the Afrims who took your women?'

'Yes.'

'Then I think I know where they might be.' He glanced at me, as if to judge what my reaction might be. 'I've heard – though it is only a rumour – that the Afrim command has authorised several brothels of white women for its troops.'

I said: 'Rumours are reliable.'

He nodded.

I started at him, shocked and silenced. After a moment I said: 'She's only a child.'

'My wife is here,' he said. 'It's something we all have to be guarded against. All we can do is hide until the war is finished.'

I was given some food and we exchanged as much information about troop movements as we knew. They wanted to know details about Lateef's group, and I gave them directions to where I had last seen them. I was told that the reason for this interest was that a consolidation of the two groups would strengthen their defence of the women, but in my own mind I felt that it was because I had told the leader about the rifles.

I regretted this, and saw that perhaps I had inadvertently helped sponsor a move to which I did not subscribe.

I found out as much as I could about the rumoured brothels. I knew instinctively that this was the fate that had befallen Sally and Isobel. It disgusted and frightened me, but in one sense it was reassuring since there was a chance that if the brothels were at the direction of the command there would be at least a chance of appeal, either to the command itself or to one of the welfare organisations.

I said: 'Where are these brothels?'

'The nearest, I've heard, is to the east of Bognor.' He named a seaside town, the one in which I had discovered the bungalow with the petrol-bombs.

We consulted our maps. The town was ten miles to the south-west of us, and Lateef's last position was a similar distance to the north. I thanked the group for their food and information, and left them. They were breaking camp and preparing to move.

The part of the coast to which I was going was not one I knew well. The towns run into one another and sprawl back into the countryside. In my childhood I had spent a holiday in the neighbourhood, but I could recall little about it.

In a few miles I encountered the edges of urban development. I crossed several major roads and saw more and more houses. Most of them appeared to be deserted, but I did not investigate further.

When I estimated I was about five miles from the coast I came across a well-made barricade built in the road. There appeared to be no defenders, and I walked up to it as openly as possible, prepared always to take evasive action should there be any trouble.

The shot, when it came, caught me by surprise. Either the cartridge was blank, or the shot was intended to miss, but the bullet came nowhere near me.

I crouched and moved quickly to the side. A second shot came, this time missing me narrowly. I dived gracelessly to the ground, falling awkwardly on to my ankle. I felt it twist under me and an agonising pain ran through my leg. I lay still.

* * *

Later, my friend told me some amusing stories. He is a large man, and although he is only in his early thirties he looks a lot older. When he tells jokes, he laughs at them himself with his eyes closed and his mouth wide open. I had known him only a few months, since falling into the habit of drinking in the evenings. He was a regular at the pub I went to, and although I did not particularly like him, he had often sought me out for company.

He told me about a white man who was walking along a road one day when he encounters this big buck nigger carrying a duck. The man goes up to the nigger and says: 'That's an ugly-looking monkey you've got there.' Whereupon the nigger says: 'That's not a monkey, man, that's a duck.' The white man stares up at the nigger and says: 'Who the hell's talking to you?'

My friend started laughing and I joined in, amused in spite of myself at the absurdity of it. Before I had finished he began to tell me another one. This was about a white man who wanted to shoot gorillas in Africa. As gorillas were very rare in that part of the jungle, everyone considered it very doubtful that he would find any. After only ten minutes he comes back saying he's already shot thirty, and can he have some more ammunition? Of course, no one believes him, so to prove it he shows them the bicycles the gorillas had been riding.

I had seen the end of that one coming, and anyway did not consider it to be very funny, so I didn't join with my friend in his laughter. Instead, I smiled politely and bought some more drinks.

On my way home that evening, I saw with the clarity that alcohol can sometimes bring how our modes of behaviour had already adapted subtly to allow for the presence of the Afrims and their sympathisers. To tell me the stories, my friend had taken me to a quiet corner of the bar, as if about to divulge something of the order of a state secret.

Had he told the stories in the main part of the bar it was probable that trouble would have been started. There was an Afrim settlement less than a mile from the pub, and its presence had already caused apprehension amongst local residents.

My walk home took me within a few hundred yards of the settlement and I disliked what I was forced to see. Groups of men and youths stood about on street corners, waiting for an excuse to provoke an incident. In the last few weeks there had been several cases of attacks on Afrim sympathisers.

A police-car was parked just inside the entrance to one of the houses in my road. Its lights were off. There were six men inside.

I felt distinctly that events were picking up a self-destructive momentum, and that no longer was a humane resolution possible.

*　　*　　*

Sally was happy to be reunited with her mother, though Isobel and I greeted each other coolly. For a moment I was reminded of a period in the early years of our marriage, when it had seemed that the presence of the child would adequately compensate for the disquieting lack of rapport between us. I talked now with Isobel about practical things, telling her of our attempt to return to London, and the events subsequently. She told me how she had joined Lateef and his group, and we remarked again and again on the good fortune that had brought us together again.

We slept together that night, the three of us, and though I felt we should make some effort to re-establish a sexual relationship, I was incapable of making the first move. I do not know whether it was Sally's presence that caused this.

Fortunately for us, and for all the refugees like us, the winter of that year was a mild one. There was a lot of rain and wind, but only a short period of severe frosting. We had established a semi-permanent camp in an old church. We were visited several times by Red Cross workers, and both military sides knew of our presence. The winter passed uneventfully, the only severe handicap being the continuing absence of news of the progress of the civil disorder.

This period, too, was the one in which I first saw Lateef as some kind of social visionary. He would talk of enlarging our group, and establishing a recognisable unit which would be self-sufficient until the resolution of the troubles. By this time, all of us had abandoned any hope of ever returning to our homes, and we realised that we would be ultimately in the hands of whichever side succeeded in creating a working government. Until that time, Lateef convinced us we should sit tight and await developments.

I think I grew complacent in this period. I was directly under Lateef's influence and spent many hours in conversation with him. Though I grew to respect him, I think he despised me, perhaps because I was so evidently incapable of committing myself to a firm political viewpoint.

Several other groups of refugees came to the church during the winter, staying for varying periods of time before moving on. We came to see our establishment there as being a kind of nucleus of the situation. In our own way we were prospering. We were rarely short of food, and our semi-permanent status enabled us to take time to organise proper foraging parties. We had a good supply of spare clothing, and many items which would be useful as barter.

With the coming of the spring, we soon saw that we were not the only faction which had used the lull in the hostilities to consolidate a position. In late March and April we saw many aircraft in the sky which, by their unfamiliar appearance, were presumably of foreign origin. Troop-activity renewed, and during the nights long columns of lorries would pass. We heard heavy artillery in the distance.

We had acquired a radio and it had been made to work. To our frustration, however, we were unable to learn much of use from it.

The operations of the BBC had been suspended, and replaced with a one-channel station called 'National Voice'. The content of this was similar to the tabloids I had seen: political rhetoric and social propaganda, interspersed with hours of continuous music. All continental and foreign stations were jammed.

We learned at the end of April that a major attack had been launched against rebel and alien groups in the south, and that a major offensive was under way. The forces loyal to the crown were reported to be sweeping through the very area in which we were established. Though our own observations of military movements lent disbelief to this, we were concerned to a large degree as if there were any truth in the reports there could well be a further increase in activity in the near future.

One day we were visited by a large delegation of United Nations welfare organisers. They showed us several government directives which listed the groups of participants in the hostilities which were to be treated as dissident factions. White civilian refugees were included.

The organisers explained that these directives had been issued some weeks before and, as had happened on several occasions previously, been withdrawn soon after. This lent a great uncertainty to our status, and we were advised either to surrender ourselves to U.N. rehabilitation centres or to move on. The advice came at this time, they said, because large numbers of Nationalists troops were in the area.

The question was debated at some length. In the end, Lateef's wish that we should continue to live outside the law was carried. We felt that while large numbers of refugees remained in this state we retained a large but passive pressure on the government to resolve the conflict and rehouse us. To surrender to U.N. rehabilitation would be to deprive ourselves of this small level of participation. In any event, the conditions in overcrowded and understaffed camps were by all accounts worse than we were presently experiencing.

Several of us, though, did go to the camps . . . mostly those people with children. But the majority stayed with Lateef, and in due course we moved on.

Before doing so, we had agreed on our daily tactics. We would move in a broad circle, returning to the vicinity of the church every six weeks. We would go only to those places which, either from our own experience or from what we had heard from other refugees, we knew were relatively safe for the overnight encampment. We were equipped with as much camping-equipment as we would need, and had several handcarts.

For four and a half weeks, we travelled as planned. Then we came to an area of flat farmland which was reported to be under Afrim control. This had no effect on our policy, as we had often passed through Afrim territory before.

The first night we were not molested in any way.

*   *   *

I spent the afternoon at the college in a mood of withdrawn depression. I conducted three tutorials, but found myself unable to concentrate fully. Isobel was uppermost in my mind, and it was not pleasant to associate what I felt with a sense of guilt.

I had finished an affair two weeks before. It had not been complicated by emotional overtones, but had been a negative expression of the sexual frustration induced in me by Isobel's attitude. I had spent several evenings at the woman's flat and one whole night. I had not particularly liked the woman, but she was proficient in bed.

At this period I was still lying to Isobel about my activities and was not certain whether she knew the truth.

By four in the afternoon I had reached a decision, and telephoned a friend named Helen who had sat for Sally on the various occasions when Isobel and I wanted to spend an evening out together. I asked her if she would be free that evening and arranged for her to call at seven.

I left college at five and went straight home. Isobel was ironing some clothes, and Sally – who at this time was four years old – was having her tea.

'Get rid of that as quickly as you can,' I said to Isobel. 'We're going out.'

She was wearing a shapeless blouse and a worn skirt. She had no stockings on, and was wearing her slippers. Her hair was tied back with an elastic band, though stray wisps fell about her face.

'Going out?' she said. 'But I can't. I've all the ironing to do, and we can't leave Sally.'

'Helen's coming round. And you can do the rest of that to-morrow.'

'Why are we going out? What's to celebrate?'

'No reason. I just feel like it.'

She gave me an ambiguous look, and turned back to her ironing. 'Very amusing.'

'No, I mean it.' I bent down, and pulled the socket of the electric iron from the wall. 'Finish that off, and get ready. I'll put Sally to bed.'

'Are we having a meal? I've got all the food in.'

'We can have it tomorrow.'

'But it's already half-cooked.'

'Put it in the fridge. It'll keep.'

She said quietly: 'Like your mood?'

'What?'

'Nothing.' She bent over her ironing again.

I said: 'Look, Isobel, don't be awkward. I'd like to spend the evening out. If you don't want to go, just say so. I thought you'd appreciate the idea.'

She looked up. 'I . . . do. I'm sorry, Alan. It's just that I wasn't expecting it.'

'You'd like to go then?'

'Of course.'

'How long will it take you to get ready?'

'Not long. I'll have to have a bath and I want to wash my hair.'

'O.K.'

She finished what she was doing, then put away the iron and the ironing-board. For a few minutes she moved about the kitchen, dealing with the food she had been cooking.

I switched on the television and watched the news. At this time there was speculation about the date of the coming General Election, and a right-wing Independent M.P. named John Tregarth had caused a controversy by claiming that the Treasury accounts were being falsified.

I saw to Sally and washed up the dirty dishes in the sink. I told Sally that Helen was coming over to look after her and that she was to behave. The child promised solemnly that she would, and then became very placid and happy. She liked Helen. I went into the bathroom to get my electric razor and Isobel was already in the water. I leaned over and kissed her as she sat in the bath. She responded for a second or two, then pulled away and smiled up at me. It was a curious smile; one whose meaning

I could not easily identify. I helped Sally undress, then sat with her downstairs reading to her until Isobel had finished in the bathroom.

I telephone a restaurant in the West End and asked them to reserve a table for us at eight o'clock. Isobel came down in her dressing-gown while I was speaking to them, looking for her hair-dryer. Helen arrived on time at seven, and a few minutes later we took Sally up to her room.

Isobel had brushed her hair down straight and was wearing a pale-coloured dress that fitted and emphasised her figure. She had put on eye make-up and was wearing the necklace I had given her on our first anniversary. She looked beautiful in a way I had not seen for years. As we drove off I told her this.

She said: 'Why are we going out, Alan?'

'I told you. I just felt like it.'

'And suppose *I* hadn't?'

'You obviously do.'

I detected that she was not at ease, and I realised that to this point I had judged her mood by her behaviour. The cool, beautiful appearance betrayed an inner tautness. As we stopped at a set of traffic-lights I looked at her. The drab, almost sexless woman I saw every day was not here . . . instead I saw the Isobel I thought I had married. She took a cigarette from her handbag and lit it.

'You like me dressed up like this, don't you?'

'Yes, of course,' I said.

'And at other times?'

I shrugged. 'You don't always have the opportunity.'

'No. Nor do you often give it to me.'

I noticed that the fingers of the hand that was not holding her cigarette were picking at each other's nails. She inhaled smoke.

'I wash my hair and put on a clean dress. You wear a different tie. We go to an expensive restaurant.'

'We've done it before. Several times.'

'And how long have we been married? Suddenly it's an event. How long to the next time?'

I said: 'We can do this more often if you like.'

'All right. Let's make it every week. Build it into our routine.'

'You know that's not practical. What would we do about Sally?'

She put her hands to her neck, scooped up her long hair, and held it tightly behind her head. I glanced from the traffic to her. She held the cigarette between her lips, her mouth turned down.

114

'You could employ another drudge.'

For a while we drove on in silence. Isobel finished her cigarette and threw it out of the window.

I said: 'You don't have to wait for me to take you out before you can make yourself look attractive.'

'You've never noticed it at any other times.'

'I have.'

It was true. For a long period after we were first married she had made a conscious effort to retain her attractiveness, even during the pregnancy. I had admired her for that, even as the barriers were forming between us.

'I despair of ever pleasing you.'

'You're pleasing me now,' I said. 'You've a child to look after. I don't expect you to dress like this all the time.'

'But you do, Alan. You do. That's the whole trouble.'

I acknowledged that we were talking in superficialities. Both of us knew that the subject of Isobel's manner of dressing was only peripheral to the real problem. I fostered an image of Isobel as I had first seen her and I was reluctant to let it go. That much I accepted, and felt that within certain limits it was common to many married men. The real reason for my disinterest in Isobel was something we had never been able to discuss.

We arrived at the restaurant and ate our meal. Neither of us enjoyed it, and our conversation was inhibited. On the way home afterwards, Isobel sat in silence until I stopped the car outside the house.

Then she turned and looked at me, wearing the expression she had had before, but had then concealed with a smile.

She said: 'I was just another of your women tonight.'

*　　*　　*

I was carried to the barricade by two men. I had one arm around each of their shoulders, and though I tried to put weight on my sprained ankle I found the pain was too great.

A moveable section of the barricade had been opened and I was carried through.

I was confronted by several men. Each carried a rifle. I explained who I was and why I wanted to enter the town. I did not mention the Afrims, nor that I feared Sally and Isobel were in their hands. I said that I had been separated from my wife and daughter, that I had reason to believe they were here and wished to be reunited with them.

My possessions were searched.

'You're a scruffy sod, aren't you?' one of the younger men said. The other men glanced at him quickly and I thought I detected disapproval in the way they did this.

I said, as calmly as I could: 'I've lost my home and all my property. I've been forced to live off the land for several months. If I could find a bath and clean clothes I'd gladly use them.'

'That's all right,' one of the others said. He jerked his head to the side and the younger man moved away, glaring at me. 'What did you do before you were displaced?'

'My profession? I was a lecturer at a college, but I was obliged to do other work for a time.'

'You lived in London?'

'Yes.'

'It could have been worse. You heard what happened up north?'

'I heard. Look, are you going to let me in?'

'We might. But we want to know more about you first.'

I was asked several questions. I did not answer them entirely honestly, but more in a way that I felt would provoke a favourable response. The questions concerned my involvement with the war, whether I had been attacked by any troops, whether I had initiated sabotage, where my loyalties lay.

I said: 'This is Nationalist territory, isn't it?'

'We're loyal to the crown, if that's what you mean.'

'Isn't it the same thing?'

'Not entirely. There are no troops here. We've been able to handle our own affairs.'

'What about the Afrims?'

'There aren't any.' The direct flatness of his tone startled me. 'There were, but they left. It was only carelessness that allowed the situation to get out of control elsewhere.'

Another man came forward. 'You haven't said what your stand is.'

'Can't you imagine?' I said. 'The Africans occupied my home and I've lived like an animal for nearly a year. The bastards have taken my child and my wife. I'm with you. All right?'

'O.K. But you said you've come here looking for them. There aren't any Africans here.'

'Which town is this?'

He named it. It was not the same one as the other refugee leader had mentioned. I told him where I had thought I was going.

116

'That's not here. There aren't any blacks here.'

'I know. You told me.'

'This is a decent town. I don't know about the Africans. There's been none since we kicked the last lot out. If you're looking for them, you won't find them here. Understood?'

'You've told me. I've made a mistake. I'm sorry.'

They moved away from me and conferred in private for a minute or two. I took the opportunity to examine a large-scale map which was attached to the side of one of the concrete slabs forming the barricade. This region of the coast was heavily populated, and though each of the towns had a separate name and identity, in fact their suburbs ran into one another. The town I had been heading for was three miles to the east of here.

I noticed that the map was marked with a zone outlined in bright green ink. Its northernmost point was about four miles from the sea, and it ran down to the east and west until it reached the coast. My objective, I observed, was outside the green perimeter.

I tested my ankle and found that it was almost impossible to stand on it. It had swollen, and I knew that if I removed my shoe I would be unable to get it on again. I suspected I had not broken any bones, but felt that if possible I should see a doctor.

The men returned to me. 'Can you walk?' one of them said.

'I don't think so. Is there a doctor here?'

'Yes. You'll find one in the town.'

'Then you're letting me in?'

'We are. But a few words of warning. Get some clean clothes and tidy yourself up. This is a respectable town. Don't stay on the streets after dark . . . find somewhere to live. If you don't, you'll be out. And don't go around talking about the blacks. All right?'

I nodded. 'Will I be able to leave if I want?'

'Where would you want to go?'

I reminded him that I wanted to find Sally and Isobel. This would necessitate passing through the eastern border into the next town. He told me that I would be able to leave along the coast road.

He indicated that I was to move on. I got to my feet with some difficulty. One of the men went into a near-by house and returned with a walking-stick. I was told that I must return it when my ankle had healed. I promised I would.

Slowly, and in great pain, I limped down the road in the direction of the centre of the town.

* * *

At the first sound I was awake and moved across the tent to where Sally was lying asleep. Behind me, Isobel stirred.

A few moments later there was a noise outside our tent and the flap was thrust aside. Two men stood there. One held a flashlight whose beam was directed into my eyes, and the other held a heavy rifle. The man with the flashlight came into the tent, seized Isobel by her arm and dragged her out of the tent. She was wearing only her bra and pants. She shouted to me for assistance, but the rifle was between me and her. The man with the flashlight moved away, and around the other tents I could hear shouting voices and screams. I lay still, my arm around the now-awakened Sally, trying to soothe her. The man with the rifle was still there, pointing the weapon at me without any movement. Outside, I heard three shots, and I became truly frightened. There was a short silence, then came more screams and more shouted orders in Swahili. Sally was trembling. The barrel of the rifle was less than six inches from my head. Though we were in almost complete darkness, I could make out the shape of the man silhouetted against the faint glow of the sky. Seconds later, another man came into the tent. He was carrying a flashlight. He pushed past the man with the rifle, and outside, only a few feet from me, another rifle fired. My muscles stiffened. The man with the flashlight kicked me twice, trying to push me away from Sally. I clung to her tightly. She screamed. I was struck across the head by a hand, then again. The other man had hold of Sally and tugged her violently. We clung to each other desperately. She was shouting at me to help her. I was incapable of doing more. The man kicked me again, this time in the face. My right arm came free and Sally was pulled from me. I shouted to the man to leave. I said again and again that she was only a child. She screamed. The men stayed silent. I tried to grab the end of the rifle, but it was thrust violently into my neck. I backed away and Sally was dragged struggling through the flap. The man with the rifle came into the tent and squatted over me, the barrel pressing against my skin. I heard its mechanism click, and I braced myself. Nothing happened.

The man with the rifle stayed with me for ten minutes and I lay listening to the movements outside. There was still a lot of

118

shouting, but no more shots. I heard women screaming and the sound of a lorry engine starting up and driving away. The man with the rifle didn't move. An uneasy silence fell around our encampment.

There was more movement outside and a voice made an order. The man with the rifle withdrew from the tent. I heard the soldiers drive away.

I cried.

*   *   *

In addition to the pain from my ankle, I was experiencing a growing feeling of nausea. My head ached. I was able to take only one step at a time, pausing to recover my strength. In spite of my discomfort I was able to observe my environment, and registered surprise at what I saw.

Within a few hundred yards of the barricade I found myself in suburban streets which, because of their façade of normality, appeared strange to me. Several cars drove along the streets, and the houses were occupied and in good repair. I saw a couple sitting in easy-chairs in a garden, and they looked at me curiously. The man was reading a newspaper which I recognised as being the *Daily Mail*. It was as if I had been transported somehow to a period two years before.

At an intersection with a larger road I saw more traffic, and a corporation bus. I waited for a lull in the traffic before attempting to cross the road. I managed it with great difficulty, having to pause half-way across to rest. When I reached the far side the nausea grew to a point where I was forced to vomit. A small group of children regarded me from a near-by garden, and one of them ran into a house.

As soon as I was able I limped on.

I had no idea where I was heading. Perspiration was running down my body, and soon I retched again. I came across a wooden seat on the side of the road and rested there for a few minutes. I felt utterly weakened.

I passed through a shopping precinct where there were many people drifting from one store to another. I was disoriented again by the outward normality of the streets. For many months I had not known any place where there were shops, where it was possible to find goods available for purchase. Most shopping areas I had seen had been looted or under strict military control.

At the end of the row of shops I halted once again, suddenly aware how unusual I must look to these people. Already I had earned several curious stares. I estimated that I had left the barricade an hour and a half before, and that the time now would be around five or six in the evening. I realised how tired I was, in addition to the other symptoms I was experiencing.

Because of my dirty clothes, my unkempt hair, my unshaven face, my two months' odour of dried perspiration and urine, my limp and the flecks of vomit on my shirt, I felt unable to approach any of these people.

The pain from my leg was now almost beyond bearing. I became obsessed with the thought that I was an offensive spectacle to the people, and turned off into a side-road at the first opportunity. I carried on as long as I could, but my weakness was overwhelming. A hundred yards from the turning I fell to the ground for the second time that day, and lay helplessly. I closed my eyes.

· In a while, I became aware of voices around me and I was lifted gently to my feet.

*   *   *

A soft bed. Cool sheets. A body cleaned with a bathful of hot water. A painful leg and foot. A picture on a wall; photographs of smiling people on a dresser. Discomfort in my stomach. Someone else's pyjamas. A doctor winding a bandage around my ankle. A glass of water at my side. Comforting words. Sleep.

*   *   *

I learned that their names were Mr and Mrs Jeffery. His first name was Charles; hers was Enid. He had been a bank manager, but was now retired. I estimated their ages as being in the middle or late sixties. They were remarkably incurious about me, though I told them I had come from outside the town. I said nothing of Sally or Isobel.

They told me I could stay as long as I wished, but at least until my leg had healed.

Mrs Jeffery brought me all the food I could eat. Fresh meat, eggs, vegetables, bread, fruit. At first I registered surprise, saying that I thought they were impossible to obtain. She told me that the local shops had regular supplies of groceries, and could not understand why I had thought this.

'Food is so expensive though, dear,' she said to me. 'I can hardly keep up with the price-rises.'

I asked her why she thought prices had increased.

'It's the times changing. Not like they were when I was younger. My mother used to be able to get bread at a penny a loaf. But there's nothing I can do about it, so I just pay up and try not to think about it.'

She was marvellous to me. There was nothing that was too much to ask of her. She brought me newspapers and magazines, and Mr Jeffery gave me cigarettes and some Scotch whisky. I read the journals eagerly, hoping they would be able to give me some information on the present social and political scene. The newspaper was the *Daily Mail* and was, as Mrs Jeffery told me without any apparent surprise, the only one available at the moment. Its editorial content was mainly foreign news and photographs. There was no mention anywhere of the civil war. There were very few advertisements, and those were in the main for consumer-goods. I noticed that the price was thirty pence, that there were only four pages, that it was printed twice a week and that it was published from an address in Northern France. I passed on none of these observations to the Jefferys.

The rest and comfort allowed me time to think more objectively of the situation. I realised that I had been concerned mainly with my personal life, and had given no thoughts to what our long-term prospects would be. Though I fretted mentally at my inactivity, I recognised that it would serve no useful purpose to move until my ankle had healed.

The questions were the same whether or not I was able to find Isobel and Sally. In my unwitting role as refugee I had of necessity played a neutral role. But it seemed to me that it would be impossible for this to continue in the future. I could not stay uncommitted for ever.

In what I had seen of the activities and outlook of the Secessionist forces, it had always appeared to me that they adopted a more humanitarian attitude to the situation. It was not morally right to deny the African immigrants an identity or a voice. The war must be resolved one way or another in time, and it was now inevitable that the Africans would stay in Britain permanently.

On the other hand, the extreme actions of the Nationalist side, which stemmed initially from the conservative and repressive policies of Tregarth's government (an administration I had distrusted and disliked) appealed to me on an instinctive level. It had been the Afrims who had directly deprived me of everything I had once owned.

Ultimately, I knew the question depended on my finding Isobel. If she and Sally had not been harmed my instincts would be quieted.

I could not directly contemplate the consequences of the alternative.

I felt the dilemma was largely of my own sponsorship . . . had I been able to come to grips with it earlier, I would not now be in this position. On a personal, practical level I could see that whatever future there was for us, it would not be one in which we could settle until the larger issues around us were resolved.

* * *

On the third day at the Jefferys' I was able to get up and move around the house. I had trimmed my beard, and Enid had washed and repaired my clothes. As soon as I was mobile I wanted to pursue my search for Isobel and Sally, but my ankle still pained me when I walked.

I helped Charles with light tasks in the garden and spent several hours in conversation with him.

I was continually surprised by the lack of awareness displayed by both him and his wife. When I spoke of the civil war, he referred to it as if it were a thousand miles away. Remembering the injunction given to me by the man at the barricade not to speak of the Afrims, I was cautious about discussing the politics involved. But Charles Jeffery was not interested in them. As far as he was aware, the government was dealing with a difficult social problem but that the solution would be found in the end.

Several jet aircraft flew over the house during the day, and in the evenings we would hear distant explosions. None of us mentioned them.

The Jefferys had a television set which I watched with them on the evening of the third day, fascinated to learn that the service had been restored.

The style of presentation was similar to that which had once been adopted by the BBC, and in fact the station identification was given as that. The content of the programmes was largely American. There was one short news-bulletin in the middle of the evening, which touched on issues local to the south-coast towns, making no mention of the civil war. All the programmes were pre-recorded, and consisted in the main of light entertainment.

I asked the Jefferys from where the programme were transmitted, and they told me that they were part of a closed-circuit wire system, broadcast from Worthing.

On the fourth day I felt that my ankle had healed sufficiently to allow me to move on. I had a growing restlessness in me, emphasised by a feeling that I was being seduced by the friendly comfort of the Jefferys' house. I could not believe it to be real, but thought of it as an artificial restoration of normal life in an abnormal state. The Jefferys would be incapable of appreciating this, and I said nothing of it to them. I was genuinely grateful for what they had done for me, and while they were able to maintain their illusion of normality I wanted to have no part in breaking it.

I left them in the late morning, knowing that I could never fully express either to myself or to them what the short stay had done for me. I headed for the coast road.

* * *

I encountered no difficulty at the barricade. The men who guarded it were unable to understand why I wished to leave the town, but once I had made it clear to them that I genuinely wished to leave, they allowed me through. I told them that I may be returning later in the day, but they warned me it would not be as easy to re-enter as it had been to leave.

* * *

I walked for two miles through what had been suburban streets. All the houses were empty and several had been damaged or destroyed. I saw no civilians.

On several occasions I met small groups of Afrim soldiers, but I was not accosted.

At midday I entered an empty house to eat the beef sandwiches and salad which Mrs Jeffery had given me. I drank the flask of tea, and washed it out afterwards, realising that it might be useful in the future.

I went down to the beach and walked along it until I came to the place where I had found the bungalow with the makings for petrol-bombs. Out of curiosity I entered the bungalow and looked for the bombs, but they had been taken.

I moved on down to the beach. I sat on the pebbles.

Half an hour later, a youth walked along the shore and approached me. We engaged in conversation. He told me of a large group of refugees about eight miles to the east who had commandeered a ship and who were planning to sail to France. He invited me to join him. I asked him if the group were armed, and he told me they were.

We spoke for a while of the Afrims, and the youth told me that this had once been a garrison town but that their organisation was not good. Though there were still many hundreds of black troops here, they were ill-controlled and undisciplined. I asked him if he knew anything of the reputed Afrim brothel, and he confirmed its existence. He said there was a large turnover of women, and that the Afrims had no compunction about murdering those who would not co-operate.

He told me that the brothel was less than half a mile from where we were, and that he would take me to it if I wished.

I thanked him, but turned down his offer. In a while he left me, giving me detailed instructions on how to find the group who had the vessel. I told him that if I was going to join them I would be there by the next evening.

I waited until he had disappeared from my sight before I moved off in the same direction.

I walked slowly towards where the youth had said the brothel was situated. This necessitated leaving the shore and walking up into the streets of the town. There were many more Africans in this neighbourhood and I discovered that I was not going to be able to get near the building. I tried approaching it from several directions, but each time I was stopped and told to move away.

Tiredness was growing in me, and I returned to the shore. I sat down on the pebbles and looked at the sea.

There was much crude oil on the water, and in many places the beach was covered in thick black sludge.

The silence appalled me. There were no sea-birds, and the oily waves that broke on the shore were sluggish and without foam. The tide was receding. Far out to sea there was a large warship, but I was unable to determine what type or nationality it was.

My attention was first drawn to the bodies by the presence of a squad of Afrim soldiers, who moved down to the beach about a quarter of a mile from me, then returned to the town. I stood up.

As I walked, my feet were continually sucked by the thick layer of oil on the pebbles. The bodies were not easy to see, and had I not known they were there, from a distance I would have mistaken them for large pieces of congealed oil. They were all black and there were seventeen of them. They were naked, and all but one of them were female. The blackness of the skin was not that of natural pigmentation or of oil, but of paint or pitch. I moved amongst them, soon finding Isobel and Sally.

I noticed no reaction in me. Later, I felt a sadness, and later than that a disturbing combination of terror and hatred.

I slept that night on the beach. In the morning I murdered a young African and stole his rifle, and by the afternoon I was again in the countryside.

EARTHLIGHT

THE DREAM ARCHIPELAGO

CHRISTOPHER PRIEST

In a world at war, the Dream Archipelago marks a neutral zone, a lure to the young men on both sides of the conflict. In this interlinked collection of stories, Christopher Priest explores war, relationships and forms of reality.

A soldier comes to doubt that the right is on his side; a young woman remembers peaceful times in the archipelago; a man discovers the evil that women can do to each other. Over all looms the time vortex which makes the reality of this world so different from our own.

Newly revised and added to by the author, and published in book form for the first time, *The Dream Archipelago* shows a writer at the height of his powers.

Price £5.99

ISBN 0 671 03388 3

EARTHLIGHT

THIGMOO

EUGENE BYRNE

What an idea – the Museum of the Mind. At the University of Wessex, Sir John Westgate and Dr Katharine Beckford have used computer power and AIs to create over 200 fictional characters from all periods of history, known as 'erams'. Soldiers, parsons, lawyers, even a Victorian tart with a heart. For Dr Beckford, it's a wonderful use of artificial intelligence and a superb learning tool. For Sir John, it's a superb way to make money (and gain personal honours).

Something was bound to go wrong.

When a number of erams escape from the system, becoming self-aware, it seems that the outbreak can be contained. But the University should never have attempted to destroy them . . .

'I really enjoyed this humane and humorous tale of a socialist Singularity. Sharp satire, bold futurism, and some very serious points about the world we live in and how it can be changed'
Ken MacLeod
Bestselling author of *The Cassini Division*

Price £5.99

ISBN 0 671 02862 6

EARTHLIGHT

OMNIBUS 1

CHRISTOPHER PRIEST

Christopher Priest is one of Britain's
outstanding novelists.

Earthlight are proud to present the first of two
omnibuses, featuring his SF novels *The Space Machine*
and *A Dream of Wessex*, each of which shows a very
different side of England.

The Space Machine is both homage to H.G. Wells and
wonderful imaginative fiction. It was praised by *The
Times* as 'compulsively readable . . . a mutation
between *The Time Machine* and *The War of the Worlds*.'

In *A Dream of Wessex*, the author conjures up an
alternative reality where his characters find both
peace and fulfillment, until a disruptive force arrives.

Price £6.99

ISBN 0 671 03389 1

The British Fantasy Society

EARTHLIGHT

A SELECTED LIST OF SCIENCE FICTION AND FANTASY TITLES AVAILABLE FROM EARTHLIGHT

THE PRICES SHOWN BELOW WERE CORRECT AT THE TIME OF GOING TO PRESS. HOWEVER EARTHLIGHT RESERVE THE RIGHT TO SHOW NEW RETAIL PRICES ON COVERS WHICH MAY DIFFER FROM THOSE PREVIOUSLY ADVERTISED IN THE TEXT OR ELSEWHERE.

☐ 0 6710 1783 7	Komarr	*Lois McMaster Bujold*	£5.99
☐ 0 6710 1607 5	Memory	*Lois McMaster Bujold*	£5.99
☐ 0 6710 1605 9	Escardy Gap	*Peter Crowther & James Lovegrove*	£5.99
☐ 0 6710 1784 5	Quicker Than The Eye	*Ray Bradbury*	£5.99
☐ 0 6710 2207 5	Driving Blind	*Ray Bradbury*	£5.99
☐ 0 6710 1791 8	The October Country	*Ray Bradbury*	£5.99
☐ 0 6710 1790 X	Something Wicked This Way Comes	*Ray Bradbury*	£5.99
☐ 0 6710 1788 8	Golden Apples of the Sun	*Ray Bradbury*	£5.99
☐ 0 6848 4028 6	The Sum Of All Men	*David Farland*	£9.99
☐ 0 6710 1787 X	The Lament of Abalone	*Jane Welch*	£5.99
☐ 0 6710 1785 3	The Royal Changeling	*John Whitbourn*	£5.99
☐ 0 6848 5169 5	Sailing to Sarantium	*Guy Gavriel Kay*	£16.99
☐ 0 6848 5167 9	Beyond the Pale	*Mark Anthony*	£9.99
☐ 0 6848 5168 7	The Last Dragonlord	*Joanne Bertin*	£9.99
☐ 0 6710 2208 3	The High House	*James Stoddard*	£5.99
☐ 0 6848 5817 7	Superscience	*Michael White*	£9.99
☐ 0 6848 5828 2	Green Rider	*Kristen Britain*	£9.99

All Earthlight titles are available by post from:

Book Service By Post, P.O. Box 29, Douglas, Isle of Man IM99 1BQ

Credit cards accepted. Please telephone 01624 675137,
fax 01624 670923, Internet http://www.bookpost.co.uk or
e-mail: bookshop@enterprise.net for details.

Free postage and packing in the UK. Overseas customers allow
£1 per book (paperbacks) and £3 per book (hardbacks).